A
FRAGILE
ENCHANTMENT

Also by

ALLISON SAFT

Down Comes the Night

A Far Wilder Magic

A
FRAGILE
ENCHANTMENT

ALLISON
SAFT

WEDNESDAY BOOKS
NEW YORK

First published in the United States by Wednesday Books, an imprint of St. Martin's Publishing Group

A FRAGILE ENCHANTMENT. Copyright © 2023 by Allison Saft. All rights reserved. Printed in the United States of America. For information, address St. Martin's Publishing Group, 120 Broadway, New York, NY 10271.

www.wednesdaybooks.com

Designed by Devan Norman
Needle and thread illustration © ArtMari/Shutterstock.com

The Library of Congress Cataloging-in-Publication Data is available upon request.

ISBN 978-1-250-89283-6 (hardcover)
ISBN 978-1-250-89284-3 (ebook)

Our books may be purchased in bulk for promotional, educational, or business use. Please contact your local bookseller or the Macmillan Corporate and Premium Sales Department at 1-800-221-7945, extension 5442, or by email at MacmillanSpecialMarkets@macmillan.com.

First Edition: 2024

10 9 8 7 6 5 4 3 2

For everyone taking it
day by day

A
FRAGILE
ENCHANTMENT

1

As Niamh leaned over the railing of the ship's deck, she was struck with the sinking feeling that she had forgotten something.

She'd folded all of her best pieces in delicate cream paper, packed her bobbins and fabric shears, and—most importantly—tucked the invitation safely away in her reticule. That was everything. *Surely* that was everything. But then again, she couldn't be certain. Keeping track of things had never exactly been her strong suit. And as much as she hated to admit it (and although she was secretly convinced her reticule did indeed contain a portal to a stranger realm, filled only with broken pencils and stray pocket change), there really was no arguing with the truth: everything she held dear, from her favorite pair of scissors to precious years of her life, had a way of slipping through her fingers.

It couldn't hurt to check for the invitation again.

Niamh rummaged through her reticule and sighed with relief when she found the letter there. Its edges curled in the harsh sea air, and although the parchment looked yellowed with time, in reality it had only been the victim of at least five tea-spilling incidents. By now, she had memorized every inch of it, from the unbroken wax seal of the royal family, worn smooth and glossy by the restless pads of her fingers, to the smudged ink of its contents.

Dear Niamh Ó Conchobhair,

You are cordially invited to Avaland as an honored guest of the royal family, to serve as the royal tailor for the wedding of His Royal Highness the Prince Christopher, Duke of Clearwater, and Her Royal Highness Rosa de Todos los Santos de Carrillo, Infanta of Castilia . . .

Even now, she could hardly process it. *Her,* a Machlish girl from a backwater like Caterlow, the tailor for the royal wedding. Finally, all her hard work had paid off.

Two years ago, one of the girls back home, Caoimhe Ó Flaithbertaigh, had traveled to Avaland to visit a distant relative. And when she'd worn one of Niamh's designs to a ball—a lovely dress of yellow silk, embroidered with metallic thread and enchanted with memories of early spring—she'd ensnared the most eligible bachelor of the Season, the young Duke of Aspendale. Since then, Avlish clients had trickled in steadily, all of them hungry for a taste of the magic that had turned a lowly Machlishwoman into a duchess. Niamh had made gowns for nobles desperate to make their powerless daughters irresistible, for young gentlewomen aiming to marry into the aristocracy, for matrons clinging to their faded beauty. Their ambitions had kept her family afloat these last two years—just barely. After all, few people in all of Machland could afford gowns enchanted by Ó Conchobhair magic anymore.

But now she did not need to worry about her mother, with her swollen joints and fading eyesight, or her grandmother, who grew frailer and more bitter by the day, or the roof that still needed thatching, or the cracked window courtesy of the neighbor boy Cillian and his goat. By some miracle, her work had captured the eye of the Prince Regent of Avaland himself.

Tailoring the royal wedding would give her the clout to open her own shop in the heart of the Avlish capital—and enough money to move Gran and Ma out of Machland and into a cozy townhouse. They'd never have to work or suffer another day of their lives. It was the opportunity of a lifetime.

Niamh only wished she did not feel so wretchedly selfish for taking it.

When she'd told Gran she was leaving, she'd looked at Niamh as though she didn't recognize her. *Your grandfather died fighting the Avlish to guarantee that you would have a life here in Machland. You and your magic are what those monsters tried and failed to snuff out. And now you want to use your craft to make clothes for them? I will never recover from that shame.*

Bringing shame to her family was the very last thing Niamh wanted to do. Every day of her life she'd been reminded of how lucky she was to live freely on Machlish soil, of just how much she owed to people like her grandfather. A good, obedient granddaughter would have torn the invitation to shreds right then and there. A good, obedient granddaughter would have instead proposed marrying someone who could give her stability—and children who might inherit the same magic flowing through her veins. She might not find happiness, but at least their culture would survive another generation.

But in that moment, with a letter from the prince regent in her hands, Niamh could not content herself with obedience. Whether Gran approved or not, whether it meant betraying her ancestors or not, she had to take care of her family in the only way she could.

She had to pay back the debt she owed them.

Niamh tucked the letter away and turned her face into the salt-laced wind. Out in front of her, the Machlish Sea rippled like a swath of gray fabric, foam stitched like a panel of lace across its surface. Glittering in the predawn light, all that water felt as endless as possibility.

"Docking in Sootham ten minutes!" a ship hand called. "Ten minutes to Sootham!"

She startled, banging her hip against the railing. "Oww . . ."

The pain faded quickly enough when she fixed her gaze on the city rising from the sea. Mist trailed off the coast, as white and gauzy as a bridal veil, and the barest thread of sunlight illuminated the jagged skyline. Niamh curled her fingers around the railing, practically vibrating with anticipation. It was all she could do to keep herself from swimming the rest of the way to shore.

When the ship at last ground to a halt and the dockhands tethered it to the pier, she collected her belongings and headed toward the gangplank. Her fellow passengers surged around her, shoving and shouting. More people than she'd ever seen in her life thronged on the deck. People cradled their squalling babies against their chests. Children with their bones pressing against their skin clutched their mothers' skirts. And girls no older than her glared right through her, with dirt beneath their nails and eyes as hard as iron. They all reeked of desperation and hope. All of them had no doubt left their homes and families behind to seek work here in Sootham. For the first time, Niamh feared that Gran was right. Perhaps she really had never learned that the world was cruel.

Niamh did her best to stay afloat, crushed as she was between shoulders and traveling cases. At one point, her feet lifted off the ground entirely. The rank, sharp stench of bodies was nearly unbearable, and by the time she stumbled onto the docks, her legs wobbled as though she were still out at sea.

She made her halting way forward, her fingers digging into the damp, fraying ropes that corralled them. Despite her disorientation, she managed to step over the rats scurrying across the dock and, by some miracle, resisted the impulse to apologize to them. At last, her feet touched solid ground. She looked up—and considered the possibility that she had boarded the wrong boat out of Machland.

The Sootham waiting for her at the end of the pier was nothing like she expected. Where was the glamor and gloss? The sprawling parks and bustling streets? Here, buildings slumped together wearily, as though they could barely manage to hold themselves up. The scent of sewage and brackish water settled thick over her.

No, this *had* to be Sootham. But if she could not find her way to the palace, she had nowhere else to go. She did not have enough money to return home, not that returning home was an option at all. She couldn't bear to watch her mother work through another sleepless night, magicless but determinedly sewing by the sallow glow of the shop's lacemaker lamp, or to see what even the simplest enchantment took out of her grandmother. Their livelihood rested on Niamh's shoulders now. She was strong enough to bear it.

Niamh drew in a deep, steadying breath and squinted through the gloom. There, a short distance away, she spied a carriage beneath the dim glow of a streetlamp. It was unobtrusive but lovely, painted an elegant lacquered black that shone even through the haze. Embossed on its side, in ruby red and brilliant gold, was the royal insignia: a rose, its petals pearled with golden droplets. She could almost believe that the carriage was something out of a fairy tale—that as soon as she looked away, it would settle down onto the earth, transformed back into a pumpkin by the cruel light of day.

As she approached, a footman stepped down from the back. He cut a statuesque figure, serious and stark and impossibly tall

in his fine livery. Niamh shivered. Standing before the carriage in
the dull lamplight, he looked for all the world like one of the Fair
Ones, ready to spirit her away to the Otherworld. He peered down
his nose at her with cold blue eyes, and at last, with the utmost
condescension, he asked, "Miss Niamh O'Connor?"

Clearly, he'd expected someone different. Niamh fought every
instinct she had to smooth down her hair or adjust her skirts. Four
days at sea, she was certain, had not been kind to her. She offered
him her most winning smile. "That's me."

He took her traveling case from her, holding it as he might a
wayward kitten by the scruff. "Well, then. I suppose you had better
come with me."

The exterior of the royal palace was all resplendent white stone,
with rows of windows and massive columns standing like soldiers
beneath a portico. It looked like something from the ancient world,
clean and precise and utterly imposing. The very sight of it took her
breath away. It was magnificent, but in truth, it rather hurt to look
at. In the ruthless glare of sunlight, everything shone.

"Wow," she whispered, pressing her face against the cool glass
of her window.

How could so much wealth possibly exist in the same city she'd
landed in? She couldn't believe that *this* was to be her home for
the Season. Perhaps, if she was lucky, she would run into someone
she knew from home. The last she'd heard, her friend Erin Ó Cinnéide was set to be transferred to the palace. How glorious it'd be,
to see her again after so many months apart.

Every noble family hired an enormous temporary staff for the
Season, and most of them came from Machland. From what she'd
gleaned from her friends' letters, it was brutal work, but at least
it was work at all. Machland might have its independence, but

it didn't have much else. The earth was still recovering from the Blight and the people from their losses. Nearly everyone Niamh grew up with had deserted Caterlow, off to pursue dreams of a better life across the Machlish Sea.

The carriage slowed to a stop before the palace, and Niamh spotted a woman—the housekeeper, she assumed—lurking by the doors with her arms crossed primly behind her back. In her stodgy black gown, she was a bruise against all that blinding white.

The footman hopped down from the carriage and opened the door for her. Another standing in wait in the driveway collected her belongings. All of her luggage was ferried away before she could open her mouth to thank him. As soon as she stepped out of the carriage, Niamh felt entirely overwhelmed. Without her traveling case, she had absolutely nothing to do with her hands. In the face of complete disorientation, it was somehow the only thing she could worry about. Niamh ascended the stairs to the veranda, doing her very best not to gawp at the splendid gardens or the artfully weathered statues in the yard. But when the housekeeper turned the full brunt of her gaze upon her, Niamh drew up short.

The housekeeper was a formidable woman, no older than her grandmother but built like a draft horse. Her hair was pulled back severely from her even more severe face. Her attention gave the impression of a knife aimed directly at Niamh's throat. She had no idea what to do. Erin worked in a grand house, and while her letters home contained veritable tomes full of court gossip and noble entanglements, Niamh had never paid them much mind. She began to suspect she should have.

Niamh curtsied. "A pleasure to meet you. Niamh Ó Conchobhair."

No reply came. When Niamh finally dared to look up again, the housekeeper was frowning at her with grave disapproval. "Can you do anything about that accent?"

For a moment, Niamh was too stunned to speak. Gran had warned her that the Avlish harbored just as much resentment as the

Machlish did. She had not, however, expected their disdain to be so transparent. "I'm afraid not, ma'am. My apologies."

"Pity." She clicked her tongue. "You may call me Mrs. Knight. His Royal Highness, the Prince Regent, has asked to see you. There are some things he wishes to discuss about your employment."

Her spine went ramrod straight. The Prince Regent of Avaland wished to see her? About her *job*? Surely Mrs. Knight could fill her in on anything regarding her stay here. "Me? Are you certain?"

"Quite," Mrs. Knight said dispassionately. "His Highness likes to be involved in the running of his household. He is a particular man."

Now Niamh saw the shape of it. By particular, she meant meddlesome. If he saw fit to concern himself with the affairs of one Machlish seamstress, she couldn't imagine how he ran an entire country.

She knew little about the royal family. Only that eight years ago, the king's health suddenly declined, and he never returned to public life. His wife died four years ago in a tragic accident. Their oldest son, Prince John, had been appointed by Parliament to rule as regent until his father recovered or—gods forbid—died. As for his younger brother, Christopher, Niamh knew nothing of him— only that he was to be wed in a month's time.

But if the prince regent was a particular man, she couldn't meet him in this condition. She smelled—if she was being generous— *stale* after four days on a ship. Gods only knew what her hair looked like. It was surely more knot than braid by now. "I fear I am not fit to be seen—"

"That much is apparent. However, His Royal Highness does not like to be kept waiting once he's set his mind on something. Come along."

Without waiting for a reply, Mrs. Knight disappeared into the house. Niamh followed her—and then stopped cold in the doorway. On the other side was another world entirely, as shimmering and strange as the realm of the Fair Ones, Domhan Síoraí.

"Oh," she breathed.

The palace surpassed her wildest imaginings. Everything was elegant and opulent, from the ornately carved wainscoting to the bright fabric of the upholstery and curtains. Every piece of furniture glittered: a gold inlay on a pillow here, a chair leg capped with a brass lion's head there. And the rosewood herringbone floor . . . It deserved an apology for enduring the soles of her filthy traveling boots.

"There is no time to gawk," Mrs. Knight said.

"Sorry!"

Mrs. Knight veered off down a corridor. Goodness, the woman could *move*. Niamh had to stumble to keep pace with her. As they passed, servants threw themselves out of their way and snapped to attention. Some of them even bowed, as if Mrs. Knight were the prince regent himself. Others, however, glowered at her with a barely leashed resentment. Niamh startled, training her gaze instead on the hard set of Mrs. Knight's shoulders. She supposed that no boss could be universally loved.

Finally, Mrs. Knight stopped in front of a door twice as tall as Niamh. Mounted above it was a golden statue of a hawk, its talons extended toward them. It seemed rather excessive, but the portent was not lost on her.

"His Highness will receive you here," Mrs. Knight said. "You will address him as such, and afterward as *sir*. Do you understand?"

Niamh nodded. Never had condescension been so welcome. Her stomach twisted itself into a knot, and her throat felt entirely too dry. She hoped she didn't vomit on this beautiful rug. That would almost certainly get her sent back to Caterlow—or straight to debtors' prison.

Slow down, she reminded herself, just as Gran had told her a thousand times before. *If you slow down, you'll make fewer mistakes.* She rocked her weight onto her toes and shook out her hands to dispel her nervous energy. Then, with a deep breath, she entered the drawing room.

Niamh opened her mouth to announce herself—and promptly tripped over a run in the carpet. She swallowed a sound of surprise and caught herself before she toppled headlong into an urn full of greenery.

"Are you quite all right?" Her host, His Royal Highness, the *Prince Regent of Avaland,* asked with a note of mild alarm.

Her cheeks burned furiously with humiliation. "Yes, Your Highness. Thank you."

By the time she regained the courage to look up again, he had risen from his seat. She guessed he was no older than thirty, but his weary, dour bearing belonged a man twenty years his senior. His dark brown hair was combed uncompromisingly into submission, with nary a strand out of place. His coat was simple and black, tailored in perfect, straight lines. Even his wedding ring, a simple band of gold, revealed no sign of wear. Everything about him, from the slash of his eyebrows to the harsh angles of his cheekbones, screamed *order.* He looked like a man carved from marble, perfectly at home in a palace from an era long gone.

But it was the young man standing beside him that Niamh couldn't look away from. He was no older than her own eighteen years. In the morning light, his golden eyes burned with an intensity just north of hostile. And when his gaze locked with hers, she swore her heart stopped. She steadied herself on the back of an armchair.

His features were narrow, as sharp and steely as a blade, almost . . . Well, she'd call him dangerous, but in truth, he was built like a sewing needle. She could break him in half if she really set her mind to it. He wore a black coat with peculiar notching in the lapels, a waistcoat of charcoal silk, and a black cravat knotted unfussily at his throat. She had never been one for a monochrome palette—it was quite unfashionable for daywear, not to mention *boring*—but his clothes were so impeccably tailored, she almost didn't mind it. His hair, the near-black of damp earth, was swept back into a bun at the nape of his neck.

He was the most beautiful man she had ever seen.

But the moment he opened his mouth, the spell he'd cast over her shattered.

With positively glacial hauteur, he asked, "Who are *you*?"

2

Surely, Niamh had misheard him.

Or perhaps he was joking. Yes, that had to be it. No one, especially a noble, could be so unaccountably rude. But when she forced herself to laugh, the mood didn't lighten. The young man stood there with his arms crossed and his knifepoint eyes leveled at her. Glinting within them was a challenge—and also an obvious trap.

Only a fool would take that bait.

"Niamh Ó Conchobhair." She curtsied as low as she could, hoping that was the proper thing to do. Oh, why had she not *listened* when Erin prattled on about the intricacies of Avlish high society and their absurd formalities? "It is an honor to meet you."

This clearly did not answer his question. If anything, it only served to displease him further. "I'm sure," he said acidly. With that, he turned to the prince regent again. "Why am I here?"

"This," the prince regent said, with barely restrained irritation, "is your tailor, Kit."

Your tailor. All the blood drained from her face as the reality of her situation set in. This horrible, abrasive man was the prince regent's brother. The second son of the King of Avaland. Prince Christopher, the Duke of Clearwater. The *groom*.

Kit did not deign to look at her. "Ah. So this is an ambush."

"I did not realize that an introduction would be such a terrible imposition to you." The prince regent lowered his voice. "You will have to forgive me for thinking you might like to speak with her before I had her take your measurements."

"Why would you think otherwise?" Kit's expression grew downright mutinous, and every syllable bristled with resentment. "I am yours to command."

That was when Niamh heard the sudden splinter of ceramic— and a brittle crash as it struck the floor. She turned toward the sound and nearly leapt out of her skin. The holly in the corner of the room had begun to seethe, and the veins of its leaves glowed gold with magic. Its roots pushed viciously through the crack in its container. New growth burst forth and arranged itself into perfect, layered topiaries. The prince regent's anger, it seemed, was as neat and fastidious as the rest of him.

Niamh recovered from her shock enough to pray that her jaw had remained shut. With every new generation, magic faded a little more from the world. It was rare indeed to encounter such potent magic in this day and age.

She had grown up on horror stories of the Avlish royal family's power. How it had caused the Blight by depleting the soil. How during the War of Machlish Independence, briars had torn from the earth and skewered men like living bayonets. Niamh had always suspected those legends were exaggerated. Now, she wasn't so certain what the Carmines were capable of.

How could the prince regent's father have wielded such power so callously? If he hadn't, maybe her family would not have known such hardship. Maybe fewer of her people would have had to board that ship. Maybe she wouldn't have had to leave behind everything she knew to care for the ones she loved. Anger roared to life within her, so suddenly she shocked herself.

But the prince regent seemed far too preoccupied with his brother to take any notice of her. He sighed through his teeth. The sparks of gold dulled in his eyes, and once again, he became the very picture of composure. As if by conjuration, a footman detached himself from the shadows and procured a pair of shears from his breast pocket. He set to work pruning the holly back into a manageable size, and the steady *clip, clip, clip* of the blades cut up the silence. Another servant appeared to sweep up the broken shards of the vase, there and gone in a matter of seconds.

"We will finish this discussion presently. In private." The prince regent, clearly beyond finished with Kit, turned to Niamh. His expression was unbearably earnest, as though he was speaking to a slighted highborn lady rather than a Machlish girl. After the dark turn of her own thoughts and how dismissively his housekeeper had treated her, it knocked her off-kilter. "I am terribly sorry, Miss O'Connor. My brother has forgotten himself."

Kit made a sound that was not quite a laugh. "Whatever you want to say to me, you can say it here."

Indignation swelled within her. She was a *person,* not a piece of furniture or a pawn in his ridiculous war-by-proxy. Perhaps he should think twice before treating his brother—the de facto ruler of the kingdom, no less—with such blatant disrespect in front of a stranger. Before she could think better of it, she said, "I take it you are not interested in fashion, then?"

The very air rang with tension. Both princes regarded her with open surprise, and she did her best not to wither beneath their attention.

Oh, gods. What had she done?

Kit's scowl slotted back into place. "No. I think it's a waste of time."

His curt dismissal stunned her. He didn't even bother with perfunctory politeness as he insulted her life's work. As cheerfully as she could manage, she said, "I am quite passionate about it myself."

"Is that so?" He sounded surprisingly curious, which gratified her enough to actually consider her answer.

There were far too many ways she could answer that question. Because sewing was the only thing she was good at. Because she was the only one in two generations who had even a glimmer of her family's dying craft, and it fell on her to preserve it. Because despite all the pressure, all the long hours, all the tears, little in the world made her happier than making other people happy. In the end, she settled on something safe but true. "I like beautiful things, and I like making things that make people feel beautiful."

"What nonsense." He spoke with such sharp and sudden disdain, it was as though she'd pressed on a bruise. "Beauty is nothing worth dedicating your life to. It's the domain of sycophants and peacocking fools."

Niamh recoiled. He was not just rude; he was *mean*. And entirely unreasonable, frankly. *He* was the one who was getting married. *He* was the one wearing shoes that cost more than she made in a month. *He* was the one wearing a silk waistcoat that practically begged to be engraved in a fashion magazine. Silk! In summer, no less. She hoped he would sweat through it. She hoped he—

"Show some respect to our guest, Christopher," the prince regent said sharply. "She is common, but she is divine-blooded."

Niamh had never heard the term *divine-blooded* before, but it was obvious what he meant: an ceird, the craft, *magic*. If the Avlish believed their magic came from the divine as well, perhaps Avlish

and Machlish myths were not as different as she'd been led to
believe.

Long ago, so the stories went, hundreds of gods sailed to Machland and made it their home. Before they hid themselves behind
the veil to the Domhan Síoraí, some had taken mortal lovers and
passed down their magic to their children. Every person with an
ceird claimed they could trace their ancestry back to one of the
Fair Ones. There was Luchta, who crafted swords and shields that
turned the tide of battle; Dian Cecht, whose remedies could cure
any wound; Goibnu, whose feasts could satisfy a man's hunger for
a decade; Bres, who could end any quarrel with his silver tongue;
Delbaeth, who could spit fire like a dragon; and of course, her
namesake, Niamh. She had always thought it cruelly ironic that
she was named after the Queen of the Land of Eternal Youth.

"As you wish, Jack." Kit rounded on her once more. "Let's see
it, then."

She understood his unspoken threat: *Give me a reason to not
put you back on that ship.* He didn't think himself above her; he
knew he was. From the moment she'd received the prince regent's
invitation, Niamh knew it was not a reward for what she had
achieved but the beginning of a new trial. Here, as a commoner,
as a Machlishwoman, she would have to work twice as hard to
earn her keep. Determination burned up all of her fear, and all
that remained, smoldering within her, was the need not only to
prove herself—but to prove Kit *wrong*.

"Gladly." It came out with far more fire and venom than she
intended. "But I will need my things brought to me."

The prince regent—Jack—hardly even lifted a finger before a
footman slipped out of the room. "At once. Please sit and make
yourself comfortable."

She sat gingerly on the edge of an armchair. "Thank you, Your
Highness."

After only a minute, the footman returned with Niamh's traveling case. She pawed through her meager worldly possessions, painfully aware of how coarse her life must have seemed to them, until she found her embroidery hoop, a pair of scissors, a spool of thread, and a pincushion. She measured out and snipped off a length of thread. When she dared to glance up, Kit was staring at her with an intensity that almost made her lose her nerve.

No, she reminded herself. *He will never have seen anything like you.*

Hers was far from the flashiest magic in the world. Once, in a time irrecoverable, perhaps a cloak made by an Ó Conchobhair could bring entire armies to heel. But Niamh had never wanted to change the world. Her clients sought her out for her designs but also for her craft. Whatever she sewed possessed a subtle compulsion. No one could quite describe it, other than this: when you saw some-one in a Niamh Ó Conchobhair piece, you felt something. Niamh had transformed a young widow into the very picture of sorrow. She had allowed wallflowers to vanish into the recesses of a ballroom. And two years ago, she had made Caoimhe Ó Flaithbertaigh into a duchess.

Niamh blew out a calming breath. She could do this.

A half-finished handkerchief was pinned in her embroidery hoop, one she'd worked on during the long voyage to Avaland. She'd painstakingly stitched wildflowers into it, so vivid that they seemed to be real, pressed and forgotten in a scrap of silk. She'd used thirty different colors of thread, after all. Just looking at it filled her with a longing for things she'd had and lost. As magic swelled within her, she thought of summer. It was always the best time of year in Caterlow, when all the children would run wild and barefoot through the fields, when the breeze off the sea cooled the sweat beaded on her forehead. Those days had always seemed end-less and brimming with possibility, happy in a way that felt inex-haustible. She'd stitched those memories into this piece, memories that had kept her afloat on the black waves of the Machlish Sea.

She was ready.

Something tugged sharply in her chest, no more painful than the prick of a needle. And then, her magic spooled out of her. The thread shimmered, as though she held a delicate beam of sunlight between her fingers. Its soft glow bathed the room, dancing on all the golden picture frames, on all the gleaming brass buttons studding the couches.

Kit swore, so quietly she nearly missed it.

Everything else fell away but the two of them and the tender ache of yearning threaded into the eye of her needle. His lips parted, and the light of her magic made his eyes luminous. Heat bloomed across the back of her neck, and her stomach fluttered strangely. If she did not know better, she'd say his expression was full of wonder.

No, she had to be imagining things. She tore her gaze away from him and began to sew little embellishments of gold into the design. By the time she finished, the petals looked shot through with sunlight, and all the leaves pearled with dew. As carefully as she could, she snipped off the loose thread and removed the fabric from the hoop.

"It isn't much, but I do not want to keep you here all day." She thrust the handkerchief in Kit's direction. "I hope this will give you a sense of what I can do."

When Kit took it from her, he looked five years younger in an instant. His eyes clouded over with a memory, one that transported him somewhere far away. But the effect was there and gone almost faster than she could blink. He dropped the handkerchief as though it had burned him. Niamh's heart twisted to see it lying on the floor in a crumpled heap. For a moment, he stared at it with a flush crawling up his neck.

"That," Kit said venomously, "is some sort of trick."

Jack, at least, spared her the indignity of having to defend herself.

"I will not hear another word from you. Miss O'Connor is the best seamstress I have found, and the best is what you will have."

Kit rose from his seat with all the coiled aggression of a cornered animal. He stood a full head shorter than his brother, but he filled the room with his anger. "I would sooner wear nothing to my wedding than anything she has so much as looked at."

Anger and confusion boiled within her, until she trembled with the effort to contain it. Her eyes welled with reflexive tears. A *trick*? She had learned to sew at her grandmother's elbow before she could even walk. She'd dedicated her entire life to mastering her craft, and it was the purest, truest thing she knew. She'd stitched a piece of her very soul into that handkerchief, and he'd acted as though she'd spat on his boots. What hurt the most was that he didn't even have the decency to address her directly. He wouldn't even look at her.

"Enough," Jack snapped. "My mind is made up. The court is already enamored with her work, and the King of Castilia is arriving with Infanta Rosa in two days' time. You have been away from court for too long, brother. I expect you will want to make a good impression."

Kit's expression shuttered. To Niamh's shock, he said nothing.

Away from court? It wasn't unusual for young nobles to go on grand tours, but the way Jack said it . . . It sounded almost like a punishment.

"As for you, Miss O'Connor," Jack continued wearily, "tell my staff what you need, and I will have it brought to you. That is, of course, if you have not changed your mind."

"I have not, sir. Thank you!" It came out far too loud. Struggling to rein herself in, she curtsied to him. "I will not waste this chance."

Just then, a tentative knock sounded on the door. It creaked open a fraction of an inch, and a muffled voice said, "A message for you, Your Highness."

"Do not hover there like a wraith. Come in." Jack closed his eyes, as though searching for some inner reservoir of patience. "What is it?"

The door opened just enough to admit a page boy, who lingered in the threshold with his gaze riveted to the floor. An envelope hung limply from his fingers. "Another letter from Helen Carlile, sir."

"For God's sake . . ." Jack crossed the room and snatched the letter from his page. *So much for courtly grace,* Niamh thought. "Another one? Another letter from Helen Carlile is what you interrupted me for?"

The page cringed. "I'm sorry, sir! This is the third in as many days, so I figured it was urgent."

"You were sorely mistaken." Jack tore the letter neatly in half. "I do not have time for her self-righteous screeds today—or any other day, for that matter. The next time you see one of these, send it back. Better yet, burn it. I do not want to hear even a whisper of the name Helen Carlile—or Lovelace, for that matter—in these halls. Do you understand?"

"Yes, sir." The page did not leave immediately. He glanced at Kit and Niamh, as though he were afraid of saying too much. "There is another thing. Your valet, sir . . . I thought you might like to know as soon as possible, given the circumstances."

Jack muttered something under his breath. For a moment, he looked quite exhausted, but by the time she blinked, he'd righted his stoic expression. "Very well. Send for Mrs. Knight at once. I will speak with her in my study."

"Yes, sir."

"Good. Dismissed." When the door slammed shut behind the page, Jack let out the most long-suffering sigh she had ever heard. "If you'll excuse me."

How could a valet and one woman, Niamh wondered, possibly cause a prince such frustration? And who was Lovelace?

She glanced at Kit as though he might provide some insight. But his gaze was trained like a marksman's rifle on his brother's retreating back, and it was filled with loathing. Her breath caught at the sight of it. It was not the petty sort of hatred children professed for their strict older siblings. This was as bitter as a winter night—and old, with roots going all the way down.

Kit had nursed this grudge for a long time.

When he caught her looking, he scowled. "What are you staring at me for?"

"I . . ." Her mouth hinged open. One of these days, she might just stick him with a needle out of spite. If anything, *he* was the one staring at *her*. "I am not!"

"Right." With that, he got up and stalked out of the room.

Niamh buried her face in her hands. This was the opportunity of a lifetime, and of course she was assigned to the most curmudgeonly, unsociable client in the entire *world*. Perhaps this offer truly had been fairy-tale perfect, exactly as Gran warned her. A beautiful ruse, like a glass apple filled with poison.

Nothing was going exactly as she'd dreamed it.

3

A few moments after Kit's departure, a maidservant named Abigail fetched Niamh and led her to her new bedchamber. Her thoughts turned in such anxious circles, she bumped into the doorframe—hard enough that Abigail paused and asked her if she was all right. Any coherent reply, however, vanished at the sight of her new room.

The heavy curtains let in a gauzy spill of midmorning light. It sparkled on the glass beads of a chandelier and patterned the carpet with delicate slivers of rainbow. It was all she could do not to throw herself onto the bed, but getting even a spot on those immaculate linens seemed to Niamh a sin of the highest order. Even from a distance, she could see how finely woven they were. They were even embroidered with the rose crest of House Carmine in gleaming white thread.

"Shall I send for a bath?" Abigail asked tactfully.

"Please. That would be lovely."

Within a few minutes, a small contingent of servants had hauled up a claw-footed bathtub and set it beside the fireplace. Abigail wheeled over a cart cluttered with elegant glass bottles, then drew the privacy screen.

"Call for me if you need anything, miss," she said.

And with that, Niamh was left alone.

Immediately, her throat tightened, and her eyes stung. *Don't cry*, she told herself. Oh, how she hated that she cried whenever she was stressed or angry. But once she'd begun, she could not stop. Tears spilled down her cheeks, and she didn't bother to wipe them away. All she could think of were Kit Carmine's amber eyes, boring into her as though she were a rat that had snuck into the wine cellar. All she could hear was the utter contempt for her in his voice.

A peacocking fool. A sycophant.

He didn't know the first thing about her.

When she left Caterlow three days ago, her mother had cradled her face and said, *The Season is dangerous for a girl like you. If you want to go, a stor, I will not stop you. Just know that our well-being isn't your responsibility.*

Niamh had felt her fingers against her chin, the tips callused from decades of sewing and the joints swollen from hours of work. She'd looked into her mother's eyes, hooded and blue as her own were, and drank in the premature wrinkles gathered at the corners. It had struck her then as it never had before that Ma was not a young woman anymore.

Of course her family's well-being was her responsibility. Especially now that she was in Avaland, in the home of the very family who'd left them all to die. A fresh wave of guilt knocked her nearly breathless.

The Machlish had suffered greatly under seven hundred years of Avlish rule. Machland, those early colonizers had said, was lush and fruitful; its bounty could never be depleted. It had grown wild and wicked in the time its people had been left to their own devices, but with the right care, it would surely flourish. But as the centuries dragged on, the Avlish grew greedier. They exported nearly everything that grew back to the motherland, leaving nothing for the people who tended the land. They squeezed and squeezed until there was nothing left to give. The last straw was the Blight.

The Avlish called it a terrible accident. The Machlish called it slaughter.

Carmine magic, the Avlish claimed, made fallowing unnecessary. And so, they forced the land to produce until it could produce no more. One year, the crops withered. And the next year, and the year after that.

Even though his family's divine blood had tainted the very earth, Kit and Jack's father did nothing. He watched as a million people starved and a million more fled the island. The ensuing rebellion was bloody and swift. For twenty-five years, Machland had been a sovereign nation. But no one who lived through it had forgotten or forgiven.

Niamh had grown up alongside those ghosts. All her life, she'd wanted to lighten her family's burdens, to drive away the past that haunted them still. She chose to be happy each day precisely because she knew how much worse things could be. She smiled because she couldn't bear to let them believe they'd failed her for even a moment. *Of course* it was her responsibility to care for them after everything they'd been through. It was such a small thing to try to give them the comfort they'd never had as children.

It was such a small thing to be good.

When she finally exhausted herself, Niamh scrubbed the tears from her face, unlaced her gown and stays, then carefully climbed into the tub. The water sloshed against her calves, almost painfully hot. The steam billowing around her smelled of lavender and rosemary. Tentatively, Niamh sank down to her chin in the water—

and wished, for her own conscience's sake, that she enjoyed it less. It was far more luxuriant than anything she had ever experienced. In Caterlow, she'd only ever bathed with a pitcher and basin, which admittedly might be more practical. Dirt lifted off her body in clouds, but at least some of her tension melted away with the grime. Best not to look too closely at the water.

She retrieved a comb from the cart and began working out the tangles in her hair. It floated atop the murky water, as black as the tide. With a slow-mounting dread, she stared at the strand of silver that ran through it. No change yet, but soon . . .

No, it wasn't worth fretting about.

You aren't sick until you're sick.

Sighing, Niamh brushed her hair back behind her shoulder so she didn't have to look at it anymore. She draped her arms over the lip of the copper tub and pillowed her cheek against her shoulder. The metal bit into her skin with cold, but the fire crackling lazily in the hearth warmed her.

In just a few weeks, this would all be over. With the money she earned from this commission, her family could join her in Sootham. Gran might resent it at first, but soon enough, she would see that a better, more comfortable life awaited them here. She would come to appreciate all these beautiful, frivolous things.

Assuming, of course, Niamh could make something incredible enough to enchant even a cynic like Kit Carmine.

Later that afternoon, Niamh eased open the door to her room. Down the hall, sunlight flooded through the window and washed the corridor as pink and watery as a wound.

She had no idea where the kitchens were, but surely, they could not be all that difficult to find. If her friend Erin was anywhere, it'd be there. Long ago, the Ó Cinnéide clan was renowned for their healing abilities. They could brew an elixir capable of restoring a man from the brink of death or craft a poultice that could regrow a severed limb. The most impressive thing Erin had managed was a tea that soothed the inflammation in Niamh's joints for a few hours. Otherwise, she made delicious cakes.

As she made her way toward the staircase, a great sound—a sort of bellowing, if she had to describe it—echoed up from below.

And then, chaos erupted.

A flurry of footsteps thundered against the hardwood floor, and chatter zipped through the halls. Niamh seized the banister and peered over the edge. Far below her, servants hurried through the corridors, carrying plates, trays, and silverware polished to an armor-bright gleam. She couldn't help marveling at how hectic it all was—and how much easier it would be if any of them possessed an ceird. There were folks in Caterlow who could summon an object to their hand from across the room, and those who could lift three times the weight of an ordinary man. While she'd heard that some Avlish commoners possessed the craft, it was exceptionally rare. How silly that no one doing anything *practical* had any magical assistance.

How strange, it occurred to her after a moment, *that there are no Machlish servants with the craft here to help.*

"What are you doing standing around?"

Niamh startled, wheeling back from the banister. A young woman glared at her, a basket of linens balanced on her hip. Intelligently, Niamh said, "Who, me?"

The other girl hardly seemed to be listening. "The prince regent is in a foul temper, you know. Do you want him to catch you idle? Staring dreamy-eyed at nothing when we're already short-staffed?"

It was clear that she'd been mistaken for a servant. Niamh bobbed her knees and averted her eyes. "No, ma'am. Sorry, ma'am."

"Go on, then. And look alive."

Niamh nearly did as she was told, but perhaps she could find out if Erin had been transferred yet. "Pardon me, but is there a girl named Erin Ó Cinnéide here?"

"Erin," she repeated with a thoughtful purse of her lips. But just as quickly as recognition lit her eyes, her expression darkened. "Yes. She was here, but she left just two days ago."

She *left*? That could not be right. "She did? Why?"

"You tell me," the girl replied with venom. She shoved past her, muttering something about *the lazy Machlish* under her breath.

After what Kit Carmine had put her through, Niamh had no energy left to take it to heart, especially not when she was so puzzled. Erin had seemed so content in Sootham. Her letters always sparkled with her subtle humor and serene wisdom—and were pages long, at that. Surely, she would have mentioned that she planned to return to Caterlow or that she was unhappy here. But with the post as slow as it was, it was very likely the letter hadn't reached Niamh before she'd left Machland. She'd write Erin at once and get to the bottom of it.

Her stomach growled insistently. But first, a very late breakfast.

The farther Niamh ventured into the house, the more the chaos intensified. Footmen darted every which way, hefting flower arrangements and torches and even a sculpture carved from solid ice. Others balanced precariously on ladders, placing white candles on every available surface. Maids busied themselves polishing the mirrors to a lethal sheen. A beam of sunlight glanced off one mirror's surface—and flung itself directly into her eyes. Momentarily blinded, she bumped into some poor soul minding their own business.

"I am so sorry!" she cried at the same time a man said, "Why, if it isn't Niamh O'Connor!"

Niamh took a step back to drink in the sight of him. The young man standing before her clearly knew the power of good style: a powder-blue coat with cuffs that hung low over his knuckles in the Jaillean style and a high-collared waistcoat patterned with marigold plaid. He'd paired them smartly with turquoise gloves and a matching neckcloth tied at a jaunty angle. Even his hair was utterly au courant, blond and romantically wild, an effect made possible by an alarming amount of pomade. A nobleman, no doubt, with that affected carelessness and telltale accent.

"You know me?" She tried her best not to sound shocked.

"Of course I do. I've been an admirer of your work since it dazzled high society two Seasons ago. I've been dying for a piece myself, actually."

"Oh!" She suddenly felt quite flustered. "Thank you very much. I'd be happy to make you something when I have the time."

"Don't commit to anything just yet." His smile turned mischievous. "Because I've just returned from a ride with Kit and heard the most *fascinating* things about you."

The very mention of the prince's name dissolved all capacity for language, all sense. She thought she had cried the worst of her anger out, but it kindled within her anew. Clearly, it showed on her face because he said, "He made that good of an impression on you, I see."

Oh, bother. Now she had to lie. According to every fairy tale she'd ever read, princes were supposed to be gallant and romantic. The real princes she'd met, however, were two for two on being eccentrics. "Yes, indeed! He was very charming."

At this, her companion's composure broke. He barked out a most ungentlemanly laugh.

"You must be Saint Imogen herself if you genuinely believe that." He procured a handkerchief—as charmingly patterned as his waistcoat—from his breast pocket and dabbed at his eyes. "Thank you. I needed that today."

"You're welcome," she said dejectedly.

"Ah, where are my manners? I forget myself around beautiful women." He extended a hand to her and smiled wryly, as though letting her know he was playacting. "Gabriel Sinclair."

She placed her hand in his and tried not to blush as he kissed the air just above her knuckles. "A pleasure to meet you, Lord Sinclair."

"Just Sinclair will do." His easy smile faded. "You look lost. I can show you where you're going if you'd like."

At least *someone* in this palace wanted to help her. "Do you know where the kitchens are?"

"The kitchens?" He frowned incredulously. "Why don't I send for tea instead?"

"No, no, that is quite all right! I couldn't impose on you that way."

"I'm afraid I must insist. Everyone needs a friend in court." He winked. "Especially when you're an outsider."

Sinclair whisked her down another corridor. He must have been good friends with the Carmines, indeed; he navigated the palace as though he'd wandered its halls a thousand times before, and as he walked, he gave orders to their staff with a breezy, self-effacing confidence. Every now and again, however, Niamh caught one of them snickering or whispering furtively to another as they passed. Sinclair, if he noticed at all, did not react. Niamh burned with curiosity. If even the servants felt bold enough to smirk at him, perhaps he'd counted *himself* among the outsiders at court.

Once they found seats in a sunroom, it took only a few minutes for a harried-looking girl to deliver the tea service. She set down a tower of biscuits and a ceramic teapot piping with fragrant steam before vanishing once more.

As Sinclair poured them each a cup, Niamh shoved a biscuit into her mouth. "You are a lifesaver. Thank you."

"I know," said Sinclair. "Please chew. You're making me nervous."

Niamh obeyed. Now that she'd given herself a moment to actually taste it, she could appreciate the flavor: delicately floral and rich with butter. She swallowed a mouthful of tea—and immediately regretted it. It scalded her throat, but at least it left behind a pleasant note of caramel. Sinclair looked genuinely impressed.

"It seems quite hectic here today," Niamh said. "Do you know what is going on?"

"Jack is in a foul mood, and so his staff is in a foul mood." He made a face. "*The Tattler* has returned for the Season."

"*The Tattler*?"

"It's a scandal sheet of sorts," he replied. "Although, I confess, the author has a strange sensibility."

"How do you mean?"

"There is, of course, the typical Season gossip, but they always connect it to politics. Lovelace styles themself as some sort of champion for the downtrodden, but it's all fustian nonsense." Sinclair leaned back in his chair. "I don't disagree with their message, of course, but they've been pushing their political agenda for almost three years now and have gotten nothing for their efforts. What I have to admire, though, is that they absolutely *loathe* Jack. They've been poking at him relentlessly for as long as they've been writing."

"Really?" Niamh's voice dropped to a whisper. While she hardly knew the man, she couldn't imagine him abiding any kind of open ridicule for three minutes, much less three years. He seemed far too proud. "Why haven't they been stopped?"

"If Jack could catch them, I'm sure they would be imprisoned at the very least. Not even their publisher knows who they are, but somehow, they know everything about everyone." He crumbled a biscuit absently into pieces. "Anyone who's mentioned in the column is sent a copy the day before it's published. It's meant as an opportunity to bribe Lovelace for their silence. Don't ask me how I know."

"They have written about you?"

"A few times, yes, although my father, the Duke of Pelinor, took it worse than I did. It's not as bad as it sounds. There's something almost freeing about having the worst of you already exposed." She could hear the undercurrent of anger in his voice, the *lie*, even beneath his blasé tone. Although they'd just met, it hurt to watch him gloss over something that clearly still pained him. "They're a nuisance, but they can be interesting from time to time. Would you like to see?"

Niamh hesitated. It was almost certainly wrong to indulge in idle gossip about her employer, but she did love a little scandal every now and again. "I would."

He rang for a servant to bring them *The Daily Chronicle*. When it arrived, he asked, not unkindly, "Can you read?"

It was a fair question; few common girls could. Her mother had taught her, but she so rarely read anything but captions in fashion magazines. "Well enough, I hope."

He handed it to her. The paper was creased and torn from where people must have snatched it from one another's hands. Niamh fumbled to open it, trying not to feel horribly provincial.

She'd never seen a publication quite like this before. Receiving news daily seemed an unthinkable wonder to her, far stranger than magic. In Caterlow, information reached them slowly. News from the continent could take a month to arrive in Machlish cities, two weeks from Avaland, and from overseas, it could sometimes take half a year. Add another week for it to filter to villages like Caterlow, where one of the few literate folks in town recited the paper in the pub. They hadn't much need for gossip columns, anyway. Everybody knew one another's business. If you spoke a secret aloud, the wind would carry it to every home in the village before the day's end.

The Chronicle, to her dismay, proved quite difficult to read. The print was so small, as though the typesetter had struggled to cram every story onto the first page. Niamh squinted, sorely wishing she had a magnifying glass. She flipped to the last page, and there, tucked between advertisements for carriages and petticoats, was a section called *The Tattler*.

Lovelace, it seemed, referred to everyone they mentioned by

epithets, but the details seemed incriminating enough for any-one well-connected to guess their true identities. And others, she found, were barely disguised at all.

I recently heard of a disastrous breakfast at the household of one Lord W——, who you may recall from a few months ago, due to his involvement with a certain Gun in a Nursery Incident. Apparently, when it came time to serve the wine, no servants materialized, and the gathering disbanded after no more than an hour. It was a terrible embarrassment. I tell you this, not to deal in idle gossip, but to offer you reassurance—or perhaps a warning.

You may find that your social calendars are emptier this Season. Rest assured, your friends (most likely) do not hate you. Machlish workers across the city are walking out on their duties, in protest of poor treatment—and to demand reparations for the Blight, at the urging of one Mistress HC. On the topic of Mistress HC, I must put an end to these ridiculous rumors that she and I are one and the same. Indeed, we share a cause, and I admire her for organizing so effectively. But have you heard her speak? The woman is painfully earnest—and I have never been earnest a day in my life. But I digress. A Certain Someone determinedly refuses to meet with her, even as his own servants quit in droves.

CS may not live up to his illustrious father's reputation—one misses that bold confidence, if not that nasty temper—but it seems they share a certain distaste for our Machlish neighbors. Or perhaps he is too busy white-knuckling the leash of our very own Wayward Son, who has returned to us at last after four long years. It remains to be seen whether WS has improved his manners since last we saw him, but I for one have my doubts.

All I can be certain of is that discontent brews this Season, both among the Machlish and within the court. For his own sake and out of a belief in the inherent dignity of all mankind,

I urge CS to comply with the demands of some of the most vulnerable in Avlish society. As you have seen—and will continue to feel—your pleasures depend on their labor and their magic.

Niamh set the paper down with uneasiness souring her stomach. Even after all these years, it seemed the Avlish would never tire of crushing her people underfoot. But could it be true that even Jack was mistreating his Machlish servants? So far, he'd been gracious to her, but perhaps she couldn't trust herself. She'd always been too credulous—too inclined to see the best in people. Now, she wondered if the length of Erin's letters was a reflection not of her excitement but her loneliness.

How could Niamh have failed to see it?

The Tattler was an unusual scandal sheet, indeed. To suggest the prince regent was a poor ruler and to support demands for reparations so openly . . . She certainly hoped Lovelace had taken precautions to ensure they were never exposed. Even in Caterlow, she'd heard what had happened in Jaille some thirty years ago. The commoners grew sick of the magical elite, and one day, they burned their royal family alive in the streets. Ever since then, every monarch on the continent had silenced dissenters with shocking swiftness.

And yet, this was the opinion of only one person—and likely not even one of Jack's own subjects, at that. Lovelace had to be Machlish. Who among the Avlish would care enough to write in support of foreign commoners? "It seems someone as busy as the prince regent would have more pressing things to worry about than a columnist."

"Yes, well, Jack has a nasty habit of making everything his business." Judging by Sinclair's sour expression, Niamh saw she'd pressed on an old wound. "Still, he's been under a great deal of pressure. The court can grow quite irritated when their social engagements are impacted. And as Lovelace said, Jack doesn't exactly have the reputation his father did."

"He isn't popular?"

"He's not his father," Sinclair replied. "In his prime, the king was a god among men. He commanded respect—or maybe just fear. He was also a true politician. Jack, meanwhile, cares more for governing his household than his kingdom."

Niamh had noticed as much. He had both a wife and a house-keeper, who surely could run the palace without his oversight. Tentatively, she asked, "Is it customary for Avlish rulers to be so involved in the management of their staff?"

"Oh, no. Jack is a busybody in a class of his own. He trusts no one to do a single thing right." He seemed quite delighted by the question but paused to collect himself. "In all seriousness, these days, most kings are figureheads with few actual political responsibilities—unless they *want* to be involved, like Jack's father was. The royal coffers fund the civil government, and the king commands the military. Apart from that, Parliament manages the finer details of running the kingdom.

"Our rulers have found ways to entertain themselves when they grow bored of statecraft." Sinclair waved a hand. "The king had his art collection. Jack's grandfather had a kennel full of the most beautiful greyhounds you've ever seen. And Jack . . . well, he has his social calendar. Planning the wedding has kept him quite busy."

"Oh," she said, dumbfounded.

"Indeed." Sinclair raised his teacup to her. "Welcome to Avaland."

Welcome, indeed. That made her job twice as difficult. If Kit refused to wear anything she made, then Jack would surely re-place her with someone Kit would tolerate. Despite his threats, the prince couldn't very well go naked to his own wedding. Her face burned at the memory. "Sinclair, I don't mean to pry, since I know we have just met, but I must ask . . ."

He leaned in. "Go on."

"Do you know Prince Christopher well?"

Sinclair blew out a breath. "*Too* well, if you ask me. We've known each other since we were children, so neither of us had much choice in the matter of our friendship."

So that explained it. She grinned, finding herself a little charmed at the thought of them interacting. "You two don't seem to have a lot in common. I confess, I find it hard to imagine what you talk about."

"Oh, plenty. Kit maintains an alphabetized list of all my faults. He likes to nag me about each and every one of them."

Niamh laughed. "That, I can believe."

Sinclair gave her a sly look. "Why do you ask?"

"It is nothing untoward, I swear! I would appreciate your advice, if you have any to give me. It's clear His Highness despises me, and somehow, I have to make him something he doesn't hate. He said . . ." Niamh could hardly bear to repeat what he'd *actually* said. ". . . that he would rather die than wear any of my clothes."

"That certainly sounds like Kit," Sinclair muttered with the long-suffering resignation of someone who'd heard the same story a thousand times before. He took on quite a serious expression. "I'm not trying to make excuses for him, but you should understand that he's been waging a war against himself for a long time. Sometimes you get caught in the cross fire. Try not to take it personally."

"I will certainly try." She did not sound at all convincing, even to her own ears.

"That's the spirit." Playfulness lit up his eyes again. "Once you strip off all those thorns, he's not so bad. He has a sweet, tender inside. So just be yourself. You're like a pint-sized hurricane of earnestness and good cheer. It's . . . Well, it's refreshing."

Niamh was not sure which was worse: the mental image of Kit's *sweet, tender inside* or being asked to take *pint-sized* as a compliment. As if being unable to reach anything on her own was not punishment enough. "Thank you, Sinclair. I think."

"My pleasure." He grinned. "Good luck."

She had a feeling she would need it.

4

*T*he next morning, a footman escorted Niamh to her new studio and handed her a letter composed in the prince regent's immaculate handwriting.

Dear Miss O'Connor,

Please accept my sincerest apologies on my brother's behalf, and for my sudden departure yesterday. I hope you are settling in well, and do not hesitate to let my staff know if there is anything at all you might need . . .

The note went on to describe, in excruciating detail, Kit's social calendar for the Season. In addition to an outfit for the presentation of the debutantes next week—and the arrival of his fiancée, the first time in one hundred years that the Castilian royal family would stand on Avlish soil without a war banner and a navy behind them—he would need suits for two balls a week, a hunting jacket, and, of course, the traditional wedding cloak.

Before she left Machland, Niamh had cobbled together as much information as she could on Avlish wedding traditions. As part of the ceremony, the groom's best man placed a cloak around his shoulders to symbolize his new role as husband and protector. It recalled, apparently, a chivalric era, where a knight's squire would help him dress for battle. How unromantic, Niamh thought, to see marriage as a battle to be won. In Machland, they exchanged golden coins and danced until dawn. Here, a wedding ended no later than noon.

Niamh scanned the rest of Jack's note—and nearly gasped with excitement. Infanta Rosa had requested that Niamh design her wedding dress.

Details, Jack wrote, *to be finalized upon her arrival.*

It was an enormous honor, one she hadn't dared to hope for. But after a moment, it sank in exactly what had been asked of her. She would need to make ten pieces in six weeks. Even though he'd promised her a team of assistants to help assemble the garments she designed, the prospect of all that work daunted her more than she cared to admit. It took the better part of ten minutes for complete and utter overwhelm to harden into stubborn determination. Neither absurd deadlines nor difficult princes could frighten her. Not when Gran and Ma were counting on her.

Especially not when she'd been given such a beautiful workspace.

The staff had stocked the workshop with everything she could possibly need and more. There was a spinning wheel tucked into the corner—even a loom—and a gorgeous worktable situated just beneath the bay windows. The bookcases had been emptied and refilled with sumptuous bolts of fabric, everything far finer than she could've ever dreamed of purchasing herself.

She stood in the middle of the room with her hands clasped at her chest. She never wanted to leave this place. She couldn't believe that, even if only for a month, all of this was *hers*. If only for a month, she could imagine that she truly belonged in a place as beautiful as this. That maybe she even deserved it.

Niamh gathered her skirts in her hands and twirled through the open space. She'd never learned to dance, but she almost heard the swell of the string quartet now. The weightless one-two-three of the steps, the steady touch of her partner's hand at her waist, and—

"What are you doing?"

She shrieked in surprise. When she whirled toward the voice, she saw Kit standing in the doorway. She dropped her skirts and steadied herself before she trod on the hem. "Did you knock?"

For a moment, he only stared at her. He wore a peculiar expression, caught somewhere between bemusement and irritation. "Yes. I knocked."

"Well, please knock louder next time!" Blood rushed through her ears, and her face burned with embarrassment. This was precisely why she couldn't indulge her *flights of fancy*, as Gran liked to call them. Anytime she paused to enjoy something, anytime she indulged herself, something terrible happened. She'd wasted too many afternoons sketching out impractical, unsellable gowns, or daydreaming away the hours while a loaf of bread burned in the oven. And now, she'd been caught dancing alone by the most judgmental man in Avaland. "You scared me."

"You were lost in your own world. I hardly see how that's my fault."

Niamh resisted the urge to groan aloud. Surely, he had more important things to do than mock her. He was lucky his voice was as nice as his eyes, or no one would be able to stand him at all. It had a pleasing rasp to it, like the tide over a rocky shore.

She forced a polite smile. "What can I do for you, Your Highness?"

"Don't call me that. *Your Highness* is my brother."

So he and Sinclair *did* have something in common. Neither of them had much regard for things like titles or formality. Still, Kit couldn't hide his true nature. All the pride radiating off him—the upturned nose, the disdainful curl of his lip—was testament enough to his princeliness.

"My lord, then?" she tried.

He sighed exasperatedly. "Just Kit."

"Very well, my . . ." She caught herself before the very regrettable words *my Kit* left her mouth. No, it was far too intimate. She couldn't call him by his given name, so she would not call him anything at all. "Ehm . . . I'm sorry. What is it you wanted again?"

"I'm supposed to get fitted for a new coat." He said *fitted* as though it were a method of torture and *coat* as though it were an instrument of one.

All at once, the memory of his insult came flooding back. *I would sooner wear nothing to my wedding than anything she has so much as looked at.* Hurt knotted itself tight within her, but she drew in a deep breath to steady herself. Everyone deserved a second chance. Sinclair had suggested as much, in his way.

"Have you changed your mind, then?" Immediately, she wished she could wrangle he words back into her mouth. She'd meant to sound playful, but all her hurt feelings tumbled out like thread from an unraveling spool.

Kit straightened up, and his eyes narrowed distrustfully. "About what?"

You know very well what. She shoved her wounded pride down. If he wanted to believe she was nothing but an airheaded, peacocking fool, so be it. With as sweet a smile as she could manage, she said, "You aren't planning to go naked to your wedding anymore?"

"I'm here, aren't I?" he asked, entirely and disappointingly unfazed. "Let's get this over with."

"As you wish, sir."

She hadn't yet mapped out the new studio, but it couldn't be that hard to find what she needed. She flung open the drawers of her worktable and was disturbed to see everything organized by color, every tool exactly aligned in perfect little rows. Whoever did this was very fastidious indeed. Her own method of organization was . . . Well, she supposed calling it a method would be a stretch of the imagination.

After a few moments of rummaging, she grabbed a notebook, tucked a pencil behind her ear, and draped a strip of tailor's tape around her neck. Kit stood exactly where she'd left him: arms crossed, lurking halfway out the door, ready to bolt at the slightest provocation.

She gestured to the mirror. "Stand here, please."

To her surprise, he obeyed without complaint. He skulked into the room as if one of the dress forms might suddenly leap at him, or a swath of colorful silk might fly from its bolt and garrote him. It admittedly unnerved her to have him so close, with him glaring down the bridge of his nose at her. He was as lean and coiled as a wolf in midwinter and shorter than most men she'd met. But as slight as he was, she was smaller. There were a few inches of height between them. That would make things difficult.

"One moment."

Niamh retreated to the corner of the room and dragged over a footrest. She unwound the tailor's tape from around her neck, then climbed onto the ottoman. The legs wobbled beneath her weight, and Niamh swore she saw Kit flinch, as though he meant to steady her but stopped himself at the last moment. It surprised her enough that she almost knocked herself off-balance again. Perhaps he still possessed some gentlemanly instinct. Or perhaps she'd imagined it entirely. He stared resolutely at the wall, a muscle in his jaw feathering.

Her hair still hung loose around her shoulders, so she swept it back into a chignon. One glance in the mirror revealed that she looked a complete and utter mess, but she couldn't be bothered with it at the moment. It wasn't as though she could impress him if she tried.

She began taking his measurements: his height, the breadth of his shoulders, the length of his arm . . . By some miracle, he allowed her to manipulate him like a doll and wore only a slightly martyred expression. But now, she had exhausted everything safe. *Safe.* How ridiculous. She was a consummate professional. *He* was the one who would undoubtedly be fussy and awkward about what came next, so she would warn him and be done with it.

"So . . ." An unpromising start. She cleared her throat and tried again. "I will need to be a little close for the next few measurements. If that bothers you—"

"Just do it."

"Right," she replied with false cheer. "Lift your arms for me, please."

The silence ground miserably on. Her arms were too short to spare either of them the discomfort of proximity. Niamh sidled closer to him, until she pressed herself nearly flush against his back. Heat radiated off him, along with the scent of growing things—and tobacco. If only she could stop *noticing* him. Never in her life had she felt so self-sabotaging. As she looped the tailor's tape around his chest, she felt as much as saw his muscles wind tighter. As her elbow grazed his ribs, his breath hitched. The fabric of his shirt whispered against her skin, and—

"Do you have something you want to say to me?" Kit asked.

His bluntness all but crushed her every untoward thought. "Huh?"

"You've been acting skittish and strange from the moment I walked through the door. If there's something on your mind, out with it."

Skittish and strange. Oh, the nerve of him! The last of her patience snapped. "*Well,*" she drawled, "since you asked so nicely, I thought you might want to apologize."

Kit's face slackened with surprise. She watched as he pulled himself back together piece by piece, his expression darkening with understanding. "Sorry."

Sorry, spat out like a broken tooth. As though she'd extracted a confession from him under torture. If she wasn't so furious with him, she might have laughed. "Is that all?"

His eyes flashed with bitter frustration. "What else do you want me to say?"

"I don't know." Her heart beat so wildly, she could barely hear herself over its thunderous roar. Some distant part of her knew she should demur or simper or stand down, that she should not talk to a prince this way. Perhaps it was her finite days that gave her courage, or perhaps it was the seamstress in her. She'd never been able to resist tugging at loose threads. "That you regret calling my craft a *trick*?"

He fixed his gaze on the wall past her shoulder. "I was angry when I said that."

"I'm angry *now*. My work is . . ." *Me,* she almost caught herself confessing. "It is personal!"

"I'm not going to apologize for not falling at your feet with awe. I'm not the one who asked you to come here."

"That is not what I meant." Her voice trembled. If she cried now, she would never forgive herself. "It was cruel, and you know it."

"I do know it." He bristled. "I said I was sorry."

And that, she supposed, was the extent of the apology she could expect from him. How little he must've thought of her to believe that was all she deserved. A Machlish girl, after all, was worth less than nothing. In the silence, the gulf widened and widened between them.

"I need to finish my measurements" was all she could think to say.

As she continued her work, her mood darkened. Sinclair had told her that she would be caught in the cross fire of whatever war

Kit had chosen to wage. Now, Niamh saw the battlefield plainly, with two Carmine-red flags planted in the earth. His marriage to Infanta Rosa would be a union of duty, not of love.

I didn't ask you to come here.

I am yours to command.

Jack had arranged this marriage. And although Kit had agreed to it, he clearly intended to spite everyone to the bitter end.

Suddenly, Niamh felt terribly sad. She had always loved love. As much as she yearned for it, she couldn't fathom something so bright and wild. It would burn her up like kindling. Life was too painfully short. She couldn't burden someone else with the intimacy of that knowledge, which she'd carried with her since she first noticed her fingers turn deathly white in the cold. But while love was not for girls like her, the hopeless romantic within her couldn't be denied. She couldn't be entirely certain where it had come from. Machlish myth, after all, was not so whimsical and kind as to promise everlasting love. In fact, her namesake might have the most tragic romance of all.

Long ago, Queen Niamh took a mortal lover and brought him to her castle in the Land of Eternal Youth, where spring reigned forever. Nothing ever died, and nothing ever changed. But after many years together, her lover grew homesick and longed to see all the people he had left behind. Niamh warned him that his family and friends were gone, but she knew she could not keep him like a prisoner. She knew that his loneliness was more powerful than their love.

Reluctantly, she agreed to let him go—but only if he promised never to let his feet touch the earth. As he rode across the countryside, searching for familiar faces, he realized that what Niamh had said was true. Everyone he ever knew and everyone he ever loved was long dead. As he drew away from the village he once called home, his horse spooked at a rustle in the grass and threw him from his seat. The moment he struck the ground, his hundreds of years seized upon him at once, and he transformed into a feeble old man.

No good ever came from loving fragile things.

Niamh had never cared for Machlish tales. They made her terribly depressed, all of them filled with tragedy and war and the impossible weight of honor. But she'd spent many nights as a girl paging through a book of fairy tales imported from Jaille: stories about peasant girls who snuck off to balls in glass slippers, who married princes because of their goodness and beauty, who loved fiercely enough to break terrible curses. They were impossible, wondrous, romantic stories, and they'd filled her up with hopeless yearning. She very much doubted someone like Kit cared a whit for romance, but it seemed a shame he might never get a chance to experience it himself.

When the prickly silence threatened to drive her mad, she sighed. "Is there anything about the wedding you are looking forward to?"

Kit glared at her disbelievingly. "Are you *trying* to provoke me?"

"What? No! I . . ." She resisted the urge to strangle him with the tailor's tape looped around his neck. "I am just making conversation."

"Most people might try commenting on the weather," he said, with a begrudging sort of admiration. "You're impertinent."

"And *you* are combative."

He squinted at her, but he did not look angry. In fact, he seemed almost incredulous. "What, are you going to scold me now?"

Feeling ridiculous and exposed looming above him on the ottoman, she stepped down and found herself at eye level with his chin. "Well . . . maybe."

His eyes glittered with cold amusement. "Go on, then."

"I understand that you have complicated feelings and that you are under a lot of pressure, but—" He scoffed. Ignoring his flagrant contempt, she barreled onward. "*But* this process will go much smoother if you cooperate. Your brother—"

"You don't know the first thing about my brother."

Just like that, all of his walls slammed down, every weapon on his battlements trained on her. If she were less angry, if she had not read that Lovelace column, if two people had not already made her feel small for being Machlish, she might have cowered. But within her burned a resentment that refused to stay quiet a moment longer.

How could he possibly believe himself so persecuted? He was a prince, the son of the most powerful man in the world, a resident of the most glorious house she'd ever seen. He'd never known a moment of suffering in his life, and the one time he was asked to do something that did not please him, *this* was how he behaved. He could and would make her dreams into nothing but collateral damage. That bitter realization chased away all good sense.

"Maybe not," she protested, "but I know you, sir. If you have no regard for anyone but yourself, then it is no wonder you're so miserable—so much so that you are determined to make everyone else as miserable as you are!"

His lips parted in surprise, and he looked genuinely stung. That glimpse of terrible, hard-won vulnerability made her stomach twist sharply with regret. She felt no better for indulging her anger. She'd only succeeding in digging her fingers into a wound.

But after a moment, the hurt vanished from his expression, replaced with a now-familiar disdain. "That kind of naivete will bite you in the end. In the Avlish court, it's far better to only care about yourself. You'd be wise to understand that now, before you're thrown into that pit of vipers."

You're a smart girl, Niamh, but you have your head in the clouds, Gran had said on the night her invitation arrived. *You don't know yet that the world is cruel.*

The reminder hit like a sucker punch.

Her family had given her a happy life. Niamh had never endured war or starvation. As a girl, she spent carefree days tearing through the village and rolling down the sidthe, tempting the Fair Ones to steal her away. But she'd seen darkness lurking like a wraith over every adult in Caterlow. She'd seen the churn of their tempers and the unpredictable waves of their grief. She'd seen the way the mood changed come harvest season—how it swelled, dark and oppressive as the sea in a storm—and broke only when the first potato was pulled clean from the earth. Perhaps she didn't know the bite of cruelty herself, but she recognized the shape of the scars it left behind. She very well might be silly and absentminded, but she was not a fool.

"I am from Machland, in case you've forgotten. I know first-hand how terrible the nobility can be. The people you disdain so much—you are one of them. In fact, you are among the worst of them! Your family's magic caused the Blight, and your father did *nothing* while my kinsmen starved to death." She took a step toward him, until they stood nearly flush together. "And now your brother continues to do nothing for their suffering! All I have seen you do is brood and complain. If you truly think the nobility is so horrid, why haven't you done something about it?"

The air between them felt primed to ignite. They both breathed heavily, and she swore her pulse was roaring loud enough for him to hear it. When she met his eyes again, they were blazing bright with anger. And far beneath it, hazy and faint, was something that stole away her breath.

Shame?

"We're done here," he said.

"Wait! I—"

The door slammed shut.

"I'm sorry."

The tension holding her up evaporated, and she all but collapsed onto the ottoman. She buried her face in her hands and groaned aloud, just to release some of her pent-up energy. What *was* that? How could she have been so stupid as to pick a fight with the Prince of Avaland?

A fight, she realized, he'd fled from.

She'd chased off a *prince.* She felt oddly jittery, as though she'd discovered some strange new magic of her own. She'd hardly recognized herself just now: brash and confrontational. But the heat of their argument had transfigured her. She never picked fights, never chose her words to hurt. But something about Kit Carmine made her forget herself and every ounce of self-preservation she had.

If he told Jack how she'd behaved today, he could very well have her dismissed. The thought made her blood rush hot all over again. There was no choice, then. She would have to prove herself to him, once and for all.

She would make him a coat he could not help loving.

Which meant she must resist the temptation to make it magenta or marigold out of spite. She had already earned his hatred, anyway. There was no need to be excessive. Still, something bright *would* contrast fetchingly against his hair, and yellow might draw out the gold in his eyes . . .

Focus, Niamh. As she took in her surroundings, she blinked hard to help her vision adjust. It had gotten strangely dark in here.

She noticed at last that the window was half obscured by nettle. It clung stubbornly to the glass, its tendrils grasping like fingers trying to claw their way inside. Its flowers, however, bloomed golden instead of pink. Numbly, she crossed the room and worked open the casement. She pried some of the nettle loose, watching the leaves flutter to the ground far below her.

Kit's handiwork, as lovely as it was thorny.

5

*D*espite the noise rumbling through the palace's crowded reception hall, Niamh worried she might fall asleep on her feet.

It had been a long time since she'd stayed up all night to finish a garment. In the week since she'd met with Kit, she'd designed a coat that her assistants had helped her assemble with painstaking care. Even so, it'd taken her until the last minute to finish embroidering the enchantments into the fabric. She'd dragged herself to bed only when she could no longer keep her eyes open—and had pricked herself with a needle for the third time. She'd gotten no more than three hours of sleep, but anticipation dulled the sharpest edges of her exhaustion.

She wanted to see Kit.

Earlier this morning, his valet had come to her studio just as she and another seamstress put the last stitch into the lining. He'd tucked it away into a box, tied it off with twine, and taken it away.

What she would have given to see the moment Kit first tried on his new coat. The moment he realized he'd misjudged her—or perhaps the moment he decided to do away with her.

A prickle of unease skittered down her spine, but she shook it off. She hadn't been banished from the kingdom yet, after all, and Jack had even personally invited her to the presentation of the debutantes, where Infanta Rosa herself would make her first appearance in the Avlish court. His continued hospitality puzzled her entirely. Why extend it to a common girl, a glorified servant in his household at that? But she knew better than to question either him or her good fortune.

No sense worrying, she decided, until they dragged her from the palace and charged her with the crime of harassing their youngest prince.

Even though he started it.

Someone clasped her arm to get her attention. Niamh turned to face a young woman—a debutante, judging by the bouquet of Carmine-red roses clutched like a lifeline in her hands. "Pardon me, miss. Do you mind if I stand here with you? I know it must sound mad, but you have this aura of calm about you . . ."

By now, the strangeness of the request no longer fazed her. The enchantment for peace she'd stitched into her gown had proven far more potent than she intended. Evidently, looking at the gown calmed the mind as effectively as wearing it did. To Niamh, it felt like standing up to her ankles in the surf on a misty day or embroidering by lamplight before anyone else in the world was awake.

"Oh, it is no trouble at all! Please do make yourself comfortable if you can find room."

The other girl looked vaguely displeased about her accent, but self-preservation, apparently, won out over rank. "Thank you, miss. The Saints have truly blessed you."

With that, she wedged herself into the small crowd of girls that had packed in around Niamh. In any other circumstance, she might have been struck a bit moony to be surrounded by so many beautiful girls. They came in all shapes and sizes and cuts: some cunning and sharp, others blushing and wilting, several on the brink of tears, others still bright-eyed and poised. A group of them swarmed around a gilt-frame mirror, pinching color into their cheeks and fussing with their feather headpieces.

Elaborate was the word of this Season. Out were classic lines and simple silhouettes. In were all manner of decorative horrors and delights: epaulettes, frogging, flowers, flounces, lace, and of course, an abundance of beads stitched onto each and every ruffle. By their clothes alone, she could tell which ones came from money and which ones clung to their legacy like a slick rock face. Most of them were not a day older than sixteen. So young—and already prepared to marry for the sake of their families. They came from more wealth than she could ever dream of, and yet, her heart ached for them. She could empathize, if nothing else, with how heavy obligation must have weighed on them.

The footman standing guard at the entrance nodded at her. "You may enter."

The girls behind her sucked in a collective nervous breath as she entered the drawing room, taking her calming enchantment with her. At the far end of the room, the prince regent himself waited, as still and imposing as a statue. In each wing, courtiers and nobles huddled shoulder to shoulder, murmuring quietly to one another.

From beneath her eyelashes, Niamh scanned the crowd. They all wore expressions in varying shades of anxiety and pride. All of them must've had daughters being presented to Jack today. The sheer number of them astounded her. In Machland, they were

lucky indeed to have a child with magic born every other generation. But in Avaland, the aristocracy arranged marriages strategi-
cally to ensure their magical bloodlines remained unbroken.

"Miss Niamh O'Connor," the herald announced.

All of their eyes snapped to her. Whispers swept through the
room. Her nerves blunted against the enchantment woven into her
gown. Although she could hear the shapes of the words *Machlishwoman* and *dressmaker,* her magic kept her safe in a pocket of unas-
sailable calm. All that remained was a brightly burning excitement.

As she walked down the center aisle, the crystals on the gown's
bodice twinkled like moonlight on a still pond. The tension in the
room rippled, quieting and flaring as she passed, and in her wake,
the nobility stared out at her hungrily. This was going far better
than she'd predicted.

And then she spotted Kit.

His unimpressed stare slammed into her. She faltered, and indignation coiled tight within her. Even now, he was trying to in-
timidate her. Holding her chin high, she stopped before Jack and
curtsied.

"Miss O'Connor," Jack said. "Thank you for coming. I understand it is unusual, but I want to ensure that you feel welcome
here."

His courtesy once again made her feel wrong-footed. She could
not reconcile it with Lovelace's account of him. If he truly disdained her people, why would he go out of his way to be so kind to
her? "Thank *you,* Your Highness. You honor me."

As he drank in her gown, his ever-present frown faded. It was
such a startling transformation, it struck her just how frazzled he
normally looked. He was far too young to carry so much weight
with him. "I am not sure what magic you've worked on my brother,
but he looks . . ."

Niamh slid her gaze to Kit. What word *would* she use to describe him? Striking, yes. Regal, arguably. But respectable—what

she'd been aiming for when she set out to make that blasted coat—certainly not. He radiated such foreboding malcontent, no one stood within an arm's breadth of him.

That might have been her fault.

No, it was most *definitely* her fault.

The enchantment she'd stitched into his coat had vexed her like few others had before. All of her hurt and annoyance had crept into the thread so insistently, she'd spent half her time ripping out her own work. She'd wanted him to instill a sense of due deference, maybe a touch of awe. Instead, she seemed to have overshot and landed squarely in the realm of nefarious. He loomed over his brother's shoulder like some shadowy advisor. The coattails feathered into billowing darkness, the fabric as diaphanous as a wraith.

At last, Jack said, "Civilized."

"I, ehm . . . I am very glad you think so, sir."

"Allow me to introduce you to my wife, Princess Sofia."

"Your . . . ? Oh!"

Niamh would have missed her entirely had Jack not pointed her out. A young woman, no older than twenty, stood demurely at his side, with a smile so pleasant it veered on vacant. Sofia was, unsurprisingly, beautiful. But she was as colorless and insubstantial as snowfall. Her eyes shone a pale, ice-chip blue, and her hair—arranged into wispy curls around her face—gleamed white in the sunlight. She towered over Niamh with a willowy elegance more suited to a ballerina than a princess.

"It is lovely to meet you, Miss O'Connor." Sofia offered her hand.

Niamh accepted it, marveling at the delicateness of her wrist and the sheer cold of her skin. A sapphire ring glittered on her thumb. "The pleasure is mine, Your Highness."

For a moment, she stood there, with a princess's hand clasped almost tenderly in hers. Clearly, there was some step to this ritual she did not know, because Kit looked supremely (and malevolently) entertained by the awkward silence. Oh, could he not let her exist in *peace?*

Sofia released her without comment. "You have such poise. Surely this is not your first Season."

Niamh could just barely detect an accent in Sofia's clipped, precise Avlish. If memory served, she hailed from Saksa, a kingdom fresh out of a civil war. Sofia's father, after deposing the previous royal family, had emerged victorious. Then, he'd bought and sealed his alliance to Avaland with Sofia's marriage to Jack—just as Jack now intended to do with Kit.

Jack and Sofia stood a decorous distance apart, as though a solid wall of ice divided them. Niamh understood their relationship immediately: they did not love each other. No wonder Jack could neither envision nor want anything different for his brother.

"It's is only the enchantment on my gown, Your Highness, no virtue of mine."

"Your talent is truly remarkable, then. I have read that the people of Machland have an extraordinary gift for crafts, and I see it was no exaggeration. If you can find the time, I must ask you for help with my own needlework."

"Gladly!" Niamh grinned. "Embroidery is one of my greatest joys."

Sofia's smile turned shyly hopeful.

"Mr. Gabriel Sinclair," the herald called.

Mister? Niamh could've sworn he told her his father was a duke.

The murmurs in the room immediately turned disapproving. Every head in the room swiveled toward him, their expressions twisted with disgust. Niamh's heart sank. What could Lovelace have possibly written to earn him such a reputation?

Sinclair sauntered into the drawing room with his chin held high, dressed smartly in a jacket of goldenrod cotton. He gave them nothing—no second glances, no shrinking smiles, no greeting. One hand rested lazily in his pocket, but Niamh could see the tension coiled in his shoulders.

He came to stand beside her and asked, "Do you mind if I cut in?"

"Sinclair," Jack said, with flat, open dislike.

"Your Highness." His smile was all indolence, but the glint in his eyes told Niamh that the dislike was very mutual. "Did you miss me?"

Jack looked persecuted, which Niamh supposed was answer enough. "Have you given any more thought to what I said?"

"A great deal, indeed. You do not need to worry about me."

"Why do I doubt that?" Jack sighed. "Go on, then, the both of you. There are others waiting behind you."

"Yes, sir." Sinclair bowed with a dramatic flourish of his hand. It was far too formal to be polite.

What was *that* about? If only it were socially acceptable to ask any of the questions she wanted answered.

Sinclair did not waste a moment before ducking into the crowd. Niamh followed close behind him, wedging her shoulders through the other guests and muttering her apologies under her breath. But when she saw Kit was making his way toward them, she had to resist the urge to dig her heels in or flee. She did not want to speak to him after their argument a few days ago. Besides, the enchantment on Kit's jacket made her skin feel slithery and all the hairs on the back of her neck stand on end. Even Sinclair shuddered at his approach. Part of her wanted to be pleased that Kit had been forced to wear that monstrosity, but she could take no satisfaction in a job so poorly done. Never in her life had she botched an enchantment so badly.

"Kit," Sinclair said, clearly determined to push through. "Have you been behaving yourself?"

"I'm not the only one who needs to behave, apparently."

"You wound me," he replied. "And here I thought I could get through the Season with only one Carmine on my case."

Kit crossed his arms, but his expression softened. "Ignore him. He's been reading that column again. It's put him in a mood."

"He's always in a mood." After a moment, he added, "I like your coat."

"Is that so?" Kit asked, annoyed.

"Oh, yes. I don't mean to offend, but your usual wardrobe of black and only black was beginning to depress me. This one makes me feel warm and fuzzy just looking at you."

"Fuck off," Kit replied, but there was no bite to it.

Niamh snorted. Never in a thousand years did she expect such foul language to come out of a prince's mouth. Kit and Sinclair bickered no differently than a couple of Machlish lads stumbling home from the pub. Some things, she supposed, were universal.

"No disrespect to you, of course, Miss O'Connor," Sinclair said after a moment. "It is a lovely coat. It really does suit him."

"Thank you," she said miserably.

Sinclair raised an eyebrow at her tone. His gaze darted back and forth between Kit and Niamh. "Oh? I see you two are still getting along swimmingly."

Kit huffed. "Are you incapable of minding your own business?"

"Now, now, Christopher, are you sure that's how you wish to speak to me? I do know all of your secrets." Sinclair sidled closer to Niamh and dropped his voice to a conspiratorial whisper. "Do you know, Miss O'Connor, that Kit here was a very sensitive child? In fact, I recall that on his tenth birthday—"

"Stop." Kit's face turned crimson in an instant. "What's the matter with you today?"

"Me? Why, nothing." Sinclair flashed Niamh a sly smile.

Just then, the doors to the drawing room opened, letting in a wash of excited chatter and nervous giggles. The presentation of the debutantes had begun.

"Miss Selby," the herald announced, "accompanied by her mother, the Right Honorable Lady Selby."

Miss Selby strode into the room with her chin held imperiously high—most likely to balance her precarious headdress. The feathers in her hair reached nearly a yard into the air and quivered with her every step. In one hand, she held a fan made of ivory. In the crook of her other arm, she cradled a bouquet of white lilies. She curtsied to Jack and accepted Sofia's outstretched hand. Now, Niamh saw her mistake. Miss Selby pressed a kiss to the sapphire in Sofia's ring.

"Your Royal Highnesses," she said with grave solemnity, "I carry the divine blood of Saint Isolde in my veins. What would you hear?"

The nobles around them leaned in, chattering excitedly.

"What gift did Saint Isolde have?" Niamh asked.

"Prophecy," Kit said.

Niamh had never seen magic of its kind. Soothsayers had not walked on Machlish soil for centuries. The Avlish had been quite meticulous about disposing of them in the early days of their occupation. "That is incredible."

Sinclair shrugged. "Don't get too excited. Last year, her older sister predicted we'd have at least one little heir to the throne running around, and look how that turned out."

Kit shot him a disgusted look.

"Will the day of the wedding be auspicious?" Sofia asked.

Miss Selby's eyes flared golden. The dramatic silence stretched out so long it became awkward. Somewhere in the depths of the drawing room, someone coughed. At last, Miss Selby spoke.

"There is a twenty percent chance of rain on the day of Infanta Rosa and Prince Christopher's wedding." A pause. "Erm . . . Most likely. I can say so with approximately twenty-five percent certainty."

"Thank you, Miss Selby." Jack rubbed his temples as though he was fighting off a headache. "That was most illuminating."

Tepid applause pursued her out of the room.

As the next debutante began to make her way down the aisle, Niamh stole a glance at Kit. As much as she couldn't stand him, as intolerably rude as he was to her, she couldn't let him believe that

this horrid coat represented the whole of her abilities. It simply
would not do.

She leaned closer and whispered, "Your Highness."

"I said not to call me that." He sighed thinly, as though the conversation had already exhausted him. "What do you want?"

Oh! How had a prince not internalized a single thing about
good manners? Granted, she wasn't entirely sure what they taught
noble children, but she was certain there was at least a basic eti-
quette class or three on the curriculum. "I wanted to talk to you
about your coat."

"It makes me look sinister," he supplied. "I'm aware."

She deflated. "Of course you are."

"It feels like it hates me."

She winced. "I know."

"This is supposed to be a celebration. It's kind of inappropriate
for the occasion."

Humiliation and indignation roiled within her. "I *know*. It was
an accident. You do not need to rub salt in the wound."

He paused for a long while. "You should have seen Jack's face."

The image came to her in perfect clarity. Kit, descending the
imperial staircase with a dark and menacing aura. Jack, utterly
mortified and too polite to say a word to either of them about it.
She couldn't help it. She choked on a laugh, muffling it as much as
she could with her hand. To her shock, Kit's lips curled, just barely,
in a wry half smile.

He really *was* lovely.

And she had to stop noticing that. Like one of the Fair Ones,
his beauty was nothing but a glamour that concealed a rotten inside. One shared moment did not absolve him.

"Miss Beaufort," the herald called, "presented by her aunt, the
Viscountess of Grosvenor."

Miss Beaufort, by her own account, possessed the divine blood of one of the most venerated figures in Avlish history, Saint Jeanne. With a snap of her fingers, every candle in the room extinguished. The crowd tittered nervously, then erupted into delighted gasps when they blazed back to life.

Niamh turned toward Kit again. In the warm press of the crowd, they were as good as alone. "You know, you left before I could get your thoughts on the kind of coat you *actually* wanted."

"My thoughts," he repeated skeptically.

"Well, yes. We will have to discuss what you would like to wear throughout the Season—and ultimately at your wedding. But we don't have to talk about the wedding cloak just yet. Will you tell me about what you like to wear?"

"Nothing."

Some errant whimsical impulse must have possessed her, because before she could think better of it, she feigned dismay and said, "You've changed your plans again."

It took a moment for him to catch her meaning. His face went very red, very slowly, before he mastered his expression with a scowl. She hadn't realized before now that he had such a hair-trigger blush—or that, as aloof as he pretended to be, he was so terrible at hiding his emotions. "*Anything,* then. It's all the same to me."

"Surely, you have *some* opinions," she cajoled. "Colors you like and don't like, a particular cut of suit you admire, the way you want to feel when people look at you . . ."

"I couldn't care less," he replied stiffly. "I've never thought about colors in my life. I'm sure my brother will have enough opinions for the both of us."

"But your brother is not going to be the one on the altar. You are." Niamh planted her hands on her hips. "Anything, anything at all, will help me. Please?"

"What is so difficult for you to understand? I don't want people to look at me at all." He angled himself sharply away from her and glared out at the proceedings.

Seething, Niamh turned her attention back to the debutantes, but she could hardly focus. After nearly an hour, she lost track of the girls entirely. One levitated mere inches off the ground, her hair snaking toward the ceiling as though she were underwater. Another swooned immediately upon kissing Sofia's ring. It took her mother, a vial of smelling salts, and two bystanders to revive her. Nothing particularly extraordinary seemed to happen, but everyone applauded anyway.

Just when Niamh believed she would keel over with boredom, the herald called, "His Royal Majesty, King Felipe V de Todos los Santos de Carrillo."

Excitement sparked within her. She'd nearly forgotten Infanta Rosa was meant to arrive tonight.

"His Majesty is escorting his daughter, Her Royal Highness, Infanta Rosa de Todos los Santos de Carrillo, and Miss Miriam Lacalle."

Finally, what she had been waiting for all night: a glimpse of the princess. Assuming she would be able to catch a glimpse of her at all, of course. Sometimes—most times, really—Niamh hated being short.

She stood on her toes and craned her neck, hoping for a better view, but she saw nothing through what seemed to her a towering forest of hairpieces. Kit raked his eyes across her face with the cruel fascination of a child watching an overturned turtle struggle. Niamh braced for whatever scorn he saw fit to throw at her this time.

"You," he said to the man in front of her.

The gentleman looked affronted to be addressed so rudely, but when he saw Kit standing behind him, arms crossed and expression dour, his face drained of color. "Your Highness? What can I do for you?"

"Move. You're in the way."

Shock twisted Niamh's stomach into a knot.

"I—" The man looked bewildered, but he nodded obsequiously. "Of course, Your Highness. I did not realize. My sincerest apologies."

A few other nearby courtiers shuffled away for good measure, clearly eager to avoid the prince's sharp tongue. Niamh stared up at Kit incredulously. What had he done that for? He likely couldn't see much from here, either, but she couldn't imagine him keen to see the woman he'd professed no interest in marrying.

Sensing her gaze, he turned his glare on her. "What?"

"Nothing!"

At least he made it easy to swallow her gratitude.

The steady *clack, clack, clack* of heels against the wooden floors cut through the drone of a hundred conversations. When the footsteps stopped, the room fell into a strained hush. Even Jack stared at the door with an expression Niamh had not yet seen on him.

Dread.

King Felipe and Infanta Rosa stood in the threshold of the gilded double doors, framed like the subjects of an oil painting. The king, a bear of a man, filled the doorway with the broad set of his shoulders. Gold glittered on the military-style epaulettes of his jacket and the circlet resting in his dark curls. But somehow, with not a speck of gold or a single gemstone in sight, it was his daughter who commanded all the attention in the room.

Infanta Rosa's gown fell to the floor in frilly layers of watered black silk. The color was, frankly, shocking. No Avlish noblewoman wore black unless she was in mourning. A black lace veil obscured most of her features from view, but Niamh could see that the princess's lips, gloomily downturned and pouting, were painted black. Her hair, too, settled in black, glossy curls against her olive skin. She surveyed the crowd with an air of total disinterest, her eyelids drawn almost sleepily low.

Her lady's maid trailed just a step behind the Carrillos. Compared to Rosa, Miss Lacalle looked like sunshine incarnate in her scarlet gown. She had round cheeks, a mouth that looked quick to smile, and hazel eyes that promised mischief. Her thick brown curls were gathered into an understated chignon at the nape of her neck.

"My God," someone near her hissed. "She looks like the walking dead."

"Worse," their companion replied, "she looks like a *commoner.*"

Murmurs tore through the room like a cold wind. Some people looked delighted, others scandalized. Niamh was not sure what to think. Only that there must've been something in the Sootham air that infected all royals with a choleric disposition.

As the Castilian princess made her way toward Jack and Sofia, Niamh stole a glance at Kit from the corner of her eye. He looked at Rosa as though she'd stepped directly out of his worst nightmares and into his drawing room.

"Well done, Kit," Sinclair whispered encouragingly. "She's handsome."

But for once, Kit had no retort. He only walked numbly ahead as Jack waved him insistently to his side.

This was certainly going to be an interesting wedding.

Niamh strained to listen to their conversation, but as close as they were to the royals, she could not overhear a thing amid all this chatter. She could, however, make out Jack's thin smile and the sickly sheen of sweat on his forehead. He bowed so deeply to the king, she thought his nose might scrape the floor. King Felipe had a reputation for his hot temper—and his military prowess. Even so, she hadn't expected such a show of deference from a man like Jack Carmine.

"It almost depresses me to see him this way," Sinclair said, following her gaze. "I've never seen Jack so wheedling and eager to please in all my life."

"Why, do you think?"

"Infanta Rosa is the king's only daughter, and he's notoriously overprotective of her," Sinclair replied. "It likely wasn't easy to get him to surrender his precious little princess to Avaland. I'd wager it wouldn't take much to get him to change his mind. Just look at him."

Felipe beheld his daughter with such open adoration, it made Niamh's heart flutter with a strange brew of self-pity and longing. But as Kit drew nearer, the king's entire demeanor changed. It was not only the effect of that loathsome coat. No, he had taken Kit's measure at a moment's glance, and Niamh knew by the stony disapproval on his face that he'd found him wanting.

A new wave of fear struck her then. She could not provide for her family if the king decided to call off the wedding. Her dreams depended on the most disagreeable and contrary man in Avaland proving himself to someone who had already decided that nothing and no one would be good enough for his daughter.

Which meant she'd have to do everything in her power to make Kit *look* like a prince, even if he would not act like one.

6

*T*he first ball of the Season was tonight, and Niamh still had not finished the enchantment on Kit's coat.

The lack of sleep over the past few nights had begun to catch up with her, and now, her fingers had gone pale and numb. A warning. Pushing herself much further, she knew, would not end well. It had been years since her symptoms had flared up enough to truly slow her down, but then again, she'd never used her magic this much before. She didn't know what it said about her that her frustration outweighed her concern. But sometimes, the mismatch of what her body could give and what her mind and circumstances demanded threatened to drive her mad.

Most days, Niamh believed she'd accepted her lot in life: that her own body had betrayed her. There was a grim sort of comfort in knowing how she would die, even if she did not know exactly when. She and the death god, Donn, had a tenuous understanding. He would not steal upon her like a thief in the night. Instead, he would drain her slowly, like a farmer bleeding his cattle for pudding.

Many in her family—both with and without an ceird—had borne the same illness: fatigue, pain and swelling with no clear cause, a shortened life span, fingers that turned white as bone in the cold and under stress. Some had lived as long as sixty. Some had died as young as twenty. There was no surefire way of knowing just how long she had save for her hair. The leaching color was her hourglass, a reminder of how much breath she had yet within her.

A reminder to work hard.

She stared down at her sketchbook, unable to process the few ideas she'd scribbled down sometime around three in the morning. The lines rearranged themselves the longer she looked at them, and she could not convince herself that anything she'd drawn made sense. Now, if only she could recall where she'd left her pencil.

She whirled around—and crashed directly into her dress form. It wobbled precariously, but Niamh steadied it before it fell. "Oh! So very sorry."

The dress form had no eyes—and no head, for that matter—but Niamh swore it regarded her disapprovingly. Or perhaps she needed to go to bed. When *was* the last time she had slept?

No matter. She would just finish the last of the embroidery on Kit's coat, and then she would take a nap. She fished a few pins from the cluttered drawer of her worktable, then popped the ends between her teeth. As she worked, the slant of sunlight made its way across the floor like the hand of a clock.

"You called?"

Kit.

Niamh startled, spinning around in her chair. When her gaze locked with his, all the pins in her mouth dropped onto the floor with a clatter. His lips parted, and his sour expression softened into stupefaction—probably from watching her spit out a mouthful of metal. They stared at each other from across the room.

The nettle he'd grown during their last argument waved like a flag of surrender outside her window. Its leaves curled toward him, pressing against the glass, and in the dappled light they admitted, the whole room seemed to shimmer. Her heart slammed against her rib cage.

"What did I tell you about knocking loudly?" she blurted out.

"I did. *You* need to start paying attention to your surroundings."

Niamh bit down on a pert reply. She was far too tired to bicker with him right now. "Will you give me your coat, please? I want to make sure the one I've been working on fits you."

Without a word, Kit shrugged off his coat and passed it to her. The fabric was warm and soft in her hands, and it smelled faintly of turned earth and tobacco. She traded him the new coat from the dress form and tried not to watch too closely as he pulled it on. At first glance, it fit him quite beautifully. Pride kindled within her. Finally, he looked as he should: like a prince, regal and imposing.

Niamh admired the color—a navy so deep, it could have been cut from a bolt of the midnight sky—and its decisive, crisp lines. Her assistants had done beautiful work assembling it. The embroidery, done entirely in enchanted silver thread, had taken more time and patience than she'd ever care to measure. The design, a thicket of nettles blooming along the back, eluded its viewer. It became visible only if you turned your head just so, or if the light struck it exactly the right way.

It was the most of herself she'd ever poured into a garment.

I don't want to be seen at all, he'd told her, a barb she took as a confession.

And so, as much as it pained her, she'd woven memories of safety into the coat. The enchantment would allow him to hide in plain sight. If she allowed her focus to soften, to ignore the familiarity of her own power, she could see the magic begin to take effect. In that coat, the lines of his body blurred, and his face grew indistinct. It made the eye gloss over him, as though he was a stranger in a crowd, or no more interesting than a piece of furniture.

Kit studied his reflection in the mirror. She expected him to fidget—most people did, as they reconciled their expectations with the reality of what she'd made—but instead, he stood stock-still with a faraway glimmer in his eyes. She braced herself for his disgust, for him to throw the coat to the ground in a huff, the same as he did the handkerchief.

But he said nothing.

A tentative hope blossomed within her. She knotted her fingers together at her heart. "What do you think?"

She hated the anxiety that crept into her voice. She hated that she still cared what he thought.

"It's—fine, I suppose," he said haltingly, nearly choking on the words. "Can I go?"

Fine, he supposed. She couldn't help feeling disappointed. But compared to his first two reactions to her work, it was high praise indeed. "Not yet. I need to finish the design—and sew in the lining, for that matter. Twirl around, please."

Kit glowered at her, clearly objecting to even the idea of *twirling*, but he nonetheless allowed her to turn him this way and that. He tolerated it with surprising grace.

She straightened his lapels and examined her handiwork. She traced the embroidery with the pads of her thumbs, just where the cutouts shyly curved around his collarbones. His wide-eyed gaze snapped to hers, and it occurred to Niamh, belatedly, that it was a man, not a dress form, wearing this coat. She could not touch him so casually. Her face warmed painfully.

"Ehm," she said at the same time he said, "What—"

The door swung open. They sprang apart so quickly, Niamh nearly tripped over her skirts.

Jack strode into the room with the grim bearing of a military commander. Just like that, all of Kit's walls went up. The strange, startled vulnerability she'd seen on his face just a moment ago hardened into a mask of utter contempt. Jack, however, did not seem to notice. His gaze swept the room once, then again. He looked at Niamh, frowning deeply.

"What are you doing here?" Kit demanded.

"Ah," Jack said, surprised. "There you are."

Kit's brow furrowed with vague concern as Jack blinked hard. Then his eyes lit up with the realization of what Niamh had done. He looked almost grateful.

A secret thrill shot through her. The enchantment was working exactly as she'd hoped. But now that Jack was staring directly at his brother, the magic's effect attenuated. He appraised Kit like a jeweler with a loupe affixed to his eye. The cold impersonality of it almost made Niamh feel indignant on Kit's behalf.

After a few moments, Jack asked, "Are you happy?"

"Ecstatic," Kit said dryly.

"Excellent." If Jack was aware of how Kit was attempting to kill him with only a glare, it did not seem to bother him at all. He retrieved his pocket watch from the fob at his waist. "Now, then. Get yourself ready, Kit. We haven't much time. King Felipe and Infanta Rosa will be here in a matter of hours."

"Just a moment," Niamh cut in. Both Carmines looked at her with twinned looks of befuddlement, but she pressed onward. "The coat isn't finished yet."

Reluctantly, Kit surrendered it to her.

Jack regarded her like she was a puzzle he had not quite figured out how to solve. "Very well, then. Come down when you're ready for the ball."

Niamh could not be certain if it was panic or excitement that made her heart skip a beat. "I didn't realize I was invited."

"Of course you are," Jack said, as though it were obvious. "I expect you to be there. You must be seen."

Seen? she thought. *Me?*

But she was nobody. Surely, he meant her designs needed to be seen. Perhaps to drum up anticipation for Kit's and Rosa's wedding ensembles. She'd have to choose her outfit wisely, then.

"Of course I'll be there." She would have liked more time to prepare, but she could do this. All she had to do now was cut out and sew the lining into Kit's coat. Which reminded her that she never did find that pencil. Muttering under her breath, Niamh rummaged through the pile of *things* on her desk. If only she could remember where—

"Behind your ear," Kit said.

"Huh?" Her hand flew to her temple and found the pencil tucked behind her ear. "Oh. Thank you."

"Don't mention it," he muttered. And with that, he headed for the door as though he could not escape quickly enough.

That evening, Niamh laid every dress she'd brought from Machland out on her bed. She did her very best not to touch them. One could not be too careful when it came to a pile—a mountain, really, in this case—of enchanted garments. Riffling through them willy-nilly would send you tumbling through the full spectrum of emotion in the blink of an eye. She'd done it a time or two before, and she did not care to repeat the experience.

Niamh stared at her gowns with increasing dismay. This was the first ball she'd ever attended in her entire life, and Jack had extended the invitation to her so *nonchalantly*, as though it would not send her into an overthinking spiral. She needed to look elegant but not marmish, bold but not outlandish, classic but not unfashionable. Something that said, *I belong here,* without being presumptuous.

Eventually, she narrowed down her choices to two of her favorite gowns. The first was a white muslin whose spangles had taken her weeks to sew onto the skirts. She'd imbued every last stitch with the heady joy of a late-summer night, and now, it sparkled like laughter. The second was a peach cotton, embroidered with an enchantment that bespelled its wearer to appear twice as beautiful in the eyes of whoever gazed upon them. The peach would certainly be eye-catching, but she hadn't come to Avaland to ensnare anyone. The white would do.

Once she'd dressed herself, she made her way downstairs with Kit's new coat folded neatly over her arm. She paused at the half landing on top of the imperial staircase and broke out into a grin at what she saw. The staff had been busy while she was locked away in her room. Arrangements of white lilies and baby's breath bloomed on each step, and jasmine twined itself through the wrought-iron balustrades. They perfumed the air with their sweet, delicate nectar.

And then, she spied Jack, Sofia, and Kit lingering at the foot of the staircase. Kit radiated an aura of such gloom, it was as though he stood at the center of a battlefield rather than the loveliest reception room she had ever seen. Niamh tried not to notice that he was only in his shirtsleeves, with his hands tucked into his pockets. She hurried toward them, and all three drew up short at the sight of her.

"Miss O'Connor, you are like the Saksian ice fields on a bright day," Sofia said warmly. Her pale eyes glittered with delight. "I used to play there when I was a girl, chasing after the frost spirits with my sisters. Do you not think so, Your Highness?"

Jack wore a rather peculiar expression. He studied his wife as though he did not recognize her at all. "I cannot say. I've never been, much less heard you speak of such a thing."

Sofia deflated, the excitement gone out of her in a rush. Niamh's stomach twisted. She recognized the sting of that disappointment well: a hand reached out and ignored.

To Jack's credit, however, he realized quickly enough that he misspoke. "But it is a very whimsical ensemble. In fact, it makes me think of summers at Woodville Hall. Father would visit us in the summer when we were children. Do you recall, Kit?"

"Oh," Kit said darkly, "I recall."

Jack's expression turned cold. It seemed they remembered those summers quite differently.

For a moment, the four of them stood in awkward silence. Niamh desperately yearned to see the girlish wonder on Sofia's face again. It made her feel oddly tenderhearted that such a composed woman, a princess no less, melted so easily in the face of an enchantment for joy. "I will give the gown to you if you would like it, Your Highness."

Although it was more subdued this time, her smile returned. "I would like nothing more."

"That is very generous of you," Jack said, clearly discomfited.

"It is no trouble—and the very least I can do since you've been so kind to invite me to these events." She dumped the coat into Kit's hands, eager to move on from whatever wound Jack had picked open. "Try this on, please."

Without complaint, he shrugged it on. The enchantment's effect took hold immediately. Kit's outline grew hazy, his form a sketch in smudged charcoal. Jack blinked, bewildered, and then his mouth pressed into a grim line. At last, it dawned on him what exactly she had done.

"He should be able to control it some," Niamh offered meekly.

"Well, it is always good to have an escape route," Jack said to no one in particular. He checked his pocket watch and made a fretful noise. "Finish up, then. The guests will begin arriving at any moment. Shall we, Sofia?"

Sofia tucked her hand into the crease of his elbow and allowed him to guide her to the front door.

It was almost time.

Through the front windows, she watched as a line of carriages emerged from the woods just beyond the palace gardens. With their massive frames and stately horses, it felt as though a small army was descending upon them. The impression was not at all helped by Kit's exceedingly grim expression. She couldn't afford to get distracted now. She needed to focus on the task at hand . . . if she could find it.

Niamh blinked a few times to clear the enchantment from her eyes. Even though Kit was indistinct, his eyes were like a light-house: bright and amber, burning through a fog-wreathed sea. With every passing moment, he became clearer and clearer. The coat, she decided, fit him perfectly. All that remained was adding the last few decorative buttons.

"Sit, please."

He did. Niamh settled beside him on the stairs. She threaded her needle and began to stitch the mother-of-pearl buttons to his coat. As she worked, all she could focus on was the rabbit-quickness of his pulse and the steady heat of his body against the back of her hand. When she finished, she snipped the last of the thread and slipped her shears back into her sewing kit.

"That should do it," she said, pleased. "Not even a king could find fault with you."

"Great," he replied curtly.

Great. She'd worked nearly all night and all day for a week, and that was the extent of his gratitude. But as she glared at him, she decided he looked more distracted than anything. She tried not to take it personally. This time, his sour mood did not appear to be her fault.

He produced a pipe and a vesta case from his pocket, and Niamh found herself surprised.

"I didn't know princes smoked pipes," she said teasingly. "How very common of you."

He stiffened, clearly trying to decide if she was mocking him or not. "This one does. I don't like snuff, so this is the last vice I've left."

Niamh stewed in her silence. His tone did not invite any questions. And yet, he did not make any effort to leave, nor did he tell her to go. Somehow, by the gods' grace, they were existing in proximity to each other without devolving into some silly argument. Niamh did not want to ruin it, but she couldn't stomach the quiet or the stillness. Too many unwanted thoughts crept in. Ones like: how oddly fascinating it was to watch him tuck his pipe into the corner of his mouth. She forced herself to tear her eyes away from him, but it took some effort to banish the image of the wooden tip of it biting softly into his lower lip.

"Sofia seems nice," she tried, sounding only a little strangled.

"You're awfully familiar today."

Self-consciousness prickled at her. "I was not the one who broke decorum first. Besides, you haven't discouraged any familiarity between us."

"Not for a lack of trying." He struck a match and lit the bowl of his pipe. The smell of tobacco suffused the air. "I know her about as well as you do."

It took her a moment to realize he'd humored her feeble attempt at conversation. Now, that piqued her interest. She did not think Jack and Sofia were newlyweds, but Jack had mentioned something about Kit's prolonged absence from court. Had they truly not met before this summer? She knew she was being nosy now—or, as Kit had once said, *impertinent.* But she felt almost emboldened by the lazy way he leaned against the stairs, propped up on his elbow. He tipped his head back, baring a sliver of his throat above the knot of his cravat. For the first time since she'd known him, he looked almost at peace, as though he was smoking in an open field rather than the prince regent's ornate foyer.

What would it be like, she wondered, *to be so self-assured?* Or maybe, more accurately, to not care about anything at all?

"Were you at their wedding?" she asked.

He exhaled a plume of smoke. "Apparently."

Niamh waved it away. "Was it a long time ago, then?"

"Maybe a year and a half ago." He took another long drag, then sighed it out. *In, hold, out.* Each of his breaths crested and ebbed like the tide. "Are you done interrogating me now?"

Niamh's face flooded with heat. She supposed she *was* being impertinent. But even she knew she could not ask the questions she truly wanted answers to. Ones like: *How can you possibly forget something like your own brother's wedding?*

"For now," she said.

"Christopher, the guests are—" Jack cut himself off with an impatient huff. "For God's sake, put that away. This isn't an alehouse."

Kit hauled himself to his feet and pocketed the pipe again. With a passing glance at Niamh, he said, "Stay out of trouble."

"What is *that* supposed to mean?" she asked, but he'd already begun walking away. It irritated her, but at least now she could enjoy the ball without him glowering at her.

The ball. The very first ball of her life. Of course. How could she have forgotten?

Deep down, Niamh knew she wasn't allowed to be excited for such a thing. But her wildest, silliest daydreams had stubbornly survived her girlhood. She couldn't help imagining what it would be like to walk into a ballroom where everyone knew her name. How exhilarating it would be to dance with a stranger beneath the glitter of a chandelier.

To fall in love.

She shouldn't allow herself to want so much, or so many frivolous things. It was selfishness of the highest order. Even now, she could feel the weight of Gran's disapproving stare. She thought of her countrymen—like Erin—who'd left their jobs in frustration. Who was she to enjoy the comforts of the Avlish court when so many others had suffered at their hands?

She needed to work as hard as she could, as long as she could, as fast as she could, to ensure that those she loved were safe and happy, to preserve her family's legacy. If she could shoulder their burdens for them, that would make her life—however many paltry years she was granted—mean something.

Her life did not matter. Not yet, anyway.

But as the first guests filtered in through the front doors of the palace, Niamh could not tamp down her own self-destructive yearning. She had sewn enough today. Just this once, maybe she could allow herself to have fun.

Just for tonight, she could be a little selfish.

7

*E*ntering the ballroom felt like stepping out into a meadow.
Niamh touched a hand to her lips to keep herself from
crying aloud with delight.

Flowers overflowed from pots balanced on marble columns, tumbled from the balconies, and wove through plates of cakes on the
refreshment table. A few even floated in the punch bowl. Hundreds
of candles flickered all around her, casting the ballroom in an intimate glow. Firelight winked off the low-hanging chandeliers and
lacquered the hardwood floor to a breathtaking shine. And as the
sun dipped low and streamed through those glorious windows,
everything went gilded and warm.

"This dance floor will open," the footman by the doors solemnly
informed her, "when Her Royal Highness Infanta Rosa arrives."

A massive white sheet lay over the dance floor. How curious,

Niamh thought, that they could not even look at it until Rosa's arrival.

She wandered as if in a dream. Beleaguered servants milled about, carrying silver platters with bite-sized dishes she had never seen before. She sampled layered puddings in tiny glasses; sandwiches with cucumbers sliced so thin, she barely had to chew; and three jam-filled biscuits each topped with a crystallized flower petal.

As she helped herself to another, a middle-aged woman seized Niamh by the arm and all but dragged her into her group of friends. Her eyes sparkled with wonder. "I say, who designed your gown?"

"I did," Niamh said through a mouthful of biscuit. "My name is Niamh Ó Conchobhair."

A ripple of amused silence traveled through the group, and some of the genuine mirth faded from the woman's face. Cruel delight took its place.

"You? A Machlish girl?" the woman cried. "Oh, my. Why, how very quaint. I need you to make a gown for my daughter at once. No, don't speak now. I shall call on you—oh, dear me. Can you even read? How thoughtless of me to assume!"

The insult stung, but Niamh did her best to smile through it. She'd hoped for a better life here. But a better life, she realized now, came with a thousand smaller hardships. As she made her way across the ballroom, she stumbled from one horrid conversation to another.

"What a shame. Such potent divine blood but no money or status at all," one woman tutted. "However, I daresay you are pretty enough that a certain sort of family might give you to one of their younger sons. I do hear that Machlish women produce many children."

"You must come stay in my estate for a time, if I can wrest you away from your lord," an old man told her weepily. "Your gown . . . I have not felt this sort of whimsy since I was a boy. Nothing makes me happy any longer, you see, save my glorious horses."

"How strange you must find it here," remarked one of the debutantes. "We Avlish are so buttoned-up compared to your people. In Machland, I hear you run wild in the hills. And oh, the stories one hears about your rituals!"

No one asked her to dance.

Once she escaped the last of her accosters, Niamh found her way to a chair and collapsed into it, grateful to take the weight off her feet. Her skirts puddled around her, glittering so brightly beneath the candlelight they hurt her eyes. Balls, it seemed, were far less romantic and far more humiliating than she'd expected. She squeezed her eyes shut for a count of three, swallowing down the familiar burn of tears in her throat.

When she opened them again, she spotted Sinclair stumbling into the ballroom from one of the wings. It didn't take a particularly seasoned member of the court to guess what he'd been up to. His jacket was suspiciously rumpled, and his cravat was tied loosely around his neck, although *tied* was a generous word for what he'd done to it. Admittedly, she was impressed it'd taken him no more than an hour to find someone to sneak off with.

Their gazes met, and his whole face brightened. He lifted one finger, as if to say, *wait*. He retrieved two glasses of punch from the refreshment table and ambled over to her. His golden hair fell wildly across his forehead, and he all but glowed in the candlelight, as saintly as a gilded icon in an Avlish church.

"Well, aren't you a vision? You're like sunshine itself."

Niamh warmed under his compliment. "Hello, Sinclair."

He handed her a glass and clinked his own against it. Niamh sipped at the punch—and nearly spit it back into the glass. Alcohol burned her throat and roiled in her stomach. She tasted no fewer than three different types of spirits—and wine besides. Goodness, how did anyone manage to dance, much less *walk,* if they drank more than one of these?

Sinclair leaned on the wall beside her and gestured vaguely at the ballroom. "How are you enjoying yourself?"

Niamh set her glass down on a nearby table. "It has been, ehm . . . interesting? But the food is incredible."

"It looks incredible on you as well," he said good-naturedly.

She glanced down to see the fingers of her gloves stained bright red with jam. At least she hoped it was jam. "Oh, gods. Please pretend you did not see that."

"I make no promises. It is very endearing." He grinned. "Do you have space on your dance card? I'd never forgive myself if I missed the opportunity to stand up with you."

"You may take your pick." She flashed him her empty card. That stubborn, maudlin loneliness threatened to overtake her again, so she added, "It's for the best. I never learned to dance like you do here."

In Machland, parties were a more intimate affair: fewer people, faster dances, less formal clothes. Here, she imagined the dances were as prim and regimented as everything else, all of the guests twirling on their course like figures in a music box.

"Then allow me to teach you to waltz. A lovely girl like you not dancing on the first ball of the Season? I won't allow it."

A tentative spark of excitement kindled within her, but she smothered it as best she could. "I couldn't! I will embarrass you."

"That's half the fun, isn't it?" His expression turned so overwrought and pitiful, she couldn't help smiling. "Please say yes."

"Very well, but don't say I did not warn you when I step on your feet."

"I very much look forward to it." He squinted at the dance floor. The tarp laid over it remained undisturbed, like a fresh bank of snow. Some of the guests lingered at its edge, eyeing it with eager, impatient interest. "Assuming we ever get the chance."

"I was told the dance floor will not open until Infanta Rosa arrives. Is that customary?"

Sinclair waved a hand. "In a way. Every year, Jack commissions an artist to chalk the dance floor for the inaugural ball of the Season. I imagine that this year, he's asked for the design to pay homage to our Castilian guests. We cannot have it ruined before they see it."

She could envision it now. Couples turning about the room as magic sparkled in the air. Chalk dust rising in clouds around them. The artwork smeared across the floor in wild, giddy lines. The bittersweet thought of such fragile, impermanent beauty made her heart ache with longing. "It sounds spectacular."

"It is. You ought to see it when it's unveiled." He offered her his arm and smiled when she took it. "Let's get a better vantage point."

"All right," she said, unable to keep the excitement from her voice.

As he led her through the crowds, the whispers began. At first, Niamh could ignore it. But as gazes followed them across the floor—some pitying, some derisive, some amused—she couldn't deny it any longer. Her stomach dropped with shame, and her skin felt boiling hot beneath their scrutiny.

"Sinclair?" Niamh whispered. "Why is everyone staring at us?"

"Hm?" He scanned the room briefly. "Ah. That would be my fault."

"Please, do not spare my feelings," Niamh pressed. "Everyone tonight has made it very clear what they think of me. I don't want to cause you any trouble."

His easy gait faltered, then slowed to a stop. He determinedly avoided looking at her. "It isn't because of you. I don't know how to say this, but I haven't been entirely forthcoming with you."

"I see." Niamh searched his expression, half-concealed beneath the tousled mop of his hair. "What do you mean?"

"My attention to you thus far hasn't been entirely selfless. That isn't to say I don't enjoy your company. I do, but I . . ." He let out a choked laugh. "I could use some air. How about you?"

Whatever he had to confess clearly weighed on him. She squeezed his forearm reassuringly. "You can tell me. I will not be angry."

"At the presentation of the debutantes, do you recall when Jack asked if I'd put any thought into what he said?" When she nodded, he barreled onward. "He asked me to court someone this Season. More accurately, to *pretend* to court someone. I know it sounds mad. But I don't have the best reputation, and he doesn't want it to touch Kit more than it already has. Of course, I will do my best to help you navigate the Season. I could introduce you to what few acquaintances I still have, if you would like. But I would never presume—"

"Sinclair, ah . . . I am very sorry to interrupt." Her head spun. "May I ask why? You are perfectly charming. Surely, there is a woman here who would encourage your affections—"

"I don't want to court a woman." He held her gaze steadily, and it took only a moment for his meaning to dawn on her.

In Machland, no laws prevented them from loving or marrying whomever they pleased. She and Erin had never officially courted, but the night before Erin had left for Avaland last year, she'd taken Niamh to the cliffs just outside Caterlow. As the sun had dipped low into the ocean, turning Erin's red hair as brilliant as flame, she'd kissed Niamh. The languid heat of it, the fizzling, impossible happiness of that moment, had felt as fleeting as chalk on a ball-room floor. Niamh could not promise to wait for her—not when she did not know how long she had left. She could not follow her, either. Not for an ill-paying job. Not even for her own happiness.

The wounded compassion in Erin's eyes had nearly broken her.

But in Avaland, where wealth and magic intertwined, where the nobility fiercely protected its magical bloodlines, it did not shock her to learn they disapproved of such matches.

"We are of a kind," she said, which earned her a relieved smile. "But why me? I am hardly a suitable match for you."

"That is exactly why you're perfect! You're not here to find a husband. No marriage-minded mother would let me anywhere near her daughter. Besides, I'd say you and I are about equal in the eyes of society. In fact, you might be more respectable than I am. I've no divine blood."

"But you are still a noble," she protested. And yet, the herald had announced him as *Mr. Gabriel Sinclair*.

"No longer," he said bitterly. "I'm not Pelinor's son—not by blood, anyway. He raised me like a cuckoo in his home to protect both himself and my mother from the shame of her indiscretion. But a few years ago . . . Well, let us say that I wore out his generosity. A bastard without divine blood, he tolerated as best he could. A bastard with proclivities such as mine, he could have overlooked if I'd carried my mother's divine blood. But both? It could not be borne."

"He disowned you."

"Yes." Sinclair sighed, but she watched him carefully tuck away his pain behind a smile. "But Kit has made sure I am taken care of. I have an allowance from him."

"*What?*" She wasn't sure what shocked her more: that the duke would be so cold, or that Kit would be so generous. "But that's horrible!"

"You do not need to fret over me. It's a very nice townhouse that Kit bought for me. In fact, you should come and see it sometime." He winked, but she couldn't bring herself to play along with his hollow flirtations. How could he so determinedly gloss over something so painful? When he drank in her expression, Sinclair sobered. "I've upset you. My sincerest apologies."

"No, please do not be sorry. One shouldn't have to bear one's burdens alone." Niamh took both of his hands in hers. "I'm very glad you told me. And for what little it's worth, I would be honored to consider your suit."

His eyes shone with gratitude. "Ah, Miss O'Connor, I will break your heart in the end."

"And I shall hate you bitterly for it," she replied warmly. "Call me Niamh."

"Niamh."

The sound of her name, spoken with such welcome familiarity, lit her up from within. Tonight bore no resemblance to her silly daydreams. Even so, here in a ballroom full of people who disdained them both, she'd finally found a friend.

"Sinclair. There you are."

Just as quickly as her night had improved, it soured once again.

Kit hovered just a few paces away, all the fine thread of his jacket silvery and cool. All the candlelight gathered around him, softening the sharpest edges of his features. Her mouth went infuriatingly dry at the sight of him. Here, at last, was a prince stepped out from the pages of a Jaillean storybook. Or a Fair One, cruel and beautiful, with how effortlessly and maddeningly he ensnared her attention.

And then, he turned his golden eyes to her and added, "You."

You. As if he did not know her name after all this time!

"The man of the hour makes an appearance at last," Sinclair cut in. With a touch of apprehension in his voice, he asked, "What have you got there?"

"Lemonade," Kit replied curtly, "so you can stop looking at me like that."

"Right. Of course."

For the first time, Niamh sensed awkwardness between them. She inspected the glass in Kit's hand. It was indeed lemonade, garnished with a sprig of mint and a thin sliver of cucumber. Strangely, he was one of the only people in the room without a glass of punch. He'd seemed distracted earlier in the reception room, but now, he was downright agitated. His jaw ticked, and his eyes roved the ballroom, landing on nothing and no one.

"Jack is clearly determined to spite me," he said after a long moment, clearly doing his best to break the tense silence. "It's so sweet, I can hardly stand to drink it."

She gasped. "You don't like sweets?"

"No," he said, visibly taken aback by her horror.

It seemed impossible that one man could be so monstrous. "How can that be?"

"I don't know. I just don't," he said defensively. He seemed entirely flustered by the accusation in her voice, which only baffled her further. "Here."

He did not exactly thrust the lemonade toward her, but he offered it to her hastily, as though he'd been compelled against his own volition or better judgment. The ice inside rattled ominously. Too bewildered to refuse, Niamh accepted it. The glass chilled her skin, and a trickle of water slid down the side, soaking into her glove. She stared, transfixed, at the condensation beading on the rim, where his lips had left behind the faintest impression. She'd have to rotate it before taking a sip. Gods, now *she* was flustered.

Sinclair looked at the two of them with an expression warring between awestruck and nauseated. Very slowly, he took a sip of his punch, as though he had to physically restrain himself from saying anything.

A murmur swept through the ballroom. It multiplied, until Niamh could make out the content of it: *Infanta Rosa has arrived.*

"I have to go," Kit muttered. "Bye."

And with that, he was gone. What a strange man. But she could not dwell on it. Right now, she had better things to do than wonder at his behavior. She stood on her toes and craned her neck to look out over the crowd—and instantly spotted Rosa.

Once again, she wore all black like a mourner. She walked arm in arm with her pretty lady's maid, following the path her father's broad, epauletted shoulders carved through the ballroom. A thick ribbon of black banded the empire waistline of her gown, and the jet beads on her skirt caught the light with every step.

Jack waited to receive them on a makeshift dais, his hands

clasped before him and Sofia standing serenely at his side. As the king and the prince regent spoke, the guests shifted restlessly around her. Everyone was eager to dance.

At long last, Jack stepped forward and projected over the crowd in his stately cadence. "I am honored to open the floor for the inaugural ball of the Season. As many of you know, it has become tradition to mark the occasion with art chalked on the dance floor. This year, I have prepared something very special for our guests—who soon I will have the honor of calling family. Without further ado . . ."

He gestured at a pair of footmen, who lifted the corners of the tarp in unison.

"What will it be this year?" someone muttered eagerly. "Last year's will be hard to beat."

"A portrait of the princess herself, do you think? The one he had done of Princess Sofia on their wedding was absolutely exquisite."

Inch by inch, the footmen rolled back the tarp to reveal the floor.

The giddy murmurs of the crowd intensified.

And the hope dropped clean off Jack's face.

Rosa gazed out at the dance floor with a studiously blank expression. Her dark eyes, however, twinkled with amusement. Her father, meanwhile, did not look at all impressed. He turned to Jack expectantly, but the prince regent did not seem to notice him at all. His complexion brightened from ghostly pale to livid red.

From her vantage point, Niamh could see the dance floor laid out before her. In bold, angry lines, someone had drawn the sun in the style of a Machlish rune: the symbol of the god of justice and his ruthless, illuminating glory. It was an emblem even the Avlish would recognize. It'd been scrawled on buildings and hoisted up on flags in the lead-up to the Machlish War of Independence. It was a clear enough message alone, but the artist had also scrawled Machlish words beneath the sun.

Sinclair leaned over to Niamh and whispered, "What does it say?"

Niamh flushed. She could not very well repeat what it said—especially not here of all places. "I do not think you want to know."

Sometimes, she believed their language had been made for curses, for there was a spare elegance to them in the Machlish tongue. It lost some of its power in Avlish, but what it said was this:

Jack Carmine, may the gates of heaven never open to you.
May there be guinea-fowl crying at your child's birth.
May you see what you've become.

8

"W ell," Jack called above the chaos. "Do enjoy your-
selves."

He all but fled the room, with the King of
Castilia hot on his heels. Sofia's serenity chipped just enough to
reveal the barest glint of icy displeasure. Kit and Rosa, abandoned
on opposite sides of the dais, stared each other down like two
fluffed-up cats in an alleyway. Niamh could not bear to watch him
insult Rosa, as inevitably he would. The evening was already an
unmitigated disaster.

She withdrew a few paces, pressing her back against the wall. The
air had thickened with the smell of spirits and perfume and sweat.
A few bold couples stepped onto the dance floor, their shoes making
hazy smudges of the curses chalked beneath their feet. Niamh still
sensed their power as though it were real magic, ancient and raw,

crackling like lightning in the air. To some of Jack's court, the incident would be nothing more than a spectacle to be picked apart and laughed over. But others had taken it as the threat it was. Two women drifted nearby, their fans fluttering and their heads bowed together conspiratorially.

"I say, the Machlish have gotten bold lately," one of them remarked. "My staff have gotten even lazier ever since that woman Carlile decided to make a nuisance of herself. The nerve of them, to demand more when they give less."

Niamh's stomach dropped, sudden and sharp.

Sinclair rested a hand on her shoulder, startling her. She could read the reassuring but firm pressure of his fingers plainly: *Let's go, before you overhear something you'd rather not.* "May I be so bold as to claim your first dance?"

It should have been so easy to accept, to slip away and pretend she had not heard a thing. And yet, she felt rooted to the spot. The dull, shimmery sound of the string quartet reached her from a thousand miles away.

"Can you believe," another woman continued, "that the prince regent entrusted one of them with such an important task?"

"Of course I can. After all, he's trotted out his new tailor at every event like some sort of show pony. It's laughably obvious what he's trying to do. Scrabbling to appease the rabble instead of actually doing something about it. His father never would have stood for this kind of disrespect."

"Certainly not," her companion agreed. "He tolerates it from all sides—especially from that horrid brother of his. The company the young prince keeps! Did you see the three of them together? It was like the setup of some terrible joke. A pauper, a molly, and a drunk walk into a ballroom . . ."

The drone of a hundred conversations built to a dull roar in her ears. All around her swam a sea of pale faces, drinking, gossiping, flirting, laughing. Her vision blurred with unshed tears. How had she thought for even a moment that she would belong here?

"Niamh," Sinclair said gently. "Please don't let them get to you."

"I won't." But how could she not? She smiled up at him as best she could. "Will you excuse me for one moment? I will be right back."

She needed air.

She plowed through the ballroom, upending at least one drink and knocking into a floral arrangement or three in her haste. At last, she reached a door. It did not matter where it led. She shoved it open—and stepped out onto a balcony.

Outside, it was dark, lit only by the stars overhead and a few flickering candles burned down to puddles of wax. The glass doors muffled the sound of music and chatter. Niamh rubbed her arms as the night air sighed over her skin. Sweat cooled on the back of her neck.

No one else was here.

Finally, Niamh allowed herself to weep.

He's trotted out his new tailor at every event like some sort of show pony. She did not want to believe it. And yet, she couldn't believe she hadn't realized it sooner. There was no other explanation for Jack's hospitality and attention. He had chosen her not for her skill or her craft, but to make himself look *enlightened.* To slither out of any accountability. She was nothing more than a novelty to point out to her fellow countrymen and say, *Look, not all of you suffer here.*

Much good it had done him.

His Machlish servants had resorted to this—to wishing the worst of misfortunes on him—now of all times. After such a public display, Jack would surely have no choice but to hear their demands now.

She should've contented herself with that much, and yet as deep as she dredged within herself, she found only despair. How could she have been so foolish, so *selfish,* as to waste her precious time chasing some silly, girlish fantasy? She'd come here to work for her family's sake, nothing more. This pain was just as much a reminder as the lock of white in her hair: better to deny herself than face this kind of disappointment again.

The door behind her swung open, letting in a wash of muted orange light. Someone stepped onto the balcony.

Niamh hastily smeared the tears off her face. As long as she stayed quiet, they wouldn't disturb her. With any luck, they wouldn't notice her at all. But when she glanced up past the loose tendrils of her hair, she saw nothing and no one. The cool summer air turned frigid in an instant.

A ghost. It had followed her here, lured in by the scent of her sorrow.

Erin had always teased her for her superstition. Now, through the frenetic hum of her terror, Niamh felt vindicated that she'd prepared all her life for this exact moment. If she commanded it to go, it'd vanish like mist over the sunlit hills.

And then she heard the strike of a match.

A tiny flame illuminated the hazy outline of a figure. As it came into focus, blink by blink, embarrassment chased away all her fear. It was only Kit, cloaked by the enchantment she'd stitched into his coat.

He leaned out over the balustrade, a slash of darkness against the cool white of the marble. Like this, standing alone in shards of broken moonlight, he looked so desolate. Niamh had the distinct sense that she was intruding on a private moment, but it wasn't as though she could slip away without him noticing. Maybe if she just—

"I can feel you staring at me."

"Your Highness." She winced at the teary thickness of her own voice. "I'm sorry for disturbing you."

He turned sharply toward her, surprise plain on his face. He stared at her with mounting alarm, as though he'd realized too late he'd stepped onto a sinking ship. "Are you . . . *crying?*"

"No, of course not!" She sniffled but tried to lighten her tone as best she could. "I just needed some air."

He looked so helpless and uncomfortable, it almost made her laugh. The very thought of Kit Carmine trying to comfort someone was absurd enough, but the realization that he felt some faint obligation to do so . . . Well, it almost endeared him to her. *Almost.*

"Me, too." He paused. "I should go."

"You don't have to," she blurted out. The prospect of spending even one more second alone with her own thoughts sounded unbearable. "That is, I don't mind if you're here, too. We don't have to talk if . . ."

"I should go," he clarified, "because people will start rumors if they see us out here together."

"What do you mean?"

Even in the dark, she could see the blush unfurling over the bridge of his nose. "What do you think I mean?"

Oh. *Oh.* The party raged on just on the other side of the foggy glass door, but she supposed, in a moment of passion, a secluded balcony like this would serve well enough for lovers hoping to steal just a few moments away from the prying eyes of the court. Anyone who caught the two of them alone here would assume they'd arranged some sort of tryst. Would that the floor give way beneath her feet—*anything* to escape the horrible awkwardness settling over them.

"Not that I concern myself with gossip," he continued, clearly eager to move on, "but associating with me will only cause you trouble."

The very thought of gossip doused any good cheer she'd recovered. "Maybe you should," she said quietly. "Infanta Rosa's father is not pleased with you, and he is not the only one."

That horrid brother of his.

Remembering the utter disgust in that woman's voice made her feel hot all over again, and all the desserts she'd eaten sat like stones in her gut. It shouldn't have mattered to her—not when she'd been just as insolent to him. She did not even *like* Kit. She could conjure a thousand justifications for why he might have earned high society's ill opinion: his prickly demeanor, his scowling countenance, his abhorrent manners. But he was their prince. And after all the heckling she'd endured tonight, she could understand now why he held the peerage in such disdain.

A pit of vipers, indeed.

He scoffed, puffing absently on his pipe. "I'm aware."

"It really doesn't bother you?"

"No. I've never cared what other people thought of me. I have no desire to twist myself into knots to please people I don't even respect." He stared out over the lawn below them, a preoccupied frown notched in his brow. Frustration crept into his voice. "It bothers Sinclair and my brother, though. And I can tell it bothers you."

"Yes. It bothers me to be hated and ridiculed for what I am."

Her own vulnerability embarrassed her. Niamh bowed her head, letting her hair fall to shroud her face, but she could feel him watching her with a searching intensity. When she dared look up again, the glint of recognition in his eyes warmed her from the inside, out. It said, *You and I are the same.*

"They're narrow-minded fools, all of them. They aren't worth your tears," he said. "You'll never meet their standards, nor should you want to. You're too honest for your own good—and too nice, for that matter."

A smile slowly tugged at her lips. "Your Highness, was that a *compliment?*"

"Don't let it go to your head," he huffed, but his irritation fizzled out as quickly as it'd flared. "I admit I'm surprised that you've stayed this long. Why *have* you stayed?"

"The same reason everyone else has. To give my family a better life." The thought of them, alone in that cottage, made her feel heavy and homesick. First thing tomorrow morning, she'd write to them and send back a portion of her first payment. She prayed that would ease at least some of the guilt. "There is very little left for us in Machland. Once I finish this job, I'll have enough money to open a shop and bring my mother and grandmother here."

"Is that all?"

"What do you mean?"

"What, no balls and suitors?" he asked skeptically. "You hardly factor into this plan of yours."

Self-consciously, she tucked the streak of white hair behind her ear. Once she ensured her family was taken care of for the rest of their lives, she hardly knew what she'd do with herself. But it wouldn't do to get her hopes up—to even imagine more was possible. Dreaming of all the things she might have would only make it harder when her health inevitably declined. Tonight had shown her balls were not for her, and she had no need for suitors. She'd only bring suffering to any fool who fell in love with her. As much as she yearned to be cared for, she was not that selfish. No good came from loving fragile things.

"The work is reward enough for me," she said.

He did not look entirely convinced. "You're a strange girl."

"You're a bit strange yourself, Your Highness." She smiled softly when he scowled. "At any rate, I suspect I'll have my fill of parties soon enough. How can I hope for more?"

His shoulders tightened. "Right."

"I see you're not looking forward to the rest of the Season."

"No. I hate this place. I never wanted to come back."

Niamh tried to keep the surprise off her face. Had he finally given up holding her at a distance? Or was this like one of her Jaillean fairy tales, where this spell woven by their shared pain would break as soon as midnight struck? It hardly mattered now. She would hold on to this connection between them for as long as it lasted.

"You were not really on grand tour these past few years," she said after a moment, "were you?"

He took a long drag from his pipe. As he exhaled, the smoke slipped past his lips and rose in a stark, gray line. "Everyone knows that. Ask anyone in that room, and they'll gladly tell you the whole story."

"*I* didn't know. Besides, I would rather hear it from you."

"Then, no. I wasn't." Judging by his cold tone, Niamh understood that was the extent of what she'd extract from him tonight. But he'd all but confirmed her suspicions.

Kit had been sent away, and she'd seen enough to guess at why.

The gossip from those dreadful women, Sinclair's concern over his drink, Kit's insistence that smoking was the very last of his vices . . . He was sick, too. She'd no word for it, but she recognized a disease when she saw one—especially when she'd watched it tear through Caterlow time and time again. In the wake of the Blight, chronic hunger and grief had driven many to seek solace in home-distilled poitín. She'd witnessed the devastation alcohol dependence could wreak on a man. For a time, they held themselves together well enough, but it always caught them out in the end. It came for their relationships first, and then it came for their lives.

She had to admire Kit for managing it as best he could. Very tentatively, she crossed the space between them. Speaking to him so often felt like walking into a room blindfolded and praying you didn't find any sharp edges, but she had to try. "I never apologized for what I said during our first consultation. I mean, you *are* negative and unsociable, but, ehm . . . Wait. That didn't come out right. Let me try again."

"All right," he said dryly. "This should be good."

"I know it isn't so simple to change things on your own. And it wasn't fair to compare you to your father. Neither of us was born yet when Machland was under Avlish rule." She knotted her hands together. "I cannot pretend to understand you entirely. But I do know something of what it's like to feel like your life does not matter. Like it is on a set course, and there's nothing you can do to stop it."

Emotion bubbled tight within her chest and prickled behind her eyes. Whatever she expected herself to say, it was not that.

He shifted, clearly avoiding her gaze. "You don't have to apologize. You weren't wrong about me."

Niamh was suddenly too aware of how alone they were. Their elbows rested side by side on the railing, so close she could feel the warmth radiating from him. Moonlight fell like a blade between them. It silvered the white petals of the flowers blooming around them. It softened the harshness of his features.

"This wasn't supposed to be the course my life was on," he said, startling her. "My brother never would have called me back here unless he was truly desperate. He's an ass sometimes, but he's always kept his promises to me."

Niamh wondered what promise he meant, but she did not want to risk him shutting down again by asking. "Perhaps he's changed."

Kit shook his head. "No one changes that much. The man can't stand to let a problem go unsolved for five minutes, and as you just saw, he's avoiding all of his at the moment. There has to be some reason."

What reason could there possibly be? She didn't know the prince regent like Kit did, but she could not imagine anything nefarious about a peacetime wedding—or anything terribly unusual about an Avlish lord neglecting his Machlish servants. "You think he's hiding something?"

His expression went slack, as though he'd forgotten who exactly he was talking to—or that he'd been speaking aloud at all. Pulling himself together, he rounded on her with a scowl. "I don't know why I'm explaining all of this to you. Forget we had this conversation."

"I . . ." She reeled at his sudden change in demeanor. So the spell had broken at last. "I cannot just *forget*! I am not sure I want to."

He squeezed his eyes shut. "Shh."

Niamh's mouth hinged open. "*Excuse* me?"

"Be quiet," he snapped. "There's someone—"

The door opened, and the sound of the ball came spilling out onto the balcony. A woman stood silhouetted in the doorway, her arms braced against it as if to bar their escape.

"Oh my," she said. "Am I interrupting something?"

Niamh's breath escaped her in a panicked rush. The woman had seen through the enchantment on his coat—precisely because she'd been expecting to see two people. How could she have been so foolish to tarry with him here? If she was recognized, then . . .

"You are," Kit said, his voice low and dangerous, but the hard line of his mouth was all grim resignation. The light of his magic flooded her vision with gold, and the plants around them began to seethe. Ivy detached itself from the wall, and passionfruit vines unwound from the balusters. Foliage spilled across the floor like a wave.

"Go," he muttered under his breath.

Before Niamh could reply, he strode forward, quickly enough that the woman stumbled back, her upturned face pale with dread. He took one menacing step into the ballroom—and did not hesitate as he threw himself down the three shallow stairs leading up to the balcony doors.

Shocked gasps rang out in the crowd. Someone even screamed. Niamh looked on in horror. What was he *doing*?

And where, exactly, did he expect her to go? She cast her gaze about desperately until there, a few meters away, she spied another door leading into an abandoned corner of the ballroom. *Perfect.* She slipped back inside, her chin tucked low. A few brave souls were attempting to haul Kit to his feet as he groused at them, and a few more sadistic ones were watching the scene with delight.

No one paid her any mind at all.

As she made a beeline for the exit, it occurred to her, quite belatedly, that Kit Carmine had made a spectacle of himself to protect her reputation.

9

*C*onsciousness doused Niamh like a bucket of cold water. She flailed awake in bed, her heart hammering against her rib cage, and gasped into the yawning dark. *No.* She'd slept the whole day away.

She kicked free of her stifling sheets, stumbled out of bed, and threw open the curtains. Damp air whispered through the window, stirring the wispy hairs around her face. It was still, mercifully, morning—and early enough that the sun had not yet burned away the mist blanketing the lake. Thank the gods she hadn't overslept. She leaned her forehead against the cool glass and breathed deeply, trying to dispel the last of her nerves. Last night, she'd wasted far too much time.

Last night. Memories of it clung to her like cobwebs.

She'd spoken to Kit in the dreamy half light of the balcony. In his way, he'd comforted her. And then, he'd saved her from her own ruin. Her heart fluttered with—what, shame? Gratitude? She could not place it exactly, nor did she want to. She refused to spare a moment more on any of her complicated feelings about him. He was her client and a prince—an *engaged* one, at that—not some comely village lad to moon over.

She needed to focus.

Niamh forced herself to sit at her vanity. The sight of her hair dismayed her. Half of it was snarled in a knot atop her head. She'd forgotten to let it down before collapsing into bed last night, and now she must pay the price. She wet it with a small pitcher of water. Then, picking out a wide-tooth comb from the clutter, she began to work out the tangles from ends to roots. The mindless rhythm of it settled her thoughts enough to sort through them. First, she'd deal with her correspondence.

When she finished with her hair, Niamh made her way to the writing desk and sighed at the mess. She still hadn't received a response from Erin—unsurprisingly, given the state of the post—but she needed to send money back to Ma and Gran. She hated to think of the two of them alone in that cottage with its cracked window and sagging roof: Gran, swaddled in blankets even in summer; Ma, weeding the garden with her swollen, aching hands. More than anything, she wished she could be there to put on the kettle for tea, to shoo her mother inside and kneel in the dirt instead, to while away the evening mending by dim candlelight.

But soon, she would never have to fret over them again.

House servants were typically paid quarterly, but Jack had—rather generously, she thought—agreed to a biweekly schedule. She'd worked in the palace for just over two weeks now, so her payment should be buried in here . . . somewhere. Oh, why had she not organized all of this sooner? With a groan, she riffled through the papers—a week-old newspaper, countless discarded sketches, a letter she'd started and never finished. By the time she reached the bottom of the pile, a dull panic began to rise up within her. *Nothing.* Surely, she hadn't misplaced her pay; not even she would be so careless.

A knock sounded at her door.

Her held breath escaped her. That had to be it now.

"One moment," she called.

She hurried to the mirror again and blotted at her eyes with her sleeve. They were still a little glassy, but that was nothing being outwardly cheerful couldn't fix. She pulled on a simple white morning dress and swept back her hair into a loose coil. There. Perfectly presentable.

As brightly as she could, she said, "Good morning," and opened the door.

But no one was there.

She craned her neck to peer down the eerily quiet hallway. Not even a speck of dust swirled through the thin beams of sunlight trickling through the windows. "Hello?"

Frowning, she glanced down and spotted an envelope at her feet, along with today's edition of *The Daily Chronicle*. Niamh gathered the papers up. Her name was written across the front of the envelope in a deliberate hand. Incredulous, she turned it over—and nearly hurled it back onto the floor. The seal on the back winked up at her: an ornate *L* stamped into black wax.

Lovelace.

The author of *The Tattler* had written to her. The parchment felt practically incendiary beneath her fingertips. After reading their column—and knowing how much Jack despised it—she knew how dangerous this was. Still, she couldn't *not* read it. She peeled off the seal and fumbled to get the letter out.

Dear Miss Niamh Ó Conchobhair,

I hope you will forgive my boldness in introducing myself to you—for I will not be so bold as to presume you know who I am.

I call myself Lovelace, and I am the author of a column called The Tattler. My first and foremost aim is to protect the powerless against the powerful by speaking to the court in a language they understand. For better or for worse, that is gossip.

I understand you have not been here long, but since you attended last night's ball, I assume you are already aware of the Machlish's plight here in Sootham. The conflict has finally come to a head after many years of frustration—a frustration that has built due to the prince regent's stubborn refusal to engage with anything beyond the narrow sphere of his household.

Since he was appointed regent, he's all but isolated himself, avoiding audiences and Parliamentary sessions. He reemerges only to host the social events his father held in Seasons past. But lately, he has shown a single-minded devotion to his brother's upcoming wedding. I find it terribly strange, considering he and Prince Christopher have not been on good terms for many years.

Perhaps it is all baseless speculation, but it is difficult to believe he is as indifferent to politics as he appears to be. There must be some reason that he insists on turning a blind eye to the unrest brewing around him, and I intend to uncover it. And if he does not agree to meet with Carlile and advocate for reparations in Parliament, then I will use it against him. I have many resources at my disposal, but the prince regent has grown wise to my methods over the years. All of my spies have been dismissed within days of worming their way into his staff.

This is why I write to you. I humbly request your assistance in fighting for the rights of the Machlish in Avaland. There is little I would not do to that end, and I hope you might feel similarly. The prince regent cannot dismiss you. He hired you himself, both for your skill and—I assume—for your heritage. I know he cannot stand the rumors that he mistreats his Machlish staff, so he will want to keep you happy. You have his ear, if not his trust.

*I don't believe the prince regent is an evil man, just an avoid-
ant one. If you want to help me, you may leave a response at
midnight in the burnt tree just outside the palace gardens. There
is no need to make a decision tonight. I will be watching.*

> *Yours,*
> *Lovelace*

Perhaps she was still dreaming.

Because if she wasn't, then it seemed she'd stumbled into some
sort of covert blackmail operation. It was almost . . . invigorating.
Never in her life did she expect something so utterly extraordinary to happen to her. Who would have thought that a girl from
a village like Caterlow would be recruited to conspire against the
prince regent?

Oh, gods. She'd been recruited to conspire against the prince
regent.

But Lovelace had given her a choice, and she did not have to
agree. As much as she wanted the Crown to admit its wrongdoing,
as much as she wanted to fight alongside her people, she could not
risk it. She and her family depended on Jack's favor and patronage.
Besides, she possessed all the subtlety of a flock of peacocks. If she
made an earnest effort to spy on the royal family, she'd almost certainly fail. Discovery would mean a death sentence.

The man can't stand to let a problem go unsolved for five minutes,
Kit told her last night, *and as you just saw, he's avoiding all of his at
the moment. There has to be some reason.*

No, no, no. As curious as she was, she could not embroil herself
in the Carmines' affairs. Now that Jack had been made a fool of in
his own home, social pressure would force him to agree to the protesters' demands. Lovelace had almost certainly skewered him in
today's column. She paged through the newspaper until she found
The Tattler.

What an opening night. It seems, to no one's surprise, that our very own Wayward Son shall be the undisputed star of this Season. Say of him what you will, but he is more of an entertainer than his brother will ever be. After sporting an ill temper all night—and refusing to so much as glance at his fiancée—he took quite a spill down the stairs.

I've heard all manner of speculation as to why. Some of you, no doubt, will say he still keeps that custom of his. Others—if you are foolish enough to believe a word of what comes out of Lady E's mouth—will claim he was creating a distraction. Evidently, she discovered him alone with a young lady on the balcony. A paramour would certainly explain his lack of interest in his lovely bride-to-be . . . And yet, I am inclined to think that he wanted to take some of the heat off a Certain Someone.

He will need to try harder next time to compete with a Dance-Floor-Turned-Protest-Artwork. I am sad to report that our Castilian guest, an Illustrious Gentleman, did not feel honored by this year's chalk design. If you were stationed in the northeast corner of the ballroom, you may have overheard the Illustrious Gentleman scolding CS for embarrassing his beloved, obedient daughter, who—and I quote—has never asked for a thing in her life.

If this does not entice CS to meet with Mistress HC, I anticipate this is only the beginning of a very tense Season. No party will be safe—not even yours, dear reader. If you want to spare yourself the humiliation, perhaps consider paying your servants a living wage—or float the idea of reparations to Machland in Parliament's next session. But who am I to offer advice? I am a humble columnist, not a politician.

That was *her* in the *Tattler.*

This Lady E, whoever she was, had seen her. If anyone recalled a girl with a silver lock of hair slipping out of the ballroom around the time of the prince's "accident," they'd make the connection. Just like that, her entire life unraveled like a loose stitch pulled and pulled to its end. She'd leave the palace in disgrace. She'd never find work again. She'd return to Caterlow, watching more of her friends leave, until she was left to wither away in that shop while her family slowly starved.

No, she could not spiral yet.

Lovelace did not seem to know that the young lady was her, or else they would have mentioned it in their letter. Still, her heart beat wildly in her throat with exhilarated terror. How close they'd come to exposure. She'd have to be more careful from now on, which meant no spying and *certainly* never again finding herself alone on a balcony with Kit Carmine.

Easy enough, she thought.

But the problem of her missing payment remained. In the chaos of the past few days, it must have fallen through the cracks. She considered seeking out Mrs. Knight, but Jack had handled all matters of her employment here thus far. The very thought of visiting the prince regent in his study without an invitation mortified her, but what else could she do? Sinclair had told her Jack preferred to manage things himself.

It took only a few wrong turns—and a few desperate pleas for help—for a maid to take pity on her and show her the way to Jack's study. As Niamh climbed the imperial staircase, the maid called after her, "If you ask me, I'd wait until tomorrow to speak with him. He's got the prince in there now."

Well, that did not bode well.

When she at last found the study, Jack's muffled voice filtered out from within. "I do not have time for this sort of nonsense, Christopher. My court, your future father-in-law, Carlile, that insufferable columnist—even my *staff*, for God's sake—are breathing down my neck. And now, you have decided to cause problems. To what can I credit this extraordinary lapse in judgment?"

Kit's reply came too quietly to hear. Curiosity got the better of her. Niamh crept closer and strained to listen in on their conversation.

"I do not want to hear excuses from you." Jack drew in a deep breath, gathering his temper like reins in his hands. "I know this has not been an easy transition for you. However—"

"And whose fault is that?"

Jack laughed bitterly. "Who is she?"

"No one." A petulant, flustered note crept into Kit's voice. In any other circumstance, Niamh might have laughed. Gods, he was *terrible* at lying. No wonder he was always so blunt. Then, with a meaner bite, he said, "Who's to say it's a woman?"

"Do not play games with me," Jack replied icily. But the long, considering pause that followed suggested Kit had caught him off guard. "You cannot go gallivanting about with whomever you please in plain sight of Infanta Rosa and her father. You will jeopardize everything I have taken such pains to secure for you, and you will drag your name *and* mine through the mud. What were you thinking?"

"I wasn't," Kit muttered. "Although from what I saw last night, I'm not the only one who needs to worry about dragging our name through the mud."

"Enough." Jack sounded dangerous now, his voice pitched low. "You are engaged to the Princess of Castilia, which is far better than you could have hoped for. She is a respectable girl with a strong magical bloodline. I made a list of every eligible young lady on the continent, and she met every single one of my criteria."

"And was 'will Kit get along with her?' on your list?"

"That isn't important—not to mention an impossible task! I could have brought you the most beautiful, well-bred, meek woman in the world, and you would still find fault with her."

"I'm marrying her. What's the problem? Do I have to pretend to be happy about it, too?"

"The problem?" There came the sharp sound of palms slapped hard against a hard surface. "The problem is your attitude. Such arrogance and ill temper are not becoming of a man of your station."

"I don't care." Kit enunciated every word.

"I thought your time away would have given you some perspective, but I see that was naive of me. We both must deal with reality. Your choices have led you here, Christopher, and I cannot protect you from the consequences any longer. You're an adult, and by God, you're a Carmine. Now do your duty."

The door flung open, and Niamh stumbled backward in surprise. Kit stormed out of the room, his face flushed with anger and his hands clenched in fists at his sides.

"And do not think for a second that I will not find this girl," Jack called after him, "if you insist on carrying on this way!"

Jack appeared in the empty doorframe, his eyes glittering with cold rage. But as soon as Kit was out of sight, all of the fight bled out of him. He sighed exasperatedly and dragged a hand down his face. It fell back to his side, revealing an expression that struck Niamh with a bolt of pity: a crumpled, remorseful exhaustion. She had half a mind to turn back now to avoid handing him yet another problem to deal with. But before she could retreat, Jack noticed her standing there and visibly startled. He stared at her with slow-dawning horror.

Niamh wished she could disappear, if only to spare them both the discomfort. Seeing him again made her feel oddly uneasy. She'd half expected the misfortune wished upon him to hang over him like a shroud, but he looked as he had on the day she'd first met him: balanced on that knife's edge of harried and composed.

He cleared his throat, and she watched as he neatly filed away every emotion that'd spilled across his face. "Miss O'Connor, what can I do for you?"

He sounded astonishingly pleasant, all things considered. Some

✺ A FRAGILE ENCHANTMENT ✺ 107

masochistic part of her wanted to ask why he'd hired her—to find out if she'd truly earned this honor, or if she was merely his token Machlishwoman. But even if she were bold enough to ask, why court more suffering? "It is nothing important, Your Highness. Shall I come back another time?"

"Nonsense," he replied briskly. "You're here now. Come in."

Tentatively, Niamh followed him inside. There were books and papers stacked intimidatingly high on his desk, and a collection of candles burned down to stubs cluttered the windowsills. A portrait framed in filigreed gold hung in the center of the room. The man glaring out at her looked uncannily like Kit and Jack, save for his green eyes. He had a cruel set to his mouth and an expression fixed forever in disapproval.

KING ALBERT III, the plaque below the frame read. Niamh shuddered. She did not know how Jack could bear the weight of his father's stare all day.

Behind her, the latch clicked ominously in the silence. Her throat went painfully dry.

"Please," Jack said. "Sit."

She obeyed.

Jack settled into the chair behind his desk and regarded her coolly. Sunlight caught all the gold thread in his coat and sparkled on the signet ring on his thumb. Where Kit bristled with thorns, Jack presented an exterior as smooth and inaccessible as stone. It made her feel horribly self-conscious. She'd been so rattled by Lovelace's column, she'd forgotten to put her hair up properly. She tucked the strand of silver behind her ear and folded her hands in her lap.

"What troubles you?" he asked.

She wiped her sweaty palms on her skirt. "I am terribly sorry to disturb you, sir, with something as trivial as this, but I did not receive my pay this week."

For a moment, she believed she must've spoken in Machlish, or perhaps not at all, for he looked back at her with an entirely blank expression. Then he recovered with a shake of his head. "That is not trivial at all. I'm terribly sorry that happened, and I shall speak with Mrs. Knight immediately about the oversight."

Niamh tried to keep her shock off her face. Was that really all it would take? With admirable efficiency, he procured an envelope and a quill. "Check?"

"Cash, if you please." After a moment, she added, "Your Highness."

"Of course." He pulled out his own coin purse, retrieved one shining coin, and placed it in her palm. She closed her hand around it, but she swore she saw its brilliance shining through the grooves in her fingers.

"Thank you, sir," she said breathlessly.

"No, thank *you* for coming to me with this." He somehow sounded both sincere and impersonal. "Is there anything else you need?"

"No, that is everything. Thank you again, sir."

As she made to rise, he said, "Hold a moment."

She all but collapsed back into her chair. "Sir?"

"I want to apologize for what you overheard earlier."

Oh. Surely, he did not *actually* want to apologize. This had to be a test of some sort. "I'm sure you have nothing to apologize for. I did not hear a thing."

"There is no sense dancing around it." He sighed wearily. "I understand the nature of your work has given you and my brother an opportunity to become acquainted. I've noticed you seem to have a certain sway over him—and my wife, for that matter."

"Oh, no, I would not go so far as to say that."

"Your modesty credits you," he said absently. "I mention it only to ask if Kit seems . . . well."

Niamh worried her lip. She knew well enough what he meant, but she dared to ask, "How do you mean, sir?"

"I suppose it is an unusual question." He looked suddenly troubled, almost embarrassed. It was oddly endearing. "I hate to put you in this position, but I find I have little other recourse to know how he is *actually* faring."

"He seems well enough." Apart from his disillusionment with court life, it was the truth as far as she knew. And a small, selfish part of her wanted to hold on to what little Kit had shared with her. It hardly seemed hers to give away, even to the prince regent. "Is there something the matter?"

Jack smiled humorlessly. "Are you aware of what happened to my father, Miss O'Connor?"

"Vaguely, yes." Many years ago, the king took ill and never recovered. Few details had escaped the walls of the palace, however, and judging by the guarded expression on Jack's face, he did not intend to share them now.

"Then you know enough." He laid his palms flat on his desk, smoothing out an invisible crease. "If I were to die before my father, Parliament would not appoint Kit the regent. He has too much of our father in him. But marriage makes a man more respectable in the eyes of the court. I know he resents my hovering, but I am doing what I must for his own good—and to ensure the continuity of our family's legacy."

Jack sat before her, as weathered and solid as the stones on which his legacy was built. How exhausting, she thought, to insist on solving everyone else's problems alone. To bear the weight of duty and the pressure to protect the ones you loved. She knew something of what that was like.

Over his shoulder, his father's scornful, painted gaze bore into her. If the king retired eight years ago, Jack couldn't have been older than two-and-twenty when Parliament appointed him prince regent. She drank in the shadows beneath his eyes and the faint lines etched on his forehead and felt, impossibly, a sense of kinship with him.

"I understand, sir."

"I'm glad," he replied stiffly. "I've kept you long enough. Going forward, do not indulge my brother's whims too much. We *will* need to see him on his wedding day, after all."

Niamh laughed nervously. "Yes, sir. I will make sure he is visible. At the very least."

"Thank you, Miss O'Connor. That is a relief." He checked his pocket watch and frowned. "While I have you here, I should inform you that you'll be meeting with Infanta Rosa today for a consultation. I've agreed to send you to her townhouse. Will ten o'clock suit you?"

It would, and so, she was dismissed.

As Niamh walked back to her chambers, the coin still clasped tightly in her fist, her thoughts swam with what she'd learned. All of Jack's obsessive single-mindedness on this wedding, his inattentiveness to his staff and the protests, sprang from a duty to his family. She believed him, of course—even admired that kind of devotion. But could that really be the whole truth? If Lovelace had been writing about him for years, then Jack had been ignoring the injustice in his realm long before Kit was betrothed to Infanta Rosa.

No. She could not entertain any doubts. She was a seamstress, not a spy. After she returned from her meeting with Infanta Rosa, she would write to Lovelace and tell them she could not help them. Once Kit was safely married, Jack would set things to rights.

She had to believe that.

10

*I*nfanta Rosa's rented townhouse reminded Niamh of a cake: a narrow slice of white brick, iced with elegant pediments and garnished with fragrant wisteria. It sat on the west end of Bard Row, one of the most fashionable, charming districts in Sootham, all manicured lawns, colorful gardens, and trees lush with summer foliage. Wicker baskets full of cut flowers hung like pendants from the gas lamps. All of it delighted Niamh as much as it astounded her.

She lifted the hem of her walking dress as she approached the front door. Her bonnet's wide brim kept the sun from her eyes, but the ribbon fastened beneath her chin itched horribly. Sweat beaded uncomfortably at her hairline. Never had she felt less like herself. But a girl must look the part of a high-society lady when she made the acquaintance of the Princess of Castilia, even if there was nothing to be done for her accent.

The housekeeper, already lingering on the porch, promptly escorted her to the drawing room on the second floor and told her "Su Alteza Real" would be with her shortly. A tea service already waited here, as cruelly inviting as a plate of biscuits in a fairy-tale witch's hut. Her stomach growled, and she had to remind herself that it was intolerably rude to eat without her host.

The display was unlike anything she'd ever seen in either Avaland or Machland. A bitter, acrid smell wafted from the ceramic teapot. She wrinkled her nose. Scattered around it were squares of chocolate, as dark and glossy as polished stones, thick slices of fresh bread, a wedge of hard cheese, and slivers of cured meats. Gods, she wished she hadn't forgotten to eat again. Time kept getting away from her. But surely, no one would notice if she took just one tiny piece of chocolate. She popped it in her mouth and nearly moaned aloud as it melted on her tongue.

The door to Rosa's bedchamber flew open.

Niamh shot to her feet, nearly choking on the chocolate. But it wasn't Infanta Rosa but her lady's maid, Miss Miriam Lacalle, who slipped through the doorway. Miriam slammed the door shut behind her, then leaned back against it as though trapping a beast inside. "Good morning! What can I do for you?"

"Hello." Niamh did her best not to conspicuously peer over her shoulder. "Is Infanta Rosa here? I'm meant to take measurements for her dress this morning."

Miriam's eyes went round and practically sparkled. In the daylight, her face was as kind as Niamh remembered it beneath the ballroom chandelier's glow last night. "Ah, so *you're* the dressmaker I've heard so much about. The gossip columns are all aflutter about the gown you wore last night. I am sorry I did not see it myself."

"Only good things, I hope." Niamh smiled sheepishly. "It's an honor to meet you, my lady. Niamh O'Connor."

"You flatter me, Miss O'Connor, but I am no lady." She laughed. "Miriam Lacalle."

How curious that Infanta Rosa had selected a common girl as her lady's maid. "A pleasure, Miss Lacalle."

"I'm afraid she isn't in at the moment." Somewhere from the depths of the bedchamber, something crashed. Miriam winced. "What I meant to say is that the princess is indisposed."

A dolorous voice echoed from behind the door. "Miriam, con quién estás hablando?"

Miriam closed her eyes, looking as though she was praying for patience. "On second thought, why don't you come in?"

She ushered Niamh inside. When she latched the door shut behind them, it sealed them in total darkness. Niamh blinked hard to adjust to the sepulchral gloom. All the velvet drapery was drawn; only a thin blade of sunlight cleaved through the curtains. It illuminated the frankly shocking state of the floor. Dresses were piled in heaps, a stray necklace poked out from under an armoire, and a collection of shoes—some without their twin—cut a treacherous path through the room. A chess board had been set up beside the window, the pieces still arranged in an endgame. Mysteriously, one of the chairs had been overturned. Every last one of Niamh's preconceptions about nobility now lay scattered among the wreckage of Infanta Rosa's dressing room.

"I'm so sorry for the mess," Miriam said with a nervous laugh, opening the curtains. The sudden flood of light made Niamh's eyes water. "Rosa is not a morning person. I didn't want to subject you to it, but I suppose there's no avoiding it now."

"I hardly know what you mean," Niamh lied. "This looks immaculate compared to my room!"

Miriam rapped gently on another closed door. "Rosa, there's someone here to see you." After a few seconds of silence, she cleared her throat and yelled, "Rosa!"

The door creaked open, and Infanta Rosa appeared, beautiful and terrifying.

Niamh drew in a sharp breath, her face warming at the sight of the princess. If she did not guard herself against such beauty, she would forget how to speak. The princess was surprisingly tall, but the inelegant slouch of her shoulders made her seem smaller at first glance. She had on another black gown, but today, she'd foregone her lace veil. Her hair hung around her shoulders in perfectly arranged curls, but shadows feathered beneath her dull eyes—or perhaps that was just her makeup, smeared as though she'd slept in it. Rosa wore it like battle paint. Her gaze raked across Niamh's face.

"Who's this?" Rosa asked. Like Miriam, she had a subtle but unmistakable accent. Her voice, however, was flat. Not cold, exactly, but bored. "An assassin, I hope?"

"Rosa," Miriam chided, clearly hoping to move on without comment. "This is Miss O'Connor, your dressmaker."

"I see." Rosa collapsed into a chaise, as though supporting her own weight had become a burden she could no longer bear. Her wide skirts puddled on the floor like a spill of ink. "How disappointing."

"Don't take anything she says to heart," Miriam whispered to Niamh. "She has a wretched sense of humor and aims to amuse no one but herself."

Niamh tried not to let her smile waver as she curtsied. "It's an honor to meet you, Your Highness."

Intrigue lit up Rosa's expression, and her sharp, assessing gaze locked on Niamh's. The sudden attention almost made her quail. Nothing she'd said was at all remarkable . . . At least she didn't *think* so.

"And you." Rosa yawned. "My apologies. I prefer to get a full twelve hours of sleep, but I went to bed much later than I'd hoped. Far too much excitement."

"Rosa," Miriam muttered exasperatedly.

"What?" She lifted a brow. "My fiancé was charming, was he not?"

She spoke so dryly, Niamh couldn't be sure what she meant in jest. Miriam held her long-suffering silence.

Niamh did not know whether to agree or laugh or weep. "I understand entirely, Your Highness. I will try to keep this quick for you."

"Excellent." Miriam clapped her hands together. "I have a letter to finish, so I shall leave you two to your discussion."

With that, Niamh was alone with the Princess of Castilia.

Rosa smoothed her skirt over her knees and sighed. "I am at your disposal, then, Miss O'Connor. Where shall we begin?"

"Anywhere you'd like, Your Highness. I can take your measurements first, or you can tell me about what you envision for your gown. I would love to know what styles are popular in Castilia, or . . . Oh! We could—"

"Slow down, I beg you. I haven't had any coffee, and I've never heard an accent like yours before." Rosa rubbed her temples. "Perhaps we can start with measurements."

"Yes, of course. That sounds wise."

Niamh cleared a space on the floor, shoving piles of clothes out of the way, and set to work. Rosa, to her relief, was much more practiced than Kit. She barely needed to be told what to do as Niamh pulled the tailor's tape around her waist and hips, her bustline, the length of her arms.

As Niamh bent over a table to finish recording the last of the measurements, Rosa said, "You're from Machland."

Niamh whirled to face her, nearly knocking over the chair beside her. She seized hold of the back to steady it—and herself. That a princess would inquire about her personally was still jarring. "I am, Your Highness."

"I see." That calculating interest kindled in her eyes again, but her tone was all dull politeness. "How have you found your stay in Avaland thus far?"

"Very agreeable," she replied as cheerfully as she could. "The prince regent is a very generous host."

Rosa hummed pensively. "Yes, I suppose he is, isn't he?"

"And you, Your Highness? Is this your first time in Sootham?"

"It is. I find it quite fascinating. The Avlish's stuffy manners and dispassionate dances, their drab weather, their taste in art . . ." She trailed off. "Ah, but I suppose you are not here to listen to me drone on. Shall we discuss the design of the gown?"

"Of course! Did you have any ideas?"

"I would like the gown to be black lace."

A light died within her. What did these royals have against *colors*? And the thought of making that much lace . . . Niamh shuddered. Infanta Rosa's fashion sense was most unusual for a woman of her rank—at least by Avlish standards. It reminded Niamh a bit of home. Few people in Machland purchased new gowns for their wedding day. They typically wore their finest dark-colored gown. Easier to hide stains that way. But Infanta Rosa could purchase a new gown for every day of the week if she so chose.

"What about something more fun?"

"Fun," Rosa repeated.

"I don't know." Niamh inspected the heaps of black fabric scattered across the room. "Perhaps something colorful?"

Rosa pulled a face. "I don't do color."

"Whatever do you mean? You would look so lovely in—" Rosa stared at her until Niamh had no choice but to say, "Actually, a black dress sounds very au courant."

"It is the new fashion in Castilia," she granted. "I imagine it will make an impression. Everyone here is so . . . bright."

That much was true. The thought of the court's faces when they beheld Rosa in a black gown delighted her more than she cared to admit. Niamh touched a hand to her mouth to hide her laugh. "Oh, it *definitely* will."

Rosa smiled, a barely perceptible curl of her lips. "If it isn't much trouble, it would please my father if I wore a veil as well."

Niamh couldn't read her expression. From the little Niamh had seen of Rosa's father, he seemed an overbearing man. She wanted to ask if it would please *her* but decided against it. She'd spoken out of turn with royals far too many times already. "And in terms of enchantments, what would suit you?"

"Enchantments?"

"I can stitch memories or emotions into the gown. If you want to look or feel a certain way . . ."

"Is that your blessing, then? I see why they hired you." Rosa leaned back, assessing Niamh with a heavy-lidded stare. "Let's see. Can you strike fear into the heart of anyone who looks at me?"

She struggled to keep the despair out of her voice. "Well, I . . ."

"No, you're right. Another time, maybe," Rosa relented. "Papa would be displeased. I'll think about it. This wedding is shaping up to be very interesting indeed."

Curiosity burned within her. While Kit tolerated her impertinence well enough, she didn't know if Rosa would. But she and Miriam seem to be friends despite their difference in station, so she couldn't rebuff Niamh too strongly for asking questions. "How so?"

Rosa crossed the room and settled in front of the chess board. Absentmindedly, she began to reset the pieces. "I confess, what I saw at last night's ball intrigued me. I am no stranger to political unrest. When I was a child, my uncle usurped my father and banished my family from Castilia. We lived in exile for nearly a year, until my father returned and reclaimed his throne with lightning and bloodshed."

Niamh shuddered at the image. She'd grown up on stories of violent revolution, but Rosa had lived it. What a life she must've led. "Doesn't it frighten you, then?"

"Not anymore." She watched Niamh through her eyelashes, her eyes aglow with something like purpose. "I have seen three regime changes in my lifetime. I have seen the mistakes of my forebears. If anything, I find politicking less dreadful than these infernal *proceedings*. The Avlish make such a fuss over weddings. As far as I'm concerned, it would be better to sign the contract and be done with it all."

"But . . ." It slipped out before Niamh could stop herself. "That is so unromantic!"

"Weddings aren't romantic. Not for the nobility."

Niamh's shoulders sagged.

"It isn't so dreadful, Miss O'Connor, I assure you. This arrangement suits me well. I like chess, after all."

"Chess? I don't follow."

"All of us play a role in this life. Take me, for instance. I am my father's only daughter, and so, I am a pawn. I know very well what is expected of me: to be sacrificed for his ends." She examined a chess piece, turning it through her fingers. Sunlight struck the glass pawn, and a rainbow scattered in fragments across the board. "It's precisely *because* I don't care for the prince that it is an attractive marriage."

Niamh still did not follow. Her confusion must have shown on her face, because Rosa continued after a beat of silence.

"Happiness is a simple thing. When you accept your lot in life, there are no crushing lows and no soaring highs. The vacillations are exhausting—and they impede your ability to make objective decisions." Rosa placed the pawn back on the board with a resonant *clack*. "I am often called dispassionate, but that dispassion allows me to do what needs to be done. This union will benefit Castilia and Avaland's relationship, and more importantly, it will benefit me. My wedded bliss, if such a thing even exists, is immaterial. I must do this."

So both she and Kit would marry for nothing but their grim duty. In a way, it relieved Niamh that Rosa was as practically minded as Kit about the whole affair. And yet, she doubted that anyone could be so perfectly resigned to such a joyless, monotonous life.

Not even me.

She scrambled to shove that thought back down where it came from and asked, "How can such an arrangement possibly benefit you, if you do not care for him?"

"I am suited to court games, and I am eager to play." She frowned, and an emotion Niamh could not read passed over her features. "I have my reasons."

Miriam reappeared in the doorway. "Rosa, are you tormenting the poor thing? Don't make her play chess with you. It's no fun at all."

Rosa smirked. "It *is* fun. You're just a poor player—and a sore loser."

Niamh couldn't help smiling at their easy rapport. Miriam, she saw, was the ray of sunlight that pierced through Rosa's gloom. "How long have you two been friends?"

"Friends?" Rosa asked. "Oh, no. You are mistaken. Miss Lacalle is my jailor."

"Oh, hush, you." When Miriam laughed, her eyes crinkled with mirth.

Rosa's expression softened, only for a moment, before her dull mask snapped back into place and she became the dispassionate politician once again. Niamh had always marveled at the things people kept locked inside themselves. She'd never had the gift for concealing her emotions. Whatever she thought or felt showed plainly on her face. It flowed from her like water from a broken vase.

I have my reasons, Rosa had told her.

Reasons enough that she cared nothing for her own happiness. One of these days, perhaps, Niamh would uncover why.

That night, after Niamh finished her sketches of Infanta Rosa's
gown, when the candles had burned low and the clock hands crept
toward midnight, she at last turned her attention to Lovelace's letter.
It sat on the corner of her desk, a splash of cream against the encroaching dark. The wax seal shone like a newly minted coin in the
candlelight. She pulled out a fresh sheet of paper, opened a pot of
ink, and promptly spilled half of it across her desk. That, she decided, portended nothing good. Once she'd mopped up the mess
and procured *another* fresh sheet of paper, she composed her reply
in halting pen strokes.

Dear Lovelace,

*Thank you very much for your letter—and for your devotion to
us Machlish here in Avaland. I admire your cause greatly, but
I cannot help you.*

The more she wrote, the more guilt closed in on her. Denying
them felt something like selfishness—or perhaps cowardice. But
if Jack truly was hiding something, she could not be the one to
unearth it.

With a quarter hour until midnight, Niamh slipped out of her
room and out into the dark of the palace grounds. Lovelace had
instructed her to leave her letter where they could find it: in the
lightning-struck tree overlooking the lake. It loomed before her, its
starkly bare branches an etching in charcoal against the rich purple
of the sky.

She trudged through the lawn, drawing her pelisse tight around
herself with one hand and clutching the iron handle of a lantern in
the other. It was a cool night, and the grass, damp with dew, glit-

tered faintly in the warm glow of her lantern's light. In any other circumstances, it would have been quite lovely, but by the time she reached the rendezvous point, she was shivering all over with dread. If word reached Jack that she'd corresponded with Lovelace, even to decline their request for help . . .

It did not bear thinking about.

The tree was textured with grooves and veins of bubbling black, but the bark beneath her fingers was as hard as bone. She placed her letter into the hollow of the trunk and shook out her hands. There. She'd done the worst of it. Now, all that remained was to return to her room unseen—and without being accosted by a ghost, or any of the Fair Ones. One could never be too careful. When she turned back toward the palace, Niamh froze.

A ghost.

A single light burned dimly, illuminating a figure on the second-floor balcony. The hem of her nightgown drifted like fog around her ankles. Her moon-pale hair tumbled over her shoulders and into the open air like a rope.

No, not a ghost, she realized. *Sofia.*

Sofia leaned over the railing, her gaze fixed on the horizon, longing weighing down her shoulders. She looked so lonely up there, Niamh's heart ached with sympathy. How long had it been, she wondered, since Sofia had returned to those ice plains she'd described? How long had it been since she'd seen her sisters?

Niamh shook herself out of it. She could not afford to just stand there, pitying the prince regent's wife. Sooner or later, Sofia would notice a ghostly lantern floating out on the lawn. Niamh doused the lantern's flame with a breath, plunging herself into darkness. Slowly, she made her way back to the palace by moonlight. Inside, the reception hall lay as still and quiet as a tomb. She crept up the imperial staircase, then rounded the hallway to her room. Light trickled into the corridor from a door left ajar. She paused just outside. Who else was still awake at this hour?

"Couldn't sleep?"

Niamh all but leapt into the air. She laid her palm flat against her chest, relieved to feel her heart still beating, and slumped against the doorframe of what she soon saw was the library. Shelves and shelves full of leather-bound books stood sentinel against the walls, with gold-leafed titles gleaming in the dim candlelight within. Kit sat in a wingback chair by the window, one ankle hooked over his knee. He'd removed his jacket and draped it across the back of his chair, which Niamh did her best to ignore. She half expected a cigar to be smoldering between his fingers, but he only cradled an open book in his palm. The sight of him set her stomach churning as gratitude and humiliation chased each other in restless circles.

His gaze caught on her extinguished lantern. "It helps if you light it."

That snapped her out of her stupor. "Your Highness," she protested in a stage whisper. "You shouldn't be here."

"I'm reading," he said bemusedly, "in a library."

"Yes, well . . ." She floundered. "What I mean is, we shouldn't be alone together."

He seemed to consider it. "Why not?"

"You . . . !" She huffed, then cut herself off. She stalked closer so that she didn't have to feel foolish whisper-shouting across the room. "You know very well why."

"Nothing comes to mind."

She threw her hands up. "You're making fun of me now."

"It's the middle of the night," he replied coolly. *Exactly,* she might have interjected, but he continued, "No one is here to gossip. If I feel like speaking to you, why shouldn't I?"

She suddenly felt quite warm. "You want to speak to me?"

"Is that a problem?" She thought she detected a touch of self-consciousness in the hastiness of his reply.

Yes. Of course it was. A gossip columnist had already written about them—vaguely, and to question the source of the rumor, yes, but the point stood. Rosa's father already disapproved of him. His brother had threatened to hunt down the girl Kit had been seen with at the ball. Now that she'd washed her hands of Lovelace's scheme, all she wanted was to finish her work in peace. No more complications, no more distractions.

But the longer she stared at him, that almost boyish hesitation on his face laid bare in the candlelight, it occurred to her that he must've been quite lonely here. Why else would someone like him want to speak to someone like her? For her own sake, she should tell him to call on Sinclair and leave her alone. But, well . . .

Maybe she was a little lonely, too.

The realization settled heavily over her. Erin, her last friend in Caterlow, had left a year ago. It hadn't sunk in that she hadn't spoken to someone her own age in that long. What had she even done with herself besides *work*?

"If you insist," she said, trying for a playful tone, "then I should apologize."

Surprise skittered across his face. "For what?"

"I know you wanted me to forget that we spoke last night, but I cannot. I probably would have lost this job—or worse—if you hadn't done what you did."

Shame lodged itself within her, as sudden and sharp as an arrow to the heart. If she'd been strong enough to ignore the court's petty cruelty, he never would have had to humiliate himself in front of the people he so disdained to protect her. He never would have been dressed down like a child in his brother's office. Oh, how she hated herself for that moment of weakness, for burdening Kit with all her silly hurt feelings. She took care of others; she did not ask to be cared for. What good was she otherwise?

"I am so sorry for the trouble I caused you," she said. "I shouldn't have—"

"Shouldn't have what?" His tone held no mockery, but it was

sharp enough to cut. "Been standing on a balcony? Drawing breath?"

She had no reply to that. Niamh tore her gaze away from the floor to meet his. The intensity of it bowled her over. His eyes, blazing in the dark of the library, seared her like daybreak.

"Save your apologies for when they actually matter," he said. "You didn't make me do anything."

It unsettled her, for an apology to be so summarily refused. Niamh had spent all of her life sorry for taking up space, guilty for inconveniencing anyone with her emotions or needs. She supposed she had often felt tempted to apologize for breathing, but no one had ever made her feel so absurd for it. It stung as much as it relieved her, but she should have expected no different from a man so disagreeable to all polite society. Kit, she imagined, had never once apologized for existing exactly as he was.

"Then I shall have to thank you instead," she said quietly, "for your kindness."

"*Kindness?*" He looked thoroughly discomfited by the suggestion— even disgusted. "It's nothing like that. My body works faster than my mind."

How eager he was to deny even the smallest of good qualities in himself. It made Niamh smile. The urge to tease him rose up within her quicker than she could quash it. "That is quite a noble instinct you have, Your Highness."

Most impulsive men acted to sate their own appetites, pursuing pleasures or indulging cruelties. Yet here was Kit, impulsively self-destructing to protect someone else from harm. Because that *was* it, wasn't it? That grim, resigned look he'd worn last night—that reckless abandon—did not belong to someone who cared nothing for anyone but himself.

"It isn't, believe me." He spoke so coldly, she sensed she'd offended him.

"Your Highness, I . . ."

"I'm going to bed."

He rose from his chair and brushed past her. Niamh knew she should not regret driving him off, just as she should not wonder at what he meant. Ending any acquaintance between them, retreating behind the veil of professionalism, was the wise choice. The right choice. And yet . . .

Once you strip off all those thorns, he's not so bad, Sinclair had told her once. Life had been so much simpler before she believed him.

11

*N*iamh could not stop thinking about Lovelace.

They had not replied to her yet. It had been just over twelve hours, but her mind turned and turned in circles. Perhaps they hadn't received her letter. Perhaps her refusal warranted no reply. Or perhaps Sofia had seen her outside after all, and a contingent of the Kings Guard would soon arrive to arrest her for sedition. Of course, they likely would have done so already, but—

"What's on your mind?"

Niamh startled, pricking her finger with her embroidery needle. "Gah!"

Miriam's eyes widened with concern. "Goodness. My apologies."

She placed her finger in her mouth, and the taste of blood bloomed bright and metallic on her tongue. She really must focus on being more pleasant company—especially because she very much doubted she should have been here at all. Today had been meant for Kit and Rosa to become acquainted with each other, but Kit invited Sinclair, and Sinclair invited *her* (via his calling card, tucked into the most stunning bouquet of red roses—well, the only bouquet of red roses—she'd ever received), and Rosa, not to be outdone or outnumbered, invited Miriam. Thus: the five of them, their very own motley crew.

"No, no. *I* am sorry," Niamh said. "I was elsewhere for a few moments."

"Understandable," said Miriam, smiling wryly. "It is a grim day."

In truth, it was a gorgeous day, the kind made for languid summer daydreams. Niamh couldn't abide stillness, but if one must be still, there were far worse places to endure it.

Eye Park sprawled before them, glorious and green and utterly thronged with people. Niamh loved it—the frenetic energy humming like bees over the wildflowers, the breathless urgency of a season that would soon come to an end. She longed to capture it in thread.

Carriages and horses tore down the gravel roads. Groups of friends wandered the grounds in gem-bright clothes, their noses buried in scandal sheets, their lips stained with water ices, their laughter rolling over the sunlit fields. The branches of a tree spread like a loom above her, heavy with limes and perfuming the air with its bright citrus scent. And just beside them, the River Norling rushed by, sparkling and enchanted in the afternoon light.

Miriam clucked her tongue disapprovingly. "Miss O'Connor, are you still bleeding?"

"Huh?" She glanced down. A bead of golden blood welled on the tip of her finger. "Oh! I suppose so."

"Let me see." The words were hardly out of her mouth before Miriam took Niamh's hand in her own. Her eyes glowed with warm light, and a shiver of magic passed between them. Heat pulsed in her hand, and just like that, the fresh sting of Niamh's wound dissipated. "There."

Niamh turned her palm over, stunned. "You have an ceird? I mean, divine blood? Oh, bother, what do you call it in Castilia?"

"Miracle work." Her eyes twinkled. "Did you know this magic is what brought Rosa into my life? My mother saved the queen's life—and Rosa's—in childbirth. After that, she was given a position in court as the royal physician, and I was raised among the nobility. That is its own sort of miracle."

"As a commoner?" Niamh marveled.

"And as a Siradi," she added.

There were not many Siradim in Machland, but one family, the Pereiras, had settled in Caterlow. They arrived many years before Niamh was born, fleeing from religious persecution in Castilia. Some Machlish steered their children away from them on the street, but they'd shown Niamh nothing but kindness. When the weather grew cold and the nights stretched longer, she would light their hearth once a week, on the day they could not work, in exchange for the most delicious bread she'd ever eaten. She thought of candles burning softly in their windows—and most of all, their exquisite, sashed robes, embroidered all in gold.

"The Siradim have been expelled from Castilia many times before, and Rosa's father has not always tolerated us. He terrifies me. Even Rosa is afraid to disappoint or disobey him. The only time I've ever seen her stand up to him was on my behalf." Her expression grew wistful. "She has always been protective of me. I suspect that is the real reason she has brought me with her. Of course, she would never admit to such sentimentality."

Niamh's heart squeezed with unexpected tenderness. "She wants to keep you close."

"What she wants is to see me married off to some Avlishman," Miriam replied, both fond and exasperated. "I've told her I have no interest in marriage, but she can be quite stubborn when she sets her mind to something."

"I don't have trouble seeing that." Niamh laughed softly. "So you do not want to be an Avlishman's wife. What would you like to do instead?"

"I want to open a clinic and provide medical care for those in need."

"I think that would be a wonderful thing."

"It's my duty." Miriam pulled up a handful of grass and let it fall back to the earth. "God acted through my mother the day she saved Rosa, and he has protected us since. I live with the guilt of it every day, the knowledge that so many suffer where I have not. And yet, I cannot help thinking I lived because I was meant to use my station to do more. If I could influence a noble to do something . . ."

Yes, she wanted to say. *I know exactly how you feel.*

Niamh reached out and squeezed her forearm. "I can only imagine how difficult it is to live among those who have hurt your people so deeply. But you do not have to suffer just because others have. Your dream sounds very noble to me."

"I think you can do more than imagine, Miss O'Connor." Miriam smiled sadly. "You and I ought to stick together."

Niamh beamed at her. "I'd like that."

A shadow fell over them. Niamh craned her neck to see Sinclair standing there, shading his eyes against the sun. His cheeks flushed cherubically in the heat. "I bring grave news. I could not track down any lemonade."

"And you dare return empty-handed?" Miriam asked teasingly.

"I'm terribly sorry, my lady." Sinclair clasped a hand to his heart. "However, I've another idea. What do you say we conduct a rescue mission?"

He jerked his head toward Kit and Rosa, who sat side by side on a bench overlooking the river. Kit was managing to maintain a prickly distance from her, holding what Rosa had called a papelate—tobacco wrapped in maize leaves—between his fingers. She'd made some effort to please him, and Kit, who was above pleasing and being pleased, at least seemed to have accepted her gift without fuss. Rosa looked content enough to watch the swans paddle through the cattails. Her black parasol cast lacy shadows across her face.

Miriam's smile turned mischievous. "Which of them do you suppose needs rescuing?"

Sinclair tapped his walking stick against the ground. "Both, definitely."

"Probably true," she mused. "Let's go."

"Please, go on without me." Niamh retrieved her embroidery hoop from where she'd set it in the grass. She'd asked her assistants this morning to start on the lace for Rosa's gown while she was out, but she could not depend on them for everything. "I really must finish this pattern."

Sinclair plucked the hoop out of her hands.

Niamh gasped and scrambled to her feet. "Sinclair!"

He held it above his head so that she could not reach it, even if she stood on her toes and jumped. Foiled *again* by her height. He looked far too pleased with himself. "I'm afraid this is urgent, Niamh. A day like this cannot enjoy itself."

Groaning, Niamh followed them to the bench. In the shallows of the river, children splashed one another as servants filled jugs of water. Farther down, a woman fed a swan by hand—and shrieked when it bit her. Kit and Rosa, however, sat like twin shadows against the bright chaos of their surroundings.

"Hello, Your Highnesses," said Sinclair. "Can we persuade you to take a turn, or will the sunlight make you catch fire, princess?"

"A few minutes of sunlight should be agreeable." Rosa rose from her seat. Today, she'd threaded scraps of black lace and ravens' feathers into her hair. She fluttered her fan over her face demurely, but Niamh could see displeasure glittering in her dark eyes. "The river was growing terribly dull."

Miriam linked their arms together. "Then we shall have to play a game and keep that busy mind of yours at work."

When they returned to their picnic blanket, Rosa immediately collapsed onto one of the cushions and sprawled out like a drowsing cat. Kit burned the last of his papelate down to nothing, and immediately lit another. Behind the haze of smoke, his jaw ticked. Niamh watched him from beneath her eyelashes, doing her very best to seem like she was not, in fact, watching him. He had not spoken to her all day, so she could only assume he was still angry with her for—of all things—calling him kind in the library. He could be so confusing sometimes.

Mercifully, Sinclair broke the silence first. "So, what were you lovebirds talking about?"

Rosa had already closed her eyes. She draped one elbow across her face and said blandly, "I was inquiring about his opinions on recent Parliamentary referendums and the upcoming election."

"Oh?" Sinclair's smile faltered.

"It was a surprisingly brief conversation."

Kit's shoulders bunched around his ears, his expression betrayed and fuming. "I haven't kept up with politics."

"It was my mistake." Rosa spoke calmly, but their conversation had obviously frustrated her. "I'd forgotten you just returned home a few weeks ago. Your brother is kind to have granted you such a long tour. Four years, was it not?"

"I'm certain he would have liked it to be much longer," Kit replied dryly. "I didn't realize spares in Castilia had such extensive political duties."

Rosa stretched, the very picture of indolence, but she sharpened her every word to a lethal point. "Spares? No, indeed. Save the Crown Prince, my dear brothers are military officers and clergymen and poets. But while I myself am not required to assist in matters of governance, I like to know when and where to apply pressure when it is needed."

Kit glowered. He clearly felt every ounce of the insult she intended. His voice oozed sarcasm. "And how is that dedication working for you? You and I are standing in the same place."

"And your cynicism, sir?" she countered. "You have not escaped the world you so disdain."

"Continue acting righteous if it helps you sleep at night," he said coldly, "but I refuse to glorify ridiculous ideals like sacrifice and duty."

Rosa opened her mouth and closed it again. A terrible chill passed over her face. Niamh could not bear to watch a moment longer.

"So!" Sinclair clapped his hands. "About that game."

"Yes," Miriam agreed readily. "What kind of game shall we play?"

"I was thinking blindman's buff."

Kit perked up, reluctant interest kindling in his eyes. But what he said was, "Really? How childish."

"Don't let him fool you," Sinclair said. "He *loves* this game. We used to play with Jack and my sister all the time. I still remember that time you got so competitive, you rolled your ankle. Jack had to carry you back inside. That was when you both were cute." He winked at Rosa. "Can you imagine?"

"As clear as day," she said archly.

"That was a long time ago." Kit turned scarlet and exhaled a thin stream of smoke. "I seem to recall you falling into the lake. Serves you right."

"Aw, come on," Sinclair cajoled. "You're just afraid you're going to lose."

He scoffed. "No, I'm not."

"All right, then." Sinclair strode forward, squaring up to Kit. "Prove it."

His grin was roguish, a challenge. It hit its mark, because Kit's entire demeanor changed. From the glint in his eye, Niamh could see plainly the competitive boy he'd been. He dropped his papelate, then ground it underfoot. Smoke curled sinuously between them.

"Fine," he said resignedly. "Since it matters so much to you."

Niamh raised her hand. "Excuse me. I have a question."

"No," Sinclair said, "you cannot work instead of playing. Any other questions?"

She huffed indignantly. "What *is* blindman's buff?"

"I, too, would like to know," Miriam chimed in.

Sinclair stared at them in open dismay. "Allow me to expose you ladies to the finer points of Avlish culture."

It was a simple game of tag, Niamh learned. One person was blindfolded, guided—or misled—only by sound and magic. Once they caught someone, they guessed the identity of their captive. If they were wrong, the game continued. If they were right, the captive became the next blind man.

"Ah," Rosa said. "It's gallina ciega. This should be interesting."

"How fun!" Niamh clasped her hands together at her chest.

It was, indeed—and complete chaos. She couldn't remember the last time she'd had such fun.

In the first round, Sinclair and Miriam teamed up to lead Rosa in circles for a solid five minutes with nothing but their voices, shouting so loudly she eventually surrendered due to "sonic exhaustion."

In the second, Kit lingered within arm's reach of Sinclair for the entire round, pivoting and dodging like a fencer while Miriam cheered him on. Eventually, he lured Sinclair directly into Niamh. She swore she caught Kit smirking at her cry of indignation.

But, at last, it was her turn.

Sinclair tied the blindfold over her eyes. The fabric scratched against her nose, and she held in a sneeze. Once she was settled, he took her by the shoulders and turned her slowly around in a circle. She spun and spun, until she felt dizzy and a little unsteady on her feet. The darkness before her eyes listed and whirled. Her every sense sharpened. The rustle of the leaves sounded as loud as the crash of the ocean. She relished the warmth of the sun on her forehead, the scent of limes and river water.

"Here I come," she called.

She held out her hands and took an uncertain step forward. The moment her foot touched down, a gust of wind nearly knocked her over. Her braid whipped around her shoulder. Miriam's laughter was soft, slipping away sylph-like, as Niamh stumbled toward her. Static crackled through the air, and a sharp tug on the pendant around her neck guided her back the way she came. Magic shimmered around her, golden even behind the blindfold.

"This way," Sinclair taunted, in a truly terrible impression of Kit's voice.

Laughing, she lurched toward him. Her foot caught on an upturned root.

Her stomach flipped sickeningly as she hurtled toward the ground. She braced herself, squeezing her eyes shut. But the crash never came. She collided, instead, with something warm and solid. Hands clamped firmly around her upper arms, steadying her.

"Oof!"

Beneath her palm, she felt the wild thrum of someone's heart. The whisper of breath stirred the loose strands of hair around her temples, and the earthy scents of tobacco and nettle enveloped her. Whoever they were said nothing. But Niamh did not need them to speak to *know*.

"Your Highness?" She lifted the corner of the blindfold.

Kit stood before her. "Are you all right?"

As she blinked, her vision adjusted. By the time she registered that she was staring at him, his guardedness had melted into something she couldn't decipher. The sunlight turned his eyes molten. It cast his face in a golden glow.

"Ehm . . ." Her face heated. "Yes. I think so."

"Right," he said gruffly. He was still holding on to her with surprising gentleness, as though he expected her to topple over the moment he let go. He might've been right, considering that her vision still swam nauseatingly. "I swear, you're a magnet for trouble. How did you manage to find the one hazard in a five-kilometer radius?"

"That's not true!" Over his shoulder, she caught Rosa eyeing them with a very peculiar expression. It wasn't exactly anger—not at *her*, anyway. Even Sinclair looked on with a frown. Hadn't she sworn to be more careful? Niamh yanked herself out of his grip and thrusted the blindfold at him. "It's your turn."

Kit accepted it from her. His expression rearranged itself at least five different times until it landed firmly on discomfort. Then, with a sigh, he trudged toward the center of their circle and pulled the blindfold over his eyes. "This is ridiculous."

On the outside, it *was* quite ridiculous. Kit allowed Sinclair to spin him around, scowling all the while. And when the game began, it became abundantly clear that Rosa was out for blood.

Electricity sparked between her hands, bathing her face in an eerie blue light. The air crackled with magic and hummed against Niamh's skin. The clouds darkened and swelled ominously, blotting out the sun. Her ears popped, and her skirts snapped around her ankles. Across the park, umbrellas bloomed like mushrooms in the rain. People's chatter grew louder as they pointed up at the brewing storm.

If the Carmines ruled the earth, it seemed the Carrillos ruled the skies.

With Rosa's blazing eyes and her hair rising in the gusting winds, she looked fiercely, dangerously beautiful—like a goddess. Sparks surged down her arm, and a bolt of lightning streaked from her extended hand. It tore through the air, just above Kit's head. On reflex, he threw himself to the ground.

He rounded on Rosa, his lips parted dumbly. Although Niamh

couldn't see his eyes, he seemed reluctantly impressed. "Feel better now?"

A self-satisfied smirk tugged at the corner of her lips. Static still crackled at her fingertips and the smell of ozone lingered, but the wind died down around them. Loose, wild curls spilled across her forehead. "Yes, very much so. All is forgiven."

With that, the game resumed. Sinclair hauled himself onto the lowest branch of the lime tree and tucked his long legs underneath him, all but vanishing into the leaves. A few times he called out to Kit, who looked entirely puzzled until he realized where Sinclair had hidden himself.

"Cheating at blindman's buff? You have no shame."

"Cheating? Please, you wound me. This is called strategic thinking." He touched a hand primly to his chest. "You've just lost your touch."

Kit huffed, but his mouth curved into a smirk. With a flick of his arm, a vine erupted from the earth and grabbed Sinclair by the ankle. His eyes widened as it dragged him from his perch, and he went down with a yelp.

Kit tore off the blindfold and tossed it in his direction. "Your turn."

"Fair enough." Sinclair rolled over, grinning. But when he tried to stand, he winced. The vine Kit had unearthed lay like a snake in the grass, coated all over with thorns. It'd shorn away a scrap of Sinclair's pant leg. Blood—a startling, magicless red—soaked into his white socks. He sucked in a breath through his teeth.

Miriam crouched beside him. "Are you all right, Mr. Sinclair?"

"Fine, fine," he said good-naturedly, but his smile was strained. "I've definitely been dealt worse in the ballroom."

"Fuck." All of the color drained from Kit's face. "Sorry."

"It's just a scratch, Kit," Sinclair said. "Really. Don't worry about it."

"Indeed. It was quite gallant of you," Rosa added diplomatically, settling herself beside Sinclair. "I didn't have the energy for another round."

Their words, however, did not reach Kit. "I didn't mean to."

"Hey," Sinclair said. Niamh had never heard his voice like that. It sounded as though he was talking down a spooked horse. Worse, it sounded as though he was afraid. "I know. Why don't you sit down?"

"Yeah." Kit dragged a hand through his hair, his voice rough. "Yeah, fine."

He stalked back to their picnic blanket and slumped down at the base of the tree's trunk. Dappled shadows rippled across his drawn face, and the breeze swept his dark hair back. He sat perfectly still, radiating a steady aura of regret and self-loathing.

". . . gets like this sometimes . . ." Sinclair's low voice drifted in and out of Niamh's focus, carried lightly on the wind. ". . . a few minutes to calm down . . ."

Kindness? It's nothing like that, Kit had told her. *My body works faster than my mind.*

Was *this* what he'd meant? When they'd been interrupted on the balcony that night, his magic had reacted immediately to his surprise, as though it'd been primed for a threat. Concern and frustration needled at her. Kit so clearly believed the worst of himself. But whatever he'd done before he was sent away, whatever it was that plagued him now, it couldn't be catching.

Tentatively, she approached him. "May I sit here?"

Kit didn't reply, which she decided to take as permission.

She retrieved the embroidery hoop and settled beside him in the grass. This close, with their shoulders nearly touching, she could feel him trembling. If it would not cause the scandal of the century, she'd rest her hand over his. But perhaps there was something else she could do.

She hadn't meant to use her craft today after how much she'd abused it to prepare for the ball. But for someone in need, she could always find something to spare. There was always more of herself to give.

She let her eyes flutter closed and reached deep inside herself. Her magic lay curled up, drowsing, but when she called, it turned toward her like a loyal hound. It came to her, on slow and weary paws. Memories stirred within her. A cool hand against her fever-ish forehead. Tea pressed into her hands at the end of a long day. The warmth of her blankets on a frigid winter morning. A friend's arms around her after a crushing disappointment.

Her throat constricted with longing for those small comforts, and she channeled that feeling into thread. It glimmered with golden light in her hands. She embroidered, until Kit's breathing evened out beside her—until it fell quietly into rhythm with hers.

12

The next morning, before she even dragged herself out of bed, Niamh called for tea and a copy of every popular gossip column in Sootham. She scoured each of them front to back for any sign of her imminent demise, but today's reports on the royal couple's picnic were mercifully uninspired.

A mysterious storm brewed over Eye Park early yesterday afternoon, crowed one. *Could it be an inauspicious sign?*

What sort of gown will our Provincial Beauty design next? asked another. *One must wonder if one disgraced Mr. S— will prove a distraction or a muse. Only time will tell, but I, for one, always hope for a redemption story.*

No one had noticed her and Kit's friendship—if it could even be called a friendship at all. Even Lovelace had spared her. They'd focused their attention today on *Mistress HC*—Helen Carlile, she presumed—an Avlishwoman who'd begun advocating fiercely for the Machlish earlier this year. Yesterday, she'd apparently accosted Jack on his morning ride. Despite the display at the inaugural ball, Lovelace's pressure, and Carlile's best efforts, it seemed he had no intention to even consider the protesters' demands.

What would it take, she wondered, to get him to act?

Niamh sighed fretfully. When she moved aside the newspaper, an envelope slipped out from between the pages. Immediately, she recognized the black wax seal. Finally, Lovelace had replied. With shaking fingers, Niamh tore it open.

Miss Ó Conchobhair,

I understand entirely. I, after all, write anonymously. We all have things we are not willing to risk. Should you change your mind, however, you know how to reach me.

L

She almost wept with relief. She didn't know what she'd expected. Cruelty? Retaliation? Blackmail? As ridiculous as it was, she couldn't help but leap to the worst possible conclusion. But now, she was free. As the weight lifted from her, she realized just how exhausted she was. She'd pushed herself too hard yesterday at the park, but she couldn't bring herself to regret it. When she'd finished her embroidery, she'd looked up to find Kit watching her with something like reverence.

Niamh dragged herself out of bed and went to her vanity. But when she caught a glimpse of her reflection, her next breath did not come. Her freckles stood painfully stark against her wan skin, and her eyes shone a brighter blue against the sleepless red ringing her irises. But that was not what troubled her.

With trembling fingers, she pulled on the lock of silver at her temple, shockingly pale against the black of her hair. Seemingly overnight, the white had encroached farther, like cold fingers of too-early frost. Still, she couldn't breathe. Another grain of sand in the hourglass of her life, gone, and she had wasted it playing lawn games. Running amok like a *child*. She couldn't be so careless with her time again.

From the moment her symptoms began, her own ghost had begun haunting her. It waited for her, inevitable, a figure at the end of a long, dark corridor. She'd been running for so long now, she dreaded what would happen if she stopped. She couldn't face all the things that would catch up to her.

No matter what she did, it would never be enough.

Niamh turned sharply away from her reflection. The close air of her room pressed down on her. If she remained confined here much longer, she'd waste half the day on fretting. There was no way to know for certain when she would die, and even if there were, it wasn't as though she could change anything by worrying.

All she could do was go day by day.

Niamh collected her charcoal and sketchbook and slipped through the door of her bedroom. Her wanderings carried her through the labyrinth of hallways, until she found the doors to the garden terrace. Color-coordinated flower beds formed stark, geometric patterns. A gravel-lined path cut in straight, harsh angles toward a hedge maze. Farther back, a perfectly symmetrical line of trees stood guard against the unruly woods beyond the property line. And at the center of it all, a statue rose from the burbling fountain like a nymph. It stared back at her with its unseeing marble eyes. Everything was measured, clipped, tamed—just as its owner was. Despite all the green, it struck her as lifeless.

"You."

Niamh gasped. "Your Highness."

Kit stood at the foot of the terrace stairs, one hand tight on the pale stone balustrade. His expression hit her somewhere tender. Beneath all that tightly wound aggression, she glimpsed a spark of uncertainty. By now, she'd begun to learn all the textures of his glares. This one, she thought, belonged to a man bracing for either cruelty or kindness.

"You're following me."

Indignation sparked within her. He was only trying to put her on the back foot, but two could play at that game. "Maybe I am."

She could tell she'd disarmed him. He drew himself up taller. "What? Why?"

"What nobleman rises before noon?" she asked. "I had to see if you were hiding some terrible secret."

The wariness dropped off his face, replaced instead with displeasure at being teased. "Oh? Like what?"

"Well . . . For example, perhaps you turn into a wolf under the morning sun. Or perhaps you had a body to hide."

He looked thoroughly unimpressed. "Is that really the sort of thing you worry about?"

"They're legitimate concerns!" Perhaps it was different in Avaland, but Machland was the kind of place where a man really might be a monster. "At any rate, *no*, I am not following you. I just so happen to be walking the same way as you, and that is not at all the same thing."

He frowned at her as though he hadn't been listening at all. "Are you sick?"

Her every tender sentiment vanished in an instant. *Must* he always say whatever came to mind in the bluntest way possible? She hadn't slept a full night since she'd arrived in Sootham a little over two weeks ago, but he didn't need to remind her of how haggard she looked. "I don't look *that* bad, do I?"

"No," Kit said hastily. "You look . . . Your hair is different."

Her hand flew to the streak of white. "How strange. I've done nothing different with it." After a moment, she asked, "Are you feeling better today?"

Roughly, he said, "I am. Thank you."

"Good." She hesitated. "And, ehm . . . I'm sorry about the other day in the library. I did not mean to—"

"It's fine. It isn't worth mentioning."

A few beats of silence passed between them. The breeze carried the smell of roses and ruffled the hem of his black jacket.

"I assume you came out here for a reason," he said. "Walk with me, or don't."

Don't, said her good sense—but too late. The words "Oh, very well" had already come tumbling out of her mouth.

If he kept seeking out her company, it wasn't as though she could deny him. Despite her better judgment, despite all the risks, she'd almost come to enjoy spending time with him. As much as he frazzled her, he had a way of making her forget her melancholy.

She trotted to keep pace with him as he led her through the gardens, her sketchbook clutched tightly to her breast. Her weary joints ached with protest, but she forged ahead. Kit was incapable of a casual stroll. Nothing surprised her less. Then again, she supposed she was, too. A smile tugged on the corner of her mouth. However, her fondness shifted into confusion as he steered them toward the woods. "Where are we going?"

"You'll see. I want to show you something."

Now that was ominous. "In the *woods*? With all due respect, sir, this seems like a very bad idea."

"Do what you want. I'm going this way whether you follow me or not."

To that, she had no further argument.

Soon enough, she saw a greenhouse emerging from behind the tree line. It looked like a ruin, coated all over with moss and choked with thick curtains of ivy. Its glass walls shone in the sun, as brilliant as the facets of a diamond. Kit said nothing as they approached. The only sound was the wind sighing softly against the shell of her ear, the tread of their footsteps in the knee-high grass.

He opened the door and let her inside. The first thing she noticed was the heat. It nearly smothered her. Condensation beaded on the walls, and her hair immediately separated into a cloud of frizz. But once she pushed past the discomfort of the air bearing down on her, she fully drank in her surroundings.

Beautiful.

The greenhouse burst with light and color, as whimsical and lush as an enchanted wood. Every shade of green bristled and tangled and bloomed before her. The air hung thick around them, redolent with earth, sweet nectar, and *life*. Emotion pulled taut in her chest. The wild splendor of it reminded her so much of Machland. Here was a place teeming with magic.

Kit sighed the moment the door clicked shut behind them, and she sensed a weight lifting from him. As he followed the flagstone path into the greenhouse, flowers opened toward him and shook loose their pollen, as though preening for his attention. She liked the way contentment looked on him. Niamh wasn't sure if he was even aware of how much he'd relaxed, and she wasn't about to wind him up again by telling him.

"This is spectacular," she said. "I didn't realize you liked gardening."

"I don't. It's tedious. But I did a lot of it while I was gone, and Jack wants me to keep myself busy."

"What kind of garden did you keep?"

With an edge of self-deprecation, he said, "I worked on an olive orchard on some island in Helles."

"Oh. Wow!" It made sense now, she supposed, that he hardly behaved like a prince if he'd lived for years among commoners. His manners—even his speech—were more unrefined than any other noble she'd met. He was like a purebred cat, turned loose and taught to survive in the wild. "That sounds difficult."

"It was," he replied. "Granted, I was drunk most of the time, until about a year ago. Makes things a little harder." He watched her, clearly waiting for her to recoil.

"Congratulations," she said, and she meant it. "A year is an incredible achievement."

"Don't patronize me." There wasn't much heat to it. If anything, he looked unsettled by her praise—maybe even bashful. "At any rate, this place is much easier to manage. It was my mother's greenhouse. She grew everything herself from seed, so my father always thought it an expensive waste of time. Any of us could have grown it three times over for her in a matter of hours. But she was stubborn that way."

So that was where he got it from. She smiled at the thought.

So many questions bubbled up—everything from *What was she like?* to *What is your favorite flower?*—but she didn't want to frighten him off. He hadn't mentioned either of his parents to her before. Yet his tone was matter-of-fact and dispassionate, as though he was discussing the weather rather than his dead mother and ill father. Niamh stroked the delicate petals of an orchid, just to keep herself from staring at him. "It must bring back memories to be here."

"I suppose." She'd never before encountered someone who so chafed against sympathy. "Someone has to keep the flowers alive, and I don't trust the gardeners to do it. This place was a wreck when I got home."

Niamh bent over a pot and pressed her nose to a flower, a starburst of indigo petals. It gave off the slightest peppery smell. "Do you need any help?"

"No. I don't want you tripping over anything." He gave her a strange look. "If you want something with an actual scent, you may enjoy the lilacs more. They're two rows down."

"Oh." She flushed, quickly straightening up to her full height. "Thank you."

He nodded stiffly, then went to retrieve a watering can from a hook beside the door. While he busied himself with the flowers, Niamh took the opportunity to wander. She ambled through the rows of flowers, her sketchbook tucked in the crook of her elbow and her fingers trailing over the most inviting blooms, until at last she found a place to install herself: atop a pile of burlap sacks, filled to bursting with soil. Comfortable enough, she decided. She was so tired, anything was better than standing.

She rested her chin on her fists and watched Kit. The greenhouse was enormous, and she was frankly astounded that he had the patience for such time-consuming work. But he settled into an easy rhythm, watering and pruning each of his plants with a practiced assurance. The sunlight trickling through the windows turned the air syrupy and warm. If she closed her eyes for even a moment, she'd doze off. *How quaint it would be,* she thought, *to spend every morning this way.*

Kit unbuttoned his jacket and abandoned it on the worn handle of a spade. Another *pop* of buttons, pearly in the light, and he began to roll his shirtsleeves to his elbows. Just below the bun at the nape of his neck, his skin glistened with a fine sheen of sweat. Humid air trailed its fingers slyly down her collar, and her mouth went entirely dry.

Suddenly, it was quite hot in here indeed.

Niamh forced her gaze back to her empty sketchbooks, her face burning furiously. Gods, how much time had she wasted sitting here moonily, just after she vowed to focus? And yet, in those few minutes she'd stolen from herself, she had felt . . . contentment.

She shoved the thought away and set to work sketching her ideas. By the time Kit's shadow fell over her, she'd finished no fewer than five designs for a potential wedding cloak.

"You're covered in dirt," he said.

"Huh?" She glanced down at her dress. Indeed, dirt streaked her skirts like careless daubs of paint. *How could this have . . . ?* When she turned over her hands, her palms, too, were covered in soil and pollen. It must've happened sometime between touching all of the flowers and seating herself on a veritable mountain of dirt. "Oh. Oh no."

Kit rested a hand on his hip. Something unusual glittered in his eyes. Not disdain or irritation . . . But *amusement.* Her temper flared mutinously. "How did you manage that just by sitting here? It's almost impressive."

"There's *tons* of dirt in here! It's not that difficult."

"There is," he conceded. "Most of it is in pots."

"Enough," she cried indignantly, "I get it already!"

He smirked. "It's as though—"

"Stop it, K—" She cut herself off.

His expression shuttered again, sharp and assessing. "Why won't you call me by my name?"

Because calling him by his given name was an intimacy reserved only for friends in Avaland. It would cross a line they could not uncross. Her heart leapt into her throat. "Because! You don't call me by mine, either. You don't call me anything but *you.* Do you even know my name?"

He seemed unperturbed by her outburst. "It's Niamh."

Her entire face warmed at the sound of her name on his lips. Not again. Maybe she could leach the heat out of her skin—or at the very least, keep him from seeing it. She clapped her hands to her face. It was then she realized she'd only succeeded in stamping two dirt handprints onto her cheeks.

"You've made it worse. Stop." He made a soft sound—half amusement, half protest—and procured a handkerchief from his breast pocket. "Here."

It was a shockingly gentlemanly gesture coming from him. She expected him to hand it brusquely to her, or maybe toss it in her general direction, but instead, he lowered himself onto one knee before her. She watched him from outside herself as he reached forward to dab at the streak of dirt on her cheekbone.

She stopped breathing.

His skin scalded, even through the thin scrap of fabric between them. The glass walls glinted in the corner of her vision, until all the world seemed to sparkle around them with magic. All she could see were his brows furrowed in concentration and the sooty fringe of his eyelashes. All she could see was *him*. He was far, far closer than he should've been. She could feel his breath like a caress against her lips.

"There," he said. And then, as if realizing what exactly he'd done, he drew back as though burned. He shoved the crumpled mess of his handkerchief abruptly back into his pocket.

"Thank you." The words escaped her in a wheeze. She slipped off her gloves to prevent any more horrible accidents. When at last she felt she'd recovered herself, she said, "Do you *really* want me to call you by your given name? We're not friends."

He stared at her blankly.

"Are we?" Her voice climbed alarmingly high.

"I don't know. I don't have any friends."

"That's not true. What about Sinclair?"

"Him?" Kit curled his lip. "Sinclair is a self-destructive, self-deprecating good-for-nothing. He's more of a ward than a friend. Someone has to keep him out of trouble."

Just as someone had to take care of the flowers. Just as someone had to keep her from making more of a mess. She tilted her chin up at him. He'd painted Sinclair with such contempt, but she'd seen the way he reacted when he believed he'd wounded him. Sinclair himself had told her that Kit paid for his house *and* gave him an allowance.

Now, she was beginning to see him clearly. All his fretful affection was coated with acid, as if he could conceal what it really was.

"You cannot fool me anymore," she said accusingly. "You don't want anyone to see it, or maybe you refuse to believe it yourself, but you do care about people. You *are* kind."

"You don't know the first thing about me." Every flower in the hothouse shivered with the vehemence of his denial. He bristled all over: thorns around a delicate bloom.

It sent a thrill of heady delight through her, and she masked a giggle behind her hand. "You're right. Of course."

"Stop smiling like that," Kit said peevishly.

"Sorry." She bit her lip to keep herself from grinning. "For what little it's worth, I think Sinclair is a good man."

"Hardly. But he can be intelligent on the rare occasion he chooses to be." He hesitated. "And we understand each other."

"How so?"

"There are things that aren't spoken about in polite society," he said slowly. "He and I never had to pretend with each other, or to be anything we aren't."

I don't have the best reputation, Sinclair told her, *and Jack doesn't want it to touch Kit more than it already has.*

Niamh sat up straighter with the sudden realization. She did not want to presume, but the pieces fit together, and she understood the confession he was dancing around well enough. "Were you together?"

Kit looked surprised. "You already knew."

"He told me, yes—about himself, not you." She tried and failed to rein in her curiosity. "So, were you?"

"No," he said guardedly. After a moment, his expression softened some with wryness. "We would've killed each other. He was even worse when he was fifteen. So was I."

Niamh smiled. "I suppose you've more options than your friends here in the city. There were only four other girls who fancied girls in Caterlow that I knew of. It could get quite complicated."

"You're like me, then."

Like me. Being claimed so casually filled her with a warm sense of belonging.

She glanced down at her sketchbook, unable to bear the intimacy of holding his gaze any longer. "Ehm . . . Kit?"

He reacted bodily to the sound of his name. From the corner of her eye, she saw him lean toward her. It was undeniably wrong for someone of her station to address a member of the royal family by his first name, but she supposed they'd abandoned propriety long ago. She tucked a strand of hair behind her ear, finding herself suddenly shy.

"Do you want to see the sketches?"

"All right."

He took the sketchbook from her. Slowly, he paged through, his expression entirely unreadable. Anxiety knotted itself tight in her stomach. All this time, she'd wanted to prove him wrong about her and her craft. But right now, it went beyond that petty squabble, her tender wounded pride. She wanted to make him happy.

When he handed it back to her, he said, "They're . . . nice."

Niamh promptly choked on her own saliva. "What did you say?"

"I'm not going to repeat myself," he said sourly. "I know you heard me." Self-consciousness flickered across his expression, there and gone in an instant. "Do whatever you want with the design. I trust you."

It might have been the most generous thing any client had ever given her. Total trust. Her heart swelled with excitement. "Really?"

"Yes, really."

She sprang to her feet. "Are you absolutely sure?"

He took a step back. "Yes. I am absolutely sure."

"Because if you *really* let me have full rein—"

"I said I'm sure. Don't make me change my mind."

"No taking it back now," she singsonged.

He threw up his hands. "Enough. You win."

With that, he retreated to the far corner of the greenhouse, watering a plant she was sure he'd watered at least once already. She didn't know what else to do with herself. She flopped back onto the makeshift chaise of burlap and grinned up at the ceiling, flushed and dirt-streaked and giddy with triumph. She'd extracted his approval at last. And, it seemed, his friendship.

Was that really what this was?

Kit. She held the shape of his name in her mouth, her tongue pressed softly to the back of her teeth. Her skin still tingled with the memory of his touch, of the way he'd looked at her with such tender focus. There had been nothing but the thinnest layer of silk between their bare skin. He hadn't even been wearing *gloves*. Heat pooled within her. Her fingertips brushed her lower lip and pulled softly as she imagined . . .

She shot bolt upright. *Oh, no.* She had not just crossed a line today. She'd leapt clear over it and left it miles behind her. A girl like her wanting Kit Carmine would not—could not—end well.

13

When Niamh opened the door to her studio, two figures were lurking by the open window. She almost screamed but clapped her hands over her mouth before any sound could escape.

"Ah," Sinclair said. "That's what you meant by jumpy."

As she blinked the spots out of her vision, he and Kit came hazily into view, both of them dressed for riding: Sinclair, in a blue velvet waistcoat and matching top hat, his neckcloth tied in a ribbon; Kit in an olive-green overcoat and a black hat, tapping a riding crop impatiently against the leather of his boots. Sunlight fell over him like a sheet of water, drawing out the shades of red in his dark hair. Niamh nearly groaned aloud.

It had been two days since she'd seen him in the greenhouse, and time had not whittled the edge off her wanting. Up until now, she'd thought it would be easy. It *should* have been easy. After all, she'd thought him handsome the moment she first saw him. His wretched personality had disabused her of any serious attraction for a time. Only now, she understood that every last one of his emotions manifested as either hostility and sarcasm—and more damning still, she'd seen how hopelessly awkward and fussy he was beneath that one shoddy defense. She was fond of Kit Carmine, unsociable as he was, and it was becoming a problem.

Niamh slammed the door shut behind her. "What are you doing in here?"

"Waiting for you," Kit replied. The warm, familiar rasp of his voice made her feel prickly all over with heat.

"Have I missed some appointment?"

"Have you forgotten already?" Sinclair removed his hat and clasped it in front of him. "I am here to call on you."

Oh. Gods, that was *today*? She'd lost track of time again. "Oh, Sinclair, I am so sorry!"

"It's quite all right," he replied. "If you are still amenable, you should accompany me on a ride. Kit will chaperone, of course. He is hardly respectable enough for the job, but desperate times, as they say. I simply could not wait another moment to see you."

"As your chaperone," Kit said dryly, "I object to that kind of talk in my presence."

"It's all right, Kit." Sinclair smirked. "You can admit it's working."

Kit rolled his eyes. "You're insufferable."

It relieved her to see that whatever tension she'd sensed between them in the park had dissipated. Sinclair's offer was tempting, but she'd far too many things to do. Yesterday, she'd pored over her sketches with Rosa, who had a far more exacting vision than Niamh anticipated. The amount of lace she and her assistants would have to make was . . . staggering, to say the very least.

"I can see the cogs spinning in your mind," Sinclair said. "Do not fret. We shall have you home before your embroidery even knows to miss you."

"Very well," she relented. "But you should know that I am not a very accomplished rider."

Kit muttered something under his breath that sounded suspiciously like *shocking*. Niamh decided to ignore it—just this once. Few people in Caterlow could afford to own horses, save for her friend, Erin. As girls, they would take a pair of mares out at dawn and ride along the coast. It'd been many years, but she supposed it wasn't the sort of thing one easily forgot.

"You will do wonderfully, I'm sure," Sinclair said.

"I will join you shortly, then. Just give me a moment to change."

"I'd suggest something dark," said Kit. "Dirt will show less."

Her ears burned as she took in his stupid, self-satisfied smirk. He was clearly referencing her little mishap in the greenhouse. She'd say he was mocking her, but . . . No, she could not dwell on the alternative. With feigned innocence, she said, "Of course, I shall accommodate your preference, Your Highness."

"It's not—" he blustered, then cut himself off with a defeated sigh. "We'll be at the stables. Come on, Sinclair."

Sinclair raised his eyebrows but followed after Kit without comment.

Niamh lingered by the bay window. The nettle still garlanded the eaves and waved gently in the breeze. Kit must've cleared some of it away, for she now could enjoy an unimpeded view of the lawn outside. She watched the two of them trek toward the stables. They spoke animatedly—although Kit, frankly, seemed to be yelling—but the conversation ended abruptly when Kit shoved Sinclair into a thicket of gorse growing at the border of a garden bed.

She winced. He'd be pulling thorns out of that lovely coat for weeks.

Even from here, she could hear Sinclair howling with laughter and see Kit's face burning a bright, livid red.

Avlish ladies, Niamh learned, did not ride astride. It would take Sinclair, Kit, and a prayer to hoist her into the sidesaddle.

Her horse's name, the groom told her, was Ferdinand, a palfrey who boasted the dubious honor of being the most reliable, gentle gelding in the stables. He snorted good-naturedly when Niamh lifted a hand and patted him on the nose. Her powder-blue gloves contrasted charmingly against his chestnut coat.

"He hasn't had a single thought in all his life," Sinclair assured her, holding Ferdinand still by the bridle.

Kit lowered himself onto one knee and knitted his fingers together. With all his usual charm and grace, he said, "Get on."

It took her a few moments to process that he wanted her to use his hands as a step. "Are you sure, Your Highness? I don't want to hurt you."

He sighed so exasperatedly, the loose strands of his hair fluttered. She wasn't certain if her reversion to formality or her hesitation vexed him more. "You're not going to hurt me. A strong wind could carry you away."

The same could be said for you. Very nobly, she refrained from saying that aloud. However, she found it strangely difficult to argue with him when he was on his knees before her. With a fretful groan, she grasped the saddle with one hand and placed the other on his shoulder. Kit was surprisingly solid beneath her palm—and surprisingly warm, even with the leather of her riding gloves between them. She had the dim awareness that she'd frozen where she stood, if only because of the impatient stare he leveled at her like a rifle. Very reluctantly, she stepped into the foothold of his hands.

"All right," he grunted. "Up you go."

With that, he boosted her. Niamh yelped as her other foot left the floor. Ferdinand swiveled his massive head to watch her with placid confusion. As soon as she was perched on the very edge of the saddle, Kit steadied her by the waist. Warmth unfurled through her at his touch. She hurried to hook her knee in the horns of the saddle's pommel. Her skirt slid up her calf, revealing a flash of bare skin. Kit's eyes flickered down, just for a moment, before he turned abruptly away from her.

"Good?" he asked.

"Now I am," she choked out, adjusting the fall of the fabric. "Thank you for your assistance."

He ducked to retrieve a riding crop from where it leaned on the side of the stall. Above the collar of his overcoat, his neck flushed a lovely shade of pink.

"Well done, Niamh." Sinclair patted the palfrey's neck affectionately. "You look like a natural."

Kit pressed the riding crop into her hands but did not let go. His displeasure made itself plain on his face. "Don't be reckless. And keep your wits about you for once in your life. If you fall, there's no easy way out of the saddle. You'll flip underneath your mount and be dashed under its hooves."

A shudder tore through her at the image, but she couldn't fight back the petulant impulse to quarrel with him. "I will be fine. I *have* made it eighteen years without your fretting, you know."

"Fretting?" he repeated indignantly. At last, he relinquished his hold on the crop. "I'm not fretting. Just don't make yourself a nuisance."

Sinclair gave him a flat, unimpressed stare. "Shall we?"

No more than five minutes into their ride, Niamh realized that Kit might have been right to caution her. Although Ferdinand's ambling gait made it easier to balance, she still felt precarious, twisted in her seat as she was. The pleasant sensation of the wind slipping beneath her bonnet, at least, almost outweighed the nausea.

It was cool today, with thick skeins of fog drifting across the fields. Her spencer jacket, embroidered with roses in golden thread, kept out most of the morning chill. But the air still nipped at her nose and cheeks, stinging them pink. By the time they arrived at the white gates of Eye Park, Niamh sensed something amiss. Through the fog, she could see nothing. But the dull roar of manifold voices reached her through the gloom. A phantom army called to arms. Kit and Sinclair exchanged a grim look.

"We should turn back," Kit said.

"Don't be so dull," Sinclair countered. "Let's see what the fuss is about."

He did not wait for a reply before taking off through the gates. Kit huffed out an impatient sigh. But his stallion was clearly eager to run, prancing beneath his rider. Kit hardly needed to ask before he raced after Sinclair, far faster than the polite, sedate trot Niamh had been advised they must maintain on the park trails. The fog swallowed them like a coin dropped into a dark well.

"All right, Ferdinand." Niamh leaned over her palfrey's neck, and his ear flicked attentively toward her. "We can keep up, right?"

The three of them rode toward the source of the uproar. They didn't have to go far before Niamh saw them: thousands of people, gathered in the heart of Eye Park. It quickened her pulse with something like excitement—and maybe a little like fear. Never before had she seen so many people in one place. In the distance, even more of them poured off the hillside: a veritable parade marching in from all corners of the city. Some of them busied themselves pitching tents. By the looks of it, they intended to stay for a while, installed in the heart of high society's social life.

Sinclair pulled his horse up alongside another gentleman, who had stopped with a small group to watch the proceedings. "Excuse me, sir. What's all this?"

"Helen Carlile," he replied. "That woman has some gall to

establish her encampment here. She and Lovelace clearly mean to incite the Machlish into another rebellion! Look at them, gathered like an army."

Machlish? So these were all the servants who'd walked away from their jobs in grand houses. When Niamh looked out over the gathered masses, her heart squeezed with homesickness. All of them dressed like they did in Caterlow, their clothes homespun and dirtied from travel. Their skin, toughened and browned from work, made them look as though they'd grown from the earth itself. None of them carried weapons.

The gentleman's eyes found Kit, and his face broke open with astonishment. "Your Highness. My sincerest apologies. I did not see you there. If I may be so bold to say, sir, it's a comfort to know you are here. I hope you can talk some sense into Carlile. If not, I suppose that's what the Kings Guard is for. This kind of impertinence is not to be borne."

Before Kit could reply, the man tipped his hat and rode away.

Kit tightened his grip on the reins. His stallion pawed at the upturned grass. "If I call the Kings Guard, we'll have bloodshed on our hands."

Niamh's heart leapt into her throat. He couldn't. Gathering in a public space surely couldn't be a crime.

Sinclair frowned. "I'll give Carlile some credit. She has balls."

"She's a fool," Kit said darkly, "if she thinks this can end well."

"She's desperate. You know as well as I do what it's like to get Jack to listen. He's as stubborn as you are. The question is, are you as avoidant?"

It had the air of an old argument. Kit's mouth twitched like he wanted to reply, but he bit his tongue.

"The nobility is only going to get more antsy the longer this goes on," Sinclair continued. "Someone has to do something before it turns ugly."

They stood on the hill, gazing down at the growing crowd. They pressed in around a makeshift stage, made of stacked timber and shipping crates. A trio, too hazy in the mist for Niamh to make out clearly, had climbed atop it. The organizers, she surmised. Flags whipped and snapped in the breeze. UNITY, one declared in plain black thread. STRENGTH. The others bore the insignia of the revolution, the same one that had been chalked on Jack's dance floor: the sun with its searing rays. The energy crackling among the masses was unmistakable. Anger—and stronger yet, hope.

Niamh looked up at Kit. "What will you do?"

"There's nothing I can do."

"How can you say such a thing?" As best she could, Niamh maneuvered Ferdinand around so she faced him head-on. "You are a *prince*."

"A lot of good that title has done me." He met her eyes at last. "What will you have me do? I'm the second son. I've no allies or respect in court. Jack created this problem, and he clearly intends to handle it as he sees fit. I don't owe him anything."

"Maybe not." She couldn't abide his cynicism today. Perhaps it was the energy of the crowd, or being among her people again after so long, but she couldn't allow him to withdraw or turn away from this. She jabbed a finger out at the crowd. "But doesn't someone owe *them* something?"

Thirty-five years ago, hundreds of thousands of her countrymen had perished because of Kit's father. So much death, all at the hands of a man who had the power to do something and refused. She'd grown up alongside all those ghosts. And while she'd denied Lovelace's request for aid, she'd found another opportunity to fight for her people in Kit Carmine himself. Whatever strange twist of fate had granted her a prince's attention, she must try to make him see. He carried a legacy of violence, yes, but blood was blood. It was not a fairy-tale curse, guaranteed to repeat itself over and over again.

If he chose to, Kit could be different.

"I know you hate the nobility," Niamh pressed. "But so do they. Right now, precisely because you have been gone, you have far more power than you know. Even if my people despise your brother and your peers, they do not know *you*. You were still a child when you left. Now, you have a chance to show them what you have become."

Kit looked stricken. "And if I don't like what I've become?"

"Your life is yours. It is never too late to change."

He hissed out a long breath through his teeth. She could see the flash of irritation—no, of *fear*—in his eyes. "Damn you."

Then, without warning, he urged his stallion onward, directly toward the crowd.

"What did you just do?" Sinclair asked admiringly. "I have never seen him listen to someone like that."

Niamh could not take her eyes from Kit. "I . . . I actually do not know."

He pinched the bridge of his nose. "You *are* trouble. Come on."

The two of them pursued Kit down the hill, Niamh clinging to Ferdinand's mane for dear life. They caught up to him just as he slowed at the edges of the crowd. Here in the thick of it, she could hardly hear herself think over the swell of thousands of voices. Nearly all of them were speaking Machlish, and her chest ached at the familiar, comforting sound of it.

"Where is Helen Carlile?" Kit's voice cut through some of the chatter.

An prionsa. His title rippled through the crowd.

Row by row, heads turned toward him. Most regarded him with cold, hard mistrust. Others burned with curiosity, still others with tentative sparks of hope. Kit's shoulders tightened with discomfort under the attention. As the murmurs spread, the crowd began to shuffle around them, parting until a path cut straight through to the front. The woman standing on the makeshift stage craned her neck to look at them, and Niamh saw the moment realization made her stand ramrod straight. Without hesitation, she stepped down from the stage and walked toward them with brisk purpose.

This, Niamh thought, *must be Helen Carlile.*

As a commoner, she likely did not possess divine blood, but she clearly had mastered a more mundane kind of magic. She moved through the crowd as capably as Rosa wielded lightning, as easily as Kit made the earth bloom. Her supporters watched her with open adoration. Here and there, she stopped to greet people. She shook their hands and clapped them warmly on the shoulder, like each of them was an old friend.

At last, Carlile came to attend their group. She looked more ordinary than Niamh had expected. Her age-lined face was earnest and open, and her hair, a mousy brown, was swept back carelessly. She dressed well, however, in a gentleman's coat, and clutched a walking stick like a club in her hands.

"Well, isn't this a surprise," she said, and just like that, she came alive. She had a voice that commanded attention, an urgency in her steely gray gaze that was terrifyingly magnetic. "You must be Prince Christopher."

There really could be no mistaking him for what he was in this moment. He sat imperiously astride his glorious horse, his black-gloved hands tight on the reins, his chin lifted to glare down the slope of his nose at her. He was the very picture of aristocratic grace, imposing and inaccessible. After a pause, he swung his leg over the saddle and landed silently in the grass.

"Yeah," he said curtly. "That's me."

Delight stole over her face at his brusqueness. "It's an honor to meet you, Your Royal Highness." Her gaze landed on Niamh. In accented Machlish, she said, "And you must be Niamh Ó Conchobhair."

"A pleasure," Niamh replied, as charmed as she was surprised. If Carlile knew who she was—and if she'd devoted herself completely to the Machlish cause—could *she* be Lovelace?

"And I'm Gabriel Sinclair," Sinclair chimed in. "Lovely to make your acquaintance."

"Oh, I know who you are, Mr. Sinclair," she replied in Avlish. Sinclair's expression turned steely. "I must extend my sincerest apologies to you all. Have we interrupted your ride?"

"That's enough small talk," Kit said. "What do you want, Carlile?"

At that, she laughed. "I want to speak to your brother."

"So I've heard." He surveyed the crowd over her shoulder. "And is this how you plan to do it? Some might call this sedition."

"I assure you, sir, on my life, that is not my intention." She gestured out at the neat contingents of protesters. They'd packed in densely, but no panic, no hot-blooded fervor, riled them. "These are good, hardworking people, who only want to be heard. I came here to speak to the Crown on their behalf. All they want is fair treatment in this country—and acknowledgment of the Crown's role in the Blight, the very thing that has driven them here."

"You're talking to the wrong prince," Kit replied gruffly, but not without feeling.

"No, I don't think I am." Her gaze swept meaningfully over his shoulder, and Niamh felt the intensity of it pass over her face. "If you would, sir, you can pass along a message for me. Tell the prince regent that I will be waiting, right here, until he decides he wishes to talk."

The moment Kit and Niamh returned to the palace, Jack accosted them.

His hair, normally fastidiously done, was in jagged disarray, as though he'd been running his hands through it in a fit of pique. Sofia trailed after him like a pale shadow, her hand pressed anxiously to her lips. Niamh thought of her the other night on her balcony, standing at the railing like a ghost. She looked as insubstantial now as she had that night, vanishing into the heat of Jack's anger.

Jack's gaze bounced back and forth between Kit and Niamh. But whatever frustration or suspicion he harbored lost out against his concern. "Where have you been?"

"Meeting with Helen Carlile."

Jack paused, clearly stunned. "You jest."

"I never *jest*," Kit said contemptuously. "There's a mob waiting for you in Eye Park. I assume you're aware."

"Perhaps we should retire to the drawing room to discuss this," Sofia said placatingly. "I could send for some—"

Jack held up a hand. "Not now, Sofia."

Sofia's gaze dropped to the floor. Niamh felt a twinge of hurt on her behalf. To be so dismissed—by your own husband, no less . . . It seemed a cruel fate indeed. She wished she could offer her an encouraging smile, but Sofia kept her head resolutely bowed, a few wisps of white-blond hair obscuring her features from view.

"That woman," Jack continued, "has sent me ten letters a day at this rate. She has come to petition me again, I expect, but it is a waste of her time and mine. There is nothing I can do for those people."

The disdain in his voice drew Niamh up short. Even if his magic was nowhere near as potent as his ancestors', he was the Prince Regent of Avaland. How could he insist that there was nothing to be done? If he wished, he could release a statement today accepting responsibility for his father's role in creating the Machlish Blight. He could agree to reparations, or work to make his staff happier, or . . . Niamh knew it was foolish to feel betrayed, but she'd trusted him to do the right thing.

"I've been asked to tell you that she will not leave until you agree to an audience. Is that really your answer, Jack? You intend to hide yourself away forever?"

"Your idealism is dangerous." Jack's voice was strained, verging on desperate. "I beg of you, Christopher. If you will listen to one thing I say, let it be this. Do not meet with her again. This is a delicate situation, one I swear to you that I am handling. Trust me to manage this, as I have managed all things for you."

Niamh heard the plea plainly in his voice: *Let me protect you.*

He's avoiding all of his problems, Kit had told her once. *There has to be some reason.*

The flash of vulnerability stunned her. It must've knocked Kit off his guard, too, for it slapped some of the hostility clean off his face. When he spoke again, he adopted the same put-upon tone he reserved for both her and Sinclair. "How can I trust you when you won't trust me? I don't argue with you for my health, you know. One of these days, you're going to crumple from lugging all this weight around alone."

The brothers watched each other from across the atrium, the weight of a thousand small wounds pressing down on them.

"Don't worry yourself on my behalf." Jack's voice was still unguarded, but Niamh could see his trick at work again: folding all of his emotions up neatly and filing them back away where they belonged. Then, as if something just dawned upon him, he said, "I have an idea. We shall host our next ball at Woodville Hall in four days' time."

A heavy silence fell over the room.

"You can't be serious," Kit said. "I am not going back there."

"We haven't returned since Mother's death. It is about time we reopen it. Besides, it requires fewer servants to maintain. We will leave the Machlish servants behind." Jack turned to Niamh. "Except for you, of course, Miss O'Connor. You will join us."

The cruel voices of those noblewomen echoed fresh in her mind. *He's trotted out his new tailor at every event like some sort of show pony.*

"It'd be my honor," she murmured.

Sofia flinched. "I think—"

"So you intend to run if you cannot hide," said Kit. "Is that it?"

When Jack did not reply, Kit scoffed, "unbelievable," and stormed out of the room.

Sofia rounded on Jack, emanating palpable disapproval. "I do not think that was wise."

"Yes, I see that now. Do you have any other counsel for me?" Jack asked wearily. "Or you, Miss O'Connor? Would you care to chime in as well?"

Before Niamh could stutter out a reply, Sofia's bearing turned arctic. The temperature in the room dropped—quite literally. Niamh's breath misted in the air before her, and gooseflesh broke out on her arms. Even Jack paled at the sudden display of power.

"Do not mock her. You know very well she cannot defend herself against you," said Sofia quietly. "And I have thoughts, yes, if you will hear them."

"That was beneath me," he conceded, shamefaced. "My sincerest apologies, Miss O'Connor."

"It's no trouble," Niamh murmured. "If you'll excuse me, Your Highnesses."

As she walked away, she heard the dull murmur of Sofia's voice. ". . . both of you come to terms with . . ."

In the safety of her studio, Niamh curled up on a chair and shivered with residual cold. Something about it made her feel small and pathetic, and just for a moment, she indulged the thought that had plagued her since she laid eyes on that crowd.

She wanted to go home.

But no comfort or hope awaited her there. No matter how bleak it got, surviving in a country that disdained them was better than starving to death with pride. She had to stay here.

One of these days, Jack would surely relent. All she could think of were the cracks spreading across Jack's cool facade. She recognized that look of exhaustion well.

One of these days, you're going to crumple from lugging all this weight around alone.

With every day that passed, Niamh saw yet another burden piled on Jack's shoulders. A brother who challenged him. A loveless marriage. Discontented servants. A legacy heavy enough to crush him. No man, however stalwart, could endure forever. As much as she hated him for his inaction, she still dreaded to imagine what would rain down on them the moment Jack Carmine faltered.

14

The farther they ventured from the city, the more at home Niamh felt.

Within an hour's drive, the stolid gray of Sootham gave way to wide, sprawling green. The hills rippled like the sea outside the carriage window, and sunlight spilled like divine blood into the rivers, shining and gold. Over the clatter of wheels and the rhythmic plod of hooves, Niamh could hear the singing of birds, the soft, croaking nest-cry of magpies and the shrill, metallic whine of the goldfinches. If she ignored the finery all around her, she could almost believe she was back in Machland. It was, however, incredibly difficult to ignore. She'd been nestled into a pile of crushed-velvet cushions and presented with a plate of almond cakes. Although she'd polished off at least five of them, it did strike Niamh as rather excessive. It *was* only her in the carriage.

Well, her and her twenty-odd bobbins.

Rosa's gown had shaped up to be far more work than she bargained for. Lacemaking was not exactly Niamh's forte, given it required the patience of a Castilian saint and a truly alarming number of sharp objects to keep track of. A lacemaker's pillow rested in her lap, and hundreds of pearl-tipped pins skewered the pattern Niamh had sketched. It looked more like a naturalist's dissection table than the beginnings of an overlay. Delicate strands of black thread were wound around each pin, and if she squinted it almost began to resemble a trellis of roses. Rosa had requested delicate, floral lace in the Castilian style to adorn the bodice of her gown. Niamh knew what "Castilian style" was only because she'd spent all night reading a history of Castilian lace. It was not sweet and subtle in the way the Avlish liked it—but extravagant and bold in a way Rosa herself was not. When Niamh finished, it would be exquisite: the finest, most intricate work she had ever done.

It would be worthy of royalty.

Sighing, Niamh twined the threads around each pin, gathering her magic like unspun wool between her fingers. The nauseating churn of the carriage made the work twice as hard as it needed to be, and her eyes drooped and ached from exhaustion. Perhaps she'd pick it up later tonight. She tore her eyes from the pattern, just in time for the carriage to crest a hill.

Woodville Hall lay cradled in the valley beneath her. Her breath caught at the sight of it. It was nothing at all like the royal palace. Where the palace armored itself in its harsh, imposing austerity, Woodville Hall brimmed with warmth and life. Vines of climbing jasmine and purple wisteria climbed its brick face and danced slowly, pirouetting in the breeze. Niamh breathed in the sweet, heady smell of flowers. A line of carriages just as beautiful as her own spilled their contents onto the house's front steps. From here, the guests were nothing but daubs of color in their watered silks. The property looked like a study in oil paints, vibrant and dreamy in the afternoon light.

When her carriage at last made it to the front of the line, a footman in crimson livery opened the door and helped her down. "Welcome, miss. The prince regent is eager to receive you."

"Is he?" How kind. Or perhaps the footman must say that to all of the guests. She cleared her throat. "I mean—of course. Thank you."

On unsteady legs, she ascended the staircase and passed through the front door. Honeyed light fell through the front windows, making golden mosaics on the worn floorboards. Jack and Sofia waited for her in the foyer, standing side by side with matching frayed expressions. Even Sofia, ethereal in her silver gown, seemed preoccupied. Clearly, the country air was not doing either of them much good.

Sofia clasped her hands in greeting. "Welcome, Miss O'Connor. We are so happy to have you."

"Thank you for your hospitality," Niamh said, trying to blink the stars out of her eyes. "You have truly spared no expense, Your Highness. It is spectacular."

Jack stood up straighter, and Sofia's worried frown deepened. But before her husband could reply, she said, "Thank you. Shall we send tea service to your room?"

"That is kind of you, but I could use some exercise after the long drive. Do you mind if I explore the house?"

"Not at all," Sofia said, her tone brightening. "In fact, I would encourage you to. It is quite a remarkable house. It had to be, I suppose, to contain Jack for eighteen years."

Jack looked only a little put out by her teasing. "Do enjoy yourself. Welcome."

And so, Niamh wandered. As she climbed the grand staircase, sweat began to bead on the back of her neck. Woodville Hall was indeed strange and lovely. It lay bare from many years of neglect, but she felt it stirring awake around her. Warm air sighed through the open windows, thick and gauzy. Nearly all of the doors rattled, locked, when she tried them, and she encountered almost no one in the halls. They were most likely—and wisely—dozing after their journeys in the syrupy afternoon heat.

The hallways wended like a trail through a shaded wood, beckoning her deeper. They branched off into new rooms, or ended suddenly in charming and mysterious corners. She happened upon a staircase that led to nothing but a wall with a faded mural, glittering faintly with some dormant enchantment. She found a hidden balcony overlooking a ballroom, the beads of a chandelier concealing it from watchful eyes, as well as an alcove tucked away beneath a curve in the staircase. Inside, a window, caked with dust and frosted with the shapes of leaves, let in a wash of sunlight. Someone had crudely carved the letters *KC* into the wooden sill.

It was all so . . . whimsical. She couldn't imagine the Carmine brothers ever living here, much less playing here. She very much doubted Jack had ever been a child at all.

Niamh roamed into an enfilade. On each side of the hall, portraits of Carmines from generations past glared out at her with their eerie green eyes. Likely upset that a lowly Machlish girl, the stubborn remnants of a people they'd failed to stamp out, had set foot in their ancestral home. At the very end, she stopped before a portrait as tall as she was.

This, she thought, *must be the royal family.* What had been the royal family, anyway.

In the center was a man she now recognized as Kit and Jack's father, King Albert III. Beside him stood the late queen, with dark brown hair and those wolfish amber eyes Niamh knew so well. Behind her soft, mysterious smile, she looked terribly unhappy. A boy no older than ten sat between them, cradling a newborn. A fissure ran through the canvas like an old scar, just barely visible beneath the glossy oil paints. She leaned closer to inspect it—only to nearly topple into it when footsteps echoed down the corridor.

Niamh gasped. If anyone found her snooping... *Was* she snooping? No matter. She couldn't chance it. But there was nowhere to hide here—nowhere except for behind the curtains, billowing in the breeze sneaking in through the open window. She dove behind them and drew them tight around her. The *clack* of heels slowed, but the sound lingered in the empty chamber.

"Huh," Sinclair said. "It seems your curtains have grown feet since I was last here."

"Are you hiding?" Kit asked incredulously.

Niamh glanced down. The curtains fell to her ankles like the hem of a fashionable gown. She flung them open. "No, of course not! I was ... ah, taking in the scenery."

That maddening, taunting glint returned to Kit's eye. "Anything of interest?"

She turned toward the window, which opened onto a view of a wall of ivy and a few slivers of the sky beyond it. It clung to the glass, blotting all but the most stubborn bars of light. "Yes, indeed! Anyway. What brings the two of you here?"

Before Kit could fire off something else, Sinclair interjected. "Dinner will be served soon. Kit thought we ought to make sure you found your way to the dining room safely, since these halls have a way of rearranging themselves." He smirked. "Very considerate of him. And strange, given he's never once gone out of his way to be helpful on purpose."

Kit rounded on him. "What is that supposed to mean?"

"Oh, nothing." His gaze slid coyly to Niamh. "Nothing at all."

"Then stop talking for once in your life."

Sinclair obliged, but he looked far too pleased with himself.

Niamh, however, could hardly bear the silence. Grasping for the first topic that came to mind, she gestured at the portrait. "It is a striking resemblance."

Kit frowned up at it. "Between me and the old man?"

She did not think *yes* was exactly the right way to reply to such blatant disrespect for the King of Avaland, but Niamh nodded. "Except for the eyes, you and your brother both are the very image of your father."

Sinclair winced. The air grew as heavy as the moment before lightning's first strike. Niamh had the distinct impression she'd said the wrong thing.

"Some people say so." Kit's flat tone made it apparent what he thought of their assessment. He crossed his arms. "He was a mean son of a bitch."

Sinclair laughed breathlessly, clearly relieved. "That's putting it lightly."

"I'm so sorry." Niamh studied Kit's expression, but it betrayed nothing. "I didn't mean to bring up painful memories."

"It's fine," he said dismissively. "He's gone now."

"Gone?"

"In all but body," he clarified. "Banished to one of his castles to live out the rest of his miserable existence. I've thought about visiting him. I hear they keep him quite docile these days."

"I imagine it would be strange," Niamh offered. "He sounds like he was a formidable man."

"You could say that." Kit did not look away from the painting. His voice was matter-of-fact, but his shoulders coiled with tension. "He was always heavy-handed with discipline. He valued duty, honor, and reputation above all else. Couldn't abide any sign of weakness."

He said *heavy-handed* with such weight, she couldn't mistake his meaning. It was far from unusual to receive a caning for disobedience or cheekiness, but Niamh never displeased Ma or Gran if she could help it. Kit and his stubborn streak, however . . .

Do you know, Miss O'Connor, Sinclair had told her, *that Kit here was a very sensitive child?* She couldn't believe it at all. Now, she supposed it made an awful sort of sense why he'd changed.

"Even after he fell ill?" she asked quietly.

"Especially then. Sometimes, he was bedridden from pain, and those were good days. But by the time I was ten, he had fewer good days than bad. Extravagantly happy as long as it pleased him, and when it didn't, he'd speak for hours at a time, spewing all sorts of vile nonsense. Jack took the brunt of it for my sake, although he'd never admit it." Kit looked pensive. "It changed him for the worse. But I suppose when you're dealing with a monster like that every day, you can't help what you become to survive it."

Hearing that sentiment put so plainly made Niamh feel oddly off-kilter. Her chest tightened with horrible recognition. Gran and Ma had never asked for her devotion, and yet she had given it to them without thinking. What else could she have done? For years, she'd watched them ration their meals, even when their garden produced a good yield. She'd learned to be helpful, to shape herself around the edges of their dark moods in the harvest season. She'd endured every prick of the needle and every sharp word of criticism while Gran taught her to perfect the family's craft, a magic the Avlish had nearly eradicated. Sometimes, it felt as though she'd threaded all her family's wounds onto a string and hung them around her own neck.

But she could not complain, nor could she compare herself to Kit. Besides, it was a comfortable weight by now. If she did not carry it, then who would?

"It occurs to me," Sinclair said, "that Kit and I have offloaded our troubles onto you. And yet, you remain a mystery."

Niamh startled. "Me? Oh, I assure you, my life is terribly boring. I've spent half of it sewing."

In truth, it hardly occurred to her that she'd shared little of herself with them. As much as possible, she avoided too much self-reflection. It always led her to dangerous places, like the one she'd toed the edge of only seconds ago, and she'd been hurtling forward for so long, she couldn't stop now. She'd fall so hard, she'd never rise again. She could not afford to dwell on things like self-pity and ungratefulness, and the very thought of burdening either of them with any of her silly worries made her skin crawl. Kit had almost combusted when he saw her cry on the night of the inaugural ball, and she did not want to mortify him again. She infinitely preferred the satisfaction of listening to others, of doing what she could to lighten others' burdens. Little held more magic in this world than the way people unraveled for her like a ball of yarn when given enough time and patience.

"Don't be modest," Kit said.

"What do you want to know?"

"I don't know. Do you have a father?" Judging by Kit's expression, he'd aimed for sincerity, but it ended up sounding rather sarcastic. Niamh knew better by now than to take it to heart. "You've never mentioned him."

"I am sure I did, but I never knew him."

"Ah," Sinclair said. His voice took on that familiar, too-cheery note. "See? Fathers are universally good for nothing."

Kit rolled his eyes. "Be serious."

"I *am* serious. We used to wish ours dead every day, or have you forgotten?"

"One of us still might get lucky."

"Enough of this brooding." Sinclair slung one arm around each of them and pulled them close. "Who needs blood family, anyway, when you have such good friends?"

An emotion bubbled up within her. It stung at the backs of her eyes. *Belonging.*

"Don't push your luck," Kit said. But for all his grumbling, he made no effort to extricate himself. "We're going to be late for dinner."

Niamh had never been so eager for a dinner to end.

She'd spent the entire evening thus far sandwiched between two women who peppered her with questions about her gowns, how she'd managed to escape the innately Machlish trait of laziness, and her opinion on the protests. When they grew bored of her polite answers, they turned pointedly to their other neighbors and began complaining about the food.

"His Highness must have left his usual cook behind," one said, absently pushing her leek soup around with a spoon.

"Assuming he hasn't quit already," the other replied. "I heard he was Machlish."

"This is shockingly bad."

Shockingly bad. Surely, it could not be all that. Curiously, Niamh spooned some into her mouth and shuddered. Cold, limp leek slithered down her throat. The taste was indescribable. She nudged her bowl a short distance away.

Instead, she occupied herself with watching the King of Castilia and Rosa. He replied to any question directed toward her before she could open her mouth, complained on her behalf whenever she did not appear to like something on her plate, and prompted Kit to compliment her no fewer than three times. Rosa somehow managed to look mortified, irritated, and resigned all at once. Still, she said nothing to contradict him. She said nothing at all.

I am my father's only daughter, Rosa had told her once, *and so, I am a pawn.*

Between Kit and Rosa, she now understood what royal duty truly meant: to make yourself and your desires so small, they were immaterial. Niamh could not bear to watch them any longer.

More than thirty dishes were trotted out throughout the night: overdone salmon wrapped in half-baked pastry, boiled beef tongue, a pie filled with what Niamh thought resembled carrots in appearance if not in flavor, an unintegrated cake of spinach and potato, and an entire fleet of desserts, each one less remarkable than the one before it. All of it lacked style and flavor, and all of it was served at odd, too-long intervals by a staff at least half too small.

They all looked exhausted—and it showed in their work. At one point, a footman spilled wine on the baron across from her, and a serving girl set down a platter of biscuits with such a clatter, the entire conversation abruptly fell into silence. She did not look mortified, however. She looked embittered enough to rival King Felipe. They both skewered Jack with steely, unimpressed glares.

Once it was—finally—over, Niamh followed the women into the drawing room. The carpet had been rolled up and the pianoforte rolled out. A young lady perched on the stool, playing tunelessly as the stragglers filtered into the room, her fingers clumsily tripping over the keys. Her voice, however, snagged like a fishing hook in Niamh's mind. She found herself drifting closer to the girl, hungry to be closer, entranced by her undeniable beauty . . . Niamh shook herself out of the spell. The girl was divine-blooded, certainly. A woman Niamh assumed was her mother stood over her shoulder, somehow looking both proud and despairing.

Across the room, Rosa had curled up in the coziest armchair in the room, close to the flickering, warm glow of the hearth. Niamh considered greeting her—but within moments, no fewer than ten other young ladies descended upon her. A short distance away, Sofia was laying out a tea service. Sharp spears of diamond glittered at her throat. She looked as lovely and cold as a polar star—and just as lonely. When she finished, she hovered awkwardly outside the knot of women with her hands clasped loosely in front of her, the anxiety on her face deepening. She clearly meant to invite them to take tea, but no one paid her any mind at all. After a few moments, Sofia turned and slipped out of the room without saying a word.

It tugged sharply at Niamh's heart. A basket of Sofia's half-finished embroidery projects sat at her feet. Without thinking, she grabbed one and followed her into the darkened corridor. "Your Highness?"

Sofia turned toward her sharply. A flicker of surprise passed over her face. "Miss O'Connor. Is there something you needed?"

"No, nothing." She hesitated, suddenly feeling quite foolish. She averted her gaze and studied the pattern in her hands. It was as precise and restrained as Sofia herself. "But I did promise to help you with your needlework, if you'd like to sit with me. However, I cannot help but notice that your stitching is very fine. I do not think you need my assistance at all."

"How kind of you to remember," Sofia said. "And even kinder of you to say, when you make such wondrous things. To stitch your emotions so freely into something . . . It is a beautiful gift."

Something about her tone gave Niamh pause. She forced herself to meet Sofia's eyes and saw such terrible sadness there. "Your Highness . . . Are you all right?"

"Yes, I . . ." Sofia trailed off. Slowly, she sat on the lowest step of the imperial staircase. She did not speak for a long moment, and when she did, her voice broke. "I am just very tired."

Niamh took a few tentative steps closer. "Has something happened?"

"This evening was a disaster. I do not know how we are going to make it through the next three days," she said, so quickly and quietly, Niamh had to strain to understand her. "I am sure you have noticed we are short-staffed. Many of our servants have left, and the ones who remain are overworked. And when this event goes awry, the court will grow more impatient with my husband."

As the emotions poured out of her, so did her magic. Golden light danced faintly beneath Sofia's skin. The temperature crept lower, and Niamh clenched her jaw to keep her teeth from chattering. If she interrupted Sofia now, she feared she'd never open up to her again.

"I do not know what to do to fix it," Sofia continued. "He will not let me run our household, and he will not tell me what troubles him. I am useless to him. The other women in court know it, too. They have no interest in a friendship with a woman who has no influence over her husband. For a time, I had my lady's maids, but Jack dismissed all of them. Now, I have no one to confide in, and I can do nothing but smile and pretend that nothing is wrong."

The silence settled heavily over them, and a fine dusting of frost glittered on the floor. Sofia leaned her head against the iron baluster and fluttered her eyes shut. The light of her magic glinted off the facets of her diamond necklace.

Niamh's throat tightened. It struck her, then, just how young Sofia was—no more than a year or two older than her. Niamh couldn't imagine how awful it would be, to be stranded in a place where she knew no one, save a man who did not value her. A man who was supposed to love her, not isolate her in the process of isolating himself.

She perched gingerly on the step beside Sofia and rested her hand on her knee. "You can talk to me if you'd like."

Sofia flinched, either from surprise or the chill of Niamh's skin. Horror lit her pale eyes from within. "Please forgive me. I have frozen you half to death, and I . . . This is not your burden to bear."

"There is no need to apologize." She was shivering quite violently, but some of the bite had dissipated from the air. "It is not good for you to hold all of that in. It comes out, one way or another."

"Yes, I suppose it does." She sighed, and her breath fogged in the cold. Bit by bit, she regained her composure. "You treat everyone with such guileless familiarity, regardless of their station, it makes it easy to forget oneself. It is as unusual as it is captivating."

"I don't know how to do otherwise. It really is nothing to admire, Your Highness. I think it has caused me more trouble than not since I arrived."

"It is not a bad thing. You have a way of drawing things out of

people, of bringing what they wish to keep hidden into the light."
Sofia pinned her in place with her cool, assessing gray eyes and
rested her hand over Niamh's. "I believe that is your true gift, not
your sewing."

It was a sweet sentiment—perhaps the most generous thing
someone had said about her. "Thank you."

"In fact, it is we who are causing you trouble," Sofia continued.
"Although it is kind of you to watch out for Christopher. He does
not have many friends in court."

"I am not—"

She smiled knowingly. "Do not worry about us. The prince regent only wants to prove himself as capable as his father, so he tries
to handle things on his own. And I am needed here, even if *he*
does not need me. My presence ensures that he supports my father's
reign. For that, I am happy, knowing that my sacrifices matter. I
would do anything to ensure they continue to matter. You understand, yes?"

Of course she did. She understood that more than anything.
And yet, the intensity in Sofia's voice and the steadiness of her
gaze . . . It all felt somehow familiar, and it filled Niamh with an
uneasiness she could not shake.

15

The air smelled like rain—damp stone and rich soil. In the distance, gray clouds drifted over the hills like the dirtied train of a gown. Niamh made it no more than five paces onto the lawn of Woodville Hall before she noticed something amiss. A *gloom.* It was not only the weather, although it really was a terrible day for a lawn party. Everyone idled out on the grass with an air of boredom and confusion.

Niamh had never been to a lawn party herself, but Sinclair had painted the picture for her vividly enough. Guests should be playing battledore out in the fields, or clustered around tables, dealing cards and laughing behind their fans and gloved hands, or drinking themselves silly on punch. But the lawn lay empty. No tables, no games, no punch, no servants. Only a gaggle of aristocrats, waiting for something to happen.

How strange, she thought.

When she swept her gaze back over the house, she spotted Jack standing on the veranda with a grim expression, and Rosa's father clearly scolding him. He jabbed his finger accusingly at the prince regent, then out at the not-party, which Niamh took as a sign to move on. She drifted through the crowds, hoping to spot a familiar face. People murmured as she passed. Her gown seemed to be drawing attention again.

The skirts billowed slowly around her even when she stood still, as if caught in the sluggish current of a river. She'd made it years ago in a fit of frustration. It had taken her days to create the lace overlay—and days more to embroider all of Gran's exhortations to *slow down* into it. In theory, its enchantment and design were meant to embody patience itself. In practice, it only made her feel as though she were walking through a dream. She supposed her focus on *slow down* might have caused some unintentional effects. Today, it suited her fine. Last night, she hadn't slept at all. She'd finished Kit's new jacket for this event just as dawn had peered in through her bedroom window. The ache in her body and the bleariness of her eyes made her feel half-dreaming already.

At last she stumbled upon her friends beneath the shade of an oak. *Friends.* When had that happened? The word warmed her up from the inside.

Rosa sat primly on a swing rigged from a thick branch, her feet kicking in the open air. Miriam pushed her, occasionally glancing up at the ropes as they groaned beneath Rosa's weight. Kit and Sinclair leaned against its trunk, deep in conversation. Kit looked more at ease than she'd seen him in days. The enchantment she'd woven into his jacket created the most entrancing effect on the fabric. It shone all over like plated armor. Just looking at him made her feel a little braver. Last night, she'd gathered her memories of courage around her like a shield: leaping off the cliffs into ocean below, taking those first steps onto Avlish soil, telling Kit exactly how he had hurt her all those weeks ago.

It was only when he met her eyes that she realized she'd been staring at him. He raised an eyebrow, as if to say, *Well?* It did very strange things to her stomach. Perhaps she should have chosen a different gown, if only to keep her wits about her more.

Flushing, she curtsied. "Hello, Your Highnesses, Miss Lacalle, Sinclair."

"You're here at last," Sinclair said warmly, with a tip of his hat. "Are you enjoying the liveliest party of the Season?"

"About that," Niamh said. "What is going on?"

"The last of the staff quit," Rosa said blandly. "I confess I'm relieved. My father is too busy yelling at the prince regent to hover over me."

"What? But . . ."

The only staff members left were Avlish. Yet, last night Sofia had worried they were overworked and frustrated, taking on all the duties of the Machlish servants who'd already left. It left the nobility completely stranded. Niamh did not know whether she wanted to laugh or weep. All she could imagine were the skies opening up now, just to secure this party's slot in the gossip columns as the worst of the Season. It would be a disaster. All of these bright day dresses hemmed in mud, all of those silk slippers soaked through, all the hard-won paper curls drenched and ruined. She shuddered at the very thought of wet silk.

"We were just about to fetch the croquet set ourselves," Sinclair said. "Care to join us?"

Rosa dug her fingers into her temples and sighed deeply. "Oh, joy. You were serious."

"It's too dreary to sit around doing nothing," Miriam chided.

The prospect of exerting herself any further sounded onerous, but the alternative—doing *nothing*—was far worse. "How fun!"

Together, they began their trudge across the lawn. At the far end, behind a thin curtain of mist, Niamh could make out the faint shape of a shed.

The clouds continued to thicken overhead. Sinclair laughed as a gust of wind nearly tore off his top hat. "Think you can do anything about this, princess?"

"Why would I alter perfection?" Rosa asked serenely.

Miriam fell into step beside Niamh and took her arm. Her face glowed with the chill in the air, and in the humidity, her curls loosened into a halo around her. "I feel as though I haven't seen you at all since we arrived. You look like a dream today."

"Thank you!" Niamh beamed. "How are you faring?"

"Well enough, I suppose." She sighed. "Although I have to say, I feel somewhat out of place here. Burdensome, if I'm honest."

"Who could ever think of you as a burden?"

Miriam lifted a shoulder. "No one has ever said as much. But the feeling has never gone away. In Castilia, Rosa's decision to associate with me prevented her from making relationships that might have made her life in court easier. I cannot allow myself to get in her way again here."

"Anyone would be fortunate to spend time with you." Niamh rested a hand atop hers and squeezed. "Besides . . . I'd say the king is far more effective than you are in preventing Infanta Rosa from making friends here. Did you see him at dinner last night?"

Miriam snorted. "True enough."

"Still," Niamh continued, "I understand how you feel about not wanting to get in the way."

Out in front of them, Kit and Rosa walked arm in arm through the grass. Of all things, jealousy tugged at her. *Foolish,* she scolded herself. She had always known his situation—and her own station.

Miriam did not answer. She was busy watching the royal couple with a strange, wistful glint in her eyes. She exchanged a look with Niamh before hurriedly glancing away.

The five of them stopped before the shed. Weeds grew wild

around its foundation, and a rusted padlock hung from its moldering door. It looked like it hadn't been opened in half an age. Sinclair rattled it and regarded Rosa with a sly smile. "You may need to zap this thing off, Your Highness."

Kit retrieved a rock from the ground and smashed it over the lock. It fell to the ground in a shower of rust and hardened mud.

"Well," said Sinclair. "That works, too."

Rosa hummed pensively. "Certainly less of a fire hazard."

"And more style," Miriam agreed.

Kit pulled open the doors. Inside, a collection of long-abandoned tools littered the floor, along with an old croquet stand filled with mallets. Each one's handle was banded with a stripe of color. He hauled it out and stepped back so the rest of them could choose their colors. Rosa snatched up the black one covetously. Niamh selected the pink one with a rush of pleasure. Pretty things, no matter how small, never failed to delight her. While Sinclair began hammering the iron hoops into the earth, Niamh hefted her mallet. She swung it in a wide arc, testing its weight as it scythed through the air.

"Careful," Kit warned. "You could do some damage with that thing."

"Then it sounds like *you* are the one who should be careful," she said teasingly.

"Is that a threat?" he asked, matching her tone.

Her stomach twisted itself into another wicked knot. She had no pert reply to that. Mercifully, she was spared from floundering when she caught a glimpse of a figure emerging from the fog. Their coattails billowed in the wind, a dark banner unfurling over the whispering grass.

"Who is that?" Niamh asked.

Sinclair shaded his eyes and grimaced. "Well. This is awkward."

Within a few moments, Jack came clearly into view. The wind had made a mess of his hair, and his gait seemed uncharacteristically loose—almost uneven. He even smiled at them as he approached, and it gave Niamh the same impression she imagined witnessing some sort of rare cosmological event would. Rosa and Miriam immediately curtsied to him. Niamh remembered her manners a moment too late, murmuring *Your Highness* under her breath.

"No need for such formalities," he said. "May I join your game?"

Kit stared at him as though he had spoken another language entirely. For once in his life, he seemed to be entirely speechless.

Sinclair, however, recovered enough wherewithal to reply. He clapped Jack on the shoulder, a bit too hard to be friendly. "Of course, Jackie. Grab a mallet."

With that, they each took their first shots—an altogether unremarkable round, apart from Niamh almost breaking her own ankle bone with a misaimed swing. Rosa, meanwhile, abstained from effort altogether. Her ball sailed lazily through the air and thunked to the earth no more than a few yards away. But when Jack knocked his ball against Kit's and sent them both flying far afield of the course, the air went brittle.

Seething, Kit rounded on his brother. "What are you doing?"

"I am playing the game. I see you are still a terrible sport."

"No," Kit replied slowly. "What are you doing *here*? Don't you have guests to entertain—or appease, for that matter? Or perhaps you should focus on your staff first."

At that, irritation broke through Jack's unusual languor. But instead of replying to him, he turned to Rosa. "What say you, Infanta Rosa? You've seen enough of Avaland's troubles to weigh in on them. I'd like to ask your opinion."

Rosa, who had been politely pretending not to eavesdrop, regarded them with a preoccupied expression. She leaned against her mallet. "You truly want my opinion, sir?"

"Indeed I do."

"It seems to me that you are under siege, holding a disadvantageous defensive position. If you give the Machlish what they are asking for, you will end the worst of it."

Jack seemed bitterly amused. "And when my court moves against me for adopting such a weak position and insulting my beloved father's legacy? Or when the working class rails against me for treating the Machlish as their equals?"

"In the event you are replaced, a new regent will likely use force against them to appease the people—your opponents—who put power in their hands. That will only worsen the situation, potentially inciting an all-out revolt. Such mismanagement would smooth the path for your reinstatement as soon as your father passes. In the very worst-case scenario, I ask for a favor from my father, or your pretty wife from hers." She paused. "That is my humble opinion, of course, Your Highness."

"And there you have it," said Jack. "By God, she has solved all of my problems in seconds."

Rosa narrowed her eyes with displeasure, clearly aware that he was making some sport of her. Muttering something in Castilian under her breath, she hit the ball, sending it soaring toward a distant iron post.

Once she ambled out of earshot, Kit seized on Jack. "Are you *drunk?*"

"It has been a very long couple of weeks," Jack replied tartly. "Why should I not enjoy myself, on my own private lands? Mother would surely approve of getting drunk to mark the occasion of her house's grand reopening."

"Because you're making a complete fool of yourself," he hissed, "and you are about to let everything fall and crush you underneath it."

Jack looked at him for a long time, through bleary eyes. Then he laughed so hard a tear ran down his cheek. "Oh, this is rich."

Oh no. Niamh shrunk back a few steps. She had witnessed enough of their fights by now to know this would not end well.

Kit recoiled, but he masked his hurt with a scowl. "Mother would be ashamed of what you've become. You talk about family as though it means something to you, but you care more about our poisonous legacy than the family you have left, much less your own subjects."

"Mother? Ashamed of me?" Jack tilted his head. "What on earth are you talking about?"

Kit's anger fizzled, doused by uncertainty.

"If you believe Mother would have spared even a single thought for our current situation, save for what gowns she would have worn or which of her appetites could be sated, you are completely delusional." Jack smiled ruefully. "I suppose it makes sense, however. You always were her little pet."

Niamh sucked in a breath. Even the wind ceased to stir.

Thus far, it had been the unruly crash of Kit's waves against Jack's unmoving shore. She had never seen Jack remove the cool impersonality of his roles, either as a prince or a stand-in parent. She had never seen him mire himself in mortal things like pettiness or resentment. Someone had to intervene before this turned ugly. But Rosa and Miriam had quietly slipped away, and Sinclair urgently waved Niamh over to him. She felt completely rooted to the spot.

Kit's eyes darkened, a warning. "Jack."

"I do not know what's gotten into you, pretending at notions of duty." Jack sneered. "As if it's ever meant a thing to you. There was never an ounce of Father's discipline and dignity in you."

"Not like you, of course." Kit trembled with barely restrained fury. "It's like I'm looking at him now. You try to conceal it, but I see his temper caged up inside you."

Jack's expression turned dangerous.

Niamh gasped as plants shot up from the earth. On Kit's side, briars tangled around his feet, rising like a battlement, each of their wickedly sharp thorns aimed at Jack with malicious intent. On Jack's, shrubs in horrible, jagged shapes sprang up around them. They bloomed with heavy, bloodred fruits. The very color of them screamed *poison*.

Niamh stepped out of the way when a thorn pierced the hem of her skirt. "Ehm . . . Your Highnesses?"

They did not hear her.

"If you know what is good for you," Jack said quietly, "you will bite your tongue."

"What, you want to hit me?" Kit squared up to him. "Go on. Do it."

"It would hardly make a difference, for I cannot very well beat gratitude into you! These last few years, I have arranged everything *perfectly.* All you have to do now is behave yourself, but you are so selfish and spoiled, you cannot even manage that. You fall apart at the slightest provocation—and you cut and run the moment things get difficult, just as Mother did. What good were either of you to me?" He threw down his mallet. The very corner of his lip quivered before he mastered himself, all imposing, impenetrable marble once again. "You are the very worst of both our parents, Kit. From the day you were born, you have done nothing but create problems for me to solve."

The ground rumbled beneath them. A briar vine launched toward Jack, its spikes extended like claws. Jack did not even flinch. He clenched his fist, and the vine withered, its leaves desiccating before her eyes. The brothers stared at each other, all of their armor stripped off. Something passed over Jack's face. Without a word, he turned and walked away.

Sinclair trotted up to Kit and placed a hand on his shoulder. "Kit, are you all right?"

"Don't." Kit shrugged his hand off. His breaths came in short gasps. "Don't fucking touch me."

Before Sinclair could reply, he stormed off. In his wake, foul-tempered plants bloomed in riotous clusters: poison oak, nightshade, wolfsbane. They surged from the earth, only to strangle one another just as quickly.

"Kit!" Sinclair pressed a fist against his lips. When his hand dropped back to his side, his face was drawn and pale. "Damn it."

Niamh hurried to Sinclair. "What *was* that?"

"I don't know," he said quietly. "I've never seen Jack act that way."

"Should we go after Kit?"

"Yes, probably," he said, his voice hoarse and distant. "The last time he was like this . . . I don't know. I don't know what he'll do."

He sounded afraid, the same as he had when Kit's magic lashed out at him in the park. "What do you mean?"

Sinclair dragged a hand down his face. "It's not his fault, but his magic can be dangerous when he gets like this—to himself and other people. Maybe I'm a coward, but I can't do it again. Last time taught me to be a little more selfish."

A prickle of unease went through her. "Then *I'll* go. Someone needs to make sure he's all right."

"No. We need to get Jack."

"I do not think Jack is in any state to deal with this!"

As she brushed past him, Sinclair caught her elbow. She made to thrash out of his grip, but he steered her back around. "All right, hold on. I understand that you're worried, but perhaps we should think this one through together. First of all, you look like you're going to keel over. You're as pale as death."

"I am *fine*."

"I'm not done." He gave her a stern look, then sighed. "Listen. I didn't want to bring it up like this, but I don't see any other way around it. I love Kit, and you've been a good friend to me, so I won't mince words. I'm not an idiot."

Niamh stared up at him. Her breath snagged in her throat, and she had the distinct sensation of free-falling. "I . . . I beg your pardon?"

"Come now, Niamh." Sinclair looked anguished. He stepped

closer to her, until hardly any space remained between them. He took her by the shoulders and dropped his voice low, as though to speak any louder would give them away. "Give me some credit here. It's like watching an entire opera play out every time you two so much as make eye contact with each other. If I've noticed, then it won't be long before the wrong person does. Don't tempt fate."

A thousand feelings tore through her at once. Humiliation, fear, anger, sadness. She couldn't make sense of this jumble. She couldn't deal with the fact that he'd pulled her heart out and thrown it, still beating, at her feet. Right now, the only thing that mattered was that Kit was unharmed. "Then *help* me, Sinclair. It won't look so bad if it's both of us. Will you really take that risk?"

"I can't do it."

"I can handle this." She met his eyes steadily. "I am not afraid of him."

Thunder rolled overhead. The first of the rain began to fall.

"Fuck," he muttered. Sinclair shrugged off his jacket and wrapped it around her shoulders. "Fine. I'll walk with you as far as the edge of the woods. Everyone's gone inside, but there are windows everywhere. So just . . . Be careful. And don't come back together, for God's sake."

She clasped the lapels at her throat. "Thank you, Sinclair."

He nodded. And when she committed to what was quite possibly the worst decision of her life, he was right there behind her.

The sky was downright ominous, with gashes of dark clouds that blotted out the sun. The rain fell in gouts, plastering her hair against her skin. In a matter of minutes, it would soak through both Sinclair's coat and her dress. Already, her fingers had gone numb and white as bone in the chill. She could not afford a flare-up of her symptoms now of all times.

Past the tree line, the grounds of Woodville Hall grew wild and untamed. Out ahead of her, a field of pale lavender shivered in a sudden gust of wind. Niamh hiked up her skirts and waded in. With every step, the cloying scent of lavender and petrichor wafted up from the earth below. Her shoes sank deeper into the mud as she approached an old wrought-iron gate. The latch was rusted shut and groaned angrily when she tried to shimmy it open. Instead, she threw her weight against it—and promptly regretted it when her hip throbbed in protest.

She'd have to scale it, then.

Niamh drew in a breath and hoisted herself over the top, scrabbling to find footholds in the scrollwork. Her fingers resented being curled to fists. Her swollen joints cried out in protest, and it took nearly all her strength to climb the short distance. The pointed finials jabbed into her guts and tugged a few threads loose in her bodice. By the time she spilled over the other side, great smears of orange marred the front of her gown. She landed in a heap, spattering mud all over herself.

She picked herself off the ground and squinted into the gloom. Once, maybe, there had been a garden here. But now, it was all overgrown and ruined. Purple clover blossomed riotously in the garden beds, and the mint had claimed half the property for itself, the greedy thing. Dandelions pushed determinedly through the cracks in the stepping stones. How gorgeous this place must have been when there was someone around to take care of it. Still, there was something lovely about it all. The dark earth, redolent and alive. All these stubborn, wayward things, thriving in their neglect.

As she stepped carefully through the weeds, tendrils of green snagged at the hem of her dress and curled around her ankles. Another vine wound itself around her wrist almost longingly. They tried to root her in place, but they were slender enough that it required no effort to yank herself free.

Kit clearly did not want her here. She could practically feel his will coursing through the flora, even without the telltale gold running through each leaf and petal's veins. Her vision swam with exhaustion, and she shivered with cold. But she refused to leave him alone in his suffering.

"Kit!" she called, but the squall of the storm swallowed up her voice.

She passed beneath the shade of gnarled apple trees and through vegetable patches gone to rot. At last, as the trees thinned out, she spotted a figure crumpled on the ground: Kit, wreathed in silver rainwater. His jacket and cravat lay in a sodden heap in the mud beside him, and his shirt was translucent with damp. Like this, he looked so frail.

"Kit?" Niamh hurried toward him, kicking up mud in her wake.

He didn't look up. "Go away."

She came closer, tentatively. "I know you may not want to see me right now, but I . . ."

He turned toward her. His loose, wet hair clung to the sharp planes of his face. Through the rain pelting the earth between them, she saw his eyes burning bright and gold. "I said *go away.*"

Thorns shot from the earth, forming a perfect circle around him. Niamh yelped, stumbling backward. By a stroke of good fortune, she managed to keep her footing. Before she could process it, sweetbrier vines wound around him, caging him in a thicket. They were garlanded with white flowers and red berries, and water beaded on each delicate petal like droplets of divine blood.

Niamh's pulse raced, hard enough that she felt it in her wrists, in the tip of each finger. Never before had she seen magic quite like this. Powerful enough that she might believe the Fair Ones still walked among them. It was awesome and awful all at once.

Kit was nestled within the thorns and wild rose like a seed kept safe within its shell. His shoulders trembled, and when he looked at her, she saw that he was in two places at once: here and not here. It brought Niamh back to herself. This was not a god nor a prince. He looked like a frightened child. As the vines tightened around him, they cut into his skin. Blood, golden as sunlight, seeped into his shirt.

"Let me in," she said, attempting to inject some sternness into her tone. "Right now!"

He did not reply.

The wind lashed her braid against her back. Niamh had half a mind to clamber back over the fence and fetch a pair of gardening shears from that moldering shed. She was drenched and shivering with some mixture of fear and cold, but she would not abandon him here. That was only what he believed he wanted.

"I'm not going anywhere. I can be very persistent, I'll have you know."

He hardly seemed to recognize her. His eyes blazed like a lantern in a dark wood. "I can't."

"What do you mean you can't?"

"I can't control it." The thorns seethed around him, and another vine whipped toward her. Niamh stumbled back. This time, she let out a little shriek and landed flat in the mud. Grime splashed onto her, and the impact rattled into her shoulders.

Her emotions had always ruled her magic, too. Accessing it had only ever been a matter of *feeling*. But it had never hurt her like this. Even when she was sad, even when she was angry, magic lit her up from within. It felt like light, blossoming within her like petals in the rain. For Kit, it was another beast entirely.

Once you strip off all those thorns, he's not so bad. She had glimpsed that truth long ago. All his anger and aggression were the sword and shield in the hands of his fear.

"Please, Kit." She righted herself and knelt just outside the reach of the thorns. "Talk to me."

"Why? It doesn't matter," he rasped. Another vine erupted from the earth and coiled viciously around his arm. He pressed his forehead against his knees. "All I do is ruin the lives of everyone around me."

"It does matter!" Niamh set her jaw. "What your brother said was cruel. That doesn't mean you have to punish yourself, and it doesn't mean you have to push everyone away."

He was silent.

"Don't force yourself to bear it alone," she pressed. "Please."

Slowly, the vines fell away like layers and layers of armor sloughing off. His eyes faded back to amber. Somehow, they were still the brightest things she had ever seen. For the first time since he ran off, he looked at her. Truly looked at her.

Recognition lit his eyes. "You."

"Kit." As soon as she stood, exhaustion, greater than any she'd ever known, settled over her. Blackness crept in at the edges of her vision. Distantly, she decided it was a bad idea to stay up all night again. "You're going to be all right."

Kit's lips parted with surprise. "Niamh?"

Her knees went weak. She felt disembodied now, floating somewhere far above herself. Her center of gravity slipped from underneath her, as quick as a cut to the throat.

"Niamh!"

Before she hit the ground, she slumped into something solid. *Kit.* Her head lolled into the crook of his neck and shoulder. Some part of her knew she should be mortified, but it was so warm in his arms. So oddly comforting.

"Are you hurt?" As she slid into the encroaching dark, the last thing she saw were his wide, panicked eyes, and in them, the look of a man who had finally realized the worst of his weaknesses lived outside himself. "Answer me. Please. Did I hurt—?"

16

When she opened her eyes again, she was inside—and warm. Rain drummed steadily against the roof. It streaked the windowpane and glittered in the light of the candle burning low on her nightstand. Another fire crackled merrily in the grate, releasing the heady scent of woodsmoke. Shadows marbled the ceiling, swirling slowly. It was all so cozy, she considered falling back asleep. But then she remembered.

Kit.

Someone had swaddled her in a wool blanket. Niamh squirmed out of it and forced herself to sit upright. Immediately, she regretted it. Her head ached. *Everything* ached. The inside of her chest felt as though it'd been hollowed out, like a well tapped too deep. It'd been a very long time since she felt this wretched. If memory served, she wouldn't be getting out of bed for a day or two. She would live like a maiden imprisoned in her tower, watching life pass her by through a cracked mirror.

But the wedding was in two weeks.

Every second trapped in this bed, trapped in this treasonous body of hers, was one she couldn't spare. The backs of her eyes burned with unshed tears. At least she was too exhausted to run to the looking glass and check how much her hair had silvered.

You're not sick until you're sick, she reminded herself. And yet, it was getting so much harder to convince herself that she was well. If only she had not pushed herself so recklessly. If only she did not have to worry about pushing herself at all.

The faint sound of voices reached her from behind the door. There were two of them, tense and hushed. If she held her breath, she could almost make out what they were saying.

". . . really made a mess of things now." *Miriam,* Niamh thought. "Go to sleep. She will be fine."

"Let me see her first." Niamh's heart leapt. She would recognize Kit's voice anywhere.

There came the awkward shuffle of footsteps, then the soft rattle of the door in its frame. "Don't you think you've done enough for one night?"

Another low mutter.

"As you wish, Your Highness," Miriam said sourly. "I'll check on her for you again."

The doorknob twisted. *Oh no.* If Miriam caught Niamh awake, she'd know she'd been eavesdropping. Niamh scrambled for the blanket, but it was too late. The door swung open, revealing a very exasperated Miriam. Her mouth parted in a soft O of surprise. She glanced over her shoulder, then locked the door behind her. "You're awake."

"I haven't been for long."

Miriam studied her with an unreadable expression. "How do you feel?"

She winced. "I feel fine."

"Don't be brave for my sake." Her tone grew stern. "I don't mean to be invasive—it is the healer in me—but you need to rest. I have seen conditions like yours before."

Niamh supposed it made sense that her family was not uniquely afflicted, but she hadn't considered her illness might be common. "You have?"

"Do others in your family have the same symptoms?" When Niamh nodded, Miriam went on. "Then, yes. Some illnesses pass through generations. We tend to see them appear more often in families with divine blood—not necessarily because they're connected, but because stress seems to worsen symptoms. Magic use can be quite taxing on the body. There is no cure yet, unfortunately, but a good healer can help you manage your symptoms."

Her thoughts swam. She couldn't think of finding a healer right now. Until this job was done and her family was safe, she couldn't think of slowing down or entertaining even a scrap of hope that her life could be longer or less painful than she anticipated.

"My apologies," Miriam said sheepishly, clearly sensing Niamh's overwhelm. "I imagine that is not what you wanted to hear immediately upon waking up. The prince is waiting for you in the hall."

"Is he?"

"He carried you back to the house."

"*What?*"

Of all the things Miriam could have told her, this was perhaps the last she would have expected. She couldn't process it. She couldn't even envision it. Kit Carmine was most certainly not the gallant type. But how else could she have gotten here? She remembered it now: the creeping darkness over her vision, the unbearable concern in his eyes, the feeling of safety in his arms.

She shoved that thought away.

"Mm. It was quite something. He came out of the storm, wild-eyed, looking like he'd seen a ghost." She widened her own eyes for effect. "And you looked like a rag doll. I thought at first that you were dead. It took some convincing to get him to let you go."

It was all too easy to fill in the blanks from there. The thought of him carrying her, completely limp and sopping wet, all the way back to the estate . . . It was too humiliating to bear. She would never, ever be able to look him in the eye again. He would lord it over her forever.

But when what he'd done well and truly sank in, her stomach curdled with dread. What had he been *thinking,* doing something like that so publicly? Sinclair had warned her about this very situation. More people than Miriam must have seen him emerging from the fog and rain like some revenant.

She could hardly make herself ask the question she dreaded most. But she had to know. "Did Infanta Rosa see?"

"No," Miriam said quickly, "thankfully."

"But it won't take her long to hear, I am sure. If you saw him, anyone could have." She buried her face in her hands. "Oh, no . . . This is a disaster. I ought to flee the country now. I need to—"

"One thing at a time." Miriam sat on the very edge of the bed and squeezed her arm reassuringly. "She may not look it, but Rosa is quite an understanding person. If it comes up, I'll explain it to her. He was only bringing you out of the rain and nothing more. Right?"

"Right," Niamh said softly.

"He's still in the hallway now. I think he's worn a groove in the floorboards by now with all his pacing. Would you like me to send him away? *I* would like that. It reeks out there. The man smokes like a chimney when he's stressed."

"I'll see him."

Miriam sighed. "Very well. One moment."

She slipped back through the door. There was a muffled exchange outside. Then, the door all but flew open. It crashed into the wall with a too-loud *bang.* Kit kicked it shut behind him, then strode to her bedside with grim purpose in the set of his shoulders. He still wore his damp clothes, spattered with mud. His hair fell loose and damp around his shoulders, curling just barely at the ends. She'd never noticed just how long it was. And his eyes . . .

They were as wild as Miriam said—practically ablaze in the firelight. A thousand emotions passed over his face at once, too quick for her to trace, before they landed, quite decisively, on anger.

"Hello," she croaked.

"You fool. What were you thinking?"

All Niamh could do was gawp at him. Then, righteous indignation doused every one of her worries. "What was *I* thinking? Oh, you are so— Ugh! I shouldn't have expected anything different from you. If that is all you have to say to me, then you can leave!"

"You followed me through a rainstorm." Every word was an accusation, as sharp as a thrown dagger. "And then you collapsed. You're clumsy, but I've never seen anything like that. Down like a felled tree, out of nowhere. What was that about?"

"I . . ." Her throat constricted. No, she couldn't explain this to him. She couldn't endure his pity. "I was tired. That's all."

"Then why would you be so careless?" When his hair fell into his face, he raked a hand through it. "You have a death wish, clearly. There's no other sensible explanation for it."

"You've made your point, sir!" Now she felt utterly embarrassed. What a joke she was, to harbor a single tender feeling for Kit Carmine. "If you must know, I was worried about you."

"Worried about *me*? I'm fine."

"No, you are certainly not fine. What I saw was not *fine*, Kit."

The tension swelled between them like a storm cloud ready to burst. But then, she saw the exact moment his defenses collapsed. He spoke in a rush, as if he would lose his nerve if he stopped for even a breath. "What about you, then? *You're* the one who was going to die of exposure, or by tripping over a pebble. What's more, you're constantly sticking your nose where it doesn't belong and overextending yourself for no good reason." A pause, then: "Not that it's any of my concern."

Oh, he was such a liar—and a poor one at that. She recognized all this bluster for what it was, and she certainly had not missed the way he'd looked at her in the garden. Fearful and full of something like . . . No, best not to dwell on things that would hurt her worse.

Accusatorily, she said, "Then why are you fussing over me?"

He reeled back, insulted. "I am not *fussing*. I just said I don't care."

"You can't do that!" she cried. "You can't carry me through a rainstorm and then say you don't care. It doesn't work like that!"

"Well, I did."

At first, the only response she could muster was "Arghhh!" She threw her hands up. He didn't even bat an eye. He was steely and—and . . . *flushed*? It had to be from cold or from anger. She did not know and did not care. She was sick of him. He brought out all her worst, most childish impulses. "Then I don't care, either! And I *do* have a reason, by the way."

His pupils were bare pinpricks of black, even in the flickering candlelight. The room suddenly felt too small. Her heart beat far too quickly in her chest. "So explain it to me."

"It's because . . ." Niamh hesitated for only a moment before the last of her resistance gave way. It wasn't as though it was a secret, and Kit was not one to default to pity. She twisted the lock of white hair around her finger. "It's because I'm dying."

His expression went slack with surprise. "What do you mean?"

"I'm sick, and there is no cure for it. One day, it will kill me." She knotted her hands together in her lap. "I suppose you're right. I pushed myself too far. I shouldn't have been so careless. All the same, I cannot do less. Everything is riding on doing this job well."

"Because of your family."

"Yes." She squeezed her eyes shut. "My gran and I are the last of our bloodline who carry on the craft. If I cannot complete this job . . . I couldn't bear it if thousands of years of Ó Conchobhairs ended with me, a silly girl who threw away the opportunity of a lifetime. Their sacrifices will have meant nothing."

"Of course they mean something." Anger crackled beneath his every word—not at her, she could see, but on her behalf. The protective look he fixed her with now skirted too close to the one he'd given her in the garden. "Despite everything we've put you through, you're alive. They have no right to ask you for anything more."

Don't they? Her breaths came in fitful, shaking gasps. Tears spilled down her cheeks, too suddenly for her to stop them. Somehow, she hardly cared that she was weeping like a child in front of him *again*. "Of course they do. It is not enough to exist. It is my duty to be perfect. I have not been perfect—not at all."

Some of the intensity dropped clean off his face, and he looked despondent in his bewilderment. "What are you crying about now?"

"I have done my best, but I have to do more to finish this. I *can* do more."

"Listen to yourself. You're not making any sense. You can't give more than you have."

"Yes, I can." He had ripped open an old wound, and emotions she had long sealed away came rushing out of her. "I am so afraid, Kit. I am afraid that I will fail, despite all the pains I have taken. I am afraid I will let everyone down. And deep down, I am afraid that I am horribly, irredeemably selfish because I am so afraid that I will die without having let myself live at all."

It was confession and a realization both. Here, in the close darkness of Woodville Hall, she wanted more than she'd ever allowed herself to want. The good, the bad, and everything in between: all of life and its ten thousand ways to cut you. All of the things she'd never envisioned for herself. To grow old. To be hurt. To fall in love.

"Maybe you are self-centered," he said after a long moment. "Or just clueless."

A mixture of hurt and indignation dropped heavily into her gut. Niamh wrapped her arms around her middle. "You do not always need to say exactly what you're thinking, you know."

"Sorry. I'm not trying to hurt your feelings. I'm just . . ." He sighed, frustrated. "The only happiness you can imagine for the people you care about comes at your own expense. You're making yourself miserable, and don't try to deny it. You are the most obvious, transparent person I've met in my entire life."

She choked out a laugh through her tears. "Am I?"

"To me, maybe. You smile like my mother did. Your eyes . . ." He trailed off, then seemed to think better of finishing the thought. More gently, he continued, "Forget it. My point is, if your family really loves you, they'd want you to be happy. They'd be fools for not recognizing how much you've given up for them, or how talented you are. So just . . . stop it. You don't need to work yourself to the bone. You don't need to do things for people before you ever think to do a thing for yourself. Whatever you think you have to prove or earn, it's all in your head. Your existence alone *is* enough. And if you believe you've made no difference at all to anyone, you're even more clueless than I thought."

But she did not know how to believe that, and she did not know how to stop. "I'll try."

"Good," he said gruffly. "That's all I have to say."

They sat in silence for a few moments while her breathing evened out. She felt . . . awful. Yet somehow cleansed. Kit had not treated her gently, but she did not expect him to. There was something oddly comforting about his bluntness. It forced her to be honest with herself as much as it did with him. She supposed she owed him the same. "Do you want to tell me what happened out there?"

"Not really."

"It's only fair," she said lightly.

"I've had a hard time controlling my magic for a few years now, especially when I'm emotional," he said, only a little begrudgingly. "And especially when I'm drunk. Technically, *that's* why I got sent away."

She could tell it cost him a lot to tell her; it surprised her he'd told her at all. Something told her he didn't want sympathy. "I see."

"Being in this house, what Jack said . . . It pushed me." He frowned. "It's hard to describe. When I lose control, I feel like I'm somewhere else. I go back to where I was four years ago. I don't want to hurt someone like that again."

"You didn't hurt me." Niamh hesitated. "Kit . . . What exactly *happened* four years ago?"

"You really don't know." It was less of a question than it was an expression of disbelief.

She did, and she didn't. His mother had died, but there was something else. Something that Jack couldn't tolerate. Something that frightened Sinclair. Something that Kit was deeply ashamed of. She braced herself for all of his walls—all of his thorns—to go up again.

But after a moment, he let out a long sigh and sat on the edge of her bed. The mattress creaked beneath his weight. "What do you know of my mother?"

"Nothing but what you've told me."

"She was complicated." By *complicated*, Niamh sensed he meant *troubled*. "For most of my life, it was like she lived behind a glass wall. You couldn't reach her at all. It wasn't until my father's health began to decline that she came out from behind it. I hadn't ever seen her so happy, or so alive." Bitterness colored his words. "She went to every event of the Season, and soon, the gossip columns fell in love with her. They watched her every move, dissected her every word, commented on every little thing she ate and wore."

He fell quiet for a few moments, and Niamh thought that he had followed his own vulnerability to its end. But to her astonishment, he drew in a breath and continued. "One night, she left a ball early. It was a dark, rainy night, a lot like this one. Her curricle overturned, just beyond the gates there."

He jerked his chin out the window. A shiver worked its way through Niamh as she stared at the wrought-iron fence beyond the sheets of rain.

"I was too young to go to the ball, so I was here. When I heard the crash, I thought it was thunder. But when I went to the window, I saw . . ." He closed his eyes, and frustration mounted in his voice. "I can't remember exactly what I saw. I can't even remember what killed her, even now, even though they *told* me a hundred times. If it was the horse that trampled her, or her head striking the cobblestones, or . . . I just can't remember."

"Kit, that's horrible. I'm so sorry."

"Her death alone, I could have dealt with. But the aftermath was a mess. The columns were desperate for details. They were like vultures, them and the rest of our court, and I was never able to satisfy their appetite. I couldn't stop thinking about what had happened. I couldn't remember, but no one let me forget, either. It was like this crater smashed open my life, and one day, I couldn't step around it anymore. I fell into it. And once I fell, I kept falling, and thinking, until I didn't want to think anymore. I felt like they wanted me to grieve differently. It felt like they were waiting for me to snap entirely. So I gave them what they wanted."

Niamh wished she could do something, say something, that would make the pain of those memories go away. But sometimes, bloodletting was the only way to drain the poison. She reached out and placed her hand over his wrist. His pulse fluttered against her touch, but he did not flinch away from her.

"It was a bad period of my life," he said, with a bitter wryness that made her heart ache. "Jack worried a lot, and I resented him for it. Sinclair tried his best to keep me together, but then the columns started speculating that the two of us were involved. I'd ruined my own reputation enough that not even my title could stop them from saying aloud what everyone already knew. I didn't care what anyone thought of me, but Sinclair knew what his father would do if enough people talked."

"They had no right to do that to either of you." Niamh could not fathom such a violation. She boiled with anger, to know that nothing but idle gossip and small-minded hatred had cost Sinclair so much. "What happened then?"

"Apparently, someone made an insinuation about us at a ball when his father was in earshot. I'd been drinking too much and lost my temper. And then I lost control of my magic. Sinclair tried to rein me in. I almost . . . He almost . . ." He scoffed. "The worst part is, I don't even remember what I did. I had to learn about it from the columns."

Niamh did not need him to say it. The fear in Sinclair's eyes today had already told her everything she needed to know. Whether he intended to or not, Kit had lashed out at him enough to leave scars. She imagined only half of them were visible.

Kit shook his head and muttered, "The idiot. He plays at being unreliable, but he's stupidly loyal."

"He has forgiven you." She tightened her grip on his wrist. "He told me that he feels he owes you a lot."

"No, I owe *him*. He could have walked away from me a thousand times. He should have, because I was killing him long before that night, and I was too self-involved even to care. After that, Jack put me on the next boat to Helles. He was right to do it." His expression grew hard. "He was right about me today, too. The worst of both our parents. Doomed to end up either raving mad or dead on the side of the road."

"Oh, Kit," she whispered, blinking back a fresh wave of tears. "I know it's hard."

It felt so horribly inadequate. And yet, to her shock, Kit leaned forward and rested his head against her shoulder. He leaned heavily on her, but he did not seem to know what to do with his hands. He folded them loosely in his lap, as though he were afraid to touch her. Tentatively, she wound her fingers into the hair at the nape of his neck and cradled him against her. He went rigid, but as he relaxed, breath by breath, he finally dared to drape one arm around her.

"I came back for Sinclair." Kit sighed heavily. "Jack said he was going to cut off my account unless I married Rosa."

"What?" She gasped. "So you . . . ? That's—"

He pulled back suddenly, taking all his warmth with him. "I swear, if you tell him—"

"I won't!"

"I mean it. I won't hear the end of it if you do. It was almost impossible to get him to agree to accept my help in the first place."

"I do not wish to upset you any more than you already are, so I will refrain from reminding you that you are a good man." She paused. "And also that *you* are the one who told me that you should not make yourself miserable for others' sake."

He glared at her. "Thanks for that."

"Still, I promise I will not tell him."

He seemed to relax some at her reassurance. A small, selfish part of her wanted to pull him back to her and let him curl up against her. To coax him to accept more than a scrap of tenderness and comfort. Because in that secret he'd trusted her with, she'd glimpsed who he really was. Hadn't she known it all along?

In all the ways that mattered, Kit Carmine was just like her.

"But I do think you should know . . ." She cleared her throat, suddenly shy. "I meant what I said the other day. Our fates are not sealed. It is never too late to live the way you wish, and you are not doomed to anything. I understand what it's like to not want to disappoint people. But you deserve to be happy, too. Life is too short, and it is *yours*."

"You hypocrite." He sounded fond, the insult spoken as tenderly as a pet name. It made heat bloom within her.

He held her gaze with his own, then let it slide down, as if he was memorizing her face. He lingered on the curve of her lips as they parted in anticipation. Right now, there was nothing and no one but the two of them. No expectations, nothing but the desire she saw reflected in the brightness of his eyes. She had never felt less like she was dying.

Something in her face must have changed, because his body became charged with awareness. He twined his fingers into her loose hair, pushing it back from her face. His hand seared her chilled skin like a brand. She knew, down to her very marrow, that she was about to be kissed. Her head swam. It felt like a dream—a fairy tale. It didn't feel possible, that she should've been allowed to have something she wanted so badly.

"Are you sure?" she blurted out. "After everything that has happened, I understand if you are tired, or—"

"Stop talking."

He kissed her.

At first, he was impossibly gentle, his lips brushing against hers. Niamh sat up as best she could to meet him, sinking into the veritable mountain of pillows beneath her. Her fingertips skimmed his jaw. His breath shuddered against her mouth. That was all it took. A shot of pure, liquid firelight tore through her body. As he drank her in, his eyes darkened.

Perhaps this was inevitable from the moment he first stirred her anger.

When he kissed her again, all she could think was, *Of course.* The intensity of it was all Kit. He curled his hand around the side of her neck, angling her chin up to him. He was assured and uncompromising, all of his brutal, single-minded focus applied to eradicating every coherent thought she'd ever had, save *more.* When his tongue teased open her mouth, she melted completely into his hands.

Neither of them possessed even an ounce of patience. He bent over her, one hand against the nip of her waist as he dragged her closer. The brass buttons of his waistcoat were cool and rough against her fingers as she loosened them. She relished the thrill of satisfaction when she freed him of the last one—and again when she slipped her hands beneath his wet shirt. His breath hitched, and his muscles tightened against her palms.

He tasted like smoke, and he smelled like rain and damp wool, and she might very well go mad from how good he made her feel. She floated in a haze of pleasure and exhaustion. "Is this a dream?"

"I don't know," he said huskily, his eyes aglow. "Let me kiss you until dawn, and I suppose we'll find out."

Perhaps tomorrow, reality would crash down around her. But here, right now, with the patter of the rain and the whisper of the fire around them, she couldn't find it in herself to worry, to regret a single self-indulgent moment at all.

17

*N*iamh awoke to total darkness. The rain had slowed, but the fire had gone to ashes in the hearth and the candles dripped down to nothing in their iron stands. She sat up slowly, cradling her aching head. What time was it? Exhaustion clung to her like gauze, too thick to push through, and it felt as though she hadn't eaten in an age. Which meant she'd slept all day.

She shot bolt upright, her stomach twisting itself into a knot. How could she have let this happen? She was wasting so much—

Kit's voice echoed sharply through her mind. *You don't need to work yourself to the bone. Whatever you think you have to prove or earn, it's all in your head.*

Right. She *had* promised him she would try to believe that, impossible though it might be.

And then he had kissed her.

Her stomach fluttered again at the memory, and a sparkling, giddy feeling unfurled through her. *Is this a dream?* she'd asked him. Even now, she couldn't convince herself that any of it was real. He'd trusted her with his heart. And for those hazy, delirious hours, he'd convinced her that she mattered enough to take something for herself.

A terrible bittersweetness came over her then. Never once had she believed she'd get to feel that way, consumed by passion against her good sense, seen and desired for exactly who she was. Never once had she believed a girl like her would ensnare a *prince* in some sort of torrid, ill-advised affair. Of course, it could never happen again. But for one night, she'd been truly awake and alive—almost incandescently joyous. She would carry this secret with her forever, as warm and bright as a flame cupped in her hands. It was all hers, and it would burn hot enough to sustain her for the rest of her life. It had to. As much as she yearned for more, she could not stand in Kit's way. She would finish this job, and that would be the end of it.

Her very soul felt raw.

But if nothing else, she was safe. If anyone truly knew what had happened, they would not have waited to drag her out of this room by her hair and do . . . well, whatever it was the Avlish did with women who aspired beyond their station.

Groaning, she flopped back onto the mattress and stared the ceiling. Her fingers traced the outline of her chapped lips. If she closed her eyes, she could almost feel him there.

"Miss?"

Niamh startled. A girl stood in the doorway—a housemaid, from the look of her uniform, but she wore the colors of another noble family. She hadn't heard her knock at all, but she'd been so engrossed in her own thoughts. The entire world appeared to her as though behind a wall of glass. Gods, she needed to go back to sleep.

"Oh," Niamh said breathlessly. "Hello."

"I'm sorry to disturb you," she said, "but His Highness asked for you to get ready. His carriage is departing in a half hour."

Leaving already. She supposed it made sense. With no staff of his own, Jack could not entertain properly. His pride was surely smarting.

It took what little energy she had to climb out of bed and ready herself. Once she'd packed up the last of her things and had them brought downstairs, she wandered the halls of Woodville as though stumbling through a dream. She dragged herself through the front door and came face-to-face with the moonlit fields outside the estate. They shone with still, deep puddles of mud and rainwater and hummed with the song of crickets. The breeze tasted cool and sweet, and tangled in the loose strands of her hair. Niamh folded her arms over the granite balustrade of the terrace and let it support her weight. If she just laid her head down, she could drift off right here.

Someone stepped onto the terrace. "Miss O'Connor."

Blearily, Niamh turned toward the voice. Jack stood beside her, his arms crossed behind his back and his gaze trained on the horizon. Even in the dark, his amber eyes glowed, just like his brother's. His wan face and rigid shoulders brought a wave of sympathy crashing over her. Now, she could see the texture of the last five years he'd endured. No father, no mother, and a brother careening toward his own ruin. He'd lost so much, but she very much doubted he'd allowed himself to grieve at all. He'd only immediately set to work filling in the gaps left behind.

He frowned at her. "You look pale. My brother tells me you took ill?"

"I'm afraid so." She couldn't tell him the truth of her illness, lest he thought her incapable of finishing the job. So she settled on a comfortable lie, even as her legs threatened to buckle beneath her. "I caught a chill in the rain."

"We are borrowing a carriage, so I cannot send you back on your own. I see now that may for the best." He offered his arm to her. "Allow me."

"That is far too kind, sir. I have imposed on you so much already."

"It isn't worth mentioning." Jack allowed her to lean on him as he led her down the stone pathway and through another overgrown garden. The grass sighed restlessly as they passed, quivering in the wind. "I want to apologize for my behavior yesterday."

Her toe caught on a loose flagstone, and he steadied her immediately with an alarmed sound. His apologies never grew less strange or startling. "Your Highness, you do not need to apologize to me."

"But I do." Jack stopped in front of the carriage door, his brows knitted in a preoccupied frown. "You have been subjected to far too many family squabbles."

"All is forgiven. None of us can be unfailingly patient, sir." She offered him a small smile. "But if you will forgive *me* for asking, have you apologized to your brother?"

It slipped out. Jack blinked, stunned. Niamh clapped a hand to her mouth. Why, oh *why*, could she never keep her impertinent questions to herself? Her delirium did not help matters.

"No," he conceded. "But that is . . ." He cleared his throat. "That is wise counsel. I will take it into account."

He handed her off into the carriage. Sofia already waited for them inside—and there, twisted into a remarkably compact shape, was Kit. The sight of him cut through her haze and sent her heart tripping over itself. Never in her life had she so desperately wanted to touch someone—to talk to someone. She met his reflected gaze in the window, and all of the air promptly fled her lungs. The heat in his eyes obliterated every conscious thought. How could she have been so foolish as to believe that it would be easy to content herself with only one night?

"Y-Your Highness," she stammered.

An enchanting shade of red spread across his neck. "Miss O'Connor."

It took everything in her not to react. He'd never once called her that in the weeks they'd known each other, and the stilted formality of it delighted her far more than it should. Not to mention that blush—after how very bold he'd been with her.

Sofia's gaze bounced back and forth between them, looking far too canny for Niamh's taste. If she had an opinion on the matter, she did not share it.

Jack pointedly cleared his throat. It was then she realized she'd been looming in the doorway this entire time. She clambered onto the seat beside Kit. His every muscle coiled with awareness of her, and the bare sliver of space between them crackled with tension. It would be a simple thing to place her hand beside his. She longed for casual intimacy: entwining their littlest fingers, nuzzling into his shoulder, or sinking into the comforting weight of his arm around her. But she supposed she was forever cursed to long for things she could not have.

She followed Kit's lead and looked out her own window. Within minutes, the ivy-curtained facade of Woodville Hall receded behind the hills. How sad that she would never see it again. Soon enough, the thick silence and the steady rock of the carriage lulled her slowly, softly. Her eyelids drooped, and her forehead rested against the glass.

"Kit," Jack said quietly. "I did not mean a word of what I said yesterday. I'm sorry."

For a moment, she heard nothing but the rattle of the wheels against the road. Then, at last, begrudgingly: "I am, too."

"I am sorry for a great many things," Jack continued. "How you must hate me."

"Is now really the time?" Kit sighed heavily. His every word grew more and more distant as her weariness dragged her down, down into the dark. "I don't hate you. But you better have a good reason for all this."

Kit had driven her insane. She could come up with no other explanation. Since the day in the garden, she'd thought of little else but him. Even now, sitting in an armchair as she embroidered his wedding cloak, she found herself stitching all her longing and frustration into it. She supposed it suited the occasion well enough.

The wedding. It hung over them all like the executioner's blade, just about a week away now. Jack had whisked Kit away to finish up the last of the preparations. Niamh tried not to let his absence gnaw at her. It was for the best that they hadn't seen each other since the carriage ride home. It would do her no good to be reminded how out of reach he was.

She set down her work only when a housemaid delivered her tea, her letters, and the morning papers. Spooning sugar into her tea, she skimmed the gossip columns. Still, no one had written about them. It seemed this truly would be her secret, kept safe within her. She imagined closing her fist around that tiny spark of light.

Lovelace, unsurprisingly, was discussing the situation unfolding in Sootham. Carlile and the rest of the protesters remained in Eye Park, and their numbers only grew by the day. In Jack's absence, they'd blocked off riding trails, chanted, and delivered speeches. Now that he was back, they had to face the Kings Guard, which he'd dispatched to "monitor" the situation.

Niamh couldn't deny it unsettled her. Surely, Jack did not intend use force against them; they'd done nothing violent or illegal. She could see every horrible possibility burned on the backs of her eyelids. The Kings Guard's cavalry riding through the unarmed crowds, magic crackling in their palms, their sabers drawn and glinting. Screams and musket fire rending open the night. The blood of her people slicking the streets with red and gold.

She set the column down abruptly, feeling rather ill.

At the very bottom of the pile, she found a letter from Erin.

"Oh!" She hugged it to her chest.

Excitement chased away her unease. She'd nearly forgotten she'd written to her friend at all. Niamh tore it open and noted fondly that Erin was as long-winded as ever. She spent several paragraphs on each of her family members (all nine of them healthy, thank the gods) and how she'd found her return to Machland (bleak). At last, she came to Niamh's questions.

> But, oh! You must tell me everything you have been up to in the palace and everything about the wedding and the royal couple. I hear the prince is quite a menace. Is it true?
>
> I am so very sad to have missed you. It would have been such fun to work together, but I could not bear it in the palace anymore. I do hope they are treating you well, Niamh. It was fine work, with many good people, but my pay arrived later and later, until eventually it stopped coming at all. At first, I suspected it was the housekeeper, Mrs. Knight. What a dreadful woman! She treated us particularly poorly and guarded the prince regent like a dog. However, I learned that some of the Avlish servants experienced the same thing. I do not know what to make of it. Perhaps the prince regent is just a cruel man.
>
> I am proud, however, that a slew of us quitting seemed to awaken something. We are treated terribly in Avaland, and I am pleased to see us fighting back. I had considered joining up with the protesters, but I was eager to be home after almost two years. Everyone sends their fondest wishes to you!
>
> Oh, that reminds me . . .

Jack wasn't paying his staff.

Niamh supposed she shouldn't have been surprised. Her own payment had been late, and while he'd been apologetic, he must have known. He oversaw the hiring of his staff, event planning, and every single expense. Nothing escaped his notice. Perhaps Erin was right. He was a cruel man, as hateful as his father was.

But that couldn't be all. Despite his quick temper, she'd never believed him capable of cruelty. He was an absent husband and an avoidant ruler, yes. But if nothing else, he worshipped at the altar of reputation. If any of his peers discovered he was mistreating his staff so brazenly, it would be an embarrassment of the highest order. If it was within his power to fix, he surely would have done it by now.

There is nothing I can do for those people, he'd said.

My brother never would have called me back here unless he was truly desperate, Kit had told her.

Jack *was* hiding something, then. Kit and Lovelace both suspected as much. But surely, it wasn't as mundane as a little mismanagement. Niamh's head ached from thinking. If only she were clever or strategic, if only she had some useful skill beyond her sewing . . .

A knock sounded on the door.

Sinclair had called on her yesterday to ask if she'd walk the gardens with him today. It was a little earlier than she'd expected him, but taking the air sounded far better than miring in her own worries.

She crossed the room and opened the door. "I wasn't expecting you until—gah! Kit!"

"You were expecting someone else?" Wry amusement glittered in his eyes. "Who do I have to duel?"

For a moment, Niamh could only stare at him. Every question; every ridiculous, moony proclamation; every self-conscious doubt scrabbled to the forefront of her mind.

Was it a dream after all?

Do you feel the way I do when I look at you?

We should never do that again, should we?

Instead, she whispered, "Come in. Quickly," and ushered him inside. The door latched behind him. "What are you doing here?"

He avoided her gaze. "I don't know."

All of her girlish nerves went up in flames. Oh, she could strangle him. He'd kissed her like he meant to make her forget all sense, then left her a confused, flustered, lovesick *fool*. At the end of it all, she got a mumbled *I don't know* for her troubles. Kit was so utterly *predictable*. Why, then, did she still light up with longing?

She planted her hands on her hips and tried her best to glare up at him. "You don't know?"

"Maybe I wasn't really thinking," he said defensively. "I like you. I like being around you. I had nothing on my schedule this morning, so here I am."

I like you. Such matter-of-fact simplicity, a new law of the universe. It felt the same as when he'd told her that he'd talk to her if it pleased him, everyone else in the world be damned. But it was not that simple. It couldn't be.

"But you . . . I . . ." Her mind worked too quickly for her to form a single coherent thought. "It would be wise if we kept our distance from each other. The wedding is so soon, and after that, you and I will likely never see each other again. It's better for us to become strangers again."

Less risk. Less pain.

He seemed to consider it. He took a step closer to her, then another, until he loomed over her and she could feel the warmth emanating from him. The challenging glint in his eyes made her pulse quicken. "Is that what you want?"

She blinked up at him, perplexed. It should not matter what she wanted. "No . . . ?"

She had meant to say *but*. She really had. But the way he looked at her—enraptured, as though she'd put him under some enchantment—made her forget.

"Good," he said. "Me neither."

He kissed her, and she could not help the strangled noise she made—part shock, part relief, part joy. His mouth moved against hers, deliberate and urgent. He walked her forward until her back hit the wall. He braced his forearm beside her head, caging her in, while Niamh clung to his lapels—first for balance, then to pull him in closer. This was not the flashfire intensity of their first kiss, or the aimless languor they'd settled into as the hours had dragged on. No, this was pure intent. He would dismantle her entirely if she let him.

Distantly, it occurred to her that they should probably discuss what on *earth* they were doing sooner rather than later. What this meant, what arrangement they would have to come to, what precautions they would have to take . . . But when he angled his hips against hers, she felt just how much his desire matched her own, and the fire in her veins sparked higher. She'd been prepared to deny herself forever, but now that she had him again, she refused to take small sips of him now.

Another knock sounded on the door. They jerked apart.

"It's me," called Sinclair.

Kit radiated a murderous aura. "I'll tell him to leave."

"No!" Sinclair had warned her quite specifically about how *obvious* she and Kit were and if he caught them together like this, it would not instill any confidence. She couldn't bear his disapproval. She grabbed his wrist and looked frantically around the room for some solution. "Get in the closet."

"What?" He looked affronted. "No."

"Just do it!"

"I hear someone else in there," said Sinclair cheerfully.

She groaned. Too late, then. "Just a moment!"

Kit looked agonized and half-wild, but he huffed out a resigned breath. He gathered up his hair and tied it loosely back with a practiced ease. Just like that, he appeared aloof and unruffled again. She set to work trying to calm herself down in the meantime. Not much could be done for her reddened lips, but at least he hadn't disheveled her too much.

"All right," Sinclair called, "I'm coming in."

Niamh took another step away from Kit just as the door swung open. She did her very best not to look guilty, but she felt heat rising in her face.

Sinclair took in the scene before him. "You must be joking."

Kit let out a long, irritated sigh.

Sinclair strode toward the tea set, the tails of his coral overcoat trailing behind him. He poured himself a cup of tea, then selected a biscuit from the display. He took a bite, chewed thoughtfully, and then rounded on Kit. "Have you lost your mind?"

"Hello to you, too," Kit shot back.

Sinclair lobbed the biscuit at him. It bounced off his shoulder and crumbled to pieces on the floor. "Answer the question."

Kit glared at him as he brushed crumbs off his sleeve. "No. I haven't."

"Then what are you doing here, alone, in the middle of the day?"

Niamh laughed nervously. "I am sure this is not necessary—"

"I could ask you the same thing," Kit replied.

"Drinking tea, like a civilized person! *I'm* not engaged." Sinclair pinched the bridge of his nose and tipped his head back. "Dear God. Have either of you heard of subtlety? And you, Carmine, romance? I don't see any flowers here. It is hardly an excusable oversight, considering you can grow them any time you'd like."

Niamh groaned, burying her face in her hands.

Kit's composure finally cracked. He scowled, but his face burned red. "I have no idea what you're talking about."

"Oh, *please.* Don't insult me. The two worst liars I've ever met in my life are both standing in this room. You need my advice desperately, but on second thought, I really do not want to hear anything about the matter. I have seen enough to know what is going on here, and I am frankly scarred from it."

"Are you done?" Kit asked. Somehow, he'd gotten redder.

"I am sure there is more to be said about how ill-advised this is," Sinclair said primly. "But for now, yes."

"Great. Now leave."

"*You* leave," he countered. "I have an appointment."

They stared at each other for a few long moments before Kit surrendered. He glanced at Niamh and said lowly, "Tomorrow."

She tried not to shiver at the promise in his words. She could do nothing but nod before he retreated into the hallway. Sinclair observed their exchange from the chaise longue he'd claimed. As soon as the door fell shut behind Kit, Sinclair placed his teacup back on its saucer with a brittle *clink* and quirked a brow at her.

Well? he said without speaking at all.

"I did not mean for this to happen! It was only supposed to be one time, and then he just . . . We did not actually—" Her cheeks warmed with embarrassment. "Anyway! I suppose the particulars do not matter or interest you."

Sinclair watched her with curiosity and disgust warring on his face. "Well, now I have to know. How is he?"

"Sinclair!"

"Sorry, sorry. I know this is serious. I am only trying to cope with this very unwise thing you've both decided to do. I did try to warn you off it." He rubbed his temple. "For what it's worth, I don't think anyone knows yet. I haven't heard anything about it."

Yet. As if it were an inevitability. "How reassuring."

He seemed to be beating back the impulse to lecture her further. "I don't mean to worry you. I'm just worried *about* you. If this gets out . . ."

It would spell disaster for them both.

"I know." She sat in front of her vanity and rested her head in her hands. "I don't know what to do. Since I arrived, we've been something like friends. But I fear I have developed feelings for him that I shouldn't have."

Surprise passed over his face—and something else that looked almost like regret. "This means something to you, then?"

She nodded miserably. "I never believed he would be interested in me. Last night, I was so happy. Even though I know he cannot promise me anything, I thought I could be satisfied, knowing I had him to myself for one night. I thought I could keep my distance from him. But he is so stubborn and reckless, and he makes me feel so . . ."

Safe. Important. A thousand different things. But she could not walk any closer to that edge without falling.

Sinclair set down his teacup on the table. Gently, he said, "Come here."

Niamh approached him and settled onto the corner of the chaise longue. Without hesitation, he wrapped an arm around her shoulders and pulled her into his side. She did not offer any resistance, curling into him and resting her head against his shoulder. It felt greedy to accept comfort now of all times, but he seemed to want her near. She closed her eyes and listened to the steady beat of his heart.

"I don't think you necessarily need to do anything right now," he murmured against the top of her head, "except be careful. For the love of God. I mean it this time."

"Right." She smiled ruefully. "Careful."

"I don't want you to get hurt, Niamh. Even if you keep this quiet, it's not an easy road ahead of you. Unless you'd be content as his mistress, you're going to get your heart broken."

She frowned. "His mistress?"

"It wouldn't be a terrible life," he said lightly. "It's quite common for married noblemen to keep a lover. Most in polite society won't associate with you, but you'd have an allowance and your own home. And if you have any children, royal bastards have a better life than most."

Would it be so bad? If Kit brought her family here, it would be a peaceful existence—on paper, everything she dreamed of. And yet, *mistress* was a kind word for what Sinclair had described. It would not be what Gran or the crowds in Eye Park called her.

FraochÚn, at best. *Fealltóir,* at worst.

She didn't know if she could endure that kind of scorn. If she worked hard to bring her family here, they could learn to bear living among their enemies. But if it was because of an Avlishman's charity—a Carmine, no less . . . "My family would be ashamed of me."

"Because of his title?" When she nodded, Sinclair hummed, seemingly lost in thought. "My father was Machlish. The one responsible for my existence, I mean."

She put some distance between them so she could meet his gaze. "Really?"

"Yes. I suspect that's why His Grace hates me so much. I was a bitter reminder that his wife debased herself with a lesser being." He rolled his eyes, but true anger and hurt roiled beneath the surface. "I believe my father was one of his employees, at that. The duke runs a very profitable shipping company. The prince regent himself is an investor."

She searched his face, as though she could find something new in his features. "Why did you not tell me before?"

"I should have, but it never felt right to bring up. I didn't want to presume any connection with you I had no right to claim."

"Of course you do."

"Thank you." He took one of her hands and squeezed it. "What I'm saying is . . . To a certain extent, I understand having complicated feelings about this place and these people. But I also understand more than most that family is what you make it—and so is home. You have to choose your own happiness, whatever that looks like. You can't live your life for other people."

"I suppose not." And yet, that was all she'd ever known. She did not know how to stop, but perhaps she could try. "Thank you for not judging me harshly. You're a good friend, Sinclair."

Stupidly loyal, exactly as Kit had said.

He smiled, but whatever memories he'd dredged up still lingered. Right now, he looked so terribly sad. He tucked the strand of white hair behind her ear. "I do try."

18

The next afternoon, Niamh finished the first piece of Rosa's bridal ensemble: a black veil, trimmed all in black lace. The fibers were woven in the shapes of roses: a tribute to both her namesake and the Carmine insignia. It'd taken Niamh days—and likely years of her life—to create the pattern. It was the most intricate thing she had ever made, and she couldn't deny the swell of pride within her when she looked at it. She'd never imagined she would be patient enough to apply herself to something as time-consuming and laborious as lacemaking. She wrapped it in fine paper and packed it in a box. She was ready to show Rosa.

Well, mostly ready.

Rosa had told her she did not care for Kit—did not even want to marry him, save for duty's sake. Still, Niamh prayed her face did not give away what she'd done.

Once she chose a walking dress, Niamh made for the city on foot. Fewer people than usual milled on the streets, but the distant sound of a gathered crowd drowned out the noise of their chatter. Uniformed members of the Kings Guard patrolled the blocks nearest the park on horseback, their hands loosely resting on the pommels of their sabers. She accidentally made eye contact with one of them and nearly stumbled over herself in her haste to move on. All of Sootham seemed to be holding its breath, as if waiting for a storm to pass.

Jack, for his part, had apparently not left his quarters since they'd returned to Sootham three days ago. Niamh couldn't help feeling . . . Well, she wasn't sure what else to call it but disappointment.

When she arrived at the cozy townhouse on Bard Row, the housekeeper greeted her and ushered her into the princess's chambers. Rosa was lazing on her favorite chaise longue like a well-fed cat, the one tucked under the sunniest window in the room. She looked as though she'd just awoken from a nap, her loose curls flattened on one side. The casual intimacy of her dishevelment struck Niamh somewhere unprotected.

Rosa trusted her.

Niamh was learning that her heart was just as treasonous as the rest of her body.

"I see you are still not feeling your best," Rosa said with a stifled yawn. "What a drawn look you have. I shall send for coffee."

Niamh forced herself to smile. "I'll be fine, Your Highness. Shall I show you what I've made?"

She lifted the veil from its box and set to work pinning it on. Rosa's hair slid like silk through her fingers, and Niamh did her best to twist the frizzed sections back into shape as she went. When she slid the last pin into place, she showed Rosa to the mirror.

Niamh fussed with the fabric, letting it fan out behind her. The edges were delicately scalloped, like waves rolling in against the shore. Niamh clasped her hands together underneath her chin and drank in the sight of her. Rosa looked like a vision: mysterious, alluring, and tantalizingly out of reach.

Anxiously, Niamh asked, "What do you think?"

Rosa stood before her reflection, shrouded in black lace. A very tentative smile played on her lips. "I think you've outdone yourself."

Niamh couldn't help it. She rose onto her toes, feeling as though she could take flight with joy. "Thank you!"

"Saints," Rosa muttered. "That was loud."

"Sorry!"

"What on earth is going on in here?" The door to the adjoining suite swung open, and Miriam appeared. She froze where she stood, her lips slowly parting. "Oh! Rosa, you look absolutely stunning."

Rosa's entire demeanor changed at the compliment, and a light went out within her. She resumed her usual slouch, and her voice flattened. "We were just finishing up here. Shall we go and watch clouds?"

Miriam made a face. "I have sat idle far too much today. Why don't we go shopping? If you are on your very best behavior, perhaps we can go to the palace, and I will ask someone to row us out to the center of the lake."

Rosa's eyes rekindled with interest. Niamh hurriedly began removing the pins from Rosa's hair. When she succeeded in freeing the veil from her curls, she folded it carefully back into its box. "Have fun! I should go home and finish some work."

Rosa clucked her tongue disapprovingly. "Give yourself a moment of respite. I mean no offense, but you look like you need one."

"Yes! You should join us," Miriam agreed warmly. "It is far too lovely a day to spend it inside."

"While the point stands, I must disagree with your assessment," Rosa said gravely. "It is far too bright to be *lovely.*"

"How did you turn out this way?" Miriam asked despairingly. "Castilia is always sunny."

"That is why I am moving here." She gestured vaguely at her closet. "Borrow one of my umbrellas if you'd like, Miss O'Connor. You'll burn to a crisp in this weather."

That was how Niamh found herself walking the streets of Sootham with three of Rosa's shopping bags around her arm and a black parasol in hand. While it blocked out the sun, it did little for the heat. Her gown clung uncomfortably to her skin, and sweat dripped down the back of her neck.

Miriam and Rosa walked arm in arm beside her, peering through the shop windows and chattering in an effortless mix of Castilian, Avlish, and a third language Niamh did not at all recognize. She laughed softly to herself. Out here, away from the eyes of the royal family, they bickered like young girls, utterly carefree.

When Rosa declared that she'd "surfeited on sunlight," they stopped at an ice shop in the square. The confectioner—who immediately recognized Rosa—foisted three orange-dyed ices on them, each one molded into the shape of a perfect sphere. They even had a sprig of mint and a shaved-chocolate stem affixed to the top.

"How quaint," said Rosa, in her bland, understated way. However, her dark eyes sparkled with genuine delight. "It tastes like home."

What a bright and happy home it must have been: citrus and sweet cream, chocolate and the barest hint of rum. Niamh sighed in contentment. For a few minutes, only the burbling of the fountain filled the companionate silence between them.

But then the stares began.

Then the tittering.

People walked by with *The Daily Chronicle* tucked under their arms, others with their noses buried in it. Niamh's stomach coiled tight with dread. Over the roaring of her heart, she caught only fragments of conversation.

". . . the two of them together . . ."

". . . the gall of it . . ."

"Do you think she knows?"

One woman stared at them for so long, she nearly tumbled headlong into the fountain.

Rosa let out a frustrated little sigh and patted her lips primly with a napkin. "I trust there is nothing on my face. Do I want to know what this is about?"

"Umm . . ." Niamh and Miriam said in unison.

"Great," Rosa drawled. "I do love surprises."

"Whatever they have written today," Niamh blurted out, "I swear to you, it isn't true."

Miriam grimaced. Admittedly, she could have handled that better.

Rosa did not look impressed. "What have you two kept from me?"

Miriam seized Rosa's hand across the table. "Perhaps we should head back and discuss this at home. Or perhaps we should forget it entirely. You know how the Avlish are about their gossip."

Rosa calmly extricated herself from Miriam's grasp and rose from the table, a shadow unfurling against the brightness of the square. She moved with purpose toward the nearest paperboy, who almost fled at the sight of her. A flash of coins in the sunlight, and the column was in her hands. Niamh fought the urge to flee herself—or perhaps to grab it from her hands and pitch it into the fountain.

Rosa returned and dropped into her seat in a spill of black fabric. Miriam tried to snatch it away a few times before Rosa swatted her with it. She scanned the Lovelace column, then relinquished it to Niamh. Her expression did not change. "I don't understand the

Avlish's fascination with this nonsense. They think they are so coy and cutting. But the only insult here is that I would be angered by something as trivial as this."

While I am not one to report on society gossip, I did hear an interesting account from a Certain Someone's bucolic retreat. It seems there is turmoil brewing among a Most Illustrious Family. While I have not ferreted out the reason behind the brothers' quarrel just yet, what intrigues me is the aftermath. When our Wayward Son stormed off, a woman snuck off after him into the woods. I have to wonder now if those rumors from the inaugural ball were indeed true, and that this is the same woman Lady E reported seeing with him on the balcony. What a scandal, to dally with a man like WS in such unseemly places. I'd owe Lady E an apology, but then, I would need to overlook the embezzlement incident from two years ago. Alas, I cannot.

Forgive me this one petty indulgence. One has to maintain a sense of humor in this complete and utter madness. I confess, I cannot help wondering what this portends. I will be watching the situation with Lady R and her father closely. If the engagement is broken, perhaps it will be a blessing. God knows a Certain Someone could afford to focus less on parties and more on what is unfolding just underneath his nose.

Niamh knew it was ridiculous to feel betrayed by someone she'd never met—a gossip columnist at that. Yet seeing herself written about so flippantly, almost mockingly, by someone who purported to care about people like her . . . It stung. But that pain paled in comparison to the violation of what she'd held so dear. The precious, tiny flame of that memory in her hands went as cold as ashes. Even this one moment of joy had been taken from her. Perhaps she was a fool to believe it'd ever been hers at all.

But right now, she had more pressing matters to deal with.

"Infanta Rosa, I am *so* sorry, I—"

"Why are you sorry?" she asked. "Someone had to comfort him. Far better you than me."

It shocked her. There was not a hint of anger in her voice, nor jealousy. Rosa watched her with the same, flat look in her dark eyes. *Rosa is quite an understanding person,* Miriam had told her. But Niamh hadn't expected that meant she would not even bat an eyelash.

"You're not angry with me?"

"No." Rosa smoothed her hands over her skirts. "It is too much effort to be angry over every little thing. Besides, you two seem to be friends. I will be his wife, not his whole world."

"Thank you."

Tears stung at the back of her throat. Rosa's compassion, as understated as it was, moved her. But she didn't deserve it. She felt hot all over with humiliation—with anger, not only at Lovelace but with herself. She'd been naive to believe she'd gotten away with it. Jack would doubtless make the connection sooner rather than later. If he took it seriously, it could jeopardize her job. And Kit . . . After everything he'd told her about his past, how could she be so careless as to embroil him in another scandal?

She'd done nothing but hurt everyone around her.

Before she could well and truly spiral, Rosa said, "Miriam, will you send for the carriage? I suddenly have found myself quite exhausted."

"Why can't you do it?" Miriam protested. Niamh couldn't see Rosa's face from this angle, but the two girls seemed to confer with nothing but their eyes. Miriam plastered on a smile. "Of course. I'll be just a moment."

As soon as they were alone, Rosa turned to her. "So. Shall we speak candidly?"

Niamh's stomach bottomed out. How foolish she was, to think

anyone could be so merciful. "Your Highness, I swear to you, nothing happened—"

"Do not lie to me."

"I'm sorry," Niamh whispered. "I do not know what came over me. I—"

Rosa's hand rested softly on her knee. "Don't apologize for that."

Niamh snapped her gaze to Rosa's. Her weary face blurred behind Niamh's damp eyelashes.

"Once we are married," Rosa continued, "I don't particularly care what you do. If you choose to pursue whatever this is between you, then you have my blessing. If he buys you a townhouse right next to Sinclair's and does not come home most nights, I will look the other way."

They couldn't possibly be having this conversation. Niamh would not complain if the ground swallowed her up and spat her back out in the sea. "I . . . I could not do such a thing to you."

"You are a sweet girl." Rosa leaned back in her chair. "However, I've told you before that this is not about love. It is nothing but a very complicated game, one I intend to win. I have played it out in my mind a thousand times. But you have proven to be a most unexpected obstacle."

"What do you mean?"

"Lovelace has the right of it. My father is a conservative man. He already thinks the prince regent is an incompetent buffoon. If he feels I am being mistreated or made a fool of, he will renege on his agreement. It will not take much to jeopardize this union. Nor will it take much to remove you from the board entirely." Rosa didn't say it unkindly, but the threat in her words was plain. "I say this as a friend. Tread carefully. It is not only the column you need to worry about. The whole country is watching us. A war on two fronts is not something one should fight alone."

She knew that well now. Niamh couldn't escape her nature. She was silly and naive and scatterbrained. She'd never stood a chance against the nobility, and she never would. Ever since she arrived in Avaland, she'd been caught in the tempest of these nobles' whims. But while Rosa might have imagined a thousand outcomes of this Season, Niamh's end had always been a foregone conclusion: she could never come away unscathed.

She nodded, not trusting herself to speak.

"There are no hard feelings between us," Rosa said. "But I don't want to see you in that column again. Do what you must to ensure that."

"I understand."

"Good." Rosa tipped her face toward the sky, and some of the tension eased from her shoulders. The clouds skated overhead; the soft wisps of white spread like the wings of a dove. "There is Miriam with the curricle now."

When Niamh climbed in, she nearly sank to the floor and wept. Until today, she'd never realized that shame was a solid thing. It sat as heavy as stones in her pockets.

19

Foolishly incautious or not, Niamh couldn't wait another moment to speak to Kit, and she knew exactly where to find him.

Once Rosa and Miriam dropped her off, she circled around the back of the palace and set off determinedly toward the hothouse. But when she rounded the corner, her heart tripped over itself. Kit was emerging from the woods, his shoulders draped in the spill of late-afternoon sunlight. He was golden and flushed, the very picture of summer. They each stopped dead at the sight of the other. Anticipation coursed through her, and her toes curled in her slippers as she approached him.

"We need to talk," she said.

His gaze darted to the palace windows overlooking the back lawn. "Not here. Walk with me."

She fell into step beside him as he led her deeper into the gardens. As soon as the flowering shrubs rose high enough to shroud them, he offered his arm to her.

Niamh stared at it for a moment. "So you *do* know how to be a gentleman."

"In theory," he replied dryly. "If only so you don't keel over again."

He doesn't know about the column. How selfish could she be, to steal yet another moment? She tucked her hand into the crook of his elbow.

A hedge maze loomed above them. When he guided her inside, she breathed its sweet, delicate scent. *Jasmine.* The entirety of the labyrinth was jasmine. The loose white gravel of the path crunched underfoot as they walked, and with every corner they turned, the walls seemed to rearrange themselves. Neither of them spoke until they reached the center, where a gazebo kept its lonely watch. Vines twined up its marble columns and knotted into the lattice of its cupola.

Here, they were completely alone: no prying eyes, no one listening.

It should've flustered her, or perhaps thrilled her, how within reach all of her smallest, most breathless desires were. He'd forgone a cravat—curse him—allowing her a glimpse of his collarbone. She wanted to hold herself steady against his elbows and tip her face up to his. She wanted to feel his heart beat against her cheek when she embraced him. She wanted to pull him down into the grass beside her. To tuck flowers into his hair, to talk until the sun set, to laugh at how easy it was to fluster him now that she knew exactly how to do it. The way he looked right now, his eyes wary and hopeful, she knew he would let her indulge each and every one of them. Lovelace had ruined everything. The sheer injustice of it made her so angry, she almost began to cry.

"What is it?" Kit pressed, concern bleeding into his tone. "You look sad."

"Have you read Lovelace's column today?"

He tilted his head at her. "Lovelace? I didn't think anyone read that drivel except for my brother."

"This is serious, Kit. Someone saw us."

"What?" For the first time, he looked alarmed. "When?"

"They saw me follow you at Woodville Hall. It was quite vague. And now Rosa knows! She is not upset with us. Well, she *is* upset that her father may discover the truth of what has happened, but . . ."

He didn't seem to hear her at all. He retrieved his pipe from his breast pocket and placed it into the corner of his mouth.

Worry washed away all of her fears. "Kit?"

"I'm fine. Don't bother asking." But he opened his vesta case with trembling hands. After a few clumsy strikes of the match, the flame flickered to life with a low hiss.

"You don't have to lie to me," she said gently. "I understand that you—"

"Stop doing that."

The harshness of his tone stung. She took a reflexive step backward. "Doing what?"

"*That.*" He huffed. "Do you even realize you're doing it? The moment you see the opportunity to comfort someone else, you leap at it. You're trying to be helpful to avoid your own feelings."

"Don't be unkind," she whispered.

"This *is* kindness. I'm not interested in helping you hurt yourself." He took a drag from his pipe. When he exhaled, his magic flowed out of him, too. All around them, the jasmine petals withered. They dropped off the vine and scattered on the ground like dirtied snow. The cloying scent of rot bloomed around them. "Go find someone else to fuss over."

Was that what she was doing? Yes, she would sooner speak to someone else about their problems for hours than sit with her own feelings for a moment longer than she must. The instinct to comfort and soothe had been ingrained in her so deeply, she snapped to it immediately when she saw even a hint of distress. But with Kit, it was different. She cared for him enough to *want* to share his burdens, and right now, his biggest problem was hers, too. But Kit wounded was Kit aggressive. She would not let him get away with it today.

"Do not think I cannot see what you're doing! You are trying to push me away because you would rather be alone than hurt." She'd drawn blood. She could see it in the startled flicker of panic across his face. But the truth came to her with startling clarity. She remembered him, a drenched, pathetic heap inside his cage of thorns. *All I do is ruin the lives of everyone around me.* If he wished to deal in cruel kindnesses today, so be it. "But that is not the whole of it, is it? You would rather be alone than hurt anyone else."

Smoke flowed out of his nostrils. He said nothing, but his eyes burned with furious vulnerability behind the haze.

"You will not get rid of me so easily, unless that's what you really want." Tentatively, she crossed the space between them. "What do you want?"

"What do I *want*?" he asked incredulously. "What a ridiculous question."

"Is it?"

"It doesn't matter what I want." He turned away from her. It was like he'd slammed a door shut between them and twisted the key in its lock. "You were right. It's a bad idea for us to be around each other right now. It's too distracting."

She clutched her collar, just above her heart. "Distracting?"

"You know what I mean," he gritted out. "We can talk when all of this is over."

"Over?" Anger rushed through her. The wedding was only a

week away now, but anything could happen. "You mean when you are married? Lovelace has all but declared their delight at the prospect of your wedding falling through, and I imagine they will soon have enough information to orchestrate it! We have been too careless. Do you intend to follow your brother's example? To ignore your problems until they grow big enough to crush you?"

"And what will you have me do, Niamh?" He said her name so rarely, the sound of it growled in frustration sent a jolt through her. "You're entirely vulnerable. I won't be your ruin."

Niamh sucked in a breath at the intensity crackling off him.

"Both you and Sinclair are depending on me going through with this," he continued. "I can't give Lovelace anything else to work with. My behavior will be under scrutiny now more than ever, as will yours. For now, I have no choice but to fall in line."

She dropped her gaze to her feet. It felt like he'd punched something out of her. Shame settled into the space his words left behind. "I don't want you to be unhappy for my sake."

"It's for duty's sake, too. Ever since that day in the park, I . . ." He hesitated. "All those people sounded just like you."

"Like *me*?"

"You've made me see what I hadn't before. How can I claim to care for you if I don't care about what you've suffered?" he said quietly. "The Machlish deserve better, and Jack won't give it to you. He needs someone who isn't afraid to challenge him, someone who will hold him accountable. I don't want to get married. I've never wanted anything to do with my title. But I am going to do it anyway, because it's the right thing to do."

"Oh." Niamh's heart squeezed. Never in her life had she wished less to have instilled such noble sentiments in someone. She offered him a wobbly smile. "That is very admirable."

For the first time since she'd met him, he seemed almost a true prince—or at least, one from her fairy-tale imaginings, virtuous and determined. It suited him, this righteous fire in his amber eyes.

She could imagine his portrait hanging in the enfilade of Wood-ville Hall now.

"And what about us?" she asked quietly.

He stared at her, baffled, as if it were self-evident, but he spoke almost reverently. "I'll take care of you."

She knew he would, him and that protective streak of his. The idea of a life under his protection shimmered like a dream. A beau-tiful house, his devotion, comfort and safety for her family. He would give her anything she needed. But she would always be his weakness—another thing to worry about, another thing for the court to exploit.

She couldn't do it.

She couldn't endure the thought of him leaving her cold and alone every night, of watching him raise Rosa's children from afar, of never again selling another dress due to her tarnished reputation. She couldn't waste away in a townhouse, no matter how beautiful or how close to Sinclair's it was. Niamh did not do things by halves. She couldn't settle for half his life.

If she could not have him, then she would ensure that his wed-ding went off without a hitch. Which meant she had to stop Love-lace from sabotaging it. The question, of course, was how.

"Stay out of trouble until the wedding—and don't overextend yourself." Niamh jumped at the sound of his voice. It was as though he'd sensed the turn of her thoughts. "As hard as that will be for you."

Mutiny flared within her. She jabbed a finger at him. "You are not *my* prince. You cannot command me to do anything."

"And it would be a fool's errand to try," he said, with a flash of irritation. His hand closed over her wrist, then lowered it between them. "I'm asking you."

"Then ask nicely."

His gaze snapped to hers. He did not let go of her. Her pulse thrummed wildly against his grip, her stomach fluttering with anticipation. They stood close enough that his breath ghosted softly against her mouth. The faintest band of dirt streaked his cheekbone, and she had half a mind to swipe it away with her thumb, to let it drift down to his slowly parting lips. Desire welled within her. It darkened his eyes.

Gods. She'd never stood a chance against him.

He dropped her hand as if she had burned him, leaving her bereft. The wind sent the loose jasmine petals eddying around her feet. With a quick shake of his head, he gathered up all that new-found restraint and brushed past her with his shoulders drawn toward his ears.

Weeks ago, Lovelace had told her how to reach them. Even if they did not care about her, they cared about the good of the Machlish. Kit was sympathetic to their cause. If they knew, they'd leave him alone. How much trouble could writing a letter really cause?

In a letter tied off with delicate red thread, Niamh assured Lovelace that after the wedding, Kit would pressure Jack to do right by the Machlish—that he'd even spoken to Helen Carlile. As hard as she'd tried to contain it, some of her resentment bled into the message: *You have allies in us, if you will allow us to be.*

The reply, to her shock, arrived early the next morning. Someone slid it menacingly under her bedroom door without a knock to announce it:

> *I understand you are upset about what I have done, but I assure you, it is not personal. Surely, you can understand a small wrong for the sake of the greater good. It is clear to me now that the prince regent will ignore the political situation as long as this ridiculous show goes on. If this wedding falls through,*

he will not have anything left to hide behind. I intend to push onward. However, if you find anything of substance to change my mind—or if Prince Christopher suddenly has both the political clout and a plan to address the protesters' concerns— you're welcome to tell me.

It took nearly all of her strength not to hurl the note into the fireplace where it belonged. Oh, how she hated them and their self-righteousness right now. She flopped into an armchair to sew and to think. As darkness cut across the sky, her eyes adjusted slowly. But soon, just outside her window, the night was practically luminous. The moon overhead silvered the lawn with its light.

She imagined the day of the lawn party over and over again. The Carmines' argument had not exactly been subtle. They'd turned the croquet field into a veritable garden of their repressed feelings. Most of the guests had gone inside once the rain began, but anyone could have seen her follow Kit. Before the column dropped, the only ones who'd mentioned any untoward feelings between her and Kit were Sinclair and Miriam. But Sinclair said it was obvious. No doubt someone else had suspected them.

You have a way with people, Sofia had told her once. *You have a way of drawing things out of them, of bringing what they wish to keep hidden into the light.*

What a kind lie that had been.

Wait. *Sofia.*

Dread crept slowly down Niamh's spine. In her time at the palace, she'd seen all of the small insults Sofia endured from a court who had no interest in her. How she was absentmindedly silenced and dismissed by her husband. How she faded into the corners of a room, like the last bite of winter chased away by spring. How she stood on her balcony, longing for her homeland . . .

It was enough to breed hatred. It was enough to make one sympathize with an overlooked and silenced class of people. It was certainly enough to make her want to protect another lonely, foreign girl from the same fate she'd suffered. And in their first correspondence, Lovelace had complained that Jack rooted out their spies—just as Sofia confessed that Jack kept dismissing her lady's maids.

Could it really be . . . ?

If she unmasked Sofia as Lovelace, then she could stop her from sabotaging the wedding. But no one would accept that argument. She'd be hanged for treason for even suggesting it. Unless, of course, she could prove it. All she needed were the right opportunity, the right tools, and the right ally.

And she had just the person in mind.

20

*N*iamh eased open the glass door overlooking the terrace, and the lazy, drugging heat of the afternoon washed over her skin like a balm.

She hadn't left her bedchamber in two days, since her conversation with Kit. If someone asked her a single question, she feared that the truth of what she planned to do would come tumbling out. Instead, she'd sat by the window and eased her magic out little by little, spinning it into skeins of golden thread. She'd sewed and sewed until her joints swelled and her hands went stiff. Even if it killed her, she *would* finish Rosa's dress and Kit's cloak before the wedding. She would make sure everyone was as happy as they could be with the sad compromises they'd made.

Miriam waited for her outside, an uncertain smile on her face.

As always, she was a vision. The midday sunlight stained the lawn gold and set the dark red in her curls ablaze. It sparkled off the golden rings on each of her fingers. When Niamh stopped before her, all of her thoughts hopelessly knotted, Miriam did not hesitate. She enfolded her in a hug. The unreserved tenderness of it shocked Niamh. Her world went indistinct, a blur of light and color, as tears spring to her eyes.

"Thank you for coming," she said hoarsely.

"I did say we would stick together this Season." Her voice was quiet against Niamh's ear. "Are you all right? Has someone given you any difficulty?"

Niamh must have been far more overwhelmed than she'd let herself acknowledge. Held close and held together by someone else, all of her feelings came spilling out in a rush. Her shoulders trembled, and tears spilled over her cheeks. Miriam did not recoil. She allowed Niamh to weep in her arms, making soft, sympathetic sounds. She hadn't felt like this since she was a child, which only made her cry harder.

After a minute, once her hiccupping sobs slowed, Miriam drew back with a kind smile. "Why don't we go for a stroll? That always helps me clear my head."

Niamh nodded as she wiped her face with the back of her wrist. Together, they set off down the path through the gardens, arm in arm. Niamh half expected to see Jack here. Every now and again, she'd caught a glimpse of him patrolling outside her window, inspecting every bloom and snipping off those that apparently did not meet his standards. All of the flowers now bristled with his magic, their petals veined in gold and all of them arranged in perfect symmetry like a battalion of soldiers. He was coping with the stress in his own way, she supposed.

"How is Rosa?" Niamh asked.

"Oh, the same as always." Miriam sighed. "She and the prince regent have been talking her father down. I think they've finally convinced him it was nothing but a cruel, false rumor. It sounds like His Highness has convinced *himself* of it as well."

"I'm so glad to hear that."

"And you? What do you plan to do now?"

"I confess," Niamh said, before she could lose her nerve, "that is what I asked you here to discuss. I need your counsel."

"Oh!" Miriam's eyes went round. "Well, I can assure you that what Rosa told you is the truth. She would not object to such an arrangement, not that any wife truly can—"

"Not that." Niamh flushed. "I think I know who Lovelace is."

"You do?" Her fingers tightened on Niamh's arm. "Who?"

"Princess Sofia."

"*What?*" Miriam dragged her into a shadowed curve in the garden path. The sunflowers seemed to lean in conspiratorially.

Miriam listened silently but with increasing alarm as Niamh explained her reasoning. When she finished, the mothering disapproval in Miriam's eyes was almost enough to make her wither on the spot. Niamh buried her face in her hands.

"Oh, Niamh," groaned Miriam. "What have you stumbled into? This is a complete and utter mess, not to mention *treasonous.*"

"I know." Her words were muffled by her palms.

She sighed fretfully. "Why have you come to me with this? I am happy to listen, of course, but . . ."

"I am sorry to burden you with it. I didn't know who else to turn to." She took Miriam's hands in her own. Sinclair had already counseled her against making more trouble for herself, and he had his own history with the column. "If you want to pretend we didn't have this conversation, I understand completely. However, I know you care about Infanta Rosa's happiness as much as I do about Kit's."

Miriam looked startled to hear her say it. Her face drained of color. "I . . . Yes. I do." She recovered quickly enough, tucking a loose curl behind her ear. "Rosa is determined to go through with this; Castilia is in sore need of allies. However, I fear Lovelace may be right. I have been worrying about the prince regent's intentions myself. During the negotiations with the king, His Highness was quite insistent on Rosa's dowry."

Niamh frowned. "Why?"

"I don't know. It isn't unusual to want to talk money, of course, but apparently it was quite uncouth. And I have heard some rumors about him. Nothing substantiated, of course, but . . ."

"Jack isn't paying his staff," Niamh said grimly.

"Yes." Miriam steepled her fingers together at her lips as she thought. It was such a quintessentially Rosa gesture, Niamh almost smiled. "I wonder if it is intentional, or if he is distracted."

"No matter the reason for his behavior of late, if it comes out, it will be disastrous. The king will call off the engagement."

"Certainly he will. He has threatened to at least twice already." Miriam settled onto the lip of a granite urn. "But what can we do? You cannot baselessly accuse the princess of being a radical or, God forbid, inciting sedition against her own husband."

"There must be proof! Surely, there will be something in Sofia's chambers. A wax seal, a letter with matching handwriting, *anything*."

Miriam's brows shot up. "And how do you propose to break into the royal quarters to find it?"

The skepticism in her voice was not appreciated. Niamh scowled. "I can be very stealthy."

Miriam gave her a pitying look. It said, *Not even the gods can help you.* But she did Niamh the small mercy of keeping her thoughts to herself. Very diplomatically, she said, "You only have one chance to do this before they catch on. If you're caught, you will be dismissed or worse."

"I have to try."

"Why?" Miriam asked. "You are wading into a pool you can't

see the bottom of, Niamh. You are talented and charming, and everyone has seen how wondrous your creations are already. There will be other opportunities for you to make a name for yourself as a tailor, even if you walk away now. Neither Avaland's nor Castilia's problems are yours. Is it truly worth it?"

Perhaps not. But the Machlish's were. She couldn't turn her back on what she'd seen, knowing all the suffering she would leave behind her. She couldn't go back home to that cottage with its broken window, working away her life, watching her family wither along with the plants in the earth, mourning as more and more people left every day. There was nothing left for her there.

She'd hardly lived at all before she arrived in Sootham—until she met people like Sinclair and Miriam and Kit. Whether she was as foolish as Miriam believed or as self-destructive as Kit accused her of being, it did not matter anymore. Even if she could not truly be with him, Kit Carmine was still hers, and he deserved protection, too.

He would not be rid of her so easily.

Niamh met her eyes steadily. "It's worth it to me."

"I see there's no convincing you, then. But I suppose I understand. There is a way the prince looks at you when he thinks no one is watching." The dreaminess in her voice faded as mischief sparked in her eyes. "Yes, he has a certain *intensity* about him that I imagine could be appealing in certain circumstances."

Niamh nearly choked. She swatted her arm. "Miriam!"

Their laughter dissolved into the warm summer air. They sat side by side on the warmed stone of the urn, the heat of the sun against their backs. Somewhere in the distance, Niamh heard the faint cry of a mourning dove. She wished that she could stay like this forever, here in contented silence.

Miriam angled herself to face Niamh, wearing a serious, calculating expression she must have also picked up from Rosa. On her, it looked almost devious. "I suppose you need my help, then. Do you have any ideas?"

"I don't— Oh. Wait a minute." A plan came to her, slowly but surely. There *was* something that would make sneaking into the royal quarters much easier.

Miriam made a face that suggested she very much regretted asking. "What is it?"

"Oh, nothing," Niamh said brightly. "Do you happen to know where Kit's room is?"

In the darkest stretch of the night, the house was finally quiet. No servants bustled in the hallways or moved unseen in their secret passages. No guests lingered in the parlor, no pianoforte music drifted from the drawing room. The only sound was the soft plod of Niamh's and Miriam's slippered feet on the floorboards. Candlelight whispered against the walls and bobbed softly in the gloom, borne aloft on Miriam's lantern.

"For the record," Miriam said, "this is a very, very bad idea, and you are going to get the both of us thrown in jail."

"Don't be so paranoid," Niamh said with a wave of her hand. "I'll be in and out in a second. I just need to borrow his coat for the evening."

"Steal his coat," Miriam amended.

"Is it really stealing? I did make it for him. It is more like a gift I am taking back."

Miriam rolled her eyes heavenward but decided, apparently, that it was an argument not worth having. In all fairness, this was perhaps the worst idea Niamh had ever had, but she didn't exactly see any better options. She owed Miriam all the remaining years of her life—and perhaps her firstborn child—for very reluctantly agreeing to keep watch. If anyone caught her sneaking out of Kit's bedchamber in the dead of night, there would be no stemming the tide of those rumors.

They stopped in front of a door, the ridges of the panels outlined in gold and decorated with delicately illustrated vines. In the candlelight, the paint seemed to glow and crackle. Drawing in her breath, Niamh curled her fingers around the handle. With a *creeeeeak* that seemed to echo through the entire house, the latch popped open. Even in the gloom, Niamh could see Miriam's dark eyes gleaming with horror. It was all far less encouraging than she would've preferred.

She shimmied through the door and welcomed a sudden rush of giddiness. She'd never done anything so daring before.

But the sweet thrill of rebellion did not last long. Inside, the dark hung as thick as a curtain. She blinked against it, waiting for her eyes to adjust. When the room finally came into focus, Niamh found herself surprised. It looked nothing at all like she'd expected. It was oddly impersonal, like a guest room—as though no one lived here at all. No paintings. No personal effects. No mess. The only thing that caught her eye was the wallpaper, patterned with daisies and violets. It was lovely, but its loveliness bothered her. It was all delicate, soft, and beautiful: a shrine to a boy who'd left four years ago—one who perhaps never existed at all. Sinclair insisted he'd been a sensitive child, but she couldn't envision Kit Carmine ever being as sweet as new growth. He was of hardier stock: a weed growing through cracks in the pavement out of sheer spite.

At last, her gaze landed on the bed—exactly what she'd tried *not* to notice. Kit slumbered in a pool of moonlight. The shadows of the leaves outside his window cast dappled patterns across his face. His hair fell across his pillow like a spill of dark water. Even in sleep, he did not look peaceful. And now, his beauty was made crueler because she couldn't look closely. It would cut her if she lingered.

She shut the door behind her. It hardly made a sound as it settled into its frame. Now, all she had to do was find where he'd stowed the coat she'd enchanted with invisibility. She made her way toward the wardrobe—and promptly banged her toe against the base of it.

Pain tore through her entire body, and her eyes watered reflexively. She bit down on the whimper that threatened to escape, then darted her gaze back over to Kit. He stirred, his brow furrowing. It occurred to her then that she had not prepared any sort of excuse, should he awaken and find her here. Perversely, she wanted to know what he would do. She could all too easily imagine that hair-trigger blush of his and the furious accusation in his eyes. The way it would all melt away, and he would say something horribly unromantic but undeniably compelling, like *Come here.*

Focus, she reminded herself sharply.

Niamh opened the doors to the wardrobe. She sorted through the shirts and jackets, her breath catching at every metallic grind of the hangers against the valet pole. When she reached the end of the rack, her heart sank. It wasn't here. Could he have gotten rid of it already? But when she turned on her heel, she saw it. There, in the corner, draped over the back of his writing desk's chair. Moonlight danced on the enchantments laced into the embroidery, beckoning her closer. It would've felt like a victory if it weren't an arm's length away from his bed. Her entire face burned. Well, there was nothing to be done for it now. She had come this far already.

Niamh held her breath and crept closer. Every creak of the floorboards rang out as loud as musket fire. Carefully, she gathered the coat into her arms and hugged it to her chest. The fabric was cool and soft against her skin, and she felt the magic—the hope—shimmering within it. It felt like a different girl entirely had made this coat, one who still believed Kit to be mean and immovable.

She dared to glance at Kit again. A panel of moonlight traced his features in silver. This, she thought, was the closest she would ever be to him again. She'd never again hear the pleasant rasp of his voice or feel the brunt of his irritation directed at her. One day, maybe, she would forget what it was like to feel cared for and protected by him. She wanted to wake him now, to commit him to memory anew. But she'd tormented herself enough tonight.

"Goodbye," she murmured.

His eyes cracked open. Niamh held back a squeak of surprise.

"Niamh?" Kit's eyes were bleary, and his voice was rough with sleep. "Am I dreaming?"

"Yes," she agreed readily. "You're dreaming."

"Come here." He still sounded half-asleep, but the princely iron behind those words made her snap to attention.

What was she supposed to do now? If she fled, he'd almost certainly come to—and realize she'd broken into his room like some kind of common thief. The only thing she could do was pray he fell asleep again and forget this encounter entirely come morning. Slowly, she draped the jacket over her shoulders like a cape and sat on the edge of his bed. The mattress dipped beneath her weight.

He rolled toward her and mumbled, "I've missed you."

Her heart fluttered. Gods, she was so weak.

But when she looked down, his eyes had closed. Slowly, his breathing evened out. A pang of disappointment dropped into her gut, although she didn't know what she was expecting. With that, she rose and closed the door on what they might have had.

21

*W*ith only four days left until the wedding, the final event on Jack's social calendar presented Niamh with the perfect opportunity.

It was an intimate gathering tonight, with only the wedding party and the couple's families in attendance. From her bedroom window, Niamh watched the Carrillos arrive. They filed out of a line of carriages, one by one. There were considerably more of them than Niamh had anticipated. Rosa, apparently, had eleven brothers. They ran the gamut in age: the oldest of the infantes were in their thirties, while the younger ones were still children. She caught only a glimpse of the king and queen before an army of servants—and Jack himself—overtook them and led them inside.

When it was time to leave, Niamh tucked Lovelace's last letter into the pocket of Kit's coat, then pulled it over her shoulders. Its

weight comforted her—and warmed her, with her magic lingering in the threads. She closed her eyes and breathed deeply as the
enchantment washed over her. It was always the same. Emotion
bubbled up within her. Then: memories. Everything she felt while
embroidering this garment flooded back to her.

She remembered all the times she felt small and safe, held and
cradled: tucked away in a hollow beneath a tree's roots during a
game of hide-and-seek, curled up beside a friend in bed, dozing
in her mother's arms. The tenderness of it made her feel strangely
off-kilter. She wondered what Kit saw when he first tried it on, and
about all the things he must've hidden from as a boy. She'd never
be able to ask him herself. She'd never again see him slither out of
vulnerability, or throw up a wall of thorns, or grow flustered at her
needling.

No, she couldn't dwell on this. Not now.

She descended the grand staircase, watching the guests in their
finery filter into the drawing room. Jack had brought in a trio of
dancers from Castilia to perform. A stage had been constructed,
with three rows of chairs surrounding it on all sides. Niamh lingered, hoping to catch at least one glimpse of their costumes. But
soon enough, the doors fell shut.

No time to waste, then.

In the shadowed corridors, all the statues were bathed in blue
moonlight. Their cold, impassive eyes looked down on her in silent
judgment. The door to Jack and Sofia's wing of the palace rose as
strong and tall as a vanguard above her. She tried the handle, but
the lock held fast.

She'd expected as much, and she'd prepared accordingly. How
hard could it be, really, to break in? She fished a hairpin from her
updo, and her braid tumbled down her back. She slid it into the
lock. A shove, a twist, and *snap*. The broken half of the pin clattered to the floor.

"Oh, bother," she muttered under her breath.

"I told you to stay out of trouble."

Niamh gasped. She whirled around quickly enough that her braid nearly slapped her in the face. Kit stood there, leaning against the wall barely a foot away from her. His amber eyes seemed to glow in the candlelit dark, filled with exasperated disbelief and a thousand strangled emotions.

"Kit!"

"Still so easily surprised," he said wonderingly. "You really ought to pay more attention to your surroundings, especially if you're trying to break into His Royal Highness's quarters."

She had no idea what to say to that. She had no idea what to make of him, entirely nonchalant and as bitingly sarcastic as ever. She clutched his coat tighter around her throat. "What are you doing here? Aren't you supposed to be avoiding me?" And then, something else occurred to her. "How did you even see me?"

"I saw you in the doorway, just for a moment."

"So you were looking for me?"

"Don't get the wrong idea." He turned his face away from her, but she could see the faintest dusting of red creeping across the bridge of his nose. "I could tell you were about to do something reckless. Looks like I was right. You really can't help yourself, can you?"

Niamh's entire face burned with humiliation. "And what about you? It isn't exactly the wisest idea to follow me. People will have seen you leave."

"And? This is my house."

"Oh. Right." She paused. "Still, if anyone finds us together again . . . This is a very compromising position."

"Then we won't get caught." She recognized that look in his eye by now: defiance. "What are you doing?"

Niamh could muster no sensible excuse. She was standing in a dark hallway, in his stolen coat, holding a broken hairpin-turned-lockpick. "I am taking a look around."

"Is that what you call it? You've been doing a lot of that lately."

It took a moment for her to catch his meaning. "You . . . You were awake?"

"You almost broke my wardrobe with how hard you kicked it. So, yes."

"You . . ." If only the floor would swallow her now. If only she could burst into flames. "You were just teasing me, then, when you called me over to you! Why didn't you say anything?"

"Maybe I wanted to see how it would play out." He leaned against the wall, the very picture of nonchalance. "I'm still waiting, honestly."

Gods, why did he have to be here? She'd believed it would be simple, to aid him from afar and drift out of his life. But they were hopelessly drawn to each other like magnets. It frustrated her how easy and right it felt to fall into this pattern with him.

"I'm trying to find out who Lovelace is," she blurted out. "Are you happy now?"

He lifted a brow. "In my brother's wing of the house?"

Oh, he was *evil*. She could tell by his deadpan tone and the cool glimmer in his eye that he was enjoying this. "I think it's Princess Sofia."

All of the amusement dropped off his face. "*What?*"

She winced. "I know it is treasonous to even suggest such a thing, but I have my reasons that I cannot—"

He huffed out a breath. "You don't have to explain yourself to me. I'm not here to stop you."

"You're not?"

"No." He pushed the hair out of his face and sighed, as though he were very put upon indeed, but she did not mistake the softening of his expression. "I'm coming with you. But I want my coat back."

"Deal." She paused, and suspicion crowded in. "Wait. Why are you helping me break into your brother's chambers?"

"Because even if you're wrong, he doesn't deserve a moment's peace," he said offhandedly, "and if you're right, you're in over your head. You have no one to protect you if things go south."

"I don't need your protection." She very much did. But she would not give him the satisfaction of that admission.

"I gave you my opinion. Now give me my coat."

Begrudgingly, she handed it to him. He traded her the one was wearing. It was warm with his body heat—and smelled like him, like garden soil and tobacco. It was more than a fair trade. Immediately, she slipped her arms into the sleeves and drew it tight around herself. Kit watched her with a peculiar, almost admiring, expression.

"What?" She looked down at her feet. "I look silly, don't I?"

"No," he said, almost shyly. "I mean, it *is* huge on you. But I like seeing you in my clothes."

"Oh." She cleared her throat, determined not to be flustered. "Ehm . . . So, do you have the key?"

He smirked, and her heart fluttered in response. She didn't think she had ever seen the way mischievous looked on him. "No. But I've gotten in before. It's easy."

His eyes flickered golden, and a pulse of magic whispered over her skin. The plants around them stirred to life. Vines poured out of their pots and snaked into the keyhole. The wood groaned and splintered, and after a moment, the entire lock separated from the door. It struck the floor with a metallic *bang*.

Niamh stared at it despairingly. "Well, that is certainly one way to do it. But now he is going to know we were here. How are you going to explain that?"

"He won't ask. He'll assume I was looking for his whisky again." The mirth faded from his voice. "Come on."

He brushed past her, and Niamh hurried after him. Softly, she asked, "And you're all right with letting him believe that?"

"I hardly see how it matters what I feel about it." Prickliness radiated off him, before he dispelled it with a sigh. "I doubt he trusts me anymore—for good reason. I was a bad person before I left, to be honest. He was hardly managing himself, and it's not like our old man gave him any examples of good parenting."

She could still remember the raw, furious pain in Jack's voice on the afternoon of the lawn party. *You cut and run the moment things get difficult, just as Mother did. What good were either of you to me?*

"I am sure he is not proud of himself, either. Desperation sometimes makes people act in ways they regret," she said quietly. "Still, you were a child—and you were not yourself. Show yourself some compassion."

Their footsteps echoed in the corridors. In the dark, the marble floor was as glossy as a sheet of ice. Kit walked to the center of the antechamber, where a mosaic on the floor depicted the family crest: a rose in full bloom, a drop of golden blood beading on a thorn.

"Where to now?" Kit asked.

Niamh looked around uneasily. "Ehm . . . Well . . ."

"Unbelievable," he muttered. "You tried to sneak in here without a plan."

"Just give me a moment. I'm thinking." Three hallways branched off from the atrium. "Which one is Sofia's room?"

Kit looked as though he were about to tease her for sneaking into people's bedchambers again, so she said, "I do not want to hear anything out of you!"

Without thinking, she grabbed him by the elbow and dragged him along. It was only once they crossed the threshold into the princess's room that she realized he hadn't pulled away or fought her at all. She released him and took in the room.

Everything was upholstered in soft white and gray fabrics, as drab as a forest in midwinter. Niamh went to the writing desk first. Nothing cluttered the surface of it—nothing but half-started letters in a language she couldn't read. The handwriting did not look at all familiar. Her heart dropped. But perhaps there was something in the content of the letters that would prove her theory.

"Can you understand Saksian?" she asked.

"Some." He held out his hand. "Let me see."

She passed him the letter. While he scanned it, she rummaged through the drawers. Nothing, nothing, nothing. Just plain wax seals and sharpened nibs of pens, lined up in rows like surgical instruments.

"Nothing of interest," Kit said. "She's telling her sister she's unhappy here."

Niamh didn't need to read her correspondence to learn that. She took the letter back from him and carefully replaced it. "I see."

Maybe she was wrong. But just across from her, a floor-to-ceiling window opened onto a balcony. It overlooked a view of the sprawling front lawn—and there, like a slim ghost against the night, was the lightning-struck tree. Niamh remembered it now: how she'd seen Sofia standing out there on the balcony, the curtains billowing in the breeze, her robe clasped tight around her. Sofia must have seen her, too.

She must have.

"You seem disappointed," he said.

"It's nothing. Let's try another room."

When they tried the handle to the room next door, however, it rattled. Locked. Kit closed his eyes and pressed his hand against the door. A faint golden light shattered across his cheekbones, spidery and shadowed from beneath his eyelashes. A vine slithered through the lock from the other side. It wrenched the lock from the door, and it swung open with a pitiful groan.

"Well done," Niamh said wanly. The brazenness of it astounded her. As unprincely as he was, he couldn't completely deny his nature. She supposed this was what happened when you were raised knowing you owned the earth you walked on.

Kit stepped into the room and turned on the gas lamp mounted on the wall. Oily light settled thick over the room. Jack's was exactly as she remembered it: everything just so.

"I used to come and bother him while he was working." He scuffed the toe of his shoe against the floor. "If you moved anything even an inch, he would know. It's like a museum in here."

"Then we shouldn't touch anything. Oh. Right. The door."

Too late for caution now.

"I want to take a look around while we're here," he said.

She supposed she was curious to know what kept Jack so busy in here, too. Kit traced slow circles around the perimeter until he came to stand behind the desk. He grabbed the glass decanter of whisky from a shelf, unlatched the window, and promptly poured it out. A muscle in his jaw feathered as he replaced it on the shelf. A cool breeze stirred through the room, rustling all of Jack's papers.

Niamh joined him hesitantly. Between the shelves and the wingback chair, there really wasn't much room to navigate. Her elbow bumped against his as she began to shuffle through the papers stacked in neat piles. There were seating charts—names added and crossed out and rearranged a hundred times over—and menus with his meticulous notes (*the sponge is far too dense,* read one, *and the tea flavor is overpowering. I cannot* stand *lavender*).

It was all terribly ordinary.

She put them in what she believed was the correct order, then turned her attention to the drawers. Inside, she found ledgers—*tons* of them, all identical and bound in leather. She heaved the most recent one onto the desk. It landed with a *thump.*

"He's always scribbling away in those," Kit said. "He's never let me look at them."

"Shall we?"

They each took one. The tiny precision of Jack's handwriting addled her, and the sheer amount of numbers made her head throb in protest. She'd learned some basic math for the running of the shop. But it wasn't a strong suit of hers, and it was hard to make sense of what exactly she was looking at. Filed away here were letters and documents; each looked more official and dire than the last.

Beside her, Kit paged through them with the same unyielding focus he applied to everything else in his life. But his eyes were wide, and his skin paled with every page he turned. He read for what felt like an eternity before setting the ledger aside and flipping through another. Eventually, the color returned to his face with a fury. "This can't be right."

"What is it?"

He took a step back and glared down at the desk, as though it had bitten him. "The royal coffers are nearly empty."

"*What?*"

Kit set to work anew. He tore open every drawer and every cabinet. He unearthed correspondence from all corners of the empire. He disassembled the room with the same mercenary precision of a hunter dressing a kill. By the end of it, they were practically drowning in paper. He bent over the desk, his fingers clawed around the edges.

"It started with our father, decades ago," he said. "Machland wasn't the only colony that rebelled around that time, and the old man's attempts to crush them all at once were enormously expensive. It was a losing battle to begin with, but he was scrabbling desperately to keep his hold on the empire. He drained our resources for the sake of his own ego."

Niamh could not imagine how much bloodshed had come from so many wars. And now, she dreaded to think what would have happened in the Machlish War of Independence if the king hadn't divided his focus. They might very well have been crushed.

"And then," Kit continued, his bitterness only growing, "when he lost, he soothed himself by building pretty, useless things— such as the palace he's currently rotting away in. That thing is a monstrosity made of gold. Not to mention the expense of keeping all of his mistresses, his taste for laudanum, the art he collected . . . The debt he racked up is astronomical."

"And he left all of this to Jack," Niamh said quietly, "without bothering to prepare him."

"Exactly," he said thinly. "It looks like Jack has been struggling to plug the holes ever since, all while trying to maintain an illusion of normalcy. One of his biggest investors right now is the Duke of Pelinor. Sinclair's father."

Her heart sank. "Oh, no."

Kit set to pacing. "A man who has made half his fortune from exploiting the Machlish. He was a landlord before the rebellion, and now, he uses cheap Machlish labor to maximize his own profits."

Which meant that Jack couldn't afford to anger him.

Niamh leaned against the desk when a sudden wave of nausea came over her. "So that is why he refuses to engage with the protesters."

"Avaland is hemorrhaging money," Kit said, "and he's throwing even more of it at this wedding. *Why?*"

All at once, it dawned on her. *This* was what Lovelace wanted. *This* was what they suspected: debts, bribes, corruption. Avaland was a kingdom held together with gold paint, a prayer, and the will of one man determined to shoulder the weight alone.

Kit swiped everything off the desk. The ledgers clattered to the floor. Papers spilled across the room. "How could he have kept all this from me?"

Niamh rested a hand on his elbow. "You were too young."

"It's no excuse," he snarled. "He's an idiot. If he were to drop dead tonight, all of this would fall to whatever poor bastard Parliament saw fit to appoint, and none of them is competent enough to conceal it as well as he has. I could have helped him. But I can't step in if I have no idea what I'm up against."

"This isn't your responsibility to fix, Kit," Niamh said. "You were not even here. You didn't create this mess."

"Neither did he. Fuck," Kit muttered. "*Fuck*. Sorry."

"Are you all right?"

"Yes," he said after a moment. His anger melted away, and all that remained on his face was steely determination. "This is good."

Niamh gawped at him, stunned. "Are you feeling quite well? I hardly see how this can be good by any stretch of the imagination."

"I've never felt better. I feel like there is something I can *do*." He raked his hair out of his face. "For so long, I've felt completely powerless—like I haven't been free a day in my life. I thought I would never escape—not from my family, not from the past, not from my own mind. Before I came back, no matter if I quit drinking or didn't, living hardly seemed worth it. I was stranded on a farm in Helles, with no one I knew and nothing to do but think about all the things I'd lost and all the ways I'd failed.

"But one day, I got a look at what I'd become. The man who owned the olive grove found me passed out. It wasn't a pretty sight, apparently." He scoffed. "When I came to, he sat me down and told me, 'I've seen many men like you over the years. You don't have to hurt yourself because someone else hurt you.' I knew then I had a choice. I was either going to die there, or I was going to live out of spite."

Niamh almost smiled. How very like him, even in the depths of despair, to cling to *spite*.

"I'm still here, by some miracle. I still don't know how to be vulnerable. I still don't know how to live with myself most days. I still don't know how to be a good person. But this is a start." He looked to the ledgers he'd scattered across the floor. "I climbed out of oblivion, and my life is finally my own. I finally know what I want. I want to make things right. I want . . ."

He cut himself off. But he did not need to finish his sentence for her to understand.

I want you.

Niamh stumbled backward a step and bumped into the shelf.

An astrolabe wobbled precariously behind her. "You can't joke like that."

"I'm not joking."

They stood close enough to share each other's breath—a cruelty. Because no matter how he felt, it did not change their difference in stations. It didn't change the fact that this could never be.

"But . . . I . . ." It took her a moment to remember how to speak. "You have to be! You were right to suggest we stay away from each other. I am inelegant and silly and—and I will make a mess of everything. I already have! I am bad for you in every possible way."

"You may be the only good thing I've ever wanted."

Her breath whooshed out of her. She couldn't process it. She couldn't accept it. She couldn't allow herself to hope again. It would hurt too much. *You're going to get your heart broken.* "We should go before someone finds us here."

Without waiting for his reply, she turned on her heel to flee.

"Wait." He caught her by the wrist. His fingers were hot against her skin, his grip firm but reverent. *Stay, please.* Her pulse beat wildly as she turned around to face him. "Just . . . Wait a minute. You're always moving."

They stood in the middle of the room, but his presence enveloped her entirely. The warm intensity of his gaze pinned her in place. As long as she'd been old enough to understand the cards she'd been dealt, she had worked her life away: always preparing for the inevitable, searching for the next thing to do, another tear to mend, another hurt to soothe. She had always believed life was what slipped through her fingers while she was idle. That life was something she wasted, not something she had. But now, she understood how wrong she'd been. Her heart beat. Her lungs swelled with air. Life was here, right in front of her.

She would not move for anything.

His eyes on hers were molten, as golden and bright as sunlight itself. They were poised on the knife's edge of hunger and frustration. It sent a jolt through her, pooling low within her.

"There," he murmured. "Is that so terrible?"

"No," she breathed.

She didn't know how it happened, or who moved first, but she was suddenly weightless. She rose onto her toes, and the plane of his stomach was solid and warm against her palms. His hand slid to the small of her back, pulling her flush against him. When he kissed her, it was entirely unlike him, nothing at all like it had been before: sweet and tentative and searching. Niamh grinned against his mouth.

There were so few times when she did not resent her body, traitorous as it was. But gods, he felt so good against her. Tears gathered behind her eyes at how tenderly he held her. Happiness fizzed within her like magic. She felt practically luminous with it, her every heartbeat singing with the sound of his name. Everything was falling to pieces around them, but here, with him, she stood within the eye of a hurricane.

"Kit!"

At the sound of Jack's voice, they both froze.

"Hide," Kit said.

22

ide. It was a cold reentry into the world.

Nothing felt real at all, when her head was still swimming from his kiss. He lowered her back onto her feet, her skirts suddenly heavy and snaring around her.

Hide? There was no *time* to hide. Jack's footsteps echoed in the antechamber, growing louder and louder. Her eyes roved wildly about the room. Unless she wanted to climb out the window—which, knowing herself, would almost certainly result in some kind of injury—there was nowhere to go, either.

Nowhere but the desk.

Niamh scrambled underneath it, just as the door flew open.

"What do you think you're doing?"

Niamh's blood ran cold at the sound of Jack's voice. Growing up in a household still reeling from so much loss, she'd always been attuned to anger, all the ways to make herself small to avoid it, to weave between its volleys. But Kit faced Jack down with the stoicism of a soldier.

"Taking a look around," Kit replied flatly.

She tried to adjust herself more comfortably, but she'd drawn her knees to her chest and cranked her neck at an odd angle to even fit under here. If she pressed her cheek flat to the floor, she could make out a thin sliver of the room. Just the floorboards, slick with moonlight and strewn with all of Jack's documents, and the shine of their black shoes.

The silence stretched out between them. Jack must've noticed the empty decanter on the shelf because he said, "You're drunk."

Jack's voice wavered in a way Niamh had not thought him capable of. In truth, she hadn't thought *anyone* could inject so much feeling into two words. It crossed every shade of grief, from anger to despair and back again.

"Don't look at me like that," Kit snapped, but there was something raw in his voice: guilt, born from a pure and awful self-loathing. "I poured it out."

"I don't believe you." Jack spoke steadily now, pulling on all his armor piece by piece. But the damage had been done. Too many cracks had spread across it, where the helplessness, the heartbreak, seeped through. Niamh's throat tightened, to hear a man like the prince regent so undone by love. "How can you possibly expect me to believe you?"

"Believe me or don't. I don't care." But Niamh could tell that he cared very much. She could picture them now, standing on opposite sides of the room as though it was a ravine they couldn't cross. "I can already see the gears turning in your mind. But I'm not a problem you have to solve. I'm not some mess you have to sweep up. Don't you get it? You couldn't have fixed me. I still resent you for it, but now I see sending me away was the right decision because you would have killed yourself trying."

"Kit—"

"Shut up," he said roughly, emotion still thick in his voice. "I don't want to talk about this right now. You have problems enough of your own, don't you?"

"What problems could you be referring to?"

Kit let out a derisive sound. "This kingdom is on the brink of financial collapse, and you can't stop it."

Niamh didn't need to see to know Jack was taking in the room. The papers and ledgers scattered across the floor, everything on his desk pried open and shaken loose.

"You have no idea what you're talking about." He sounded breathless, not with anger but with relief. "God. You do not know the weight I have had to carry since Father took ill. He spent money as though it were no object. All of his failed colonial projects, all of his bribes, all of his *vices*. Avaland is a house of cards, Christopher. It is a beast with an endless appetite. Every time I patch one hole, another rift opens. I would not have summoned you back here if I had any other choice. I was trying to shield you from this as much as I could."

"So this wedding . . ."

"Yes. It is another patch," Jack said wearily. "I can invest Rosa's dowry."

Kit's temper sparked again. "So how the hell did you convince King Felipe to agree to this engagement?"

"Because I promised him military support, the same as I promised Sofia's father."

"Military support you can't give," Kit said, disgusted.

"Correct. It is a gamble, one that will pay off enormously if Castilia does not embroil itself in some conflict before my investments bear fruit. I expect it to be five to ten years. After that, we will be free of this."

"Five to ten *years*?"

"Until then, we must maintain appearances. If Parliament were to find out the true state of things, do you know how quickly I would be replaced as regent? I will sooner die than see four hundred years of our family's legacy crumble. I will not disappoint him."

"Why do you idolize him, even now? Why do you excuse the things he did to us? He wasn't just an imperfect man. He was a monster." From her vantage point, she could see a sliver of Kit crossing the room. "Don't believe for a second I didn't know what he did to you, no matter how much you tried to hide it. And now he's left you with a corpse to drag behind you, and somehow convinced you that you needed to shoulder the burden of it alone. Look where it's gotten you."

Jack said nothing.

"I'm not your pawn anymore," Kit spat. "You've wanted me to do my duty. I'm doing it—and I will do yours as well if you're not equal to it."

Jack let out a startled, vicious laugh. "Be careful what you're implying, Christopher. I just might begin to take you seriously. Enlighten me, then. Do you think it would make everything better if I agreed to pay the Machlish reparations we cannot afford? If I abdicated out of some misguided sense of honor? Can you even fathom the bloodshed that would ensue with that vacuum of power? Which foreign rivals will take advantage of the tumult? How quickly Castilia will retaliate? We are in too deep to turn back now."

"If you are so determined to fix Father's mistakes," Kit said lowly, "then meet with Carlile. You can still do *something* to make things right with Machland."

"My hands are tied. I am the shield between ruin and our subjects. They may not like it, but I am all they have."

"Get over yourself. What must it be like, to know what everyone needs better than they do? Your martyrdom has made you a shortsighted, egotistical fool."

"Enough. No matter how righteously you argue, whether you

like it or not, you cannot escape from the fact that you are of royal blood. You have obligations. Do not think I do not know what you have been up to. I wish I could believe that Lovelace published nothing more than a scandalous falsehood, but I know you well enough by now. You will not have your judgment clouded by a lowborn—"

Niamh winced, bracing for the impact of his insult.

"Don't you dare. Don't say another word about her."

"You are marrying Infanta Rosa." Jack's tone darkened. "You do not have a choice."

"I refuse."

"I am the prince regent," he thundered. The window splintered with a high, ringing sound. Glass shards and vines poured into the room. They skittered at Niamh's feet, reflecting the cold moonlight. "Hate me if you must, but you *will* obey me."

"Look at the ledgers, Jack. You're the prince of nothing."

"Get out," Jack said, with deadly quiet. "I am tired of this insolence."

"That's it?" Contempt dripped from every word. "Who's the one who cuts and runs now?"

"Get. *Out.*"

Niamh sensed Kit's hesitation. She could almost feel him searching for her anxiously in the dark. Gods, if only she had kept that coat, she might have been able to sneak out with him.

"Fine," Kit said. "This conversation isn't over."

After a moment, the door slammed. The impact rang in the silence.

Niamh held her breath. At any moment, Jack would chase after him. Surely he couldn't let the conversation end on that note. But he let out a long, defeated sigh. She could hear the soft rustle of fabric as he shrugged off his coat. It landed in front of her, crumpled on the back of his chair.

Oh no.

He approached the desk. From here, Niamh could see him silhouetted in the lamplight. He'd stripped to his shirtsleeves and loosened his cravat. He looked completely and utterly exhausted, with his bloodshot eyes and miserable expression. He reached for the decanter perched on the bookshelf, but when he remembered it was empty, he swore.

"The spiteful wretch," he muttered under his breath. "I knew I should have sent him to the navy instead."

And then his gaze landed on Niamh. All the blood drained from her face. For a long, horrible few moments, they stared at each other without speaking. She felt like some tedious ghost he'd thought was already banished.

When he finally recovered, his shock melted fully into rage.

"*You*." He hauled her out by her elbow. As soon as she stumbled to her feet, she put some distance between them. "What are you doing here? Did you put him up to this?"

"No, I swear!"

"You have done nothing but cause me trouble since the moment you first arrived, you meddlesome little chit."

"I'm sorry." Niamh pressed herself flat against the wall. Her mind blackened with fear at the wild look in his eyes. Right now, she didn't know what he was capable of. She'd never been struck in her life.

She hardly recognized the smallness of her own voice. Jack, at last, seemed to notice her cowering. Remorse flickered in his eyes, chased quickly by shame. He glanced down at his hand, clenched into a fist, and shook it out, as though dispelling a bad memory.

"I am sorry for frightening you. It has been a long night." His eyes fell shut, and he rubbed his temples. "Am I such a joke that no one—not a commoner, not my own brother—will give me any respect? You have done nothing but take advantage of my leniency. You have given Lovelace more ammunition for their crusade, and now, you have filled my brother's head with all sorts of pretty nonsense."

His cool dismissal of Kit roused within her an obstinance hadn't realized she possessed. "I am terribly sorry for the trouble I have caused you, but I have only ever acted with the best of intentions for your family," she said hotly. "All I have done is treat the prince as he wants to be treated: like a person, who has feelings and ideas of his own."

"Spare me, madam." He sounded weary now. "Surely, you must have enough conscience, enough basic *sense,* to understand my position. You are entirely unsuitable for him in every regard. I did not take you as an ambitious girl, but the gall of you . . . To aspire so far above your station. To brazenly attempt to tear apart a match made by those who have the common good of all in mind."

"What could you mean by all of this, sir?" she asked before she could think better of it. "The prince has made me no offer."

Jack flushed, clearly incensed by the very suggestion. "And am I meant to understand that if he had, you would accept?"

She'd be a fool to reply in anything but the negative. She had always known what his duties as a prince entailed. And yet, it was such a farce. He couldn't sacrifice so much for a kingdom that did not love him—for a marriage that would make both parties miserable and trapped. She couldn't quell this quiet, desperate fury burning within her. If she was to die young, why should she live pleasing everyone but herself?

"And why should I not?"

"Miss O'Connor, do not test my patience." He radiated powerful, unrelenting malice, determined to make her feel the weight of every drop of his royal blood, all of his intimidatingly regal bearing. "If it's money you're after, you now know there is nothing to be gained. Did you not, after all, overhear every sordid detail of our plight? Do you not understand what is at stake? I know Avaland has not historically been kind to your people, and I very much regret my father's mismanagement of your troubles. But you cannot be so cold as to doom us all because of your foolish, romantic *whim*."

"Perhaps there is another option you have not considered! One that does not require such sacrifices, or one that will allow for a more just world!"

"And marrying my brother would accomplish that?" he asked derisively.

"I . . ."

"So this is how you show your gratitude. In what world could you even conceive of it? A prince of Avaland, with a commoner. A Machlishwoman, no less!" The moonlight pouring through the broken window highlighted all his cold austerity. "I cannot even begin to imagine the scandal—the disgrace—such a thing would cause. How can you claim to care for him when you know it will ruin him? Has he not suffered enough from the contempt of society?"

"Do you truly believe he cares at all what people think of him? If he suffers at all from their contempt, it's because he fears what it will do to *you*."

"As he should," Jack snapped. "If he carries on this way, the Carmine name shall never recover—after all of the pains I have taken. It cannot be endured. You are a nothing girl from a nowhere town. Apart from your divine blood, you have absolutely nothing to offer him."

"I may not be suited for him, but I love him! Is that truly nothing?"

I love him.

It had happened. Niamh had always imagined love as something sparkling, something all-encompassing and glorious as daybreak, as sudden as a knife to the heart. But love was somehow more magical and more banal than she'd dreamed it. It crept up on her, out of sight, until it was completely undeniable—until it was already out of her mouth and solid as a stone to strike her down with.

Jack looked horrified. "What am I going to do with you?"

Niamh had come too far to back down now. Despite the trembling of her hands, she tilted her chin up and met his eyes. "You cannot make his decisions for him forever."

He smiled ruefully. "Can't I? My will is the strongest force in this universe. You have not yet seen the depth of it, the things I am capable of when pushed, the lengths to which I will go to protect what is mine. I will not let him get hurt again—not by such an obvious, horrible mistake."

She saw him plainly then, as immovable and unbreakable as stone. Even now, he was trying to protect Kit. Since he was a boy, he'd made himself into a wall: one that stood between Kit and their father, between Kit and all of the burdens of ruling, between Kit and *himself*, between his father's sins and the public. In the hard set of his shoulders and the stern line of his jaw, she could see all of the calculations he had made and all of the things he had denied himself in the name of duty. Here was a man convinced of his competence and secure in his conviction that his careful control was the only thing keeping the world spinning properly on its axis.

It hurt to both understand him so perfectly and to loathe him so bitterly. How could she blame him? She, too, had carried the weight of generations on her shoulders. She, too, had withstood the pressure not to squander what she was handed. Tears welled in her eyes. "There has to be another way. Please, give him a chance to help you fix this. If you force him to go through with this wedding, he will only resent you more than he already does."

"Enough," he said, soft as a plea. "I do not have time to find another tailor. You will finish what you were asked to do. You will say nothing to anyone about any of this. You will go nowhere without my permission. Do we understand each other?"

What was there to understand? No matter what she did, no matter what she said or how hard she railed against him, he would send her away. But if she refused now? She would be escorted from the palace, with no chance to say goodbye to her friends, no chance to have any of her designs featured in the wedding, and no chance to tell Kit how she felt. She would be exactly what he said she was: a nothing girl, sent back to her nowhere town in shame.

"Yes," she choked out.

"Good." He leaned against his desk and set to work unfastening his cuff links. "The moment you have put the last stitch in that gown, you will be back on the boat to Machland. We will all move on with our lives, and soon this will be a distant memory."

A distant memory. Just as she was always destined to be.

"Will you let me talk to him? Please."

A horrible silence descended over them. His stony expression cracked, and she could see his better judgment warring against his affection for his brother. Niamh steeled herself for his denial, but at last, he sighed.

"Let no one say I am heartless. Go. But if you have loved him for anything but his status, do the right thing and walk away." He dragged a hand down his jaw. His weary, haunted eyes fell shut. "This charade must continue, whether any of us wants it to or not."

23

As she made her way through the darkened corridors of the palace, Niamh could still hear the faint strains of the musicale below: the applause of the guests, the stomp of the dancers in their beautiful dresses, the mournful strum of a guitar. It carried through the halls like the halting, faint tune of a music box. The shadows sparkled and swam in the watery light. She felt as though she were wandering through a dream—or perhaps a nightmare.

At last, she emerged into the atrium. Kit waited for her there, pacing restlessly. As soon as he heard her approach, his gaze snapped to hers. She'd never seen him look so relieved. "Did he see you?"

She didn't trust herself to speak. She nodded.

He closed the gap between them and pulled her in to him. All of the tension flowed out of her body, and it took all her strength not to weep with relief. Slowly, she wound her arms around his waist and nestled her head on his chest. His lips moved against her ear when he asked, "Are you all right?"

She let out a strained laugh and drew back enough to look up at him. *No.* "I think so, yes."

What could she truly tell him? *Your brother cornered me with the intention of breaking off our engagement, one that does not and never will exist.* It had certainly felt nice in the moment, to see the prince regent fuming mad at the very idea of it. But Kit would do his duty, regardless of his feelings for either her or Rosa. All of her wildest imaginings, all of her silly daydreams were just that: wild and silly. There was no world in which a Machlish tailor got to marry an Avlish prince. Still, she couldn't bring herself to say goodbye just yet.

"He is not pleased with me, but he will let me finish the job," she said. "However, I feel as though I understand him better now. I have never seen him as truly afraid as he was for you."

His face fell. "I could kill him right now, but it made me sick to see him like that. I don't want to put him through that again. There's no guarantee I won't."

Niamh smoothed her hands against his lapels. "All you can do is take it day by day. At least, that's what I try to tell myself when things seem overwhelming, or when I cannot remember why I am doing half the things I do, or I grow afraid that I will be gone sooner than I like."

"Day by day," he repeated, as though trying out the idea.

Perhaps, she thought, *even moment by moment.* She would make every last one of them with him count. "Do you want to go somewhere else?" she murmured against his chest.

Without a word, Kit twined their fingers together and led her through the halls. In the uppermost level of the palace, he showed her to a solarium, tucked away like a gown in the back of a closet: lovely and forgotten. The rose window overhead let in a wheel of moonlight, spoked with shadow. The room was scattered with threadbare settees and chaise longues with faded cushions. A harp sat in the corner, still polished to a glossy sheen, uncovered as though at any moment, someone would come sit at the stool and play.

"This was my mother's solarium," he said.

No wonder it made her feel so wistful. It was forlorn, but she could tell someone came to dust the furniture and air out the room. Back home, her mother had kept her father's things. His militia jacket folded the same as when it was delivered to her upon his death; his favorite rocking chair; his pipe. But she cherished them and kept them close. She'd been happy to take them from the shelf anytime Niamh asked. Jack, it seemed, kept even his discarded memories orderly, preserved and impersonal like a museum exhibit. Somehow, it was even sadder than if they were left to molder.

"It's lovely," she told Kit.

She wandered to one of the bay windows. Outside, there was nothing but a black-satin sky and the golden curve of the moon. She crawled onto the seat, scattered with worn pillows. She hugged one against her chest, feeling childish for how much it comforted her. Kit came to sit beside her. The moonlight brushed him delicately with silver.

In the silence, Niamh was all too aware of how their thighs were mere inches from touching. He wore such a pensive, somber expression, she couldn't help herself. She knocked their knees together. "What are you going to do now?"

"I don't know."

"Then what do you *want* to do?"

"There you go, talking about what I want again," he said wryly. "What do *you* want?"

She smiled softly. "I want you to be happy. I wish your duty and your happiness did not seem so mutually exclusive right now. But

I know you will do well and that you will find contentment with Infanta Rosa."

His expression grew wary. "Why does that sound like a goodbye?"

"Because . . . because . . ." Niamh drew in a shaky breath. She had really wanted to be more eloquent than this. "This *is* a goodbye. Jack has sent me away. As soon as I finish Infanta Rosa's last fitting, I will be gone."

"What?"

"I am so sorry, Kit." She struggled to keep her voice even, but emotion swelled within her, too urgent to tamp down. "For everything. I never should have gotten you involved in this foolish scheme tonight. I never should have spoken to you so freely at all! If we never truly became acquainted, then . . ."

"Don't talk nonsense." Her protests died at the look in his eyes, panicked and furious and longing all at once. "This is not your fault. None of this is your fault. You need to stop shouldering everything and jumping to conclusions and blaming yourself for every little thing. If anyone's at fault here, it's me. I couldn't have stayed away from you if I tried."

She had never felt so grounded, nor so out of control. Her pulse roared, and her breath quickened, and her fingers dug into the cushion beside her. The air between them crackled, charged like a brewing storm.

Alive.

Her eyes fluttered shut as their mouths crashed together. Kit lifted her halfway onto his lap, and she fisted her hands in his lapels. Whether it was to steady herself or to hold him against her, she couldn't be certain. The rush of her own desire shocked her, but Kit matched her hunger. He was artless, almost desperate, as his fingers twined in the hair at the nape of her neck. The rest of her hairpins fell against the floorboards like rain. And when his teeth pulled at her bottom lip, she was too far gone to be humiliated by the moan he pulled from her. He kissed her like a man starved. He kissed her like he was running out of time.

They *were* running out of time.

Kit drew back, and her heart leapt into her throat when he met her eyes. She would *not* cry. If she ruined this, she would never forgive herself. Her mind spun with a thousand possibilities, all of the things she would never get to do with him, all of her fantasies crowding in at once. It was overwhelming, the longing he instilled in her. She hardly knew how to put a name to what she wanted. She whimpered.

"Are you all right?" His lips were kiss-swollen, and his breaths came harshly. "Is this . . . ?"

Too much? She could hear the question in his voice. His concern was more endearing than it had any right to be.

Two roads diverged before her. There was the sensible route, where she put a stop to this before it could gut her, where she did not make their parting more difficult than it already needed to be. And then, there was the selfish route, the foolish route, the route where she let herself burn.

She hardly needed to think at all.

With trembling fingers, Niamh cradled his jaw. She swallowed so hard, she heard her own throat click. "It's not enough."

"No?" His pupils were blown wide with wanting. He shifted, one knee tucked into his chest, the other dangling off the edge of the seat to make room for her. "Then come here."

When he spoke like that, she could deny him nothing. He guided her so that she was flush against him, her back pressed against his chest. She could feel the steady rise and fall of his breathing, the wild beating of his heart.

"Comfortable?" His breath stirred the loose hair around her face, and his voice was warm on the shell of her ear. A lazy shiver worked its way through her. How eagerly her body responded to him was humiliating.

"Hm . . . Not quite." She wiggled her hips back and was rewarded by a low sound and the feeling of him hard against her. When she tipped her face toward his, she grinned. A flush crept up his neck.

"There," she said angelically. "*Now* I'm comfortable."

"Good."

He caressed her ankle bone before slipping his hand beneath the hem of her skirt. It was long—far longer than she would like right now. Slowly—agonizingly slowly—he lifted it. His fingers traced fire up the curve of her calf, the swell of her thigh, the jut of her hip. The room was so quiet, she could hear the fabric sliding against her bare skin. Gooseflesh rippled across her body despite the heat, and she squirmed at the soft whisper of his breath against her throat, the soft *click* of metal as he unbuckled her garters. Anticipation quickened her pulse.

Her legs parted, and her knee knocked into the glass of the window, cold against her feverish skin. Somewhere in the distance, the sounds of the musicale far below them reached her. She became dimly aware of the thousand anxieties bubbling to the surface: what if they were caught, what if she had no idea what she was doing, what if she disappointed him, *what if, what if, what if.*

But she'd never felt so wanted. And when his hand finally, *finally* slid between her thighs, her every worry dissolved. A quiet gasp escaped her. Her eyes fluttered shut; her head lolled back against his shoulder. He kissed her neck, and her limbs grew airy and useless. His free arm snaked around her waist to support her weight as she melted into him.

She turned to catch him by the mouth, but she couldn't focus, couldn't quite get a good angle on him. She drifted through a haze, and it felt so good, she never wanted to be anywhere else, never wanted it to end. There was nothing but the heel of his palm flat against her stomach, the steady rhythm of his fingers, her hips moving of their own accord against him. Never had she despised her stays more than when he traced her breast through the boning. Never in her life had she wanted to be touched more. His breathing quickened in time with hers. Pleasure coiled tighter within her. It built, slowly—and then all at once. She bit down on a cry as it crested.

He eased his hold on her, letting her unwind from him. His eyes were hooded and clouded with something like wonder. "You're incredible."

Heat zipped into her face. As the haze cleared from her thoughts, the embarrassment caught up to her. For the last few minutes, she hadn't had a single coherent thought. Now, they sprung upon her with a vengeance. Was she too loud? Too needy? Too much? She didn't even want to consider what she must've looked like—or how she looked now, with her hair in disarray and her cheeks stung pink. "*Please* don't make fun of me right now. I'm vulnerable."

He blinked, as though she'd struck him upside the head. "What are you talking about?"

"You're teasing me, aren't you?" She buried her face in his neck. "I bet you're filing all of this away for later."

Kit choked on a laugh. "Maybe. Not for any of the nefarious reasons you seem to have in mind, though."

She groaned. "Kit!"

"Believe me, I'm not making fun of you. That was . . ." He ran a hand through his hair, searching for the right word. He seemed to come up short and only looked at her helplessly. "It was good."

"Oh." Her face felt hot. "Well, then."

It boosted her confidence, at the very least.

Drawing in a shaky breath, she shifted back onto his lap and straddled him. Her knees pressed tightly against his hips, and she watched with a small shiver of satisfaction as his throat worked. It was all she could do not to chase the movement with her lips. His hands reflexively rested on her thighs, but what nearly undid her was the quintessentially *Kit* glint in his eye. A challenge: *What next?*

Niamh ran her fingers through his hair until she found the lace holding it back. He let her do it without comment. When she tugged it loose, his hair cascaded past his shoulders. She nearly sighed aloud at his unaffected beauty. *Gods,* was the only dreamy thought in her head, *it is so unfair.* He probably never thought twice about how stupidly soft his hair was. The moonlight spun it into silver. It lit his eyes with pale fire.

She pushed his jacket off his shoulders; next, she unfastened his neckcloth. She could feel his eyes on her, watching her every move. He somehow looked amused and embarrassed and entirely undone by the slow reverence with which she undressed him. Rain began to fall steadily, muffling the shaky sounds of their breathing and the rustle of starched linen. His cravat came loose at last, and his shirt parted to reveal a thin sliver of bare skin below his throat. She wanted to taste it. She wanted to make him feel the way she did. Gods, if only it were easier to say. Her hands trembled from nerves. But beneath it all, there was excitement.

Certainty.

She allowed her palm to roam down his chest, over his waistcoat's warm silk and cool wire buttons. "Kit?"

He didn't answer her. He only turned his eyes onto her like a blade. Her mouth went dry.

"Do you want me?" She hardly recognized the sound of her own voice, shy and wanting despite the boldness of her words. "Because I want you."

At first, his only reply was to cradle her neck and kiss her as though tomorrow would not come.

"Yes," he murmured against her lips. "Yes."

24

Rain drummed steadily against the roof. The rose window overhead looked like a small lake suspended above them, and on the other side of the glass, the sky was a dreamy swirl of violet. Through the cracked-open window and the lace curtains, she could smell the rain: damp soil and damp grass, the world stirring awake around them.

Sweat cooled on her skin and shone on the lines of Kit's shoulders. He was so lovely, with shadows feathering soft against his cheeks and his eyelashes a fan of black. His breath flowed evenly against her, and his heart beat steadily against her cheek, where it rested on his bare chest. She reached out to brush his loose hair off his forehead. There was a sort of languid serenity about him now. It filled her with fondness so bright, it strained against her ribs.

She could've stayed here forever, with the weight of his arms around her. But this contentment was another fragile and imper-manent thing—another thing she'd never truly had. She traced the line of his jaw, determined to commit every detail of his face to memory. He was just like one of the Fair Ones. Tonight, he'd spir-ited her heart away, and she'd be left sick and lovelorn all her life.

"What are you thinking about?" he asked huskily. "It's loud, whatever it is."

Niamh shot upright. "Oh, nothing."

He seemed skeptical but didn't push. He only took a lock of her hair and twisted it slowly around his finger, as though he meant to reel her back down to him. "Come here."

She almost complied, if only to kiss him again and marvel at just how low that lovely flush of his traveled, but from her vantage point, she spied something familiar—and strangely colorful—in the pile of his clothes.

She leaned over him, her hair spilling heavy over her shoul-der, and plucked out a scrap of silk. The moment she touched it, a strange feeling seized upon her. A warm, steady happiness, touched at the edges with the bittersweetness of loss. Even with-out the enchantment stitched into it, she would've recognized this anywhere: the handkerchief she gave him on the day she arrived in Avaland.

"Why have you kept this?" She couldn't keep the accusation out of her voice as she dangled it in front of him. "You hated it."

Panic passed over his face, and she could practically see him wrestling his impulse to be snappish back into its cage. After a long moment, he said, "I didn't hate it."

"What do you *mean* you didn't hate it?" She smacked his arm with it, which earned her a glare. "I have not forgotten for a moment what you said to me, or the look on your face when you took it, *or* your terrible apology, for that matter!"

"I don't know," he said defensively. "It made me . . . uncomfortable. Your magic makes me feel things."

"That is rather the point!" she cried. "But what could have possibly set you off? This is a silly little charm for . . . for . . . longing?"

What do I want? He'd scoffed at her once. *What a ridiculous question.*

"I didn't want to feel much of anything when we met, least of all *longing*." He sounded frustrated—but not at her. "But it hasn't let me out of its grip since. I hardly remembered what it was before you crashed into my life. I hardly knew what I wanted at all."

Her heart beat too fiercely against her ribs. Her eyes burned again with the threat of tears. "But now you do."

"Yes. Now I do." He raised himself onto his elbow. His next word was a bare exhalation against her collarbone: "Stay."

She shivered. "You know I can't."

His jaw set, and his eyes blazed with defiance. "He can't send you away so easily. Not if you're mine."

Maybe he could make her his. Maybe Jack would see the value in placating him, in giving Kit something to distract himself with while his brother continued his machinations. How sweet it sounded on the surface. But Niamh had already made up her mind.

"I can't be your mistress, Kit."

"Then be my wife."

Her mind went entirely blank. She couldn't be certain if she'd heard him correctly, but no . . . No, she had. It was a far, *far* cry from the romantic proposal she'd envisioned as a girl, brimming with fervid declarations and perhaps a touch of begging. Oh, she ought to reject him outright, just for his utter lack of passion! But the impetuousness of it all seemed far from the point at present; she couldn't even be cross with him for ruining her very first—and likely last—offer of marriage. Because he couldn't truly mean it, and if he did, he was entirely delusional. Right now, both of them gloriously naked, he would've surely promised her anything.

She pulled the curtain of her hair over her shoulders. "You are not thinking clearly right now. You shouldn't promise me things that aren't yours to give."

"My life is my own." His voice was fierce, argumentative, and it was so utterly *him,* it made her heart flutter. "Someone once told me that."

"Still! You cannot say that."

"I can say whatever I want," he countered. "I'm a prince."

"That is exactly the problem. What will they say?"

Walking out of the cathedral with his hand in hers would be as good as the first spark of revolution. A commoner—a *Machlish* commoner—marrying an Avlish prince? It was not just irregular. By all the rules of high society, it was completely unnatural.

"Let them talk. It's time things changed." The conviction in his voice enthralled her. "I've been thinking about this. This would be a symbol that we're committed to making things right with Machland. It would prove that we believe there's nothing fundamentally different between us. You'd be at my side as we change things."

It sounded too good to be true. "But Castilia . . ."

"Doesn't need me to marry Rosa to have our assurance that we will ally with them."

Her head spun. "And the kingdom's financial troubles . . ."

"Can be dealt with in other ways, when its regent is not committed to preserving the status quo above all else."

"Your brother will never allow it."

"If we elope, his opinion makes no difference."

Niamh slumped against the window. "You *have* been thinking about this."

He seemed at once satisfied and anxious. "Any other objections?"

"Kit, I don't think I . . ." *I don't think I deserve this.* She lowered her gaze and buried her face in her hands. "It's too selfish."

"You have never done a selfish thing in your life. Why can't you see what I see? I have never met someone half as accomplished or virtuous as you are." He took her face in his hands, and his tone softened. "Stop criticizing yourself and undercutting your own achievements. Stop cutting off pieces of yourself, when you're already more than good enough."

You are a nothing girl from a nowhere town.

You cannot be so cold as to doom us all because of your foolish, romantic whim.

The whole world would be set against them. And if only it were so simple to *stop*. Contentment was stagnation. It was surrender. It was death. What lay ahead of her was dark and uncertain. But behind her was a collapsing bridge, and underneath, a rising tide she could not outswim. The only thing to do was run blind.

In his eyes, she saw her every hope and her every fear reflected back in equal measure. "Don't deny me only for the sake of denying yourself."

Her breath caught. Desperate to lighten the mood, to keep herself from dwelling too much on that exhortation, she said, "It isn't fair, when you look like this and you have addled me so tonight. Ask me again tomorrow so I have time to think."

His eyes fluttered closed, and his brows creased in a troubled frown. She ached to smooth it away. "Fine."

He helped her redress, lacing her stays with surprising dexterity and fastening up all of the buttons on the back of her gown. She could hardly stand the heaviness of their silence.

"You know," she said, "you are quite good at that. You could have another, more scandalous life as some sort of lady's maid."

He snorted. "And you, the world's most unprofessional valet."

Once she'd finished straightening his neckcloth and tucked the handkerchief back into his waistcoat, she stooped to retrieve his coat. A sheet of paper tumbled from the pocket. Her heart dropped.

Lovelace's letter lay in the spill of moonlight at their feet.

Don't. The word was halfway out of her mouth by the time Kit picked it up. It was there in his hands: her name written in that elegant handwriting, the black wax seal on the envelope. His eyes flickered over it before he held it out to her.

She did not touch it. "Ah. My love letter."

"I'd believe you if it wasn't for the handwriting. It's Sinclair's."

Her thoughts evaporated into nothing. Her head rang with a metallic whir as she tried to make sense of what he had just said. "What?"

Kit frowned. "What do you mean, *what?*"

Niamh leaned against the wall. The whole room was spinning now, and she could feel her heartbeat in about five different places. When she finally felt able to speak, her voice was painfully small. "You're certain it's Sinclair's?"

He looked lost. "Yes. He's written me hundreds of letters over the years."

Sinclair was Lovelace.

Suddenly, it all made perfect sense. Why Lovelace knew her name so quickly and where she was staying. How they knew so much about every event. Why they despised Jack. Why they were determined to expose the Crown for corruption and defend the Machlish.

Lovelace was Sinclair.

He wrote about her, after everything she'd confided in him, after all the time they'd spent together, after all the kindness he'd shown her. The betrayal carved open a hole within her. How could he do such a thing to her? How could he do such a thing to *Kit?*

"Kit," she said. "I have something to tell you. Perhaps it's better to show you. But it will look very bad, and you will need to let me explain—"

"Slow down. You're not making any sense."

She could end this now. Take the letter from him and smile sweetly and pretend this never happened. Kiss him good night and let herself accept everything he'd offered her. Allow him to go through life, never knowing that his best friend conspired against him. Be happy. But if he was determined to have her, he should go into it with his eyes wide open. He should know all of the people who hurt him and kept secrets from him.

Including her.

She drew in a tremulous breath. "Open the letter."

Although he still seemed confused, he did as she asked. She watched his face, and she saw the moment he realized what he was reading. Slowly, he leveled her with his stare. It felt like an iron gate slamming shut between them. There was nothing of the man who'd treated her so tenderly, nothing of the man who'd argued with her to accept his suit.

"*If you find anything of substance.*" His voice was hard and detached. "You've been an informant for him."

"I swear, I told him nothing about you. Only that you supported the Machlish."

He looked at her as though he didn't recognize her at all. "Is that why you were so kind to me? To figure out if I was hiding something?"

It felt like he'd punched her in the gut. "No! I would never. Kit, please . . . I spent time with you because I *wanted* to."

"As if you've ever done anything you wanted to. Tonight was just . . ." The scorn in his voice faltered. "You've made a complete muddle of things. You've made me . . ."

Of everything he'd said to her, all the rude and petty things, the way he cut himself off stung the worst of all. "I've made you *what*?"

"Nothing," he said sharply. "It doesn't matter anymore. You've made this situation impossible."

"You can't do that. That isn't fair." She felt like a child, protesting so helplessly. "You cannot shut me out just because being angry is easier than being hurt!"

"You're no better! You've isolated yourself, Niamh. You throw yourself into work just so you don't have to look too closely at yourself."

She reeled back from the bitterness in his voice. Kit knew her too well to overlook the worst of her. A second idle was a second wasted, yes; such was the curse of her short life. But a second idle was also an open door for the truth to slip through like a thief: that no matter how much she did for others, no matter how much of herself she gave, no matter how much of their burdens she carried, she would never be worthy of love.

"I can't deal with this right now." By *this,* he clearly meant *you.* He crumpled the letter into his fist and shoved it into his pocket. "Stay here. I'm going to kill Sinclair."

Right now, he might very well mean it. Men had dueled over much smaller slights. Duels weren't especially common in Caterlow, but even she had heard of the politician who'd killed his rival for calling him a liar during a Parliamentary session. And in Avaland, where they cared so much about things like propriety and honor . . . She could not imagine how many had died over petty insults and wounded pride. The offended party chose the weapon (pistol, saber, or magic), as well as the victory conditions (first strike, first blood, or death).

Sinclair did not stand a chance against Kit. The thought made her mind blacken with terror. She grabbed his arm. "Kit, *wait.*"

He wrenched away from her. "Don't touch me."

The pain in his eyes gutted her. She curled her hand into a fist and cradled it close to her chest. "You don't have to forgive me. I wouldn't ask you to. But please listen to me. If you confront him now, in front of all these people . . . That is a very, very bad idea— for both him and for you."

"Strangely enough," he said, "I don't care anymore."

Without another word, he stalked out of the room.

"Kit!"

As she gave chase, he swiped an arm out in front of him. The window to her right splintered, and a tide of nettle spilled into the hall. Their vines knitted tightly together, trapping her on the other side of a wall of spines. Niamh staggered backward in surprise. Oh, he was playing dirty. She slipped on her gloves and tore through the barrier, but her skin burned through the thin fabric and the spines snagged determinedly in her hair and gown. She wriggled free of them and set off sprinting down the halls.

By the time she caught up to him, he'd already dragged Sinclair from the drawing room. From the top of the staircase, she could see them making their way into an abandoned hallway. Kit walked determinedly ahead, his every muscle tense with anger.

"Do I even want to guess where you've been?" Sinclair's voice filtered up to her. The playfulness in his voice was strained.

Kit moved faster than Niamh could blink. He shoved Sinclair into the wall so hard the paintings rattled. Kit was a good six inches shorter than Sinclair, but his simmering anger filled the room to bursting.

"What the hell, man?" Sinclair spluttered. "What is this about?"

"What do you *think* this is about, Sinclair?" Kit snarled. "Or is it Lovelace?"

Niamh had never seen Sinclair caught off guard. But now he went deathly pale. His body slackened against the wall, and he lifted his hands placatingly between them. "Kit . . ."

"Don't use that voice on me. I'm not your dog to call off." Kit dug the flat of his elbow into Sinclair's neck. He was incandescent with rage, but his voice quavered with a horrible, betrayed vulnerability. "And don't lie to me. You're not weaseling your way out of this. How could you try to sabotage *everything* and pretend to be my friend this whole time? What the fuck is wrong with you?"

Sinclair wheezed uselessly, and his face grew blotchy.

Niamh barreled down the stairs. "Kit, enough!"

Kit's shoulders tensed. He let him go and took a step back with a disgusted sneer on his face, as though Sinclair was a filthy puddle he'd narrowly avoided stepping in. Sinclair slumped to the floor, coughing. "Well?"

"Because I thought you were just like me," Sinclair rasped. "Empty inside."

Kit flinched as though he'd struck him.

"When you first came back, you were so angry," Sinclair continued. "I didn't think you could see anything outside that. There was so much injustice all around us. I didn't know how you could stomach it. So I thought, fuck it. I may be anonymous, but at least I'm trying to do something.

"But then you two started spending time together." He ran a hand fretfully through his hair. "Caring about Niamh made you start caring about the Machlish. I knew you'd stand with us if I asked you to, but it still felt hopeless. Jack still wasn't listening to you. If you held no sway over him—if you couldn't actually change anything—what did it matter if you cared or not?"

"Why would you write about us?" Niamh demanded. "You knew how much it would hurt."

"It was something to take advantage of. I didn't know you actually . . ." He looked at her pleadingly. "That day we talked, I'd already sent the column to the printer. It was too late to take it back. I'm sorry."

The silence stretched out. Kit's hands clenched to fists at his side.

"Nothing to say for once?" Sinclair asked, but he sounded defeated. "So, what now? Are you going to tell Jack? Have me thrown in jail for libel and sedition?"

"No." Kit's answer came without hesitation. All of the rage drained out of him, until there was nothing but hollow resignation, flat and cold. "I trusted you, and I trusted her. I'll live with the punishment for my own foolishness."

Sinclair's face went slack with surprise.

"Was our friendship ever real," Kit asked, "or have you been manipulating me from the beginning?"

"Of course it was real." Sinclair's voice was desolate. "It was to me."

Kit's expression did not change. "Don't publish another issue. I mean it. You're in over your head. I'll take it from here. Now stay out of my business."

Niamh watched him walk away. Neither she nor Sinclair said a word. She did not know how long she stood there, with tears drying against her cheeks and her chest blown open. But eventually, a stern-faced footman appeared. "The prince regent has asked that you be seen off to your chambers."

So she was to be a prisoner for the rest of her stay.

Niamh cast her gaze to Sinclair, still huddled in on himself on the floor. The betrayal still sat heavy within her, but the sheer guilt emanating from him softened her. He'd hurt her and lied to her. He'd ruined any chance at her and Kit ever being together. Even so, she did not want him imprisoned for it. He'd been her friend once, and he'd tried to fight against the hatred that wounded them both so deeply. Vengeance would not bring Kit back to her. It would not patch this rift within her.

"Good evening, Sinclair," she said quietly. "Your secret is safe with me."

He did not look up when she left.

She followed the footman, seeing and hearing nothing. When they reached her room, he shut the door behind her and turned the key heavily in the lock. Niamh slumped onto the cold hardwood beneath her and wept until nothing remained within her.

This had been a fairy tale, after all. Only it ended where it should have begun: with a maiden locked in a tower, tending her spinning wheel alone.

25

The wedding was tomorrow.

But when her eyes swelled so much it hurt to blink and her every muscle ached from the force of her sobs, Niamh decided she'd cried enough over it. There was nothing to be gained by dwelling on that which she couldn't change. So, just as she always had, she launched herself into her work.

Looking at Kit's wedding cloak made her feel faintly ill, so she pulled Rosa's gown into her lap and began to sew: flourishes on the bodice she hadn't planned, more enchantments secreted away into the lace, emotions spilled recklessly into each stitch. It was indelicate, messy work. She pricked her fingertips more times than she could excuse at this point in her career, but it barely hurt at all. By the time she finished, she felt more like a husk than a girl. She looked it, too. In the mirror, the streak of gray fissured through her hair, wider than it was yesterday—and paler, too, like a bone left in the sun to blanch.

The gown, however, was absolutely exquisite. The fabric was a perfect night black, but in the sunlight, it shimmered with magic, each stitch like spider's silk shot gold with daybreak. It was the most elaborate, ambitious thing she had ever made. It was terrible and true. Looking at it made her ache all over with longing.

She wanted Rosa to love it.

She wanted Rosa to hate it.

It was the most ridiculous and impossible of her fantasies: that Rosa thought the whole ensemble so hideous, she called the wedding off entirely; that Kit would be free of both her and Rosa; that Castilia could go on without dragging Avaland's corpse behind it for five miserable years. But no, she realized, that wasn't the whole of it. Her selfish desires went far deeper than she'd ever imagined. When Rosa walked down the aisle, Niamh wanted Kit to feel everything he'd locked away within himself. She wanted him to remember her.

A sharp knock on the door announced a visitor. She hadn't been expecting anyone, but perhaps Rosa had come by for another fitting. Dread coiled tight within her. Niamh had no idea how to face her. The truth of what she knew would write itself indelibly across her face, the same as it always had, or else Rosa would divine it instantly with her keen power of observation, and where would that leave them? When she discovered how thoroughly Jack had schemed to use her and her family, she would—

The knock sounded again, more urgently this time. A key turned in the lock with an ominous *thunk*. Niamh launched herself out of her seat and opened the door. "Infanta Rosa, I . . ."

But there was no one there—just the dust swirling languidly through the thick columns of light. The world seemed to be sleeping, the very air dyed a hazy pink in the flush of late afternoon. Niamh blinked. She must've imagined it. She'd finally exhausted herself to the brink of madness. But then, the door imprisoning her here had been unlocked. And there, at her feet: a letter with her name scrawled prettily across the front. Lovelace's—Sinclair's— handwriting winked up at her.

Cold anger doused her confusion. How dare he write to her after all the trouble he'd caused? What kind of game did he think he was playing? She had half a mind to tear it to shreds and throw it to the wind. But curiosity got the better of her. Niamh opened the letter.

> *I will not waste your time or test your goodwill by opening with anything but an apology. I am so sorry. I cannot begin to tell you how much. If you're willing to let me grovel in person, my invitation from a few weeks past still stands. There's a carriage outside for you, and it will take you to my townhouse. I know you have no reason to want to see me, but perhaps bad company would be preferable to none at all. Moping doesn't suit you, Niamh. I dread to think of what you are doing in there all alone.*
>
> *GS*

Either he underestimated her intelligence or overestimated her capacity for forgiveness if he expected her to walk into such an obvious trap! And yet, what could he truly do to her now? The more she read it over, the less fault she could find with it. It was surprisingly genuine, with none of his usual affectation and only the barest hint of cheekiness. And if nothing else, he was right. Anything beat tormenting herself in this stuffy room.

But what to do? There was no way she could slip out of the palace unseen. Nothing in this room could help her. Nothing but . . .

That's it.

Niamh snatched the veil from where it hung and pinned it hast-ily into her hair. Beneath the delicate fabric, the world appeared as indistinct and gauzy as a dream. Hazy memories and feelings drifted across her mind like smoke, but the intricate black lace obscured her features entirely. Yes, this would do. Niamh was a solid head shorter than Rosa, but even if anyone noticed, they surely would not prevent a princess from going about her business. At least she hoped not. She was not confident in her ability to do a remotely convincing impression of Rosa.

Drawing in a breath, Niamh slipped into the hallway. Outside her room, it was utter chaos as the household prepared for the wedding night's ball. Valets of visiting lords and borrowed help bustled through the halls. Footmen carted in luggage and gowns, sculptures carved in ice and sugar, crates of food deliveries—smoked meats and sardines on ice; tomatoes and cabbages and potatoes—and more flower arrangements than a botanical garden could hold. Flower petals dusted the floors like snowfall and perfumed the air. The scents of beeswax candles and silver polish made her head swim.

As Niamh wove her way through the crowds, dragging yards of fabric behind her, she couldn't help a giddy grin from stealing across her face. No one dared glance at her for more than a moment. Sneaking around as a princess was *easy*. The front door loomed just ten paces away, then five, then—

"Infanta Rosa?" Sofia called.

Niamh stiffened and slowly turned to face her. Her cold, austere beauty, as always, chilled Niamh to the bone. The princess stood perfectly still and poised amid the flurry of motion around her. Her gown, a snowy white, practically melted into the marble floor. Her delicate hands were clasped anxiously in front of her, and the purple shadows beneath her eyes were starker for how pale her skin was. It looked as though she hadn't slept at all.

Somehow, the sight of her—as fragile and weary as ever—filled Niamh with more guilt than dread. She couldn't believe that she had been foolish and flighty enough to leap to the worst possible conclusion: that a young woman's grasping attempts to escape her own loneliness were signs of some sort of villainy. A small part of her longed to fall to her knees and apologize. The more sensible part wanted to flee from those probing silver eyes. They struggled to meet hers through the veil.

"My sincerest apologies for not greeting you sooner," Sofia continued. "No one informed me that you had arrived."

Gods, what *now*? She searched for some idea for how to gracefully escape this conversation. Niamh cleared her throat, and in the most dispassionate voice she could summon, replied, "I did not want to disturb you, since my visit was so brief."

An unusually quizzical look crossed Sofia's face, but she nodded, very determined to remain polite. "Are you ill, Your Highness? You sound congested."

Niamh feigned a delicate cough. "I must have caught a chill."

"How terrible," Sofia said. "Please, join me for tea before you leave."

"Oh, no, I couldn't impose on you." Niamh winced. That did not sound like something Rosa would say at all. "I meant to say, of course, that tea is so very dull. It does not agree with me. Ehm . . ." She winced again as her own stubborn accent slipped through. "I really must be going now. Good day!"

Understanding broke open Sofia's coolly skeptical mask. She touched her fingertips to her lips, as if to hold in a gasp. "Miss O'Connor, is that you?"

"Not so loud, if you please!" Niamh hissed. "Your Highness, I—"

Sofia cast a look around the room, then took a hurried step closer. She rested a hand on Niamh's arm. The weight of her touch was impossibly light, but the chill of it rippled over her skin. As she bent down to Niamh's height, she dropped her already delicate voice to a bare whisper. "Go. If the prince regent asks about you, I will come up with something to tell him."

"What?" Niamh blinked up at her, struck senseless with surprise. "Why would you . . . ?"

"I do not think my husband has any right to keep you locked away like a prisoner. You have committed no crime, so why should you be punished as though you have?"

"But Your Highness . . ." Niamh wrung her hands together. "Since I arrived, I have done nothing but cause trouble for him."

"Trouble," Sofia mused. "I am not convinced that all trouble is bad."

"What do you mean?"

"The prince regent does his best to keep everything under his control. It distresses him greatly when he cannot. But last night . . ." She hesitated, but a tentative hope buoyed her voice. "Last night, for the first time since we have been married, he confided in me. A great many things weigh on him, but he has always been determined to shoulder them alone."

Niamh dreaded to imagine what exactly he'd told her. But Sofia, miraculously, did not seem to despise her and her supposed ambitions as much as Jack did.

"Both he and his brother are very stubborn men," Sofia said. "Their estrangement has pained both of them, not that they would admit it. But because of you, I believe something has begun to bloom in what has lain fallow."

When she'd first arrived, Kit had lashed out at his brother like a cornered animal. But as the weeks had worn on, he'd grown far less petty and far more cutting in the ways that mattered. Last night, they seemed to almost argue as equals. And Jack . . .

Enough, he'd all but begged her when she beseeched him to think of Kit's happiness.

She did not see how any of it mattered now. "I did not know you were so poetic, Your Highness."

"I was a whimsical child, if you can believe that. My father hardly knew what to do with me." Niamh could believe it, actually. She remembered, so vividly, Sofia's account of her childhood joy: running through the snow, pink-nosed and laughing, chasing after spirits glittering just out of reach in the flurries. Sofia's warm expression sobered. "However, I beat it out of myself over the years. So thank *you*, Miss O'Connor, for reminding me. I meant what I told you. Your divine blood is extraordinary—but your compassion and patience for others more so. You make things lighter wherever you go."

The kindness of those words struck her like a knife to the heart. Thank every merciful god in the Otherworld that she had no more tears within her to cry. "Thank you very much, Your Highness."

"Where are you going now?" she asked, almost eagerly. "Are you hoping to speak to Kit?"

No, Niamh wanted to say, *I have lost that right entirely.*

But whatever pathetic feeling showed on her face made Sofia's eyes sparkle softly with—of all things—*delight*. "I thought so. Infanta Rosa is a lovely young woman, but it is very clear to me that they are ill-suited for each other."

"As are we," she protested. "I cannot ask him to abandon his duty for my sake."

"I married for duty. I knew that was my lot in life from a young age, and I made my peace with it. Love can grow, given time and space. But if you will allow me one of my childish sentiments . . ." Wistfulness played at the edges of her smile. "If there is any other option, if love already exists, who are we to stand in the way of it? You have given much to those around you. I wonder what you may discover if you showed yourself the same gentleness. Will you find out for us both?"

If you believe you've made no difference at all to anyone, Kit had told her once, *you're even more clueless than I thought.*

She thought she'd given everyone nothing but trouble. But perhaps kindness was not nothing.

Niamh wound her arms around Sofia and hugged her close.

Sofia startled, but very tentatively, she placed a hand on the small of Niamh's back. The scents of newly fallen snow and the fragile bloom of snowdrop washed over her.

"Do not delay any longer," Sofia said softly. "I sincerely hope we will have a long time to get to know each other."

"Thank you," Niamh whispered.

With that, she gathered up the veil around her and hurried through the front door. In the circle of the driveway, a carriage waited for her, just as Sinclair had promised. And when the horses took off toward the city, those first, juddering steps felt like the waves of the Machlish Sea: as uncertain and endless as possibility.

An archway of bougainvillea shrouded the path to Sinclair's town-house. Pink petals were scattered across the flagstones, bright and curling as they dried in the sun. They crunched pleasantly beneath her boots as she approached, a taste of autumn in late spring. Kit had chosen the property well. Niamh had to admit she was pleasantly surprised.

When she reached the top stair, she tripped over her own foot. She gasped but caught herself on the front door at the last moment. Her palms slapping against the wood must've alerted Sinclair's staff of her presence, because the door swung open to reveal his very concerned housekeeper. She was led to the drawing room and within a minute, a tea service was brought out for her. The very sight of it reminded her that she was famished. She grabbed one of the delicate finger sandwiches and placed the whole thing into her mouth. Rude, she supposed, but she supposed politeness was the last thing she owed Sinclair at this point.

"You came."

Niamh nearly choked at the sound of Sinclair's voice.

He leaned in the doorway. His hair had fallen just short of its usual intentional wildness. Today, he only looked harried. He was still in his shirtsleeves, with his cravat loose around his neck. A bruise in the shape of Kit's elbow blossomed along his throat.

She winced at the sight of it. "Are you all right?"

"I'm fine." His fingers fluttered to the bruise, as though just remembering its existence. *Liar.* It must've pained him terribly to swallow or speak. He entered the room and sat across from her, his elbows propped up on his knees. As he drank in her expression, his own softened. "Are you?"

"Not yet. I believe I was promised groveling."

"Right." Self-consciously, he rubbed at the back of his neck. "I will say that I am sorry as many times as you need to hear it. I never should have taken things as far as I did with the two of you. But ever since the Duke of Pelinor disowned me, I've been so angry. Lovelace was supposed to help ensure that no one would suffer the way I have. Punished and hated, just because they're not 'fully' Avlish." He paused. "For years, I've been treading water. But when I realized I had a chance to hit Jack where it hurt, I got carried away. I didn't give either of you the benefit of the doubt in telling you what I was doing. I'm paying the price for that now."

"Did you really believe either of us would turn you in?" she asked quietly. "Your cause was just."

"I suppose I've gotten too used to hiding over the years."

"Both of us care for you a lot, Sinclair. You were the first person to show me kindness in Sootham." She lowered her gaze. "I have not had many friends in my life. The time I shared with you and Kit was meaningful to me. I suppose that is what stings most of all. What you did tarnished what I'd held so dear."

"I know. It was meaningful to me, too." His voice broke. "I am so sorry. For so many things."

"I didn't tell him we'd exchanged letters, either," Niamh murmured. "We've both made mistakes, and I can see you regret them as much as I do. I forgive you."

He lifted his head and stared at her with red-rimmed eyes. "You do?"

"Of course." She offered him a tentative smile. "I am still hurt. But your intentions were good. They *are* good. And, well . . . You were right."

He looked surprised. "What do you mean?"

"Jack was indeed hiding something." The story poured out of her. It felt good to share the burden with someone else: the mess that Kit and Jack's father had left for them and the ways Jack was trying to manage it. He listened without interrupting her, even when she shared his father's role in it, his expression growing stormier.

When she finally finished, he let out a low whistle. "That son of a bitch. That's enough to sink him forever. If this gets out, Parliament will remove him as regent. And they'll almost certainly try to block his succession when the king does finally die. Barring that, the King of Castilia may do worse than call off the engagement. He doesn't strike me as the type to take entrapment lightly."

"Yes." Terror knotted in her chest when he laid it all out like that. "That all sounds likely."

Sinclair frowned. "So why are you telling me all this, when you know what I could do with it?"

"Because." She clenched her hands to fists in her lap. "I believe you want to earn forgiveness. And despite everything, I trust you. I know you don't want to hurt Kit, and I know you want what's best for our people. And maybe . . . Maybe there's a way to fix all of this. Jack still has the opportunity to change his mind."

"Change? Jack Carmine?" Sinclair laughed derisively. "You're talking about the same man I know?"

"I believe he wants to do better," she said. "I believe he *is* better than his father. He just doesn't know how to be, and he certainly doesn't know how to stray from a path he's begun walking down."

Sinclair rose from his chair and rummaged through his bar

cart. Glass and metal rattled softly together. "I need a drink. You look like you need one, too. I have brandy. Want some?"

She'd never had brandy before. "Please."

He poured her a glass and pressed it into her hands. Outside, the flowers whispered against the windowpane. Warm evening light flooded into the room.

Sinclair swirled his drink. "I will grant that Jack has a conscience. Parliament won't take a chance on Kit. He's too young. Which means Jack is the best shot we have for making things right with Machland. But only if we save him from his own stupid scheme."

Deep down, she had to admit this was all terribly exciting. Here in a leather wingback chair, sipping her brandy from its snifter, she could almost imagine she was an influential gentleman discussing politics at a club. "And how do you propose we do that?"

Sinclair's eyes glittered with mischief. "What else could I mean? We have to stop the wedding."

Niamh nearly spit out her brandy. "*What?* No. We cannot do that."

"Why not?" He leapt out of his chair, practically crackling with energy. "If there's no wedding, Jack has no plan. The situation with the protesters shows no signs of letting up, which means he will have to make concessions somewhere—either by getting funding elsewhere than Pelinor, or by letting his advisors actually help him. The way I see it, Castilia isn't getting anything out of this arrangement, so stopping it is the only ethical thing to do." He paused. "Besides, have you seen the way Rosa looks at Kit? She'll be thrilled to be rid of him."

"I suppose I haven't noticed," she lied wanly.

"Granted, it might take a bit of a delicate touch," he continued, undeterred. "We somehow need to pull this off without causing a collapse of international relations between Avaland and Castilia, or the complete destruction of Jack's reputation. It's almost impossible, but it's a risk I'm willing to take."

"But *why*?"

"I could use a little excitement." He smiled bitterly. "And despite everything that's happened this Season, Kit is still my best friend. Is that sad?"

Kit's voice echoed in her mind. *Sinclair is stupidly loyal.* And well, she still loved Kit, too. "No, not at all. Unless you consider me sad, too."

"Kit has his charms, I suppose," he said teasingly. "I'll allow it."

Niamh grinned back at him.

Sinclair tapped his chin. "The easiest way is to get either Kit or Rosa to call it off. Young people change their minds all the time, so it wouldn't raise too many eyebrows. I don't know Rosa. But I know Kit." He fixed her with a lingering look. "And I haven't seen him this happy in a long time."

Niamh's face burned. She hadn't told him about Kit's proposal, mostly because she'd longed to forget it herself. "You saw him after the party. He will never want to speak to either of us ever again. Whatever you are implying, I have no sway over him, I assure you."

"Come, now! Where is that can-do attitude of yours?" Sinclair crossed his arms. "Just bat those pretty blue eyes at him and apologize. He's had a few days to cool off, and he's a complete pushover for you, in case you haven't noticed."

She very much doubted that *batting her eyes* would improve this situation, but she supposed anything was worth a try at this point. "Say he *does* accept my apology. Then what?"

"Jack is afraid of being found out," Sinclair said. "I threaten to expose him. Kit refuses to go along with his plan. Just like that, he has nothing over anyone. I'll even write a little column about how, oh, I don't know, Kit has a grand new vision for Avaland. No one will dare to touch Kit. There's absolutely no reason he has to be a martyr for his father's mistakes."

Niamh heaved a long sigh. "All right. I'll try to talk to him again."

"Excellent! And as a matter of fact, I just so happen to know where he is right now."

Niamh perked up. "Where?"

"At his stag party at Nightingale's." Sinclair made a face. "I was disinvited. No surprise there."

"I see . . . What is a stag party?"

He looked at her with exaggeratedly wide eyes. "It's only the most important day of a man's life. His last day of freedom!"

He explained it to her, but she had a hard time following. From what she could glean, a bunch of people sat in a room, drinking and eating until they lost all sense. Then, maybe, in a wine-drunk haze, they hunted a deer, skinned it, and presented it as a gift to the bride the next day. Niamh suspected he was having one over on her, but she didn't want to embarrass herself further by pressing the issue. The image of Rosa, holding a deer skin in her arms, un-impressed and completely bemused, nearly killed her.

"You should count yourself lucky," said Niamh. "In Caterlow, we parade the newlyweds through the streets and cover them in mud and flowers. Then we chase them into a lake."

"That sounds infinitely more fun."

A silence fell over them, and Niamh buried her face in her hands. This was an entirely ridiculous idea. Kit had already proposed to her—horribly, yes—but she would never have the honor of ex-pecting another. If he called off the wedding, she would have noth-ing at all. All her work, wasted. Her one chance to give her family a better life, gone.

"Is it really wise to risk so much?" she murmured. "Jack's plan will work."

"All right." Sinclair frowned. "Let's play it out, shall we? Kit and Rosa get married. Castilia stays out of any military conflict for five years. You go home, knowing you had something real and you let it go, but at least you didn't rock the boat for anyone but yourself. That's it for you? True happiness?"

That sounded absolutely dreadful. "I . . . I don't know."

He raised an eyebrow. "When you're on your deathbed, do you think you're going to reflect on how proud you were to put everyone's needs before your own? Do you think you'll wish you'd given up *more*?"

Hope blossomed within her, but she crushed it in her fist. "How can I possibly live for my own happiness, when I have so little of it left? How can that possibly be meaningful, when my family is counting on me?"

"Because it's not meaningful to kill yourself little by little to make people happy!"

Niamh reeled back at the sudden fierceness in his voice.

"Believe me, I've tried. I've tried so many fucking times." He sank back down into his chair, as if suddenly exhausted. The quiet pain in those words made her heart lurch. "I tried to be the son Pelinor wanted. I tried to save Kit from himself when he didn't want to be saved. But that's not love. That's madness. That's cruelty—to you and everyone else around you. Can't you see that?"

Niamh choked on a sob. When she thought of what made her happy, *truly* happy . . . It looked like this: brandy in a cozy room with someone who might be her friend again. It looked like playing lawn games in the summer, or curling up beside Kit in the rain, or embroidering absentmindedly while he tended to his greenhouse. It looked like a thousand quiet moments, each of them as small as a candle flame. But together, they were luminous—as expansive and bright as a galaxy. How could such beautiful, tender things be selfish?

Happiness looked nothing like sewing by a lacemaker's lamp long after her body had begun begging for mercy. It looked nothing like aching fingers and swimming thoughts. It looked nothing like sinking deeper and deeper under the weight of exhaustion and *regret.*

Sinclair sighed and offered his handkerchief to her. "I've seen a lot of horrible things growing up in Sootham. The lengths people will go to in order to protect their legacy. The things they'll do, the people they'll hurt. But I've seen a lot of beautiful things, too. There's this lake near my family's country home. This may sound ridiculous, but I used to love to watch the ducks."

When Niamh laughed, he smiled encouragingly. "When they hatch, they imprint on the first living thing they see. Most of the time, that's their mother. But one season, an egg got left behind in the nest, and when the duckling hatched, it imprinted on the duke's hound. Whatever they imprint on, they swim toward it headlong. Even if it's dangerous, even if they're completely wrong, they follow that instinct. It's the first thing they ever do. They live for love.

"Nothing is guaranteed, Niamh. We all die. You and I are dying right now, but we're also *alive*. Love is what makes life worth living. Love is what makes us act when we most need to. That's what your legacy is. It's how you love the people around you, not how much you've sacrificed for them."

Niamh dabbed her eyes with his handkerchief. "Thank you, Sinclair. Really."

"Don't mention it." When he smiled, he looked like the god of mischief himself. "So, what do you say? Shall we pay Kit a visit at Nightingale's?"

26

*D*espite the late hour, the streets of Sootham were teeming and alive. Niamh, however, kept her eyes trained on her feet. The cobblestones were treacherous tonight, glistening with damp. Rainwater—and a slurry of other unseemly liquids—pooled in the cracks and reflected the oily, golden light of the streetlamps.

She would not ruin either another hemline *or* a pair of slippers. She would not look like a careless child on the one night of her life it mattered. She stepped carefully off the curb—and immediately was jerked backward by a firm tug on her elbow. Niamh stumbled back into Sinclair, just as a carriage tore out of the night itself. It clattered by, a blur of horses and crushing wheels. Her heart slammed against her rib cage.

"Careful." He offered his arm to her, and she gratefully accepted.

He led her around puddles and the gentlemen pouring out of the gambling dens and clubs, loud and merry and unsteady with drink. Never in her life had she felt so completely out of her element. This, she understood, was not a place girls like her were supposed to be. But on the arm of one of the most infamous political columnists in the city—and with little reputation left to lose—she felt oddly safe.

Sinclair leaned down conspiratorially and said, "This is where all the nobles take their mistresses. You'll find the best gossip here."

"Revealing your trade secrets, Sinclair?"

"Hardly," he scoffed. He jerked his chin toward a building across the street. "Here we are. The doom of high-society men."

Tucked away between dark-windowed shops and busy coffee-houses, Nightingale's rose up out of the gloom and the protective arms of the oaks, all ostentatious white stone and imposing crenelations. On the other side of a wrought-iron fence, twin gas lamps burned like the eyes of a massive beast in the dark. Out front, a massive bow window, nearly opaque and streaked with black beads of water, overlooked the street. If she squinted, she could see the shapes of people moving just beyond it. It made even Sinclair's lovely home look like a dollhouse.

"That does not make me feel better," she said weakly.

"*You* have nothing to worry about, my darling, innocent companion. Men come here to gamble and bicker among themselves. Mostly cards or hazards. There's also betting books. They wager on things like who's going to get married this Season, or whose marriage is going to collapse. I heard Lord Bowsworth once made a two-hundred-guinea bet on a raindrop race."

Those were the kinds of men she would anger, if she succeeded tonight. Or perhaps some of them had already betted against Kit and Rosa. She swallowed down the knot of nerves in her throat. "Right."

He tapped his walking stick against the wet cobblestone, then gestured toward a lattice that ran up the side of the building like a ladder. Wisteria threaded through its rungs, its sweet scent carried on the breeze. "See that there? You can climb up to get to the balcony. In the meantime, I'll create a distraction. As soon as Kit is left to his own devices, he's going to make a beeline for it. I guarantee it. You use your wiles. He realizes what a stubborn ass he's been. He calls the wedding off. Crisis avoided."

She nodded.

Sinclair frowned up at the balcony. "Are you sure you can do this? You have a way of tripping over air."

"Ghosts push me, I'll have you know!" She huffed. "Have a little faith."

"Very well," he said skeptically. "I'll see you soon."

As he strolled through the gate, the very picture of confidence, Niamh slipped around the side of the building. Here, the light hardly reached the narrow alleyway, and as the mist scythed lazily over the streetlamps, the darkness guttered around her. A shadow cleaved from the others and glided toward her. Niamh bit down on a scream. But it was only a black cat, trotting busily past her. It registered her presence with a soft, inquisitive *mrow?*

She blew out a breath, beyond exasperated with herself. For the good of her people, Castilia, and the man she loved, she could do this.

Niamh grabbed the lattice. The iron was slick and cold against her palms, and when she eased her weight onto the first foothold, the entire structure groaned in protest. She did her best to ignore that as she hauled herself up rung by rung. This close, the scent of the wisteria turned cloying, and the flowers tickled her nose as she climbed. Her breath grew thready, but she refused to think of how far below her the ground was. At last, she closed her shaking fingers around the railing of the balcony. As carefully as she could, she eased herself up onto it—then all but melted onto the floor. She lay on her back, chest heaving, as the stars spun overhead and her vision pulsed black. Remembering to breathe while climbing had not been high on her list of priorities.

Maybe Sinclair had been right to worry. This was by far the worst idea she'd ever gone through with, in a very long list of very bad ideas.

Once she caught her breath, she got to her feet and waited. Light from inside spilled out onto the floor a bare meter away from her. From here, she could just barely make out the club within. A miasmatic haze hung over everything, but she could hear the clink of glasses and the laughter and shouts of men as they staked their fortunes. Most of them clustered around tables and lingered at the bar. There were, disappointingly, far fewer hunting tools than Sinclair had led her to believe. She should've known better than to listen to a single word he said.

The balcony doors flew open. Niamh swallowed a squeak of surprise.

Kit stalked to the railing and leaned over it. He took in a ragged gulp of air, as though he'd been holding his breath all night. He carried the smell of the club on him: acrid tobacco smoke and the sickly sweet sharpness of liquor. It couldn't have been easy for him to be in this environment. His skin was paler than usual and slick with sweat. No one paid him much mind. They were too deep in their card games and their cups.

But as miserable and stressed as he looked, her heart still gave a desperate lurch at the sight of him. His sleeves were rolled to his elbows; his jacket must've lain forgotten on the back of some chair. She wished she could touch him again. She wished she had any right to. The lit end of his cigar burned like a will-o'-the-wisp. He puffed restlessly at it, too absorbed in his own thoughts to take notice of her standing in the dark like a fool.

"Kit."

He nearly jumped out of his skin. She had to admit it was satisfying to be *doing* the startling for once. He blinked, then blinked again, as though she were a horrible vision he might dispel with enough effort. But when that failed, he stared. She couldn't track the emotions that passed over his face. Each one of them bludgeoned her. At last, he predictably settled on anger. "What the hell are you doing here?"

I wanted to see you. The words hovered right there, on the tip of her tongue. *I wanted to speak with you.* But he hadn't fled at the very sight of her. Now that she'd hurdled that first obstacle, she couldn't jeopardize this opportunity.

"I wanted to apologize. I'm sorry."

"Yes," he said dismissively. "You've said that already. Now that you've gotten what you've come for, you can go."

"Wait, please." She took a step toward him, and he threw himself against the railing as though she'd aimed a knife at him. Chastened, she retreated a few paces, where the wisteria tumbled down like a curtain. His wary eyes flashed like a cat's in the dark, but he did not move again.

"I wrote to Lovelace—to Sinclair—when you told me to be careful," she continued. "He wrote to me when I first arrived, but he never forced me to spy on you. I never intended to, and I never did. But I was foolish to believe that I could handle everything on my own. You're right that I am a coward. I *am* always running, without any regard for my own well-being. But this time, I hurt someone else, too." Her voice trembled, and she squeezed her eyes shut to hold back her tears. "I should have said something much sooner. I regret every moment I didn't trust you with the truth. It was my own recklessness that landed us here. I'm so sorry."

Kit fell quiet for a long moment. He tapped the ashes of his cigar off on the railing. "There's no sense dwelling on what you should have done. It's over."

"It doesn't have to be," she said breathlessly.

He listened without interruption as she described Sinclair's plan. Kit had always been terrible at hiding his feelings, but as she spoke, he remained unsettlingly blank. With the cigar smoke shimmering before his face, it was as though they stood on opposite sides of the veil between worlds.

"No," he said. "Sinclair has tried it his way for years. I'm done playing these games. I'm done. I'm not making a fool of myself again—especially not for you two and your harebrained schemes."

"You didn't even consider it!"

"I don't need to."

Tension slipped between them like a knife. The last time they were alone, he'd looked at her so tenderly, his hair and eyes washed cool and silver. She did not want to remember it all so vividly. The gentleness of his callused hands against her skin, the reverence of his gaze on her. But now, Kit glared at her with pure and utter reproach. She didn't know how to cross this gulf, or if there *was* any crossing this gulf. There was nothing to do but pound on the door he had slammed shut between them.

"Why not?"

"I can't let Jack take the fall for what our father did," he said lowly. "He's spent his whole life protecting me. It's time to repay the favor."

Of all the foolish, self-sacrificing things he could do . . . ! If he would not call off the engagement for her sake, perhaps she could appeal to him in another way. "But there is no guarantee Jack's plan will work! Besides, it is wrong of you to drag Infanta Rosa into this unknowingly. If you had any honor at all, you would let her go free of this engagement."

Coldly, he asked, "Have you gotten everything out of your system yet?"

"No! Why are you so determined to be unhappy? Why do you think you deserve nothing better?" Her voice wavered. "I know I have lost all claim to the ability to make you happy. But if there is any other way to do your duty, to fight for what you believe in, then why are you doing this to yourself?"

Kit looked stricken. "I can't risk it."

"Risk *what*, Kit? Can you truly tell me you want to do this?" She felt wild and reckless, like she was standing on the edge of a cliff, rather than a balcony. The force of her feelings swelled like a storm within her. If anyone were to find them here, it would be beyond ruinous, but she couldn't bring herself to care. She couldn't let it end like this. "Tell me you do. Tell me you will be content. Tell me you will have no regrets, and I will wish you well. I will leave Avaland at once, and I will not look back. I will remember you fondly, and I will not wish for you to think of me more than you ought."

He was silent.

"Tell me," she whimpered, "*please*."

"It was cruel of you to come here."

"Cruel?" She clenched her fists at her sides. "What is cruel is befriending me and treating me like an equal. What is cruel is—"

In one fluid motion, he dropped his cigar and crossed the space between them. Her back hit the wall. He loomed over her, all coiled tension, and the heat of his body flooded over her like a wave. He must've read the longing in her, for his pupils dilated. By now, she knew intimately what hunger looked like on his face. There was a fire kindling in his eyes, and fool that she was, she was all too eager to burn. His breath trembled against her lips.

This, she thought. *This is cruel.*

"What's cruel," he said, "is that you let me hope."

When he spoke, his mouth moved against hers. The softest, feather-light pressure. The ghost of a kiss she would never have again. A punishment—whether for himself or her, she couldn't be certain. The agony was greater than she ever could have concocted for herself in her worst nightmares.

But then his mouth captured hers, hard and insistent and *angry*.

Niamh's eyes widened, riveted on him. Desire turned her molten. Indignation filled her with stubborn resistance. But as his teeth tugged on her lower lip, as he slid a knee between hers, her eyes fluttered helplessly shut. She arched up to mold herself against him. The rough moan she drew from him pooled low within her. Faced with his fervent, unyielding *want,* she couldn't remember for the life of her what she'd come here for, or what they'd been arguing about.

Then, she heard a terrible sound: the creak of the balcony door opening.

The noise of the club flowed out: laughter, the clink of glasses and coins.

Kit pulled back sharply. Golden light—and panic—sparked in the depths of his eyes. Before she could blink, the wisteria *seized* her. Its vines looped around her arms and waist, then all but dragged her back into the shadows. New growth shot out, delicate and glittering faintly with magic, to conceal her entirely from view. Their petals made her nose itch, but she held her breath and stifled the sneeze. She could hardly resent the rough treatment when he'd saved her. Again.

Jack stepped outside. "There you are. What are you doing out here?"

"Nothing," Kit said, sounding just a little breathless. "Just getting some air."

Jack eyed him suspiciously, but came to stand beside him. He rested a hand on Kit's shoulder, and Kit did not pull away. "I know this has been difficult, but you are doing the right thing."

Kit's jaw worked, but he made no reply.

"How can I make things right between us?" Jack hunched over the railing. "After tomorrow, you will go on to live your own life. I do not want us to part like this, with so much regret between us."

"Just let it go, Jack," Kit said wearily. "Don't torture yourself anymore. Not for my sake. These past few days have helped me to understand you more. On some level, I always have understood."

"I hope you know that I love—"

"Yeah. I know." Kit tensed. He stared out into the night, but even from here, Niamh could see sadness overtake his expression. "I do, too."

Jack turned to face him. "Kit, I . . ."

"If we're done here," Kit said, "let's go."

He turned and walked back inside. Jack lingered for only a moment before following him.

Little by little, the vines around her slackened. They eased her onto the ground so gently and apologetically, she had the impression of them dusting off her skirts and rearranging her hair. Purple and gold blossoms drifted through the air and settled at her feet. For a few long moments, Niamh stayed slumped against the balcony railing, the pads of her fingers pressed to her swollen lips. Her face burned with what she was certain was a magnificent flush. Anger and fondness tangled so wretchedly within her, she couldn't breathe.

Kit Carmine was the most insufferable, contrary, *confusing* man ever to live.

But she'd given him an escape route—a chance to cut her free forever—and he had not taken it. He'd kissed her with the furious, terrified desperation of a man clinging to life. He'd protected her as if it were as ingrained in him as breathing.

Don't deny me only for the sake of denying yourself.

Tomorrow, he couldn't waver any longer. He did not have to love her as she loved him. But he deserved, for once in his life, a chance to build a life on his own terms. He deserved a second chance to take his own advice.

She would give him one.

And then, if she must, she would let him go.

27

*T*he night before felt like yet another fairy tale: a girl spirited away and returned before her cruel family could be the wiser.

At eleven o'clock, Sinclair had snuck her into the palace. During the ride back, he'd fumed at Kit's stubbornness—then, when he'd exhausted himself, fallen into an uncharacteristically sullen silence. For once in her life, Niamh had not minded the quiet. A plan, taken root on the balcony, began to blossom in the dark of the carriage. A stupid, impossible plan—but a plan all the same. As desperately as she wanted to, she could not involve Sinclair. If it went sour, her disgrace would not touch him.

By three in the morning, she'd finished embroidering and assembling Kit's cloak. At six, she'd been awoken and delivered to

Rosa's townhouse, with the wedding gown and Kit's cloak each tucked into a delicate box like a jewel in its case.

Now, she walked into Rosa's chambers, fearing she might fall asleep on her feet. One of Jack's footmen followed close on her heels like a fussy hound. Once the door shut behind them, he stationed himself in front of it and kept his gaze pinned on her. In it was a warning: *The prince regent is watching. Do not say or do anything you will regret.*

Rosa waited for her behind her privacy screen. A bouquet of roses sat on a table beside her, ready to be woven into her hair. All of their thorns had been carefully removed and their stems twirled to loosen the petals. Rosa had painted her lips Carmine red. She looked elegant, even in nothing but her thin dressing gown. But upon closer inspection, her olive skin possessed none of its usual luster. Beneath the rouge dusted on her cheeks, she was waxen.

"Good morning," Niamh said, her voice little more than a croak.

"Indeed," Rosa said absently. "Shall we?"

Niamh unpacked the dress carefully. The long train of the skirt tumbled across the floor like a rivulet of dark water. Rosa inspected it with an unmistakable look of appreciation. Niamh worked as quickly as she could to lace Rosa into it. Of course, she tripped over the hem no fewer than three times and almost popped a sequin or three off the sleeves. When the last of the jet buttons was fastened at the base of Rosa's neck, Niamh climbed onto a wobbly stool to place the veil on her head like a crown. She adjusted the draping of the fabric before pinning it in place. It flowed down her back and fanned out across the floor, all of the intricate lacework on display.

"There." Niamh took a step back to admire her handiwork. "You are ready."

Rosa stood before the mirror. Imprisoned within its enormous gold frame, she looked like a portrait done in oils—or she would, if it weren't for the very peculiar look on her face. She scrunched her nose as though she had tasted something quite bitter. "What an unusual magic you have."

"What do you mean?"

"I am feeling," she said, with equal parts disgust and awe, "quite a lot of feelings. Is this what the inside of your head is like? No wonder you are so *busy* all the time."

Admittedly, the enchantments in the gown were quite strong. The gown filled her up with yearning for all the things that could have been and sorrow for all the things she'd failed to do. In hindsight, perhaps she should not have finished it immediately after Kit had dismissed her. It was rather inappropriate for a wedding, but at least it matched the elegant solemnity of the gown. Rosa could be the goddess of night herself.

"Sorry," Niamh said sheepishly, "I may have gotten carried away. Should I—"

"No. Don't change a thing. It's everything I wanted."

"There certainly won't be a dry eye in the church," she offered.

Rosa stared at her reflection, turning her face this way and that. "I almost feel like a bride."

Her heart gave a painful lurch. "I'm glad. You look beautiful."

It was only then—with the wobble of her voice and the tight burning in her throat—that she realized she was already weeping. Rosa looked utterly bewildered, even alarmed. Then, with a grave air, she pushed aside the privacy screen to address the footman lurking by the door. "You. Send for tea at once."

"My apologies, Your Highness," he replied. "The prince regent says I'm not to leave the girl unattended."

Rosa drew herself to her full height and lifted her chin. In her gown of all black, she cut a striking figure indeed, and her tone rang out with regal condescension. "What, is she a prisoner? Or are you afraid I shall besmirch her honor?"

An uncomfortable beat of silence passed before he relented. "No, Your Highness. Of course not."

"Then go, before I tell my brother-in-law that I was treated brutishly. I'm famished. I daresay I'm beginning to feel a swoon coming on."

He paled. "At once, Your Highness."

As soon as he vanished, Rosa all but wilted into a chaise and leveled Niamh with a flat stare. "What was that? What exactly is going on here?"

"Nothing at all!" Niamh scrubbed her face dry and pinned on a smile. "Weddings make me emotional, and the enchantments on your dress . . . I will do my best not to embarrass myself any further."

"Do you think I'm stupid? That is not a rhetorical question."

"No! Of course not."

"Then why are you lying to me? You are stumbling all over yourself—more than usual. And you are . . ." Rosa gestured hopelessly at her. ". . . leaking."

Rosa is quite an understanding person, Miriam had told her. And she was. Niamh envied how nothing rattled her. But somehow, she did not think even a woman as patient and pragmatic as Rosa could take *I am in love with your fiancé, and if one of you does not call this wedding off, your union may very well shackle you to a financially insolvent kingdom for half a decade* in stride. She couldn't risk it.

So she sat beside her and said, "It's the stress. I've hardly slept in days."

Rosa placed a hand awkwardly on the top of Niamh's head, which Niamh supposed was meant to be reassuring. "You have worked yourself too hard for my sake."

"Do not trouble yourself over me. Today is about you."

"Is it now?" she asked wryly.

Just then, Miriam nudged the door open with her hip, holding in her arms the tea service she had clearly wrested from the beleaguered footman. Her tongue poked out in concentration as she fumbled with it. But when she saw Rosa, her lips parted and the tray nearly fell from her hands. The teacups wobbled precariously.

"Rosa." Tears glimmered in Miriam's eyes. "God above, you are a vision."

Rosa laughed thickly, fond and rueful. She reached beneath her veil to sweep her fingertips beneath her eyes. "Stop. Soon *I* will start leaking."

Niamh felt like the greatest fool who ever lived.

She wasn't sure how she hadn't seen it—truly seen it—before now: the reason Rosa had endured everything like a soldier preparing for battle, the reason Rosa cared little if Kit's heart was elsewhere, the reason Miriam had helped Niamh without question. Now, it was so beautifully, breathtakingly, heartbreakingly obvious. An invisible thread looped the two of them together.

Love.

The day on which Infanta Rosa de Todos los Santos de Carrillo and Prince Christopher Carmine, Duke of Clearwater, were to be wed was, by all accounts, perfect.

It was a bright and cloudless morning—an Avlish rarity—and the streets, from the royal palace shining on its green lawn to the white-stone Cathedral of Saint John, were lined with people. Nobility and commoners alike gathered, drinking and chattering, cheering and singing, weeping and shoving. They carried wicker baskets at their hips and tossed herbs and flower petals onto the road. Every bloom represented a wish—for health, fortune, fertility, and happiness. In Avlish tradition, the groom led the wedding guests in a parade from his home to the cathedral.

To Niamh, it felt as grim as a funerary procession. Today, she could lose Kit forever.

She followed the parade alone. The crush of people all around overwhelmed her. Her ears rang, her pulse pounded in her wrists, and her eyes felt as though they were going to leak out of her skull from exhaustion.

The dark cloak she'd dredged up from the back of her closet suited her mood and served well enough to disguise her, but she sweated feverishly in the wool. A wide bonnet—and a wispy cluster of baby's breath tucked behind her ear—obscured her features. Still, it would not take more than a few moments' inspection for either Carmine to recognize her. She clutched a box tightly against her chest, Kit's wedding cloak tucked safely inside.

Out in front of her, Jack rode a white stallion that seemed perfectly at ease beside the Kings Guard in their green-and-gold livery and their muskets. Today, he wore his full regalia. His red tailcoat billowed in the wind, and the golden crown nestled into his dark hair blazed in the sunlight.

And there, just ahead of him, was Kit.

Niamh couldn't see him clearly from here. Only the grim iron set of his shoulders. From the moment she first realized who he was, perhaps Niamh should have known it was destined that she would find herself here. Her, heart twisting itself into lovesick knots. Him, impossibly out of her reach for a hundred different reasons.

As the Carmines passed, flowers sprouted in their wake, pushing through the cracks in the cobblestones and flooding the lawns. The crowds cheered, their eyes alight with magic's golden glow. It drifted through the air, dreamy as early-morning mist.

Niamh caught a glimpse of the cathedral's spires as they rounded a corner. Its buttresses and towers extended heavenward like accusatory, reaching fingers. The closer the procession drew, the denser and rowdier the crowds got. They jostled and jeered like a sea whipped to madness by the wind. It didn't take long for Niamh to realize why.

The protesters waited in the cathedral's courtyard.

Clever, Niamh thought. Jack couldn't oust them all without causing a scene. Besides, a massacre on the wedding day would be a most inauspicious start to a marriage.

They hoisted flags into the air and planted them in the cathedral's immaculate lawn. Despite their numbers, the protestors stood in orderly contingents, facing down the wedding procession like an army making their last stand. And at the front of them, radiant and tall on the makeshift stage of an overturned crate, was their general: Helen Carlile.

Jack drew his horse up short. His mount pawed restlessly at the cobblestones. He stared imperiously down the bridge of his nose at Carlile. Niamh had been on the receiving end of that stare a time or two before; she knew the effect it had. But Carlile met it head-on.

"What is the meaning of this?" he asked.

"I'm here to demand an audience with the prince regent." She gave him the most perfunctory of bows. "I suppose that would be you."

He dismounted from his horse, his boots striking the cobbles with a decisive *clack*. The Kings Guard rested their hands on their sabers in unison. An anxious murmur rippled through the wedding guests.

"Good day to you, madam," he said coldly. "You are in no position to demand a thing from me. It is my brother's—your prince's—wedding day."

"I mean no offense, sir. It's only that I have asked to speak to you a great many days before this," she said earnestly. "You're a difficult man to pin down. One can almost begin to suspect that you're hiding from me."

"Give me one reason to not have you arrested for sedition here and now." Jack lowered his voice; Niamh had to inch forward to even hear. "What do you mean by this display? It serves no other purpose but to excite discontent and vex me personally."

"An hour of your time is all I ask." A pleading note entered her voice. "These good people have gathered here to have their concerns heard. If that is a crime, I do not recognize you any longer. No matter what they say about you, sir, I did not take you for a despot."

"Meet with her." Kit, at last, spoke. He addressed his brother almost wearily, without a hint of petulance or imperiousness. "Consider it my wedding gift."

Carlile's gaze darted between them.

The silence stretched on. A bead of sweat ran down Jack's temple. But whatever he saw in his brother's eyes must have moved him. "Very well. I will speak with you after the ceremony. You and your *ilk* can wait for me outside the Parliament building. I will receive you in my office there."

Niamh could hardly believe it.

Carlile's entire face lit up, all sunny gratitude and stunned satisfaction. "Thank you, Your Highness. Sincerely, thank you. I very much look forward to it." She bowed to Kit. "And congratulations to you. Much happiness to you and your new bride."

"Thanks," he said tersely.

She turned back to the protesters, and with a single gesture, they fell in line around her. They marched toward the Parliament building, parting around the wedding procession like a river flowing over a stone. Their disciplined silence astounded Niamh. As soon as the last of them cleared the cathedral's gates, the tension in the air dissipated.

And as if on cue, the wedding bells tolled overhead.

They *gong, gong, gong*ed, a deep, mournful sound that resonated within Niamh's rib cage. As the last toll of the bell shivered into the morning, the doors to the cathedral opened wide.

Niamh's breath quickened. She didn't know if she could do this. She couldn't face Kit again. And if she failed, she didn't know if she could bear to see the moment he was bound to Rosa forevermore. She would not survive that heartbreak.

But she had no time to hesitate. Once the Carmines entered the cathedral, the guests behind her all but shoved her through the threshold and into the vestibule.

The ceiling loomed high above them, supported by white columns and laced up like stays with ribbing. Flames floated and drifted through the air as though they were candles borne on a current. Flowers were woven into the pews, and garlands were draped over every alcove, all the blooms done in sumptuous white. Everything glittered, from the dust motes drifting through delicate threads of light to the gilt on the saintly icons on the walls.

But it was the altar that truly stole her breath away.

Kit stood silhouetted against the backdrop of the stained-glass windows. They filled the entire apse, from the wooden wainscoting to the dramatically arched ceiling. The light they let in enfolded him, softening all his hard edges. It painted him delicately. He wore a white waistcoat and cravat, with a golden pin in the shape of a blooming rose. He looked like a fairy-tale prince.

Sinclair stood beside him on the altar. As livid as he was with Sinclair, he hadn't disinvited him from the wedding.

This is it.

Niamh found a seat in the back of the cathedral and tucked her chin so that her bonnet hid her face from view. Her palms were clammy in the delicate silk of her gloves. Chatter and laughter swirled around her as guests filed in. She did her best to drown them out.

A flutter of movement at the front of the cathedral snagged her attention. A member of the Kings Guard approached Jack and bent down to whisper something in his ear. Immediately, he swiveled around in his seat with a startled fury. His gaze raked across each person's face. He was looking for someone. Looking for *her*, she realized.

He knows.

Jack and his guardsman exchanged a few words before the guard nodded grimly. Niamh sank down in her seat. If they found her, they would escort her out. She couldn't go back to Machland— not until she saw this through. But there were hundreds of people in this cathedral and a ceremony the Guard couldn't so brazenly interrupt. She'd be fine.

The harpist began to play. The song soared to the rafters, sweet and ethereal and glittery: the announcement of the bride.

Every head in the church turned.

And the doors to the vestibule opened, framing Rosa in a brilliant square of light.

28

*G*asps broke out. Then, more quietly, sniffles.

With her hand in the crook of her father's elbow, Rosa lurked at the rear of the nave, beautiful and terrible, dour and elegant, and utterly magnificent. Every thread of her gown, every fiber of her veil, radiated pure emotion.

Memories, all of them bittersweetly painful, washed over the crowd. Even King Felipe's eyes glimmered with unshed tears. Niamh did not know what Rosa made of her reception; her features were almost entirely hidden behind her veil. She began to process.

The train of her gown lapped against the floor like cold, dark water. It whispered softly with every step, dragging the petals strewn across the marble floor beneath its tide. Hushed, reverent murmurs followed her down the aisle. *That gown,* Niamh heard, over and over again. A strange brew of pride and sadness threatened to bowl her over. Was such beauty worth such suffering?

When they arrived at the altar, Miriam approached and took Rosa's bouquet of red roses from her. She retreated a few paces back, folding herself into a column of shadow, but even from here, it was obvious that she was bereft. Sinclair caught Miriam's eye across the dais and winked reassuringly. Miriam offered him a brave smile in return. The king placed Rosa's hand in Kit's. The grim finality of it twisted like a knife in Niamh's stomach.

Kit clasped her hand weakly. In Caterlow, the wedding ceremony began the same way. They would drape a rope around their wrists, and strand by strand, they would knit both their hands and their souls together. But nothing happened. Kit only grew paler and paler as he stared at Rosa, blank-eyed, as though watching a well-trodden nightmare play out before him.

With the wedding party fully assembled, the bishop stepped forward. He carried himself with utter self-importance, his nose upturned and his mouth pressed into a solemn line. A golden stole hung around his neck like the pelt of a skinned animal, and a black cap was perched atop his head like a grizzled old bird. Niamh despised him immediately, but she couldn't exactly trust herself to be a solid judge of character at present.

With a grave air, the bishop said, "Dearly beloved, we are gathered together here in the sight of God, and in the face of this congregation, to join together this man and this woman in holy matrimony; which is an honorable estate, instituted of God in the time of . . ."

The ceremony droned on. Niamh hardly absorbed a single word of it. Panic and despair made a muddle of everything. There were at least five pauses where she believed something, *anything* new would happen. But each time, the bishop audibly cleared his throat and flipped to another page in his prayer book. The congregation sighed and shifted. Ivory-boned fans fluttered all around her.

Niamh dug her nails into her knee to ground herself. She could hardly process that this was happening, that she was *here,* sweating in this uncomfortable pew, as the man she loved was marrying another woman. And unless she wanted to mortify everyone in this church—herself most of all—she could do absolutely nothing. Never had she felt more powerless.

Your magic makes me feel things, Kit had told her. No matter what happened, all she could do was pray that he'd feel all the things she did not get a chance to say.

A low murmuring a few rows ahead of her jolted her back to awareness. The Kings Guard had begun to sweep the perimeter of the church, drawing stares and speculation. They made a valiant effort to be subtle, but between their bright livery and the sabers glinting menacingly at their hips, it seemed to Niamh wasted effort. Her skin prickled all over with dread. She tugged her bonnet down over her eyes.

At the altar, the bishop finally set aside his prayer book in favor of a chalice. Unlike anything else in the room, it was elegant in its simplicity: a vessel of pure, unadorned silver. Sinclair had explained this to her last night. The cup was empty, but Kit and Rosa each held a glass vial filled with water. Traditionally, the vials contained honey mead, as golden as the nobility's divine blood, but Niamh understood the substitution for Kit's sake. He and Rosa would each pour their vials into the chalice and drink, symbolizing the joining of their bloodlines. And once it was finished, Kit would don his cloak and enfold Rosa in his protection. With that, they would be wed.

The corner of the box Niamh held dug into her hip.

The chanted prayer blurred into nonsense. Kit and Rosa unstoppered their vials. They drained them into the chalice in perfect unison. Neither of their hands shook. Each moment spanned an eternity: Rosa lifting the cup and drinking, Rosa passing it to Kit, Kit barely touching it to his lips before setting it hastily down again.

"We will now begin the recitation of the vows." The bishop paused for only a moment before fixing Sinclair with an impatient look. "The cloak, sir."

Sinclair jumped, startled. He scanned the floor at his feet. When that turned up nothing, he whirled around to check the seat behind him. By now, people had begun to murmur openly. Someone stifled a laugh. Others coughed. The Kings Guard drew closer and closer, row by row. Niamh's heart pounded against the box, hugging it closer.

"The cloak, if you please," the bishop said, more desperately this time.

Genuine panic flickered over Sinclair's face. "Just one moment. Sorry."

Ready or not, she could not draw this out any longer. She launched to her feet. "I have it!"

The entire congregation turned to face her. Niamh avoided Kit's gaze. It would strike her down like an arrow driven straight into her heart. She did make the grave mistake of looking at Jack instead, which indeed almost struck her down like a rock hurled at her head. Ice ran through her veins, even as her face warmed with humiliation. Niamh stepped over the other people in her row, muttering her apologies under her breath, and walked down the aisle.

A few paces away, she finally dared to look up at Kit. His eyes fixed on hers with a desperate longing. In that moment, no one existed in the world but the two of them. Under the spell of his gaze the music faded away. The crowds faded away.

And then her slipper caught the hem of her gown.

She strangled a yelp. The box slipped out of her hands, and she left her feet behind as she toppled forward. Shouts of surprise echoed through the cathedral, and Niamh thought, distantly, that it would not be so bad to die at this very moment. Together, they seemed to fall through water, slowly plunging toward the floor. The box clattered against the marble with a sound as loud as shattered glass. Niamh squeezed her eyes shut and braced for impact, but it never came.

The flowers lining the altar and twining through the pews had sprouted new growth. Vines twisted around one another like a rope and wound around her waist. When she blinked open her eyes, she was floating just inches above the floor.

The sound of approaching footsteps forced her gaze back up. Kit bent down and helped her to her feet. As he steadied her, she caught the softest glitter of fond exasperation in his eyes.

"Another high-gravity day?" He spoke so close to her ear, a shiver rippled down her spine. The vines around her unwound slowly and dropped to the floor one by one.

How infuriatingly *typical,* to mock her even now. She nearly wept at the familiarity of it. Although she had found her footing again, he did not let go of her. His hand lingered, his thumb pressed to the center of her palm, as though he meant to pull her in close. There was something so peculiar about the way he was looking at her. He seemed . . . focused, and yet, a hundred miles away.

"Your Highness?" the bishop called.

"Kit?" she whispered.

"Your Highness!" The bishop raised his voice, clearly desperate to regain control of the situation. He looked sweaty beneath the sunlight, clutching his prayer book with a white-knuckled grip. "Would you care to rejoin us, in mind as well as body?"

The mood in the room shifted. Everyone was practically giddy now, whispering and giggling in their seats. Kit blinked. "Right. Of course."

Niamh retrieved the box from the floor and pressed it into his hands. "For you."

He nodded stiffly, his expression once again unreadable, then returned to the altar. He all but shoved the box into Sinclair's chest. Sinclair fumbled with it, then removed the lid.

"Wedding-day nerves," Sinclair said self-deprecatingly. "Where's my head?"

A few people laughed, if only to break the tension.

Niamh perched gingerly in a pew. She could *feel* Jack's eyes furiously stabbing into her, but she kept her focus trained determinedly ahead. Sinclair removed the cloak from its box and unfurled it. Rosa's gown was beautiful. But this, she knew, would be the finest thing she'd ever make.

The cloak was a swath of dark green velvet, lined with silk and structured with panels of intricate golden lace. Sprays of embroidered nettle and thorns bristled along the sleeves and down the back. Niamh had worked on it nightly since Kit had said he trusted her sketches in the hothouse. But while the design had come easily to her, she never could settle on its enchantment. She'd threaded in countless memories and feelings, only to pull them out again. Nothing suited him. Not well-wishes, not vitality, not stateliness or honor or civility or anything at all Avlish or proper or polite.

But last night, she'd spun and spun her magic into thread. Into every delicate petal, every leaf and thistle, she'd woven a small piece of her heart. Regret at having broken his trust. Anger at his sharp withdrawal. The pain of losing him. The fear upon seeing him within his cage of thorns. The warm, languid peace of watching him tend his plants. The lightness of teasing him. The contentment of sewing as he breathed steadily beside her. The quiet intimacy of a rainstorm, lying side by side as the breeze sighed through the open window. The comforting sadness as they gave their burdens to each other. The giddy joy of kissing him. All of life, in its thousand ways to cut. Everything she had ever dreamed of and denied herself.

Every shade of loving Kit Carmine.

Sinclair held it up to Kit. He slid one arm in, then the other.

The cloak settled heavily on his shoulders. His expression

morphed slowly, then all at once. She watched him experience every emotion, every memory, every hope she'd stitched into the fabric. Kit found her in the crowd. In that moment, it was not only his eyes aglow with magic. His entire *being* seemed to emanate a bright, golden light.

Niamh's breath caught.

Flowers burst into bloom around them, a riot of color: forget-me-nots and roses, sunflowers and camellias, lilacs and carnations, irises and dahlias, snowdrops and honeysuckle. She could scarcely keep track of them all. They flowed down into the aisle like a long carpet shaken out and unrolled. They unfurled from the rafters like royal banners. They twisted playfully above the nave, enveloping all the guests in a shroud. Petals eddied through the air and settled into her hair like a dusting of snow. For every feeling she'd given him, they poured out of him tenfold, an answer to every question she had asked:

Yes, I forgive you.

Yes, I miss you.

Yes, I still want you.

Her heart swelled with joy and stupid, stubborn hope. The whole world blurred behind a shimmery veil of tears. The guests' chatter intensified, with shouts of delight and shock.

"Should anyone present know of any reason that this couple should not be joined in holy matrimony," the bishop shouted over the ruckus, "speak now, or forever hold your peace!"

Niamh let those words wash over her. She had done everything she could to land herself here, to give them both one more chance at happiness. She had risked everything. She had humiliated herself and undoubtedly gotten herself barred from the Kingdom of Avaland forever. And yet, she couldn't bring herself to regret it. Falling in love with Kit Carmine had been the most painful, most worthwhile thing she had ever done. She would do it a hundred times over.

Kit opened his mouth to speak. But before he could say a word, a voice cut through the clamor.

"I do. I object."

King Felipe V rose slowly to his feet, radiating a cold, bitter hostility.

29

The king, risen to his full towering height, glowered at Jack from the opposite side of the cathedral. His hand curled around the back of the pew, digging in tight enough that Niamh feared the wood would splinter. His entire body quivered with the effort of holding in his rage.

"A brief recess, then," the bishop said meekly, his prayer book clutched limply in front of him like a shield.

No one moved.

Jack stood and added, "*Now.*"

The guests scrambled to their feet and began shoving their way out of the cathedral with surprising swiftness. Niamh adjusted her tilted bonnet and wedged herself into the flow of the crowds, but a member of the Kings Guard seized her arm with bruising force. She gasped, and cold, sudden terror flooded in.

When the doors banged shut and the last of the guests cleared out, the cathedral looked like a carcass picked clean. The guardsman hoisted her up and all but dragged her to the apse. He deposited her at Jack's feet with a rough shove. This time, Kit couldn't catch her. She went down hard, her hands scraping the marble and her knees smarting from the impact. Her breathing echoed too loudly around her, but she kept her head bowed.

"What is the meaning of this?" the king thundered. "I do not know how things are run on this blasted island, but I did not consent to this *farce*."

"Your Majesty," Jack said placatingly, "this Machlishwoman is behind all this. I am certain now this is some sort of vengeance, and I will have her——"

"We do not want excuses from you." Felipe cut his hand through the air emphatically, and Jack fell silent like a chided schoolboy. "Even if that is true, how can you be so incompetent? Look at her. How can you not manage even one sniveling girl?"

"Well," Jack blustered, "I . . ."

"We have never seen such madness. Your subjects have gathered like an army to appeal to you. Your brother has clearly taken up with this common girl," Felipe continued, with a disdainful look at the flowers that had sprung from Kit's magic. "You assured us he did not inherit your father's constitution. But now we see that madness is all relative. All of you must be as mad as loons if you believe we will accept such treatment!"

"My apologies, Your Majesty. I do not know what has come over everyone today, but I assure you it is most unusual."

"Enough." Felipe rested his hand on the hilt of his sword. "Whether or not you intended this, whether or not it is typical, you have insulted me today. Worse—and most unforgivably—you have insulted my daughter."

At last, Rosa lifted her veil. Her dark eyes glinted with newfound purpose. "Father, please be reasonable. I am entirely unharmed."

Felipe continued as if she had not spoken at all. "My Rosa is a good, obedient girl. She has never once spoken out of turn, and she is far too meek to say you've wounded her. But if she will not speak, I will. She is my only daughter, my crown jewel, and you do not deserve her."

Rosa's face twisted with anger and regret. It was the most emotion Niamh had ever seen from her, and yet, the fight drained out of her in an instant. How could she let her father go on believing she had no opinions or dreams of her own? How could she possibly let him speak for her, even now? The king loved her. If she found the courage to speak, surely he would listen.

"I understand you are unhappy," said Jack, "but a bungled ceremony is no grounds to call off this engagement."

"This is not a political matter. It is a personal one." The king pulled off his glove. "And so, we will settle this like gentlemen."

He threw it down between them. His eyes blazed golden, and the air within the cathedral surged. Static crackled through Niamh's hair. The stained-glass windows trembled, and the petals whirled through the air as though lashed by a storm.

"Christopher Carmine, on my daughter's honor, I challenge you to a duel."

Kit paled. "What?"

Niamh clasped a hand to her mouth. *What have I done?*

She couldn't kneel here and do *nothing*.

"Absolutely not." Jack stepped forward, throwing out an arm in front of Kit. His eyes glittered with cold, determined fire. "If you must duel someone, you will duel *me*. I made this arrangement, and as you said, I failed to manage it properly. I will deal with the consequences."

Felipe ignored Jack entirely. His focus was trained on Kit.

"I accept," Kit replied flatly. "Your terms?"

Panic, at last, erupted through Jack's facade. "Sabers, surely. To first blood."

"Magic. To the death," the king said. "You will meet me in one hour in the field to the north of the city. Bring your second. I will be waiting."

With that, he swept out of the cathedral.

No. Niamh nearly collapsed against the stairs of the altar. After all of this, she couldn't let him die for a debt of honor. If anyone was to blame, it was her. It had always been *her.* The petals scattered on the floor beneath her—and the joy they'd sparked within her—seemed a thousand miles away.

The bishop peered out from behind the altar. In a tremulous voice, he asked, "I take it there will be no wedding today, Your Highness?"

"Do not go anywhere," Jack snapped. He set to pacing down the length of the aisle. He wrenched his crown off his head and pulled his hands through his hair. "I can fix this. I will fix this. I do not yet know how, but we have an hour to—"

"There *is* no fixing this," Kit said. "What he said is true."

Rosa laughed bitterly. "Your magic is powerful, but it is nothing compared to ours. If you face him, he will strike you down in a second. What good is your honor to you? If you value your life at all, you will flee while you have the chance."

Kit sat on the stairs of the altar and busied himself with lighting his pipe. He smoked for a few moments, and while he seemed to settle, the color didn't return to his face. When he sighed out his third lungful, he sounded grimly resigned. "I don't care about my honor, but I can't very well deny him. Any alternative will involve other people."

Jack placed his hands on Kit's shoulders and shook him. "This is not your responsibility, Kit. It never has been. It's mine."

"For once," Sinclair chimed in, "I agree with him. This is absolute madness, Kit."

Kit shrugged Jack off and glared up at him with horrible, tangled affection shimmering in his eyes. "I think it's about time someone protected you instead. You can be my second if you insist on hovering." He glanced at Sinclair. "Sorry."

"As if I *want* to watch you die," Sinclair snapped, his voice thick with emotion. "You noble idiot."

"Enough." Jack looked stricken. "We should not discuss this now. Come with me. Sinclair, you, too. Such business is not fit for young ladies to overhear."

Jack strode purposefully toward the door, with Sinclair trailing reluctantly behind him. Kit hesitated for only a moment before approaching Niamh. He offered a hand to her. Even through his glove, his touch was electrifying. She didn't know if she could bear to look at him.

When he steadied her on her feet, she said, "Kit, I am—"

"Stop overworking yourself," he told her sternly. "I mean it."

Before she could even think of how to reply, he followed after his brother. Her breath left her in a shaky rush. Of all the horrible, unromantic, ungallant things he could say in this moment . . . She bit down on the hopeless flare of affection. She would not succumb to despair. She refused to believe that this was the last time she would ever see him alive. She refused to let him get away with *those* being the last words he ever said to her.

Niamh couldn't read Rosa at all.

Since they'd retired to the chapel with Miriam, there had been no outburst, no tears, no anxious chatter. She sat in the front pew, her elbows planted on her knees and her fingers steepled at her lips. At first glance, with tiles of multicolored light playing across her face, she looked almost supplicant. But Niamh knew by now that she was only lost in thought.

When Rosa opened her eyes, no spark of an idea, no stroke of genius, animated them. Niamh saw only defeat. "You have quite a knack for causing trouble, Niamh. Do you know that?"

"Yes," she said wearily. "Everyone has made that quite apparent to me by now."

"Ten more minutes," Rosa said with a rough edge of impatience, "and we all would have been free of this nightmare."

"But I—"

"Do not insult my intelligence. I know very well that you planned this." Rosa slumped further into her seat and scrubbed at her face. "I just did not expect Kit to be so . . . unknowingly complicit. Why have done this? I thought we understood each other."

"I could not bear to see either of you so miserable," Niamh protested. "Both of you play at being so cool and unfeeling, but you are as obvious as he is."

Rosa skewered her with a warning look, and a jolt shot through Niamh at the realization. Miriam didn't know. Or did *Rosa* not know?

Niamh chanced a look at Miriam, who had drifted to the back of the chapel. She sat at the base of a statue of some saint whose name Niamh did not know. It seemed impossible—absurd, even— that either of them should have an ounce of doubt about the other's feelings. Perhaps this was how everyone else felt, watching her and Kit dance around each other for half the Season. The urge to shake them both nearly overpowered her.

"Once again," Rosa said darkly, "I thought we understood each other."

Niamh slowly crossed the room and sat beside Rosa in the pew. She unlaced her bonnet and set it aside. "I could not live with that arrangement. For many reasons, selfish and otherwise."

Finally, she unburdened herself of the truth: Lovelace's identity, the reality of Avaland's financial situation, all the ways in which Jack had tried to salvage it.

"So they intended to use us as human mortar for all their prob-lems," Rosa said quietly. "Those snakes. I can almost admire that sort of cunning."

"I had hoped to stop the wedding, but I didn't foresee it going quite like this."

"Thank you for telling me now," Rosa said miserably, "although I could have stood to know *before* the ceremony."

"I'm sorry! I didn't know how you would react."

"I might have been furious, or perhaps I would have had some brilliant scheme. We shall never know. It's too late now." Rosa pinched the bridge of her nose. For the first time, a note of despair crept into her tone. "All this time, I endeavored to protect those I love. To secure Avaland as an ally and keep violence from our door, if only for a few years more. And this is where my choices have carried me: exactly to the fate I tried to avoid. My father will either die the proud fool he is, or he will kill Kit. The prince regent and my father may claim to be men of honor, but when it comes down to it, I cannot imagine either side will not retaliate. Conflict seems unavoidable now."

"That's all, then?" Niamh demanded. "Are you truly willing to give up so easily?"

"This does not involve you." Rosa's expression shuttered. "In fact, you have done quite enough. You should leave now while you still can. Return to Machland and abandon us to our fate."

"I can't do that."

She laughed disbelievingly. "You're still trying to protect them? Even though you know what they are capable of?"

"This scheme was entirely the prince regent's, and now, it's ruined. Besides, he has agreed to meet with the protesters. That is a small start."

"That is not reassuring. You should know by now that I am not a sentimental person." Rosa slouched further into her seat. "You truly care for Kit *this* much? I don't mean to offend you, but surely you could have chosen more wisely. You have unfortunate taste in men."

Her directness snatched every coherent reply from her mind.

"He is . . . pretty, in his way, I suppose. In theory," Rosa conceded. "But I am shocked at his poor breeding. He is gentlemanly to no one but you. To the rest of the world, he is peevish and extraordinarily rude, and possesses no grace or decorum."

A protective impulse seized hold of her. Niamh drew herself up taller. "I beg to differ, Your Highness. He *is* all those things, yes. But he is also kind, even when he is not always nice. He is forthright and loyal. And although he would never admit it, he worries about those he loves constantly. He's rather like a mother hen at times. And . . . Well, he has such an intensity about him. When he looks at you, it feels like you are the only person in the world. Oh! And his voice—"

"Niamh." Rosa looked jaundiced. "Saints, enough. I implore you. I will never scrub this conversation from my mind."

"Sorry!"

"You are truly smitten with him, then." With only a touch of puzzled wonderment, she said, "Good for him."

"Yes. I love him." It hit her all over again that he was currently marching to his death. "Rosa, you have to stop your father."

"No, indeed," Rosa said, looking quite alarmed. "He will not listen to me. He has never once listened to me."

"Do not be a coward, now of all times." Miriam snapped back into herself. She emerged from the shadows and into a wash of multicolored light. "How do you know unless you try? All these years, you have let him believe you are demure and in need of his protection."

Rosa startled. "Miriam . . ."

"I have never known you to back down from a fight you *know* you can win." Miriam glared at her with a ferocity Niamh had never seen on her. A curl escaped from its updo as she advanced on the princess. "Your father is doing this for you, misguided as he is. He believes you've been insulted. Naturally, he is furious on your behalf!"

"He cannot give me what I truly want. He would not accept it." Niamh heard the unspoken fear in Rosa's voice. *He would not accept me.* "It is far easier to be his weak-willed daughter."

"He believes you want Kit to be punished for how today went," Niamh pressed. "If nothing else, you can ask him to spare his life."

"I can't." A pall came over Rosa, and melancholy oozed from her every word. "You are wrong about me, both of you. I am a coward and a masochist. I have never so sorely miscalculated in my entire life. I have failed everyone."

Miriam stood in front of Rosa's pew. "You haven't failed me."

"I have failed you most of all."

"Rosa, I cannot pretend I am unaware of what you're doing anymore." Miriam planted her hands on her hips. "I am hardly qualified to be a chaperone! You had some scheme to have me married off this Season. I have told you a thousand times that I don't *want* to marry. So why are you punishing yourself?"

"I don't want you to marry, either. But bringing you here was the only plan I could come up with," Rosa said desperately. "Perhaps that is why I do not like Kit Carmine. Because he and I are the same. We are utter fools for love. We are selfish and self-destructive to the highest degree."

"I . . ." Miriam opened her mouth, then closed it. When she spoke again, her voice was very small. "What are you talking about?"

Rosa threw her head back and laughed breathlessly. "I have never once acted with my heart over my head. And doing so, just this once, has ruined me. I wanted to give you a chance to seek your own happiness, far away from a place that has hurt you so deeply. I thought this was the best way to protect you, but I see now it was only greed."

"What," Miriam repeated more vehemently, "are you talking about?"

"I love you!" Rosa seized hold of the pew between them. "Do you not see? How can you not? All this time, all these years . . . My sweet Miriam, it has always been you."

Miriam gawped at her. "You love me?"

Rosa quailed. She gathered her veil around her arms, shrouding herself in shadow again. "I am sorry. I have forgotten myself entirely. If you cannot accept it—"

Miriam leaned over the barrier between them and took Rosa's face in her hands. She kissed her, and Rosa's eyes widened with shock. Miriam drew back, her chest heaving against her stays. "I love you, too, you stubborn wretch! Seeing you there on that altar, in that gown, was the cruelest torture I could have ever imagined."

"Perhaps," Niamh interjected, "I should give you two a moment?"

"Oh, Saints. I'm sorry." Miriam hid her face in in Rosa's shoulder. Rosa's hand lingered at Miriam's waist.

"We don't have a moment to spare. The duel will begin in thirty minutes." Rosa pursed her lips. "I'm afraid to confront him."

"If you aren't ready, you don't have to tell him." Niamh gave her an encouraging smile. "But if there is one thing I've learned, it's that making yourself miserable to please others isn't worth it. You deserve to live on your own terms."

Without warning, Miriam pulled both Rosa and Niamh into a crushing hug. Niamh clung tight to her, a fizzy happiness filling her up from within. Rosa, however, endured it for all of two seconds before wriggling out of their hold. She took great pains to smooth out the front of her gown.

"All right, well, that is quite enough of that." Rosa sniffed, once again the embodiment of dignity. "Shall we put an end to this?"

30

*W*ithout a single hitch, Rosa commandeered the pair of horses meant for her and Kit's carriage back to the palace. When Niamh climbed onto the mare, too petrified to care if anyone found her riding astride, she could practically feel the energy thrumming beneath her. The horse was ready to run.

Good, Niamh thought. So was she.

Niamh threaded her fingers into the mare's intricately braided mane to steady herself, and her horse followed hot behind Rosa's. Their hooves ate up the earth as they galloped past throngs of confused paraders still waiting for the newlyweds to be announced. A half-hearted cheer rose and died like a very unsatisfying sneeze. Others tossed handfuls of grain in front of them, which the rock doves promptly descended upon in droves.

They tore out of the city and into the open fields. Out in front of Niamh, Rosa looked positively ethereal. The train of her gown billowed behind her, and the rose petals woven into her hair came loose and danced through the open air. Overhead, the clouds began to swirl and darken. The temperature dropped, and the humidity bore down on them heavily. Her eyes stung from the sudden gust of wind. The tall grass hissed at her urgently: *hurry, hurry, hurry.*

Niamh bent over her mare's neck and urged her on. She could barely hear the horse's snorting breath above the thud of hooves against the earth and the wailing of the oncoming storm in her ear.

"Come on," she pleaded.

The King of Castilia had won wars with the powerful magic he wielded. Kit had never seen combat in his life. It was not at all a fair fight. It would take no more than thirty seconds for Felipe to kill him, as easy as extinguishing a candle. In the distance, she could see four figures, dark against the rising gloom. Two silhouettes—Kit and the king—stood back-to-back.

Please don't be too late.

The figures took one step away from each other.

The sky itself seemed to spin ominously, eager to obey their king's command. Rain began to fall, slowly at first. A fine mist clung to Niamh's eyelashes.

Another step.

The trees looming over the men hunched closer with malicious intent, their very roots straining and groaning against the earth.

Another step.

Hurry, the grass hissed, *hurry, hurry, hurry.*

The skies opened, and rain pelted them in sheets. Mud splattered the hem of Niamh's dress, and water streamed down her face in rivulets. Through the hair plastered to her face, she could see the whites around her mare's fearful eyes—and every horrible detail of the dueling grounds.

Kit and Felipe now stood on opposite sides of the field, looking

for all the world like gods among mortals. Lightning crackled in
Felipe's palm. His features were skeletal in the white light of his
magic. The wind had torn Kit's hair free of its tie, and it lashed
his face. A thicket of briars tore free from the earth, flinging clods
of damp earth like ballistae fire. Its thorns seethed like a serpent
prepared to strike, every one of them primed to shred the king to
pieces. A deadly storm pitted against the ravenous earth. The sky
overhead and the ground below, each a roiling sea.

Kit and the king slowly turned to face each other.

No. Niamh searched desperately for Rosa through the squall,
and she saw them realize it at the same time. Someone they loved
was about to die.

Rosa's eyes flashed golden. Lightning gathered in her fist. "*Stop!*"

The king whirled toward his daughter, his face slack with surprise. She loosed her magic like an arrow. It crackled through the
field, so bright that Niamh's vision flashed white.

But it was too late. Rosa's magic exploded against a tree, setting it ablaze. Her father's cut clean and true across the dueling
grounds—and straight toward Kit.

"No!" Niamh shouted, her voice ragged with terror.

When Kit crumpled to the earth, her heart did, too.

31

*E*mbers and blackened bark rained onto the field. Through the smoke, Niamh couldn't see Kit anymore. A desperate, impotent feeling welled up within her, somewhere between rage and despair. For as long as she could remember, she had been assured of death's predictability. It was not meant to cheat or surprise her. It was not meant to come and leave her behind.

She was not supposed to outlive the people she loved.

Kit couldn't be dead. He couldn't be. *He couldn't be.* She refused to believe it—not until she saw him.

Niamh did not slow her horse as they barreled into the dueling grounds, a flurry of mud and water and stomping hooves. Shouts of confusion rang out around her—none of them Kit's. Where *was* he?

A burning branch snapped off the tree and struck the earth

like a fist. Niamh's mare spooked, darting sideways away from the flames. She lurched in the saddle and gasped. On instinct, she dropped the reins and scrabbled frantically for the pommel as the mare danced beneath her, eager to bolt.

"Whoa!"

Her heart gave an answering lurch.

She knew that voice. *Kit.*

He emerged from the smoke and snatched the loose reins. The horse stilled and snorted. Her fingers slipped off the pommel, and she very slowly slumped off her seat and into Kit's shoulder. He glared up at her in furious amazement, then all but shoved her back upright. "What are you doing here? It's too dangerous."

"Clearly!"

The king might have missed once, but they would not be so lucky twice. Wind gusted through the field, and the smoke parted like a curtain. Rosa stood between her father and Kit in her ruined wedding dress. Her chest heaved, and electricity still crackled down the length of her arm. Jack and Rosa stared at her and Kit with twinned looks of relief.

It was over—at least for now.

The rain lightened, moment by moment, until Niamh could hear her own ragged breathing and the ends of her hair dripping against the saddle.

"What are you doing here?" Kit repeated.

No words came. She wanted to shake him, or maybe to kiss him. She couldn't tell at this point. A sob of pure relief escaped her. His face was streaked with ash and rainwater and his eyes were wild. But by some miracle, he was *alive.* "Saving you from your own terrible decision—again! Gods, Kit. I thought I lost you."

The anger—the panic—in his expression gave way at last to guilt. "Then why are you crying? You don't have to mourn me yet."

Not yet. But she could see now just how close death had come. Beneath the ruined fabric of his sleeve, a jagged scar mottled his upper arm. Her breath snagged in her throat at the sight of it. Rosa had saved his life.

"Rosa," the king spluttered at last, clearly as outraged as he was impressed. "You could have gotten yourself killed!"

She lifted her chin. "I can't let you do this."

The king's shock slowly rearranged itself into exasperation. "I know you love him. But I promise you, it is not worth it to marry a man whose loyalty lies elsewhere. These wounds heal. I will find you a much better—"

"No. Saints above, I do not love him." She sounded a little nauseated. "He would have very much displeased me as a husband."

Kit suddenly looked very weary.

"I have been dishonest with you for many years." Rosa slowly dismounted from her horse. She leaned against her father, and for the first time, her lips quivered with barely restrained emotion. "I have many things I want to say to you, but not here. For now, will you please let this go?"

"That is the one thing I cannot give you," he said gravely. "I cannot let them go unpunished for how they humiliated you."

"Papa, I beg you." Her voice trembled. "I am tired. Peace is all I ask for on my not-wedding day. That is all I have ever wanted."

As Niamh took in his hard expression, she understood that he meant what he said. He could not ever truly let it go.

He studied each of them with mounting displeasure. Niamh, a common girl hardly worth his notice. Rosa, his usually stoic daughter, shivering and on the verge of tears. Kit, battered and soaked to the bone. The Prince Regent of Avaland, apparently too stunned to speak at all. For the rest of her life, Niamh would wonder what exactly he saw in their faces that moved him, or which of the Fair Ones had intervened on their behalf. But whatever it was—whether pity or exhaustion or the god Donn himself—slowly, and with great effort, King Felipe laid aside his rage.

"Very well, Rosa." He wrapped his cloak around Rosa's shoulders. "If that is what you truly want."

"Thank you," Rosa whispered.

All of the affection in his eyes withered when he looked up at Jack and Kit again. Burning in them was a soul-deep resentment. "We will discuss how to move forward from this tomorrow."

"Yes, sir," Jack said wanly. "And thank you. I will find some way to make it up to you. I swear it on my life."

As the king climbed onto the horse and helped Rosa up alongside him, Kit's grip tightened on the reins of Niamh's mare. A muscle worked steadily in his jaw as he watched them vanish into the fog.

Beside them, a branch groaned and detached itself from the smoldering trunk. It collapsed onto the earth and shattered into ash. The wind and rain, mercifully, had put out most of the flames, but a swath of grass still sizzled. Jack stared out at it all—the rising smoke and choking steam, the ruined fields with its deep, gashed trenches, the broken branches—and began to laugh.

Kit watched him with a disgusted sort of sympathy. "You've gone mad at last."

"What else can I do?" Jack asked, his arms outstretched over the wreckage. "Everything is ruined. Absolutely everything. I don't know what to expect anymore. I don't know what to do."

Kit held his silence for a moment. "Don't you have a meeting to go to? That's a start."

The two of them regarded each other. Niamh braced for a protest or an argument. But Jack's expression softened, and a fluttery hope swirled within her. Jack slicked his wet hair back from his face. "I expect it'll be hours before I make it back at this rate."

Kit angled his chin toward Niamh. "Come down from there."

She huffed, sitting up straighter in the saddle. "Is that really how you're going to speak to me after all this?"

"Please," he added.

"That's better." Niamh swung her leg over, and as she eased herself down from the stirrup, he steadied her by the waist. Through the damp of her gown, his skin was impossibly warm. Kit passed the reins to his brother.

Surprise flickered across Jack's face. "You expect a young lady to *walk* in this weather?"

So she was a young lady in his book again. Niamh smiled. "I don't mind."

"Very well," he said reluctantly. He climbed into the saddle. Loftily perched above them, he regarded them with a peculiar expression. "Do I want to know what you are up to?"

Kit patted the horse's neck absently, clearly avoiding his gaze. "Do you?"

"I suppose not." Jack rubbed his jaw. "I will be occupied for God knows how long, thanks to you. I cannot stop you."

Kit nodded tightly. Jack nodded back. Niamh, entirely lost by now, felt as though she was intruding on something.

"Well, then. Good day, Kit." Jack circled his mount around. "Niamh."

She startled at the sound of her own name and dipped into a quick curtsy. "Thank you, Your Highness."

"You might as well call me Jack," he said wearily.

With that cryptic offer, he rode off toward the city. Niamh stared after him, wondering at how her choices had carried her here: an invitation to call the Prince Regent of Avaland by his given name. It was an honor she would never have the courage to take advantage of.

Then, she remembered his younger brother. They stood together in the middle of a ruined field. Sopping wet. *Alone.* Kit looked like a drowned cat, but the fabric of his white shirt clung distractingly to his narrow frame.

All she could think to ask was, "Does your arm hurt?"

"No." As terrible a liar as ever. "Let's go."

They set off toward the city. It took two of her strides to match one of his, and he moved with brisk purpose. His jaw was clenched and his eyes were fixed on Sootham. Niamh couldn't tell if he was angry, and if he was, if he was angry at her. Nerves buzzed within her. There were a thousand things she wanted to say to him. Not a single one of them came to her coherently. Her slippers squelched in the mud and wet grass, but she couldn't bring herself to care. The silk was too far gone to be saved, and her toes might soon join it at this rate. Her teeth chattered in the cold.

Kit huffed out a breath. "I can't even offer you my coat."

"At least you had the good sense to leave the cloak behind," she said. "I would have never forgiven you if you'd destroyed it—or died in it, for that matter."

His incredulous stare felt like the press of a blade against her skin. It flustered her horribly, especially when she couldn't tell what he was thinking.

"I owe you yet another apology," she blurted out. "Your wedding was a disaster, and you nearly died. This is all my fault."

"I'm still alive, for better or worse," he said dismissively. "And is it really my wedding if it didn't happen? I can't say I had any hopes of it being pleasant to begin with."

She stopped walking and rounded on him. "But I *am* sorry."

She hated how wretched she sounded. But she couldn't understand how he could forgive her so easily when she hardly knew how to forgive herself. She'd gone behind his back *again*. She might have been trying to protect him and Rosa both, but she'd done it on her terms.

"I have humiliated you and your family in front of the entire court. And now, everyone knows what has happened between us.

You and I will be embroiled in a scandal. I will be the fallen woman who ruined you. A demon, hardly fit to be seen in public with you. A—"

"All right. I think you're getting carried away now." He scowled at her. "If you recall, *I* was the one who set the king off. All you did was hand me a cloak."

She sniffled. "I'm sorry."

"I know. You've said so at least three times now." He sighed impatiently but took one of her hands in his. Her whole body warmed at his touch. "I can't blame you for doing what you had to to get through to me. So I'm sorry, too."

Niamh blinked through her damp eyelashes. "For what?"

"For pushing you away. What you said the other night . . . You're right. I *am* a coward, and I can rarely find it within me to put my faith in people, even when they've proven themselves worthy of it." In the light streaming through the thinning clouds, he looked so vulnerable. His smile was rueful, almost ashamed. "I'm all thorns."

"I don't know about that. I think you're more like a weed."

He made a sound she wasn't sure was a laugh. "Is that supposed to make me feel better?"

"Yes! Weeds are . . . tenacious. They survive against the odds, wherever they land, no matter how many times you cut them down. And sometimes they can be quite beautiful." Kit watched her with ever-growing amusement. Gods, she was humiliating herself. She needed to stop babbling immediately. "That is how I think of you."

"Who would have thought? A tailor *and* a poet."

"Oh, you're terrible!" she cried. "I'm trying to be romantic. Let's see you do better."

He frowned, clearly unable to back down from even the most ridiculous challenge. "You're like . . . a flower. Too delicate for this world."

"What, you think I don't belong here?"

"That's not what I said." His shoulders curled inward with discomfort. "I . . . I don't know what I'm saying. It's impossible when it comes to you."

"Excuse me?" Niamh glared up at him. "You're not so easy to deal with yourself, you know!"

He barreled onward. "Nothing makes sense anymore. My life should have crumbled again, but somehow, I'm still here. I'm still alive. All because of you."

Where *was* he going with this? She'd rarely known him to ramble. "That is . . . good. Right? You sound angry."

"I'm not angry," he said, although he really *did* sound it. "When it comes to you, my thoughts go in circles. None of my words come out right. I can't explain it. I feel . . . insane. It's like you've cast a spell on me. Some kind of psychic hold, or—"

"That's horrible!"

"No . . . Argh!" He glowered at her. "Don't you get it by now, you fool? Are you really going to make me say it?"

"Say *what*?" Her face felt hot, her chest oddly tight. "I can't read your mind."

"Fine. *Fine.* Now listen carefully, because I'm not going to repeat myself."

He took a deep breath. And when he held her gaze, she saw the truth of what he felt laid bare. What he'd felt, perhaps, from the moment he first saw her. Suddenly, she felt very dense indeed.

"I love you."

"What?"

"I said I wasn't going to repeat myself." There was no bite to his words now. His expression was unbearably earnest. "Marry me. I never got the chance to ask you again yesterday, but I assume you've had enough time to think about it by now."

Niamh burst out laughing, but she teetered on the knife's edge of tears. Those words stabbed through her with a longing unlike any she'd ever known. One proposal from a man like him was more than she could've ever hoped for. But a second, upon being rejected and betrayed and humiliated? No creature on this earth could be so stubborn, so . . . so . . .

"That is a cruel joke, Kit Carmine!"

"I'm still not joking."

He was frowning at her with mounting concern. He *was* serious. Her eyes welled with tears. She tried to blink them back, but they escaped despite her best efforts. She scrubbed at them, but they slipped down her cheeks faster than she could keep up with.

He cradled her jaw, angling her face up to his. His touch and expression were so uncertain, she couldn't bear it. "Did I say something wrong?"

"No! It isn't that." Niamh curled her fingers weakly around his wrist. Of all her terrible fears, there was one she had yet to vanquish—her constant companion. "I just don't understand *why*. You have always seen the heart of me. I *have* been running, and now that I've stopped, I see exactly what was waiting for me. I am afraid to be loved. I don't know how much time I can give you. Right now, I have more good days than bad. But I may decline. I may leave you suddenly. I don't want to hurt you that way. It's not fair to ask you to undergo that kind of pain."

"I can't avoid pain. I'm done trying." He made a soft, frustrated sound and tucked the strand of white behind her ear. "You are so full of life, Niamh. The wide-open way you smile. The way you dance through empty rooms. How you put all of yourself into everything you do. I feel like I've lived a thousand years in the time I've known you. I feel like I'm awake for the very first time. Even if you were gone tomorrow, even if you took my heart with you when you went, I wouldn't regret a single moment I've spent with you. How could I? You've changed me. I will carry you with me forever."

Now *that* was the proposal she'd dreamed of as a girl. "I love you, too."

She stood on her toes and kissed him. His eyes widened, and

his mouth was slack against hers as his mind caught up with his body. But then he wrapped his arms around her, pulling her tight against him. When she finally released him, he regarded her dazedly. "So . . . Is that a yes?"

"Yes," she breathed. "Yes."

It was the easiest decision she'd ever made.

32

*N*ot an hour later, in the Cathedral of Saint John, they were married.

It had seemed a shame, after all, to let such meticulous preparations go entirely to waste. And so, the guests were called in like cows from the courtyard, drenched from the waning storm and with glasses of lemonade in hand. They were inordinately merry. Their laughter and chatter filled the cathedral to bursting. It suited Niamh fine. She was a bit merry herself. Even in her stained gown, even with her bloodshot eyes and her hair half a ruin, everything was perfect. Well, almost everything.

The bishop presided over the ceremony with a pinched expression and his peculiar hat knocked askance. He looked as though he were there under duress and spoke as though he were about to perform some mortal sin. Perhaps both were true. When they'd found him in his office, he had been sprawled on the floor in supplication, a thread of prayer beads wound tight around his bloodless hands.

"This is most irregular, sir! Never in my fifty years of service have I seen the like. It is scandalous! It is unnatural! God, surely, is loath to see one of his favored children debase himself in such a manner! I should refuse you. I *will* refuse you!"

Kit had glared at him implacably. "Will you now?"

The bishop's passion had fizzled as it occurred to him exactly who he was speaking to. "Erm . . . I *would,* that is, Your Highness, if you were any other man. But you are not. And so. Shall we, then?"

It was all Niamh could do to keep a straight face as the bishop carried on with the interminable, grim business of an Avlish wedding.

"Now," he said, with a vague wave at the chalice on the table between them, "we shall commence with the blessing."

Niamh turned over the glass vial in her hands. Kit uncorked his and poured it into the chalice. The gentle slosh of liquid was the only sound in the cathedral. "I, Christopher Carmine, thee wed. With my body I thee worship, and with all my worldly goods I thee endow."

Niamh's hands were trembling as she uncapped the vial.

Don't drop it, she prayed. As she emptied it into the chalice, she held his gaze. By some miracle, not a drop spilled. "I, Niamh Ó Conchobhair, thee wed. With my body I thee worship, and with all my worldly goods I thee endow."

She lifted the cup and sipped. The water tasted as cool as spring—like honey and heather. She passed it to Kit, who watched her over the rim with lovesick golden eyes.

This time, Sinclair had the cloak ready. Niamh did not miss the misty look in his eyes as he helped Kit into it.

"Kneel," the bishop said.

They did. The floor was cold and hard against her knees, but when Kit snuck his hand into hers, a flame kindled within her.

"Those whom God hath joined together," the bishop said wearily, "let no man put asunder."

Before the words were fully out of his mouth, Kit tugged her close and folded her into his cloak. She pressed her hands flat to his chest to steady herself. With a faint smirk, he kissed her. A few in the audience gasped. Niamh grinned like a fool against his lips. It was bold and irregular and contrary—exactly as he was. Her cheeks ached from smiling.

"All rise," a herald called, "for the Prince Christopher Carmine, Duke of Clearwater, and Niamh Ó Conchobhair, the Duchess of Clearwater."

By the time they escaped the crowds, the last of the daylight had dwindled.

Niamh would never disentangle all the petals from her hair. White flowers drifted across the streets like snowfall. They were crushed into the cobblestones, releasing their sweet fragrance. They spiraled in the breeze, tantalizing and free. Niamh had half a mind to pluck one from the air and tuck it behind Kit's ear. With the unusually good mood he was in, she suspected he'd let her. The thought made her smile.

Sinclair's townhouse welcomed them, cozy and bright in the warm light of dusk. The front porch was like a bower, enclosed by the limbs of the bougainvillea. The master of the house himself heaved a long, dramatic sigh as they ascended the stairs. "I understand you don't want to return to the palace yet. But did you really have to come to *my* house?"

"Technically," Kit countered, "this is my house."

Sinclair, apparently, had nothing to say to that. He unlocked the front door and instructed his housekeeper to have a guest room prepared for "the happy newlyweds." Kit bristled at the suggestive emphasis he put on the phrase. His housekeeper looked positively delighted, but Sinclair gave a good show of being put-upon despite the fond glimmer in his eyes. Once they were divested of their hats, gloves, and coats, Sinclair ushered them out of the foyer.

"I'll be barricaded in my study if you need me," he said, "although I suspect you'll be otherwise occupied."

Kit choked. "Can you be civilized for ten minutes?"

"No, indeed." Sinclair gave a careless wave and disappeared down the hallway. "Congratulations, you two."

"Shall we?" Kit asked, clearly flustered.

Even in the low, romantic flicker of the candles, Niamh noticed how he'd gone scarlet. His skittishness both charmed and surprised her. She threaded her fingers in his and leaned against him.

"Nervous for what comes next?" she teased. "I'll be good to you."

The color on his face deepened. "Hardly."

Niamh allowed him to lead her through the halls. Delicate shards of pink light played across the floorboards. When they reached the top of the staircase, exhaustion finally caught up to her. Her ankle—somehow—rolled. Without batting an eye, Kit bent over and scooped her into his arms.

She laughed breathlessly as he lifted her off the ground. "Kit! Don't drop me, please!"

"I won't. I've done this once before, remember?"

"Oh. Right."

At that, he preened. She nestled into his shoulder. She could hardly believe that this was her life now—that they truly belonged to each other. The world swam in a dreamy haze, and try as she might, she couldn't keep her eyes open.

Kit's laugh was a bare exhalation. It rustled the loose hair at her temple. "Rest. It's been a long day."

"I'm not going to sleep," she mumbled.

"As you say," he said indulgently. But she felt so warm and safe in his arms. To the rhythm of his heart, she drifted off.

Moments or hours later, Niamh awakened to Kit gently shaking her. She shot bolt upright in bed. Outside the window, the sky was dark and the gas lamps glowed hazily. How long had she been out? Groggily, she looked up at Kit.

"The prince regent and his wife have called on us," he said by way of explanation.

In the drawing room, a painful scene greeted them. Sinclair had crammed himself into an armchair at the farthest corner of the room, his shoulders bunched around his ears. Jack waited on the opposite side of the room, one hand loose at his side and hovering dangerously close to the wrought-iron basket of fire pokers. The hearth crackled, casting the entire room in a gentle glow. Sofia warmed herself by it, a peacefully content smile on her face. The rain drummed on the window, stained a watery red in the firelight.

"Finally," Sinclair muttered.

Over the past few hours, Jack had pulled himself together nicely with a regal black jacket. His hair had once again been tidied, his feelings once again tucked away behind that assessing amber stare. The only welcoming thing about him was the cheery bouquet he'd brought, but he clutched it with such grim forbearance, it seemed as though he were about to deliver it to a funeral. The flowers were already limp from their rough treatment.

He slowly dismantled Niamh with his gaze. She could only imagine what faults he found. Her sleep-mussed, wild hair. Her gown, still crumpled and streaked with mud. Her face, freckled like a commoner's and creased from the sheets.

Unworthy, the set of his jaw said.

Unsuitable, said his deepening frown.

Anxiety made her pulse flutter. Even if he did not like her, even if their union offended his sensibilities, she couldn't squash that childish desire to please him. More than anything, she wanted Jack to believe she could make his brother happy.

Sofia removed herself from beside the fireplace. Her eyes sparkled with pleasure as she pulled Niamh into an embrace. "Congratulations. I am so happy for you, sister."

Sister. Niamh held her close as she turned the word over and over again. She'd never had a sister before. "Thank you."

"Your Grace," Jack said coolly. It was the first time anyone had addressed her by her title. Gods, she had a title now. She might never grow accustomed to that.

"If you wish to be called by your first name, it's only fitting you should call me by mine."

"Right." He cleared his throat, then went on stiffly. "Carlile wishes to pass on her enthusiastic congratulations on your nuptials. She is quite charmed with your choice of bride, Kit, and expects others will be as well. It makes us look very good to her contingent." He sighed. "I will have a great many more messages to pass on, as we now have a standing appointment."

"That's good to hear," Kit said warily, as if bracing for the *but.*

Sofia cleared her throat pointedly. Jack shifted uncomfortably on his feet and held out the bouquet to Niamh. Neither of the Carmine brothers, it seemed, had any idea how to properly express any real sentiment. "I suppose I should offer my congratulations as well. These are for you."

Niamh gathered them close to her chest. "Thank you. They're beautiful."

The conversation died miserably. The logs popped in the fireplace and the floorboards creaked as Sinclair bounced his knee.

"Forgive me," Jack said at last.

Kit's face twisted with surprise. "What?"

"I wanted to put aside the resentment between us, but I realize that a share of it is mine as well. All these years, I resented you so deeply for crumbling, for not feeling the same pressure or sense of duty that Father beat into me. Instead, I used you. I have behaved monstrously toward you." His expression grew haunted. "My duty should have been to you, not to what Father would have wanted me to preserve. You are the only family I have left. For that, I am truly sorry."

"It's fine," Kit said gruffly, although he sounded quite emotional himself. "It's behind us."

"I promise I will make it up to you." Jack glanced at Niamh, and his mouth twitched with displeasure. "I cannot say I approve of this match. But . . . you are good for each other. Niamh, I owe you an apology for how I spoke to you the other day, as well as my gratitude for your interference in a misguided and unethical scheme." He reached for Sofia's hand. "You've reminded me of what's important."

Sofia smiled very tentatively at him. To Niamh's shock, he returned it.

That was a start. "Thank you, Jack."

He winced at the sound of his name but did not comment.

"Where's *my* apology?" Sinclair asked. Jack did not know Lovelace's true identity—and hopefully never would—but that did not mean the impulse to annoy him would die easily.

Jack pointedly ignored him. "Well. That is all I have come to say. Be prepared, Kit. When you return from your honeymoon, it seems you and I have a great deal of work ahead of us to reestablish a relationship with Machland and its people living here."

Kit straightened up with surprise. "You want my help?"

"If you will lend me your time. For now, you are my heir. If we're to keep the throne in the family, you should be prepared for any eventuality." He hesitated. "And I would value your insight. You have never been afraid to challenge me."

"Fine. I'll do it." Despite his begrudging tone, Niamh watched the smallest of smiles curl on his lips.

It wasn't perfect—far from it. But here, in the cozy warmth of the drawing room, it felt like family.

When Jack and Sofia at last took their awkward leave, the three of them lingered. They sat in the bay window, watching the rain sparkle off the cobblestones. Kit and Sinclair passed a cigar back and forth. Niamh curled into Kit's side, trying determinedly not to drowse while he traced patterns on her hand.

"What do you think?" Kit leaned over her and tapped the ashes into a glass tray. "Will he keep his word?"

"He seemed sincere enough." Sinclair snatched the cigar back from him and smiled with catlike slyness. "But if he doesn't, there's always Lovelace to keep him accountable. That goes for you, too."

Kit rolled his eyes. "You're a prick."

Sinclair laughed, a full-throated sound Niamh hadn't heard in a while. "Tell your husband to be nice to me, Niamh. That kind of language isn't becoming of a good, respectable politician."

Niamh sprawled out languidly and rested her head in Kit's lap. With a yawn, she said, "Be nice, husband."

As if on reflex, he began to stroke her hair. He scoffed. "When have I ever been nice?"

33

By some miracle, the sun has risen on Avaland.

My sources inform me that tensions are still running high with Castilia. However, while Illustrious Gentleman F has returned home, Lady R has elected to extend her stay in Sootham and has managed the situation with surprising deftness, vigor, and, indeed, grace. She and her former betrothed were spotted strolling the gardens outside of the Parliament building just last week. They are apparently working closely with each other on a number of economic policies, particularly in the agricultural sector, given how nicely their magic works together. I confess, "working" may be a generous term. They seem to spend half of the time bickering.

Mistress HC's band has dispersed from the park, now that a Certain Someone has finally succumbed to pressure. The topic *of reparations to the Machlish has been opened for the first time in thirty-five years. I credit this development to our Wayward Son. He has proven an ally to our cause—and has effected perhaps the most surprising political development of the Season. Our newest duchess is a divine-blooded commoner—and a Machlishwoman, at that. For now, I watch and wait to see what they will do. They seem disgustingly happy.*

In the three years this column has run, I have not been able to sign off a final issue with anything resembling good news. We have a very long way to go. However, I find myself, if you'll excuse some sentimentality, oddly hopeful. For the future, for justice, for all people living in Avaland. Until next Season, I suppose. I, for one, will pray to every Saint still watching for a quieter one.

—Lovelace

*A*s Niamh put the last stitch in the gown, she was struck with the sinking feeling that she had forgotten something. She blinked hard, jolting back into her body. Her eyes watered against the surprising brightness of the . . . afternoon? When had that happened?

The Season had nearly ended, and yet, life had not at all slowed down. When she and Kit returned from their honeymoon and opened the shop on the corner of Cathedral Street and Champion, the orders started coming—and they hadn't stopped. She'd grown far more discerning with her commissions these days, of course, but she crammed in the ones that excited her when she could. Politics took up far more of her time than she'd ever expected. Despite her work on helping reestablish a relationship with Machland, her grandmother still hadn't come around to her "betrayal."

With time and with change, her mother wrote in her last letter, *she will.*

Niamh could only hope. At least she'd agreed to get on the boat. Next month, they'd all be together again.

"Welcome back to the land of the living, Your Grace," Miriam said teasingly. She stood at the counter, reorganizing all of the things Niamh had torn apart over the course of the day. Her dark curls blazed with fine threads of copper in the sunset.

Niamh rubbed her eyes. "Has it really been that long?"

Miriam made a show of thinking. "Only three hours of complete, focused silence. Well, there was humming every now and again."

Niamh flushed. "Oh, gods. Sorry."

"I'll allow it today," Miriam said. "It's the last order of the week."

Thank the gods for that. She *was* overdue for a break—as everyone liked to remind her. It kept the hours from slipping away. Still, this gown begged to be worked on. The fabric flowed through her hands as silky and cool as water. Sinclair had commissioned it for his sister ("Absolutely no enchantments," he told her sternly, "until you feel well enough"), and so, she needed it to be utterly perfect.

"I'm nearly ready to go," Miriam added. "If you finish by then, we can fetch the royals together."

"I'd love that." There was an easy rhythm to their lives here: charitable work; strolls through the park and languid teas with Sinclair; occasional evenings in her shop; and at night, waiting for Kit and Rosa outside the Parliament building. Without her noticing, Sootham had snuck into her heart and made itself home.

The bell above the shop jingled.

"Ah," Miriam said. "Never mind."

When Niamh glanced up, she almost toppled out of her seat. She steadied herself on the edge of the counter. Perhaps a day would come where the sight of Kit did not make her blood quicken and every faculty of balance escape her. Today, however, was not that day.

He had his hat tucked under his arm. On the other side of the window, Rosa lurked beneath the shadow of the awning, spinning the handle of her parasol.

Miriam smiled innocently at him. "Good afternoon, Your Highness."

He grimaced but did not correct her. He'd learned by now that Miriam had an impish streak and used his title precisely because it annoyed him. "I've come to collect my wife."

"Of course, sir," Miriam said, laughing softly at his increasingly agonized expression. "I'll see you tomorrow, Niamh."

She pulled on her pelisse and, with a wave, walked out into the afternoon. She all but skipped to Rosa and linked their arms together. Niamh watched them leave with a smile.

Through the open bow window, the smells and sounds of the city drifted in. Today, the breeze brought her the scent of horses and smog and honeysuckle. This, perhaps, was her favorite time of day. She loved the dreamy warmth of the sunlight and the rush of busyness as everyone headed home after a long day. Outside, noblemen trudged from Parliament to their clubs. Her neighbors extinguished their candles, their storefronts going dark and still. Carriages rattled down the street. When everyone retired to their country estates for the year, it would be so quiet.

For once, she looked forward to it.

As Kit approached her, the sunlight fell over him like a cloak. It was terribly unfair, how ethereal he could be when he did not even try. He set his hat down on her worktable, then pulled off his gloves.

"Your wife cannot be collected. She's busy."

He raised an eyebrow. "Is that right? Well, then. I'll be on my way in just a moment."

He joined her behind her worktable, and her heart rose to meet him. Kit dipped down to her level. His mouth hovered a bare inch from hers. As she leaned in to close the gap between them, he withdrew suddenly. Niamh bit down on a whine of protest.

"My apologies," he said. "I shouldn't distract you."

Oh, he never played fair.

"Weeeell . . ." Niamh wound her fingers into his cravat. "Maybe I can be convinced to set it aside. Just for a few minutes. You're very persuasive."

When he finally kissed her, time slowed to a beautiful crawl. Warmth unfurled through her, as slow and dreamy as a summer afternoon. The gown slid off the table, forgotten.

Ah, well. There would be time later to finish it.

These days, she was in no hurry.

ACKNOWLEDGMENTS

After a long creative fallow period, *A Fragile Enchantment* rekindled my sense of joy, wonder, and confidence as a writer. For that, it holds a very special place in my heart. Kit and Niamh were my stalwart, beloved companions over the past few years, grounding me during a very stressful time in my life. There are many people who helped make their story what it is today, and I am immensely grateful to each and every one of them!

To my editor, Sarah Grill, for your keen editorial insights, sense of humor, and our fragile en-chat-ments! Your feedback pushed me to make this the best book it could be, and I am so proud of the work we did together.

To my agents, Claire Friedman and Jess Mileo, for your steadfast support and guidance over the years. As always, you saw the glimmer of potential and pulled it from the murk of my initial idea. Y'all are seriously the best!

To the InkWell foreign rights team: Lyndsey Blessing, Hannah Lehmkuhl, and Jessie Thorsted. Thank you for being all around lovely to work with and helping to share my work with readers around the world.

To my wonderful team at Wednesday Books: Rivka Holler, Alyssa Gammello, Sara Goodman, Eileen Rothschild, Brant Janeway, Devan Norman, Eric Meyer, Melanie Sanders, Lena Shekhter, Kerri Resnick, and NaNá Stoelzle. Thank you to Kelly Chong (@afterblossom_art) for the cover art of my dreams!

To Louise Lamont, for your kindness and for finding the perfect home for this book in the UK! It's a joy to work with you and the Hachette UK team, including Polly Lyall Grant, Aliyana Hirji, and Bec Gillies.

To the First Flight for making my wildest, most impossible dreams come true. Words cannot express how much I appreciate all of you: Cossette, Taylor, Isa, Sequoia Cron (@rainbowbookdragon15), Lydia Byers, Heaven (@heavenlybibliophile), Tori (@toriandbooks), Lindsay (@PawsomeReads), Agavny Vardanyan (@agavnythepigeon), Kelsey Rae Musick, Stephanie (@stephdaydreams), Paola Camacho, Holden Fra, Paola (@anotsowickedwhich), Phoebe Ellman, Megan McDonald, Ena Jarales, Diane (D. E. Ellerbeck), Ashley Dang, Kelcie Mattson (@nerdilyinclined), Allie Williams, Paige Lobianco (@pagebypaigebooks), @zoereadss, Kashvi Kaul at Misty Realms, Holly Hughes, Courtney Bentzoni, Mariya Tuchinskaya (@msbookworld), Nihaarika, Mansi (@astraquill), Birdie Woodnyx, Diana (@chasingchapters_), Amy Sahir, Liz Griffin (@lizgriffinwords), Julie at One Book More, Isabelle Colantuonio (@isabellesbookshelf), Katie Laban, Courtney Boylan, Leah T, Grace (@bookswithgraceann), Kalie Barnes-Young, and Jae (@justjaesday).

To Courtney Gould. This one's for you, pal! I genuinely couldn't have done it without you. May every writer have a friend as talented, caring, funny, and willing to go sicko mode on word count goals as you are.

To Alex Huffman-Jones, my forever first reader! Your encouragement, generosity, and feedback mean the world to me. Thank you for seeing the magic in Niamh and Kit's story.

To Rachel Morris. It must be recorded for posterity: you're always right! I really was not happy about deleting the entire first act and changing the tense, but here we are. Thank you for your brilliant notes, your boundless enthusiasm, and of course, your counsel on Kit's arc.

To the Mighty Five: Audrey Coulthurst, Helen Wiley, Elisha Walker, and Rebecca Leach. Thank you all for your endless patience and support as I drafted (and complained all the while). Audrey and Helen, you gave me much-needed perspective when I felt very lost and very sad. Helen, this book would not be what it is without you.

To Kalie Cassidy, Emily Grey, Charlie Lynn Herman, Christine Arnold, Skyla Arndt, and Laura Brooke Robson. Your fingerprints are indelibly on this book; thank you so much for your notes! I am so lucky to know all of you.

To Mitch Therieau, for your undying support, love, and belief in me.

Lastly, to you! Thank you so much for picking up *A Fragile Enchantment*. Whether this is the first or third book of mine you've read, I appreciate your support more than I can express.